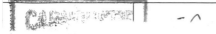

MESSIAH –
THE FIRST JUDGEMENT

WENDY ALEC

Warboys Publishing

MESSIAH – THE FIRST JUDGEMENT:
THE CHRONICLES OF BROTHERS – BOOK 2

All rights reserved

Published by Warboys Publishing Limited, 7 Thornhill Bridge Wharf, Caledonian Road, London N1 0RU

© Wendy Alec 2007

A CIP record for this book is available from the British Library.

ISBN: 978-0-9552377-3-7

First edition

Cover design by Numinos Creative and studiobox.com
Typeset by CRB Associates, Reepham, Norfolk
Production by Shirley Ferrier Ltd
Printed in Malta

Chronicles of Brothers: Messiah – The First Judgement website:
www.chroniclesofbrothers.net

Dedication

To all the thousands and thousands
of our incredible Chronicles family,
who so loved *The Fall of Lucifer*, and
have been desperately waiting for the sequel.
After many long and circuitous months, the sequel
Messiah – The First Judgement
is finally in your hands!

Your passion and love for the story has meant
more than you could ever imagine.

These pages are dedicated to you.

October 2007

'He rescued us when we were no longer able to fight for ourselves. Chronicles is His story.'

FROM 'THE FALL OF LUCIFER'
THE CHRONICLES OF
BROTHERS – BOOK 1

T HE TEMPEST BUILT with the force of a cyclone, and a torrid inferno rose out of the blackness, illuminating the entire panorama.

Lucifer lifted his forearm from his face, his mouth opening and closing mindlessly in terror as an all-consuming apocalyptic sheet of flame descended onto his angels, the scorching, incinerating flames engulfing them. 'The consuming fire!' he shrieked.

All across the chamber, spine-chilling screams resounded as the renegade angelic host were consumed by the blistering fireball.

'I'll take Man with me! I won't burn alone!'

His deranged screaming resounded through the darkness as the searing tongues of fire started to engulf Lucifer. He looked down incredulously at his hands. As he watched they blistered. His broad, manicured nails twisted into talons and yellowed with age. The chiselled alabaster features became pockmarked. The jet-black eyebrows grew together. The beautiful aquiline nose became misshapen. The passionate crimson mouth grew thin and cruel.

Frantic, Lucifer put his hands to his cheeks, feeling his mangled, misshapen features. The magnificent thick ebony tresses fell from his scalp in smouldering clumps. His gold and ruby ring burned deep into his flesh.

'Hear me, Christos!' he screamed. 'I, Lucifer, Light-bearer, chief prince, holy angelic regent of the Royal House of Yehovah, do now become Your sworn enemy, and treachery and iniquity will I bear unto You throughout eternity of eternities!'

Gale-force wind blew through the chamber. The angels with Lucifer – themselves hideously transformed – clung desperately to balustrades, marble columns, and overturned marble tables as they were sucked away from the throne room. They screamed frenziedly as the lightning raged.

Then, propelled by some unseen gargantuan magnetic force, they and everything in their wake were sucked towards the swirling black vortex beyond the chamber entrance.

The shadows had fallen . . .

1981
ST MICHAEL'S MOUNT, MARAZION
CORNWALL, ENGLAND

THE DARK, IMPERIAL figure stood on a jagged outcrop beneath the towering granite slopes of St Michael's Mount. His indigo cloak billowed in the violent gales that blew up from the raging winter storm in the English Channel.

'Our Father...' Lucifer murmured, his soft, cultured tones barely audible. A bolt of lightning flashed, illuminating the soaring pyramidal mount crowned by its medieval castle.

'...Who art in heaven...'

The heavens opened, and a driving, lashing rain hammered down.

Lucifer inhaled deeply, his face raised heavenward, bathing in the torrential downpour, and raised his hands in exhilaration to the darkening skies. Six monstrous black seraph wings rose behind him.

'My kingdom come...,' he cried, his steel blue eyes blazing with fervour.

The soaking strands of his matted locks thrashed against his face, masking the scarred imperial features.

'*His* will be done,' a soft voice echoed from behind him.

Lucifer smiled. A slow, satisfied smile.

'Michael . . . ,' he murmured, his back to his brother, 'you are late.'

Michael stood on the far side of the mount, his hand on his sword, silent. Lucifer pushed his long raven mane back from his face, turned, and studied his brother intently.

Michael wore the long white silk robes of his battalion's ceremonial regalia. The sapphires on his silver breastplate gleamed, and his flaxen locks were tied back in two platinum braids. The handsome, chiselled features were set.

Grim, pondered Lucifer. No, not grim – earnest. Earnest, noble Michael. *Nothing has changed*, he reflected. He laughed sardonically.

'You summoned me through the royal courts. What brings you here, brother?' Michael strode to and fro impatiently. Lucifer grinned his old magnificent smile, relishing Michael's frustration.

'I was passing by the area,' he said casually. He walked towards Michael, across the crests of the raging waves, in long, firm strides. 'I was *curious*, brother.' Lucifer drew his head close to Michael's. 'I would learn of the legends . . . of the white rock in the wood,' he whispered. Michael's clear green eyes locked on to Lucifer's inscrutable sapphire gaze. 'Legends of Michael the Archangel . . . '

Michael flinched as Lucifer's seductive dulcet tones penetrated deep into his soul. 'The stuff of fairytales,' Lucifer continued.

'I traverse many lands.' Michael replied.

'Ah, but you reveal yourself to so *few*.' Lucifer slowly, lazily circled him. 'They saw your apparition here in Cornwall, in the year 495.' He gestured at a lofty crag in the distance. 'You revealed yourself to a fisherman, a lone hermit ... a *monk*?' Lucifer's eyes narrowed. 'Who was he, Michael? Was he one of us?' he hissed. 'The angelic, or one of the Race of Men? Is Yehovah *compelled* to pre-empt my every move?'

'You waste my time, Lucifer,' Michael said coldly. 'You summoned me with the royal seal, yet you speak of trivia.'

Lucifer observed him sceptically.

'More than trivia, I think, brother. No matter, I will assuage my curiousity another time.' Lucifer raised his hand to the skies. 'Let us get to business, Michael – our Father's business. And like Him, I, too, would converse of Messiah's.'

He surveyed the craggy shores of southwest Cornwall. 'And of this faded empire – this weakened lion ... this *England*.' He swung around. 'For she shall yet behold a king ... this year, maybe next ... '

He grinned mockingly at Michael, as when they used to swordfight in aeons past, in worlds long departed. 'Perhaps tonight, Michael, a messiah is born in Marazion.'

'Speak plainly, Lucifer,' snapped Michael, losing patience. 'Enough of your parables.'

'Ah, but do I speak the truth, or merely a fabrication?' Lucifer needled. 'Relay to our Father that I, too, shall send a messiah.'

'Our Father is omniscient,' Michael replied. 'He knows your every conversation. Your every thought is preceded and beheld by Him.'

'Ah, yes, but I stand by the legal process. I would have my thoughts on record in the royal courts in the codices of heaven. That is why you are here – so I meet the demands of *"His"* legal system.'

Michael indicated agreement. 'It shall be recorded as you request.'

'My strength ebbs from me...' Lucifer scanned the heavens, strangely agitated.

'The Nazarene is near...' An uncharacteristic dread crossed his marred countenance. 'You came alone?'

Michael nodded. 'Time runs down, brother,' he spoke softly, sorrow etched on his noble features.

Lucifer lifted his head, his breathing easing.

'He offers repentance with one hand, yet, with the other, seeks my demise.' Lucifer's eyes filled with loathing. 'Our Father is malicious.'

'As you would have it, Lucifer.' Michael looked at him, suddenly fierce.

'Your brazen iniquity affects your judgement.'

'As your shameless naïvety does yours,' Lucifer sneered.

The two brothers glared at each other, severe, unyielding. Finally Lucifer spoke.

'My messiah shall rise from these isles,' he whispered. 'A king of politics and of industry, courted by kings and queens – a greater orator than Churchill – rises upon these shores.' He stared out past the raging black waves to a lone star that glimmered through the rising mists. 'I think I shall give him brothers,' he declared. 'Like *us*, he shall have a family.' His mood changed abruptly. 'They shall be three, even as you, Gabriel, and I are three angelic brothers.' He gave Michael a mercurial smile. 'Three brothers of the Race of Men.'

An insane fire lit his gaze. 'And *like* us' – he bowed mockingly to Michael – 'one shall be an insurrectionist, a renegade.'

Michael bowed his head. 'You will lose, Lucifer,' he murmured, 'as you lost at Golgotha.'

'*Golgotha!*' Lucifer snarled, his countenance turning at once into a mask of hatred. He turned his back on Michael, looking out to the raging winter seas. His voice was hard. 'Tell Jether when he sees the white rider in the heavens, my messiah will make his appearance in the Race of Men.'

And he vanished.

Michael turned as Gabriel strode out of the hanging Cornish mists, up the rocks and towards him. Gabriel's flaxen hair fell loose over his kingfisher blue vestments. His flawless features were finer than Michael's strongly defined one's ... gentler. But tonight his regal countenance was set.

'His messiah will be born tonight in Marazion,' Gabriel announced wearily. 'It is certain.' He stood on the rocks before Michael, the sword of justice hanging at his side. 'Lucifer's fallen angelic battalions already surround the area; our legions will do the same.'

Michael bowed his head. 'He will lose,' he said, 'at Megiddo.'

Gabriel nodded. 'Yes, Michael, he will lose – but at what cost to the Race of Men?' Together the brothers stood in silence, staring out beyond the dark, swirling mists rising off the west Cornish coast, to the blazing star that now rose in the heavens over the small village of Marazion.

⟿

2021
MONASTERY OF ARCHANGELS
ALEXANDRIA, EGYPT

Two monks stood in the portal of St Michael the Archangel, the rotating telescope dome on the observatory of the Monastery of Archangels. Their features lay hidden by the grey cowled hoods of their Coptic monastic robes. They stared through the Coronado Solar Telescope directly into the Egyptian sun, transfixed by the unsettling apparition that hovered above the sweltering desert plain.

The older monk watched, mesmerized, as the spectre materialized into a sinister waxen form astride a magnificent white stallion. The form held a bow.

'The white rider of the Apocalypse...,' the younger whispered, fingering the cross at his chest. 'The first seal is broken.'

'The Son of Perdition comes forth to rule – one from the Race of Men.' The older monk looked grimly up from the telescope into the shimmering crimson skies of the Egyptian dawn. 'The Great Tribulation has begun.'

That dusk is still imprinted in my memory. The dusk when the sign of the White Rider of the Apocalypse hung in the Egyptian skies over the sweltering desert plains. The Son of Perdition coming forth to rule in the Race of Men. For the breaking of the First Great Seal was surely to herald the beginning of the devastations of the End of Days.

And as I stood with Jether, observing the waxen apparition, my mind raced back two thousand years earlier to a different dusk. And a different sign that had once blazed high in the Eastern skies. A sign that was to terrorize the soul of my brother Lucifer, King of the Damned. For the chilling events of the coming moons were about to change eternity in the world of the Race of Men as we still knew it. And plunge the armies of the First Heaven and the Fallen into a cosmic battle that would reverberate throughout a hundred aeons.

Beyond Megiddio.

Beyond the termination of the world of the Race of Men.

Culminating in one final battle. Between my brothers.

Michael and Lucifer.

A thousand years in the future.

At the White Gorge of Inferno, on the eastern shores of the Lake of Fire.

But it here, aeons before, that our tale begins . . .

. . . For it was to be a different dusk . . .

CHAPTER ONE

PRINCE OF PERDITION

4 BC
TWO THOUSAND AND SEVENTEEN
YEARS EARLIER

L UCIFER FLUNG OPEN the colossal sapphire doors of
his throne room and walked out onto the eastern
portico of the Black Palace, overhanging the very
edge of the bloodstone cliffs of Perdition. He raised his face
to the skies as the twelve magenta moons of Perdition set in
the pale amber horizon over the desolate smouldering, lava
wastes of hell. The enormous flaming star was still fixed in
the night sky between the Second Heaven and earth.

He gazed at the nova for a long time. Silent.

Miles below, in the shadowy crypts of the sinister
Shaman-Kings, the slow, pulsating throb of hell's sinister
war drums resounded throughout the lower penitentiaries
of the damned.

A lingering smile spread across Lucifer's mangled features
as he watched the steady grey-robed throng of ghoul-like

men and women pour through two monstrous black iron gates that towered a thousand feet above the glowing red ground – the Gates of Hell.

Hundreds of jaundice-eyed, demonic gorgon seraphim nested on top of the immense black iron gateposts of hell's perimeter, their gigantic scaled brazen claws slashing at the posts, and red-hot flames issuing from their nostrils and ears. The gorgon's wings were of beaten gold, their wingspan's measured a hundred feet, and across their scaled heads, inscribed in ornate script, was written 'THE SOULS OF THE RACE OF MEN.'

Lucifer pulled his violet velvet cape tightly around him. His gleaming raven hair, plaited in thick braids and interwoven with diamonds, fell over his broad shoulders, blowing in the scorching tempests that blew from the stark onyx crags of Perdition. The diamond satanic crown of state rested on his head, and his glistening white silk robes trimmed with werewolf fur fell to the floor, half concealing his jewelled sandals. The once-exquisite countenance had been scarred almost beyond recognition in the torrid inferno at his banishment from the First Heaven. Yet still, in the rarest of moments, the haunting beauty of aeons past was strangely evident: the wide, marbled forehead, the high imperial cheekbones, the passionate crimson mouth, the imperious sapphire eyes now shadowed deep in thought.

He held out a sweetmeat idly to his favourite hellhound, the pampered five-headed Cerberus, who licked his master's hand with his coarse tongues. Then Lucifer returned to his contemplations of the star.

Balberith, his chief attendant, stood in the doorway.

'Your satanic princes are returned from earth, Your Excellency.' He bowed deeply.

Lucifer nodded and, tearing himself away from his stargazing, strode through the doors, towards the monstrous black onyx throne, the seat of Satan. He sat directly beneath the black crystal vortex that soared overhead. Araquiel, his courtier, held out his sceptre on a velvet bolster. He took it. Directly behind the throne lay the Golden Gates of the Black Necropolis which housed the great golden Ark of the Race of Men, manacled to the Black Sepulchre with monstrous iron chains. Lucifer's trophy.

Ahead of Lucifer towered the massive black iron gates of the throne room. His forbidding satanic guard, the Black Horde, stood at attention – a thousand of Lucifer's dread elite generals of his High Command, fallen from the First Heaven in millenniums past with their renegade King. After their banishment, the glory of their bravery and honour had swiftly been reduced to a depraved and relentless savagery. The corridors of Perdition reverberated with dark muttered tales of their bloody torturing and butcheries. The terror of the inmates of hell's penetentiaries. Their pale straw coloured eyes stared pitilessly out from their scarred mangled faces. Their black braided hair hung well below their thighs. Alongside the fallen horde, a pack of snarling black yellow eyed jaguars paced, chained to their depraved masters, their poisonous black fangs visible.

Dagon, commander of the Black Horde, stepped forward, helmet in hand, his black-gloved hands on his sword and bowed. 'I announce His Majesty's satanic chief Princes, the rulers of the dark world.'

The iron gates to his throne room opened, and two monstrous princes entered, followed by ten regents and their guards. The gates slammed shut, leaving the twelve regents alone before Lucifer and the Black Horde. They fell prostrate before the gates.

'I announce His Royal Highness, Prince Belzoc, champion of Perdition and satanic regent of the dark world from the kingdom of Persia,' Dagon declared.

The menacing Belzoc, satanic king of Persia, rose from his knees to his full nine feet, then strode across the gleaming lapis lazuli floors towards the throne. He was stopped twenty feet away by six of the Black Horde, who held up their broadswords. The chief magus of the Darkened Council walked forward.

'You may address your emperor.'

Belzoc fell to one knee, then pushed his coarse mane of matted black hair away from his craggy face and raised his glinting red eyes to his emperors. 'I return from Persia, Your Majesty,' he rasped, glutinous yellow saliva dripping from his thin pale lips. 'My dark slaves of the Race of Men have executed your command. Every newborn prince and royal in the kingdom of Persia is slain.' His dark demonic tones echoed throughout the chamber.

Lucifer stared at him, grim and silent.

The chief magus spoke again: 'I announce His Royal Highness, Prince Merodach, regent of the kingdom of Babylonia.'

Merodach fell to one knee. Trembling.

'Every royal house, every palace, castle, and pavilion in the kingdom of Babylonia has been ransacked – all of royal lineage are slain.'

Lucifer stood, strode over to the east side of the chamber, and flung open the heavy velvet curtains.

'Yet still the nova burns flaming in the heavens,' he cried.

'He *lives!*' He spun around in fury.

Marduk, head of the Darkened Councils and Lucifer's chief of staff, entered the gates. Marduk slunk towards the throne and bowed, then raised his hooded face to Lucifer's.

'I bring news of the nova,' he wheezed, his sibilant hiss echoing through the throne room. He bowed again deeply. Only his jaundiced, straw coloured eyes could be glimpsed under the fawn cassock hood. Lucifer waved his hand to the magi and his regents. 'Leave us.'

Immediately the twelve regents scattered to the outer court. Marduk moved closer to the throne and lifted his hood, his ravaged, sallow features now clearly visible.

'The star moves east, Your Majesty, to the Mideastern regions of Planet Earth.' Lucifer stared out beyond the hunched Marduk, past the enormous sapphire doors, to where the star still hung, 'Our battalions have scoured Persia, Greece, Babylon, sire – he is not to be found.'

Lucifer slowly turned his gaze onto a tall sinister form who now stood at the gates' entrance.

Charsoc the Dark had well earned his name among the fallen as Lucifer's Dark Apostle. Before his fall from the First Heaven, he had been one of the High Council of Yehovah's eight ancient high elders, one of the great angelic monarchs of heaven, keeper of Yehovah's sacred mysteries, second only to Jether the Just. But the treacherous Charsoc had effortlessly degenerated to the blackest and foulest of Necromancer Kings, now reigning as Chief High Priest of the Fallen. Governor of the Grand Wizards of the Black Court and the dreaded Warlock Kings of the West.

His iniquitous, wizened sallow countenance was now framed by a veil of jet black, poker-straight hair and beard. Where his eyes had been, two seared, white gaping eyeballs stared sinisterly out minus both iris and pupils. An ever-present reminder of the day and the hour that Christos Himself had visited the penitentiaries of the damned. His voluminous harlequin sorcerer's gown was of the finest taffeta and tasselled, tied in the middle with a thick vermillion satin sash. His bony, pale fingers were covered in gold rings set with sapphires, opals, and emeralds. Charsoc vanished from the gates, then rematerialized directly before Lucifer's throne bowing deeply, his hair sweeping the floor.

'Your Excellency, great Prince...' Charsoc's voice was both sinister and cultured in tone. 'The nova heralds a newborn prince; this infant king to be born of the Race of Men is one of great royal lineage.' He caressed the fire opals on his thumb ring. 'A star of this magnitude signifies a royal house of immense power.' He moved his head closer to Lucifer's. 'One so powerful that his kingdom could destroy our own...' An uncharacteristic dread fell across Charsoc's face, and he lowered his tone. '...and hasten the judgement...'

A terrible silence descended on the throne room.

'Where is the infant king to be born?'

Lucifer's words hung in the chamber. He swung around to Marduk.

'What of the Black Murmurers?' Lucifer hissed.

Marduk raised his head, his voice tremulous. 'Sire, they

have been traversing the borders of the land designated Israel in the land of Men. Your royal brothers, Chief Princes Michael and Gabriel's legions surround the area; we cannot infiltrate.'

'Michael!' Lucifer snarled. 'This infant king will be born in that parched tract of dust, I sense it.' He was silent a long moment, then turned to Charsoc, his eyes narrowed.

'The Warlock Kings of the West ... they foretell this infant has a connection with Christos?'

Charsoc stared at him, trembling. Silent. Lucifer pointed his sceptre at Marduk. 'You will seek it out, Marduk.'

He rose, resplendent in his robes.

'Yehovah continually vexes me through that spawning ground of prophets, patriachs ... and now rival kings ... And now I shall vex *Him*. Relay my royal edict.' Lucifer raised his sceptre high. 'Dagon – dispatch the Black Horde. Divert my brother Michael to the West. Release the reconnaissance legion of the vulture shamans from their hell cages. To fly east.'

Lucifer strode back through the great jewelled doors of the eastern portico. He continued his staring out at the flaming pillar of fire that blazed in the black heavens. The nova that heralded his adversary – the infant king.

Chapter Two

ARETAS OF PETRA

THE SMALL PARTY of magi journeyed on horseback for weeks across the treacherous, rocky terrain of the main Persian trade routes, following the Euphrates River, led by the strange flaming pillar of fire that hung high in the heavens. At the fringes of the Syrian desert, they met with an ancient caste of monks, who exchanged the magi's horses for ten camels.

The aged magus Balthazar led the caravan, his posture erect and regal, seated astride the leading camel. Behind him rode Gaspar, the youngest magus of the Chaldean order, next to the older, more sedate Melchior. Balista, Balthazar's manservant and six magi rode behind, their camels weighed down with massive bags of fine spices, provisions, and astronomical instruments.

Their destination, Petra.

The city that had housed the ancient relics of the Hebrew king, Solomon, for generations. The relics to be presented to the newborn king.

Days on end had melted into nights, and twilights into dusks as the magi pushed themselves to the limits of their endurance, beaten mercilessly by the scorching desert sun as they traversed the ferocious Syrian wilderness. Stopping for neither rest nor sleep, exhausted from the gruelling heat, magnetised forward by the furiously flaming nova, across the harsh and desolate wilderness, past Damascus, until the terrain transformed into a paradise of lush green valleys and babbling streams. Gaunt and weary, Balthazar lifted his hand.

'Ride ahead, Balista. Let the king's royal guard know that we are but a day's journey away. The relics of Solomon await us!' he cried, his voice hoarse from exhaustion, his eyes burning bright with exhilaration.

The caravan rounded the final mountain that dawn. There she lay, nestled in the remote, all but inaccessible valley in the mountains south of the Dead Sea: the mysterious ancient Nabatean city of Petra.

The city was surrounded by the towering rugged rose-coloured sandstone hills that rose from the desert plateau to protect the noble Arabian inhabitants from invaders. The party stared, enthralled, at the great chasm before them.

'The Shiq,' murmured Melchior in awe, 'the great cleft in the earth.'

One by one, led by Balthazar, the magi rode the long, narrow, winding route through the lofty cliffs until they rounded a bend. There, towering in front of them, was an immense thirteen story high, ninety foot wide columned monument chiselled from the pale rose sandstone cliff.

'Al Khazneh, the eighth wonder of our world,' Balthazar whispered in awe.

Then his head slumped onto his chest in sheer exhaustion, and he collapsed forward, losing consciousness into blissful oblivion.

⁓

Balthazar, now bathed and manicured and with three full nights' rest behind him, was magnificently attired in his embroidered priestly robes. His black skin gleamed like ebony, and his silver hair and beard glistened after being meticulously trimmed by one of the king's personal stewards and anointed with perfumed oils. Why – he hadn't felt this young in most of his eighty-seven years.

He rode on horseback across the royal palace courtyard, keeping up with the handsome young king, who rode ahead of him on his fine Arabian stallion, his crimson robes billowing, his steel blue eyes clear and full of purpose. Although only in his late thirties, the young monarch exuded a power and authority far beyond his years, one normally attributed to great and ancient rulers. Aretas IV, king of Petra and Southern Arabia, was pragmatic and decisive in temperament. His lean six-foot frame was burned brown by the harsh Arabian sun, his sinewy hands hardened from manual work. Long, dark ribboned locks framed his strong, dark features and quicksilver smile.

Balthazar studied him. He was different from his father, Balthazar's old and trusted compatriot, the judicious old Nabatean king. The younger Aretas was a proud king, fiery and hot-blooded, on occasion overly imperious and leaning towards inflexibility. He would mature in time, as his father had before him; Balthazar was certain of it.

He followed Aretas and the royal guard down the colonnaded street, captivated by the beauty of the ornate royal tombs and lesser palaces. Aretas pointed proudly at his newly built amphitheatre, which could easily seat three thousand. They rode through the narrow, dusty streets bounded by the towering stone walls of Petra. The stench of rancid goat's milk mixed with incense and spices invaded their nostrils as they rounded the corner to the open-air lower markets. Hundreds of Chinese, Arab, Indian, and Roman tradesmen jostled across uneven pavements, haggling boisterously at hundreds of stalls over the price of incense, silks, and spices. Balthazar stared in wonder at the paradisos, Petra's magnificent ornamental pool and gardens.

Ahead of them loomed the imposing triple-arched Temenos gateway, decorated with sculpted busts and ornately engraved inscriptions.

Aretas veered right and dismounted outside the imposing Temple of the Winged Lions. Balthazar stared up at the exquisitely carved winged lions and griffins that decorated the limestone capitals of the colossal temple pillars. Aretas led the way up the temple's wide, gilded steps, striding up the nave, with Balthazar and the other magi behind him, until they reached the silver-clad pillars of the inner sanctuary. A huge magenta veil hung from gold rods above the darkened stone altar. Aretas, uncharacteristically solemn, dropped to one knee. Immediately, two high priestesses draped in gossamer white robes reverently opened the purple veil, then flung themselves prostrate on the marble floor, followed by the magi.

Aretas slowly rose, and the high priest drew open the gossamer inner veil. Facing them on the dark, damp stone altar was an ornate silver casket carved with cherubim and seraphim. Aretas turned to Balthazar and nodded. Slowly he lifted the great silver lid to reveal a golden cup, a small stone box, and a golden rod. He stared in undisguised awe.

'Daniel's wonders...'

'The cup of frankincense, the alabaster box of myrrh...,' Aretas murmured.

'And the gold rod of Aaron...' Balthazar raised his head to Aretas, his countenance radiant. 'The relics of Solomon's temple...'

'It has been over half a millennium since the Hebrew Daniel entrusted them to our royal house for safekeeping.' Aretas hit his golden staff twice on the ground, and the stewards rose immediately.

Balthazar turned to Aretas, tears welling in his eyes, overcome with emotion. 'The great magus Daniel's prophecies must be fulfilled. We must present the relics to the newborn king.'

Aretas nodded. The high priest clapped his hands, and immediately six priestly stewards reverently placed the casket onto their shoulders.

Aretas walked slowly back through the temple. He stood on the steps, staring out over the Nabatean city, deep in contemplation. 'My father's house looked eagerly to this day,' he murmured.

Balthazar nodded. 'Your father, my old and trusted compatriot.'

'Revered Balthazar, you know that I do not share his religious sentiment.' Aretas turned to Balthazar, an unusual vulnerability on his face. 'But for My father's name's sake, I would accompany you to Jerusalem.'

Balthazar nodded, moved by the offer.

'Who knows, old friend?' Aretas smiled. 'If this babe is the future king of the Jews, I could make an alliance with him and stop the eternal disputes over our borders.' Aretas stopped as his royal household chariot drew up outside the temple steps. Four royal maidservants alighted.

A toddler struggled vigorously out of her royal maid-servant's arms, ran over to Aretas, and flung herself headlong into his arms. 'Papa, Papa! I go with you...'

Aretas' countenance immediately softened as he embraced the tiny girl long and, then held her at arm's length, gently brushing the unruly dark locks that tumbled down her face. 'Jotapa! At all times you are a princess of the royal household of Aretas. You have been playing in the *dirt* again?'

Jotapa giggled. 'Jotapa build castle ... for Papa, the king...'

Aretas threw back his head, laughing loud and long. 'I go to visit a young king, Jotapa, a king of the Hebrews.'

Tenderly he stroked his daughter's pretty heart-shaped face. 'If he is gracious and just...' Aretas looked adoringly at Jotapa. '...and handsome...' He sat her on his knee. '...very, *very* handsome, we could arrange a marriage, an alliance of the houses of Arabia and Judea.'

Balthazar smiled and shook his head, gently laying his hand on the king's shoulder. 'My dear Aretas...' He gazed strangely into the distance. 'This is no earthly king we seek...'

'You speak as my father spoke. You are aware that I am not a religious man, Balthazar. Your deep sayings are best left for the evening feast, when I can digest them with jugs of wine!'

Aretas raised Jotapa from his lap high into the air and, amid her squeals of laughter, remounted his stallion and placed her in front of him, where she sang softly to herself. Balthazar rode at their side through the colonnaded streets until they reached the gleaming marble courtyard of the royal palace.

Gaspar and Melchior strode through the courtyard towards them. Gaspar bowed low. 'The star ... the star, it moves, my lord Balthazar!'

Both Balthazar and Aretas looked up at the heavens. Balthazar dismounted, exultant. 'It moves towards the northwestern regions, Your Majesty. It is there we will find the Messiah, our compatriot of whom Daniel spoke.'

Aretas dismounted and placed Jotapa firmly on the stone floor of the palace courtyard.

'We must make haste to the councils of Jerusalem, Melchior,' Balthazar instructed.

Aretas lifted his hand. 'My ambassadors are in contact lately with him they call Herod the Great, vassal king of Judea.'

Melchior's face grew somber. 'Herod the Edomite?' He frowned.

Balthazar's brows furrowed. 'The stories of his cruelty have circulated even to Persia, Aretas. He murders chief priests of the Sanhedrin. Even his wife and three sons...'

Aretas paced the courtyard, hands behind his back. 'You have heard, I am sure, from my father, that Herod's mother,

Kufra, was a Nabatean princess . . . that Herod spent time in our midst as a boy.'

Balthazar nodded. 'This I know. I know also that when Herod was forced to flee Jerusalem, your father repulsed his request to find asylum in Petra.'

'Yes, there has been bad blood – Cleopatra . . . Syllaeus . . .'

'It is precarious at best. Be assured in this matter,' Balthazar stated grimly.

Aretas nodded. 'He is a cruel and ruthless tyrant, of that I am aware. Not to be trusted – but various political relations exist between our countries, and the disputes over our borders have intensified these last months. He presses to meet with me.'

He knelt down and caressed Jotapa's chin gently. 'Now learn a king's wisdom, my princess. The size and dignity of our caravan will at least bid him be hospitable until he searches out our real purpose. He will aid us in our search, with the intent of using us for his own . . .'

Gently he handed Jotapa to his royal steward, amid much protest. He kissed her lovingly on both cheeks and waved them away.

Aretas stood upright and looked at Balthazar soberly. 'Rather, we will use him for ours!' He clapped his hands, and servants presented themselves immediately. 'Prepare the caskets of gold and spices for the king of Judea . . .'

He turned to Balthazar and smiled. 'We shall receive a king's welcome in Jerusalem, old friend – and Herod the Great himself shall summon us!'

〜

2021
ALEXANDRIA, EGYPT

Nick De Vere pressed down on the accelerator of the rented silver 2009 sport Range Rover. He had arrived in the Cairo airport this morning from Heathrow, exhausted, to find this, the only four-wheel-drive vehicle left in the car rental bays.

'Not bad for an old girl,' he murmured as he roared up the sprawling western desert highway at high speed towards Alexandria. It had been eight years since he last visited Alexandria, the 'Pearl of the Mediterranean'. Then the road had been desolate, traffic free and truly barren but now great swaths of agricultural land, horse-breeding farms, and palatial estates lined the roadside. Thirty kilometres outside Alexandria's city limits, just before the Desert Roads City Gate toll station, he made a sharp right turn, pushed the gear into four-wheel drive, and sped across the desert plains, leaving a huge cloud of dust behind him.

Nearly an hour later, far in the distance, the formidable fortification came into view. The ancient granite walls of the Monastery of Archangels, carved from the huge mountain behind the monastery fortress that had withstood centuries of Roman persecution against the Egyptian Christians, stood between ten and thirty-five metres tall and three metres thick. And now this was the final resting place of the greatest archeological discovery of the twenty-first century: the secret annals of Lucifer.

Five weeks ago, the priceless antiquity had been moved from the high security archeological vaults of the Royal palace museum in Amman, Jordan to the monastery, immediately after the tenuous cease-fire pact following the bloody Pan Arab-Russian – Israeli War. And here the antiquity would remain.

Nick's jaw clenched. It had been *his* discovery, three and a half years previously, from his archeological excavations at Petra. And the entire world was oblivious of the fact – and would remain so, thanks to the royal household of Jordan. Nick sighed. And to his overriding need for the inordinate sum stashed in a Swiss Bank account in his name – in exchange for his silence.

He slammed his hand on the steering wheel in frustration. Pulling to a stop directly outside the towering western gate, he found it deserted. He eased his tall, lanky frame out of the Range Rover and walked over to the gate.

Nick De Vere would be twenty-nine next month, the youngest of three brothers belonging to an inordinately wealthy banking dynasty, *The De Vere Family*. He was handsome, almost pretty, with intelligent deep-set grey eyes above an aquiline nose and high cheekbones. Fine sunbleached hair, cut long, grazed his dark grey T-shirt.

Life had recently dealt Nick De Vere two hard blows in succession. His trust fund had been frozen by his father, James De Vere, the evening before his fatal heart attack. And now Nick, too, was dying. Of AIDS. He had been on the most advanced antiretroviral therapy for four years, but now his body was failing rapidly. He swiped the blond fringe impatiently out of his eyes. Peering upwards, he could vaguely make out two Bedouin men playing backgammon, gesticulating and talking in rising voices, oblivious to his presence.

Nick got back into the Range Rover, slammed the door, and leaned on the horn. Instantly the two Bedouins scrambled to their feet and hurried to the gate, their long robes flying behind them. There was a loud scraping and groaning of wood as a huge lift contraption descended over the side of the monastery wall.

Nick looked in disbelief up at the swaying lift. The older Bedouin pointed down at him.

'You get in . . . ,' he said giving Nick a wide, toothless smile.

'Open the gates!' Nick demanded.

'Gates no open – you get in.' The man pointed to the wooden contraption, then pointed upward to a door in the wall, thirty feet up.

Nick closed his eyes in disbelief, then banged on the car hood.

'My car?'

'Only foot . . . and helicopter.' The Bedouin shrugged. 'No motor,' he stated emphatically.

Nick slammed the car door, rolled his eyes, and walked into the wooden lift, which started to swing wildly as the two Arab men hauled it up by a system of pulleys towards the small door.

'This way! This way!'

An elderly priest gestured for Nick to follow him through the fields, ripe with vegetables, pomegranates, and herbs. They walked past rows of date palms and olive trees, past an olive press, then through a second inner courtyard. Nick had the distinct feeling he was being watched . . . observed.

As they continued past the monks' refectory, towards an ancient watchtower, Nick slowed down, staring up towards the rotating Solar Telescope dome on the monastery observatory. The priest frowned, motioning him forward.

Nick obediently followed the hunched figure through a walled garden of sycamore trees onto a small stone path that twisted past a vast pond filled with exquisite pink lotus blossoms that rose above the murky waters. They stopped at a rusted metal gateway, the entrance to the sprawling ancient wing of the monastery. Nick watched intently as the priest reverently made the sign of the cross, then swiftly entered a code in the sophisticated security system. The metal gates slowly opened. They made their way along numerous winding ancient corridors, permeated with the aroma of inks and leathers mingled with myrrh, then through an enormous library occupied by hundreds of monks silently archiving data into state of the art Apple Mac computer systems. Nick ducked as they continued through a low dank tunnel. Finally they reached what appeared to be a crypt door.

Two broad-shouldered soldiers holding submachine guns materialized, as if from nowhere, on either side of Nick. Their heads were clean-shaven, and he immediately recognized the digital pattern on their uniforms. Jordan's elite special operations command. The old priest handed a document embossed with the Royal Hashemite seal to the taller soldier.

'He has been granted access to photograph the annals.' The old priest lowered his eyes to the floor, bowed, then scurried away.

Nick frowned. Suddenly he was shoved hard against the

31

stone wall, his arms splayed out, and rigorously searched by the first soldier. The second grabbed his camera and unceremoniously dumped the contents of Nick's pockets and bag onto a tray, which he sent through a sophisticated-looking scanner.

He glared at the guard. Five seconds later, he was pushed roughly back towards the door. The first soldier gestured for him to remove his belongings from the tray. Seething, Nick bent down and stowed them back in his bag. He held his camera tightly.

The taller soldier gestured to Nick to follow him through the door. There he found himself in an enormous ante-chamber, surrounded by at least twelve separate smaller chambers containing the most magnificent collection of antiquities he had ever laid his eyes on. Egyptian, Etruscan, Persian, Assyrian, and Chaldean artefacts, Arabian mosaics and frescos, Greek and Russian icons, original works by Raphael, Leonardo Da Vinci, Titian, Perugino. Priceless treasures.

But ahead of him was the largest chamber, Nick stepped inside, his attention caught by a diorite statue to his right. He frowned. It seemed strangely familiar ... Now he remembered. Its photograph had been circulated through-out Europe on Interpol's red list of looted Iraqi antiquities. Fascinated, he moved nearer. Hundreds of volumes of manuscripts lay stacked from floor to ceiling. He caught sight of a stone tablet lying inside a glass case. He stared at the tablet, enthralled at the wedge-shaped depressions.

'The lost legacies of ancient Mesopotamia ... the price-less collection of cylinder seals...,' he stared at the tablet, mesmerized, feeling in his pocket for his camera. Slowly, carefully, he lined up the palm-size digital camera directly with the tablet. 'Unbelievable.'

Slim manicured fingers snatched the camera firmly from his grasp.

'No photographs here, Mr De Vere. You must abide by our conditions.'

Nick swung around to find himself staring down into a pair of flashing brown eyes. He bowed his head respectfully. 'Your Majesty . . .'

'We don't suffer fools gladly, Mr De Vere. Please make sure you respect our agreement, or I can assure you that all licences that we, the Jordanian people, have approved for your work shall immediately be revoked.'

Nick studied the princess before him. She seemed young . . . much younger than in any photograph he had ever seen of her – twenty-two, he guessed, definitely not more than twenty-four. She was petite and slim, fine-boned, her high cheekbones and regal features framed by gleaming black tresses that fell past her shoulders. She was understated, dressed only in a pair of faded jeans and white cotton T-shirt, the only sign of inordinate wealth the slim diamond Audemars Piguet watch on her left wrist.

She watched him surveying her, and a slight smile flickered across her mouth.

'The cuneiform tablets with the missing parts of the epic of Gilmagesh, the earliest written words, a bronze relief from 4000 BC – worth a hundred Mona Lisa's,' the princess of Jordan uttered softly, as though reciting a sacred doxology.

'Our government returned to the state of Iraq thousands of stolen antiquities that had been smuggled into Jordan during the 2002 war,' she continued. 'The sacred vase

33

of Warka, the statue of Entemena, the remainder we bought back, for hundreds of millions of dollars, off the black market in Switzerland. They emerged everywhere: Teherani bazaars, Paris. A US Airport.' She hesitated. 'We were patient. Most of the looted treasures eventually surfaced in London.'

She looked directly into Nick's piercing grey eyes.

'The world's largest centre for trade in Islamic art,' Nick murmured. 'Uncle Lawrence...'

The princess nodded.

'Lawrence St Cartier's network of contacts was extremely useful to the royal house. We now own the largest and most important collection of illuminated manuscripts in the world, apart from the Vatican's.'

She continued walking. 'In 180 BC, the Nabaeteans were bequeathed this monastery by an ancient caste of priests connected with the Royal Courts of Egypt. Egyptian governments throughout the centuries have held its historical heritage in high esteem and continue to honour its present treaty with the Hashemite Kingdom. The royal household of Jordan has kept its priceless treasures hidden from the prying eyes of the outside world, confined behind these walls, in these crypts. We are deeply indebted to your sister-in-law's uncle' – she hesitated – 'and, of course, to you.'

Safwat, her chief of security walked towards the princess. He was lean and clean cut.

'Your Majesty,' he spoke in a low voice in clipped Arabic tones. 'Your helicopter arrives in fifteen minutes.' She nodded in acknowledgement, then turned to Nick. 'Follow me.'

She walked briskly back into the antechamber and turned left down a narrow, dimly lit tunnel.

'Your English is impeccable, Your Highness,' Nick said. 'I read that you were educated at Oxford.'

'Ancient history and classical archaeology.' Nick followed close behind, keeping pace with her through the narrow winding corridors. He could distinguish the faint aroma of myrrh.

'An English education ... like your father...'

'Ah,' the princess replied, 'but you, like us, are not British, either, Mr De Vere. Let me see...' Her English accent carried only the faintest Arabic inflection. 'You were born in Washington, DC, into the De Vere dynasty. Your father was named American ambassador to the United Kingdom five years after you were born. You grew up in Great Britain – Regents Park, to be precise. Educated at Gordonstoun, studied serious archaeology at Cambridge, Mensa IQ, gifted, your Achilles heel, drugs and a playboy lifestyle. Black sheep of the family, trust fund frozen. Your eldest brother, Jason De Vere, US media tycoon extraordinaire, owns a third of the Western world's television and newspaper empires.

'Middle brother, Adrian De Vere, youngest prime minister of the United Kingdom, and newly appointed president of the United States of Europe, Nobel Peace Prize nominee.

'In 2014 you were involved in an accident in which your eldest brother's daughter was permanently crippled. You were the driver; you were inebriated at the time. Jason De Vere has not talked to you from that day on.'

Nick glared in the direction of the princess' fast disappearing back.

'You contracted AIDS four years ago. Adrian De Vere paid for the best treatments in Switzerland, London, and the

Mayo Clinic, but alas, in the past five months, your body has not responded favourably to any of the treatments.'

Nick fought to control the rage building inside him at this prying teenage royal. 'My private life is no concern of...'

'You are a *fool*, Nicholas De Vere,' she interrupted sharply. 'Since your brother's stellar political ascent, your entire family has been under every government's close surveillance: Interpol, Europol, the CIA, M16, Mossad, SAVAMA, the FSB, and the Jordanian secret service – *all* are watching you.'

She turned abruptly sharp right down into a small dank stairway. Nick followed.

'My brother, the crown prince, and I meet with your brother and the United Arab Nations next month in Damascus for the signing of the greatest peace accord in the twenty-first century. For the first time, we are all at the same table: China, North Korea, Europe, the Pan-Arab Union, the United States, Russia, and Israel. There may finally be peace in our time.'

She turned towards him in the stairwell. 'We have granted your access to continue your study of the annals. However, Lawrence St Cartier asked me to return a favour – strictly business. You wished to see the cross that is spoken of in the annals?'

Nick drew a deep breath; all his anger instantaneously evaporated.

'The cross exists, then?'

Nick stepped towards the princess, a strange glitter in his eyes. 'Oh, yes, Nicholas De Vere, it exists...'

The princess walked briskly down the damp stone stairs.

'Legend has it that it possesses strange healing powers.'

Nick's voice echoed after the disappearing princess. He clambered down the stairwell after her.

'Legends are very powerful in the minds of those who believe,' the princess countered.

'Legend has it that Aretas the Fourth protected the Christ child in His flight from Egypt...,' Nick's eyes shone with exhilaration, 'that he brought Him here to this monastery, to an ancient caste of magi...' Nick stopped, sweat suddenly pouring down his brow. He grasped the stair rail to steady himself. The princess turned back towards him from the lower stairs. She held his gaze.

'...that the boy Christ himself carved a cross when He was but a child and gave it as a gift to *Aretas* before returning from this monastery to Nazareth.'

'Cartier has briefed you well. It seems you know all our legends.'

They continued descending until they reached the lower crypts, then stopped outside a solid steel door, barely four feet high. Two thickset monks, standing hidden in the shadowed corner, moved towards Nick. A third older monk raised his hand. They instantly returned to the shadows.

'Thank you, Father Benedict. He is our guest.' The monk bowed before the princess, entered a security code in the wall, then stepped back as the one foot thick steel door slid away revealing an ancient wooden crypt door.

Nick ran his hand over the doorway in wonder. 'Cedar of Lebanon,' he murmured. Father Benedict nodded. 'The ancient Fathers of the monastery imported it for the original monastery,' he said. Nick eased his lanky six-foot frame through the doorway into the tiny mausoleum. There in the centre of the chamber, under thick protective glass, lay his discovery – the Secret Angelic Annals. He gazed at the strange blue light that still flickered faintly from its pages, mesmerized. Then with great effort dragged his gaze away from the annals.

In the far left hand corner of the chamber, resting against deep-blue velvet under a glass dome, lay a small cross no larger than a DVD, perfectly carved from acacia wood.

Nick moved nearer, then frowned.

'It's been mended. . . . ' He examined it through the dome. '*Crudely* mended.'

The princess sighed. 'Two thousand years ago, King Aretas had considered that the Christ child would grow up a warrior, a colossus, and overturn Rome. But Aretas' warrior was not to be. After the Hebrew was crucified, it is said that in a moment of bitter passion and disillusionment, Aretas smashed the cross in a fit of rage.'

'There were wild, unsubstantiated tales that as Aretas lay dying, Christ appeared to him,' Nick said, staring at her curiously.

'We are a wonderfully dramatic nation, Mr De Vere.' The princess lowered her eyes. 'The recounters of Scheherazade's thousand nights and a night. Our rich culture of poetry and prose has made our people the storytellers that we have been through the centuries.' She shrugged. 'That is why we have so many legends.'

The princess's voice broke off as her Prada sunglasses slipped from her grasp and fell to the stone floor. She knelt to pick them up just as Nick did the same. He grasped them in his palm and held them out to her, then stared, fascinated, at the small, plain silver cross that slipped out from beneath her T-shirt.

'Nonetheless, Princess, you believe,' he whispered.

She stared at him, silent, frozen in her kneeling position.

'My people respect and revere Christ as a teacher and a prophet, Mr De Vere. It is common knowledge, even among agnostics such as yourself,' she snapped. The princess quickly regained her composure, snatched the sunglasses, and stood.

Nick continued relentlessly. 'Yet your critics claim you choose to go a step further ... even as Aretas the Fourth's daughter Jotapa.'

Safwat appeared out of the shadows in the doorway with Father Benedict.

'Your helicopter is here, Your Majesty.' Safwat's voice was soft but insistent. 'The gulfstream refuels in Alexandria. We must leave for the palace in Aqaba before it is dusk, Princess.'

The princess nodded. 'You are in good hands, Nick De Vere.' She gestured to Father Benedict. 'But I must remind you: all digital film is to be delivered to Father Benedict before your departure – no images leave these grounds, or I *shall* revoke your licence. Even a De Vere brother has to bow to the rules of the Hashemite Kingdom.'

She turned, but he heard her soft voice from the shadows. 'She was my namesake – Jotapa.' And then she was gone.

෴

LATER

It was nearing dusk when Nick opened the door of the Range Rover. His face was flushed with exhilaration.

The hooded monks watched him from the Observatory of the Monastery of Archangels.

'He is very sick.'

'He is dying,' the elder monk whispered, 'and yet his greatest sickness is of his soul. The identity of the Son of Perdition will be revealed to him?'

'In not so many moons he will return. The revelations concerning his brother will begin.' The old monk turned from the observatory window. 'Then he will enter the dark night of his soul.'

The setting sun illuminated Jether's ancient noble features as he drew his hood back from his face. Weary.

'He has been chosen. May Yehovah grant him mercy.'

The younger monk watched as the Range Rover roared back across the desert plains. 'He has no faith.'

'And yet still he seeks for truth.'

Jether's tone was gentle, filled with wonder. 'Such is the marvel of the Race of Men, Gabriel.' He turned back to stare through the telescope at the white apparition in the Egyptian skies. 'Lucifer's messiah is here.'

~

4 BC

Lucifer stood in the fading light of the twelve magenta moons of Perdition, playing his viol, his eyes closed in ecstasy.

The tall casement doors of his bedchamber were flung wide open, and the exquisite melody echoed across the murky lava wastelands to the vaults of hell.

Lucifer's face was raised to the heavens. His raven hair,

loosed from its diamond braids, fell gleaming over his bare shoulders, and a rare serenity rested on his countenance.

He swept the carved horn bow with long, passionate strokes over the strings of his viol, his mouth moving softly to the exquisite refrain, his long, slim fingers moving dexterously across the fingerboard.

A soft knock echoed through his bedchamber, and Balberith, his attendant, entered.

Lucifer opened his eyes, sensing the presence. 'I ordered that there be no disturbances,' he glared at Balberith, then lowered the viol from his chin.

Balberith bowed, holding out a missive embossed with the Necromancers' seal of the Warlock Kings of the West.

Lucifer tore it open with his free hand and scanned the letter, then carefully folded it closed, then nodded. Balberith walked back through the doors. Lucifer paced the room restlessly, viol still in hand.

A second courtier appeared, and unlocked the doors of the ornately carved music chamber housing Lucifer's vast collection of lyres, psalteries, dulcimers, fifes, flageolets, pan pipes, lutes, serpents, cornets, and gleaming golden shofars. Lucifer handed him the viol.

Balberith re-entered followed by Charsoc, dressed in his flowing vermillion night-robes and with a canary yellow tasselled nightcap on his head. His black shaman vulture chick rested on his arm.

'Your Majesty...' He bowed deeply, a sinister smile on his blind face.

'You may speak,' Lucifer said, turning his back to Charsoc. Balberith laced Lucifer's satin night-robes.

'Your Majesty, I have received word from the caste

of Black Murmurers who traverse the Arabian kingdom of Petra. They report a caravan of magi arrived last dusk. The magi seek the newborn king.'

Lucifer looked over his shoulder at Charsoc, as Balberith pulled a heavy white fur gown over his shoulders. His expression inscrutable. 'Magi...? What do *they* want with this king?'

'They are of the upper house of the Megistanes, Your Majesty – of an ancient priesthood. Their duties encompass the anointment of kings. They follow the star.'

'Kingmakers!'

'Your Majesty, there is one, a devout servant of ours, a king of earth – whose sorcerers consult with the Warlock Kings of the West. The magi would journey to him. They seek him out.'

'And this king who seeks our cause?' A faint smile glimmered on Lucifer's lips. He stopped under the hundred blazing perfumed frankincense tapers, inhaling deeply. 'His name is Herod.' Charsoc replied. 'He is greatly disturbed, Your Majesty. This new king threatens his power.'

Lucifer moved over to the enormous rubied windows. The nova had drawn much nearer to Earth. Lucifer watched its intensely burning light.

'Dispatch Darsoc, my sinister princeling – and my Grey Magus, to follow the magi. Instruct your Black Court Grand Wizards to accompany him. Charge the Warlock Kings to instruct Herod that on arrival, these magi must make careful search for the child, and when they find him, they must bring him word. His excuse shall be that he might worship the child.' Lucifer turned from the windows.

'Then bring me word...' A slow, evil smile spread across his features. '... that I might worship the child also...'

Chapter Three

BROTHERS

G ABRIEL WALKED BAREFOOT in silence, his feet sinking into the soft, glistening pearl sands on the celestial white beaches of the First Heaven that stretched for thousands of leagues in front of the splendid Palace of Archangels. His pale gold tresses were plaited with platinum and hung loose down his back over his shot silk oyster-coloured frock coat. His ethereal features were flawless: the perfectly carved cheekbones; the regal countenance. His clear grey eyes were gentle yet piercing.

Gabriel gazed at the reflection of the twelve palest-blue moons that glistened on the First Heaven's horizon, watching the lilac hues shift to a deep majestic indigo. Towards the eastern horizon lay Eden, its magnificent, lush hanging gardens and amethyst waterfalls barely visible from the sea's edge. Shooting stars and lightnings arced over the foaming silver waves of the Crystal Sea as clusters of luminescent diamonds the size of pomegranates washed up onto the white sands, emitting a soft luminous light.

He stared up at the soaring gold-columned palace that towered high above the western wall. This was where he and his two elder brothers had dwelt in harmony and kinship before the darkening shadows of insurrection had fallen over the realm of the First Heaven – before Lucifer, seraph, great archangel, light bearer, was banished.

Now only Michael's and Gabriel's grand wings of chambers were occupied. The majestic west wing of the son of the morning lay desolate, Lucifer's magnificent mother-of-pearl chambers deserted, their towering golden doors engraved with the emblem of the Royal House barred since the dusk of his banishment, in worlds long since departed.

Michael strode towards him down the gilded steps, his emerald cloak flying behind him.

'I am returned from earth,' he announced, marching through rows of grand white columns, past the vast crystal orangeries of the eastern wing of the palace towards Gabriel across the pearl sands.

'It is good to see you, esteemed Gabriel.' Michael kissed him warmly on both cheeks, then removed his golden war gauntlets.

'As it is you, beloved brother.' Gabriel surveyed the tall, noble warrior. Michael's gleaming, flaxen hair was tied back with emeralds and gold in two thick braids that framed the noble features; his intelligent green eyes, lost in thought.

He has grown much in wisdom of late, Gabriel reflected. *Since Lucifer's banishment.* Gone was any residue of the hot-headedness and intractability of his former years, and in its wake had grown a nobility and a graciousness that were unmistakable. This was his elder brother, Michael, his spirit clothed with honour, nobility, and valour, commander-in-chief of the First Heaven's armies – Yehovah's warrior.

Michael raised his head to the horizons and closed his eyes, a deep peace transforming his features. He breathed in the heady fragrance of myrrh that wafted across the shimmering beaches from the vast, lush plains of great white poplars far beyond the eastern plains of Eden. He was silent a long moment, then followed Gabriel's gaze up towards Lucifer's chambers.

'Lucifer's magus have alerted him.' His voice was soft. 'It was just a matter of time.'

Gabriel nodded.

'We knew it would be so.' Gabriel walked to the very edge of the Crystal sea, staring out at the indigo shooting stars that blazed overhead on the horizon.

'I can still see his raven hair blowing in the eastern breeze,' he murmured. 'It is strange – I remember Lucifer's every word as though they were ingrained in my soul.' He turned his face to Michael's. ' "Each and every dawn," ' Gabriel whispered, ' "we are tested as to whether we would serve our own will, our own desires, or would we serve Yehovah." That is what he told me at this exact spot. "Choose wisely each day, Gabriel," he told me . . . ' Gabriel lowered his clear grey eyes. ' " . . . and you can never fail Him. The greatest gift you can grant Him is your free choice to serve him in obedience, which, in turn, is your true love." '

'Yehovah, by His choice, endowed the angelic race with

free will,' said Michael. 'Lucifer chose his path, as we have chosen ours.'

'And as the Race of Men choose theirs,' Gabriel said thoughtfully. He continued his pacing along the luminous sands. A long silence fell. Finally Gabriel spoke again.

'Michael . . .' He raised his face up to the abandoned west wing, his eyes filled with intense sorrow. 'Do you think Lucifer has regret?'

'No,' a soft voice echoed.

Gabriel turned. Jether the Just, imperial angelic monarch and ruler of the twenty-four ancient kings of Yehovah stood on the gilded steps above them, his silvered hair and beard blowing in the soft zephyrs off the sea. His wizened features were gentle, but underneath his bushy white eyebrows, his pale, watery grey blue eyes glittered like an eagle's – intense, alert. Nothing escaped Jether's vigilant gaze. He well knew that the tender Gabriel had suffered much of late. The dreamings that haunted Gabriel night after night the cost of the gift he bore as Yehovah's seer, the angelic revelator. He smiled compassionately at Gabriel.

'If he has regret, Gabriel . . .' Jether walked towards them across the sands, the pearls covering his lime green jewelled slippers as he walked. '. . . it is regret for himself, as he realizes the dire consequence of his choice . . . of his fall. But true regret . . .' Jether stared upwards north of the two trees of Eden, to the colossal golden, ruby-encrusted door, ablaze with light that was embedded into the jacinth walls of the tower – the entrance to the throne room.

'True regret is based on repentance – grieving for the sin, not the consequence of sin. The two are quite contra-dictory. Completely opposed.' Jether's pale blue eyes blazed with an uncharacteristic fervour. 'And they must *never* be confused.'

He gazed up towards the towering west wing, with its grand pearl balconies that now lay abandoned. Derelict.

'Perfect in beauty,' he whispered. 'Filled with wisdom – oh, how thou hast fallen, son of the morning.'

'What is this Race of Men to Him that He is mindful of them?' Gabriel murmured. Jether placed his hand gently on Gabriel's shoulder.

'The High Council assembles. The presence of Yehovah's Chief Princes is requested.'

Michael bowed to Jether, 'It shall be so, revered Jether.' Jether smoothed his embroidered pale green satin robes. 'We gather on the Eastern sands under the Great Willows. At dusk.'

Jether studied the brothers intently.

'The old world has gone,' he said softly. 'It can never be revisited. This is a day of farewells.' And then he vanished, transported to the Tower of Winds.

Through all the aeons that had elapsed since Lucifer's banishment and our return from Perdition, there had never been a time that Michael and I had looked back to our previous world.

But somehow we both knew that this was to be a different day.

We stood – alone on the shimmering sands. In silence. Two brothers. Not Chief Princes. Not Warrior or Revelator. Just younger brothers. Remembering. All that had been. All that had transpired. Grieving.

For all that we sensed was yet to come, the memories of our triune brotherhood coursing univited through our souls like all-consuming, blistering waves. And I knew, that it was in that very moment, that we each said our final goodbyes.

For Jether was right. Our previous world could never be revisited.

The old world was gone.

Michael and I would never again look back . . .

. . . For a new world lay before us.

A world whose fate now hung by a thread.

A world with whose destiny the First Heaven was to be irreversibly entwined.

. . . The world of the Race of Men.

CHAPTER FOUR

THE FIRST HEAVEN

J ETHER PACED WITH even strides through the winding corridors of the Tower of Winds in the First Heaven, his silken white hair and beard sweeping the sapphire floors as he walked. On his head rested a jacinth crown.

Obadiah, a youngling of an ancient angelic race possessing the characteristics of eternal youth and a remarkable inquisitiveness, was Jether's attendant. The youngling scurried panting behind, hardly reaching up to Jether's waist. His stocky little legs almost in a trot to keep up, his tight orange curls flying, vainly attempting to hold Jether's voluminous willow green satin cloak off the polished sapphire floors. As they rounded a corner, Obadiah distractedly caught sight of Tirzah, another youngling, at target practice with what looked like an enormous iron cannonball.

The languishing Obadiah lost hold of the cloak just as Tirzah launched the iron ball, which arced high above their heads, plummeting down at high speed to land directly in the centre of Jether's train. Jether stopped precisely as the offending spheroid landed.

He sighed deeply and turned to glare at Tirzah.

'*Now* will you believe me that I have eyes in the back of my head, Obadiah?' He glowered darkly at the youngling, his white eyebrows knitting together. 'Take your tiffin!'

Obadiah scuttled away, Tirzah in tow. Jether chuckled softly to himself, then caught six tittering younglings hidden in the corridor, devouring their morning tea break of curds and junket. Catching sight of him, they dropped their tiffin, staring at him in awe. He scowled purposefully in their direction. They turned a furious beetroot red and scattered in four different directions. Jether hid a smile, then grasped his cloak with both hands and continued his striding. Grave.

Xacheriel, one of the First Heaven's eight high elders and Jether's close compatriot, appeared from a small door in the wall. Xacheriel was the Ancient of Days curator of the sciences and universes, one of the twenty-four ancient kings under Jether's governance. He and his wise ones were the devoted executors of Yehovah's unutterable marvels, governors of the three great portals, and custodians of the sacred vaults of the flaming cherubim and seraphim, which housed the countless billions of DNA blueprints, genome codes, and the boundary lines of Yehovah's innumerable galaxies, seas, and universes.

He fell in step with Jether, his great white eyebrows knitted together, striding the corridors in his violet experimentation galoshes. Carrying Xacheriel's train was Dimnah, a short, dumpy, freckled youngling, shuddering violently from the blue arced electrical currents that were shocking him from Xacheriel's person. Jether stopped, tapping Xacheriel on the shoulder.

'*Humph*,' he coughed surreptitiously into his hand-kerchief. Xacheriel frowned impatiently. Jether pointed to the now convulsing Dimnah, blue electric arcs swirling in and out from his tight ginger curls down to his striped stockinged knees. Xacheriel looked down at his indigo rubber gloves and scowled.

'Rakkon! Jatir!' he bellowed.

A group of younglings all attired in rainbow coloured galoshes and rubber gloves instantly appeared as if from a vapour.

'Disconnect the dullard Dimnah!'

With immense difficulty, the younglings managed to pry Dimnah free from Xacheriel's train. 'No galoshes!' muttered Xacheriel. He waved his hand towards the languishing Dimnah, now fallen to the floor in a dead swoon. 'A high-voltage experiment, and the dunderhead wears no galoshes!' Xacheriel sighed in exasperation, scrabbling beneath his oilskin in the voluminous pockets of his orange robes, and brought out a small, sticky half-eaten cake with the consistency of an English doughnut with a indigo curd centre, then thrust it between the long-suffering Dimnah's lips.

'Brain food!' he declared, rubbing his large hands together, and continued his great tramping along the corridor. Jether shook his head, his eyes twinkling with amusement and followed.

'Lucifer and his cohorts are dangerously close to the truth, Jether,' Xacheriel declared darkly.

Jether looked up at him from under his eyebrows, without breaking stride. 'Lucifer's revelation of Yehovah's ways has waned these past aeons,' he replied. 'He and his evil magus seek after one born of a royal house of Earth – one of power and nobility.'

They walked out of the sapphire corridors across the lush lawns of the lower gardens of the Tower of Winds, through the lower chambers of the sixth spire, where they were met by two more younglings, holding the reins of two white-winged chargers.

Jether raised his eyebrows to Xacheriel as he placed his foot in the stirrup.

'We have a little time yet,' he said grimly.

Jether and Xacheriel mounted effortlessly and flew above the glistening diamonds paving the vast winding road through the massive pearl gates, two hundred feet high, across the crystal bridge, finally landing on the vast eastern pearl sands on the very edge of the Sea of Zamar.

Seated on jacinth thrones, under the open heavens on the eastern sands were the high council of the eight ancient kings, Yehovah's high elders. Six ancient monarchs were already seated around a golden circular table, their heads bowed, each dressed in vibrantly coloured robes. Their lips moved silently in supplication to the Ancient of Days. Michael sat on a carved silver throne.

Jether dismounted, and the six ancient monarchs and Michael rose as one and bowed reverently to his person. Jether nodded and took his seat at the throne at the head of the table, Xacheriel at his left. Jether bowed his head, his lips moving in supplication. He nodded to Michael.

'Lucifer is suspicious of these magi,' Michael said. 'My reconnaissance informs me that the sorcerer's of the royal court of Herod of Judea consult with the Warlock Kings of the West.'

Zebulon, an elder with a long white beard and a gentle demeanour, raised his head from his supplications. 'Yes, this is true, Michael, but Dracul and his Warlock Kings also consult continually with Melsoc of Persia and Babylon, with Babiel of the Medes.'

Methuselah raised his white-crowned head. 'Dracul keeps his options open. He speculates.' His words were calm and measured. 'All they are certain of is that the prince shall be born of the Race of Men, in the East.'

Maheel, a third ancient elder, raised his bowed head; his watery blue eyes were distant.

'You may speak, Maheel,' Jether said quietly.

'Our greatest danger comes when the star stands still again, this time over its resting place, Bethlehem.'

There came a thundering as Gabriel galloped across the sands on his white steed, escorted by ten Revelators. He drew to a halt under the great willows. Gabriel dismounted and strode towards them, speaking as he walked. 'Forgive my tardiness, my honoured elders, my revered brother Michael. I received urgent word from my Revelator scouts. Our greatest danger, I regret is almost upon us. Lucifer dispatched Darsoc and the Grey Magus this very dawn, to follow the magi. It will be only a matter of time before Lucifer realizes that the newborn prince of the East, and Christos, are one and the same.'

All around the table lifted their heads; Michael and Gabriel exchanged a grave look. Lamaliel shook his head. 'His wrath will be unbridled.'

Issachar stroked his beard. 'His first action will be to investigate the constituents of Christos blood.'

'We are well aware,' said Xacheriel, drumming his large fingers, rather too loudly on the table next to Jether.

'Lucifer's evil genius is no match for the unfathomable wisdom of Yehovah,' said Jether, closing the book of Eternal Law. He placed his wizened hand softly on top of Xacheriel's to restrain his pounding.

'He bcomes blinded by his own preconceptions,' stated Issachar.

'His choice to consistently despise Yehovah's treaties struck with the Race of Men in aeons past, could ultimately lead to his demise,' Gabriel said.

Jether nodded.

'His pride renders him more careless. He is contemptuous of the accords which will be to our advantage.'

Xacheriel stroked his bushy eyebrows. 'He more easily be persuaded. His misgivings satisfied.'

Jether nodded. 'We must have faith.'

'Lucifer is become drawn to the Eastern regions,' Michael rose. 'He dispatched Dagon and his Black Horde deliberately to divert me to the West. I sent forty legions after Dagon to dispel my brother's unease – eighty of my legions remain hung well back in the First Heaven. They await my return to the East.'

'My Revelator legions are mobilised,' Gabriel added. 'The Proclaimers and scouts left for the Eastern horizons at dawn. They await your command, brother.'

Jether stood up slowly from the table, as did the seven elders. Jether clasped Michael's arm, and they followed Gabriel across the pearl sands to the marble-columned pergola, up the gilded steps to the lush tropical gardens where the archangel brothers' thrones stood beside the waterfalls of nectar. The blue gales blew violently. Jether stared out past the Sea of Zamar, at the winged stallions galloping across the pearl beaches. Far above the stallions, an enormous white eagle with golden talons soared towards them.

The eagle landed gracefully on the sands next to Jether, who unclasped a missive with the seal of Yehovah from its diamond collar. He read silently.

'Yehovah summons me,' he murmured, then turned to gaze up at the shimmering indigos and lilacs of the rainbow overarching the Crystal Palace. To the north of the two massive trees in the hanging gardens, above the labyrinths, a colossal ruby-encrusted door, ablaze with light, was embedded in the tower's jacinth walls – the entrance to Yehovah's throne room. There were few, so few, who had ever gazed upon the beauty of Yehovah's countenance.

Jether, faithful steward of Yehovah's mysteries, was one.

Jether closed his eyes. 'The codices of the White Judgement,' he whispered. 'They are to be opened.'

Michael stepped back, stunned. 'The codices of fire,' Gabriel echoed.

Jether nodded. 'The Day of the Seventh Stone approaches.' He mounted the great eagle, sitting astride the golden saddle and stroking its soft white neck feathers. The eagle looked up at Jether, its piercing brown eyes gentle, awaiting his command.

'Faithful Vespar, I would journey to the labyrinths of the seventh spire,' he said, his eyes strangely misted.

'Michael make haste to the Eastern heavens. Gabriel – meet me in the seventh spire of the labyrinths. Let us never forget, my angelic princes, that we fight on behalf of Yehovah for the greatest prize in the universe.' His voice shook with passion as Vespar ascended into the skies. 'For the redemption of the Race of Men from their tyrant king, Lucifer!'

CHAPTER FIVE

HEROD

A HUGE GROUP of the councils of Jerusalem, including the seventy-one members of the Jewish supreme council, the Sanhedrin, and all Herod's scribes and his own magus, were gathered in the palace's inner court. Herod sat on his elaborate golden throne in the inner court of his palace. He was dressed in the most ostentatious purple finery, his crown awry on top of his thick, ill-fitting ginger wig. He limped heavily over to the nearest windows to stare balefully at the pillar of fire that blazed in the night sky.

'The star burns brighter with every hour!' His face was florid with rage. 'You knew I had a rival, yet you did not *warn* me?' He slammed his sceptre down on an ornate vase, smashing it to the floor. 'There is a king of the Jews; your Hebrew writings are clear on it.'

MESSIAH – THE FIRST JUDGEMENT

He rose from the throne and swung around to the chief priest, who was shivering with terror. 'They are clear, aren't they?'

'The writings are clear, sire,' the chief priest stammered.

Herod flung open the Torah scrolls. 'Bring him nearer, that he might know his subject more intimately.'

Herod's guards grabbed the chief priest by the arms and thrust him in front of Herod. Herod pushed the Torah in front of the chief priest's face.

'Where is this king of the Jews to be born?'

Petrified, the priest fumbled through the scrolls until he found the book of Micah. Trembling, he stopped. Herod snatched the scroll away from him and scanned it avidly, his fleshy jowls shaking as he read.

'Where, *where* does it say "king of the Jews"?' He pushed his face right up to the high priest. 'Show me.'

'In Bethlehem of Judea, for thus it is written by the prophet Micah: "But you, Bethlehem, in the land of Judah, are not the least among the rulers of Judah; for out of you will come a ruler who will shepherd my people, Israel."'

'Is this ME?' Herod screamed, red in the face. 'Is it Herod the Great they prophesy? Is it Herod? Or is there...' He spun around. '...ANOTHER!' he hissed, his two chins shaking.

The chief priest gulped. Suddenly finding courage, in a holy fervour he blurted, 'There is another.' His words were soft but unmistakable. 'The Messiah, the ruler of Israel – His kingdom shall see no end.'

Herod rose, apoplectic, from the throne and smashed the sceptre against the chief priest's chest. The priest rolled down the marble stairs, blood flowing from his head onto the marble floor. The council stood terrorized, silent.

Herod lifted up his voluminous robes. 'GET OUT OF HERE! Get out!' screamed Herod. 'OUT!'

The council scattered like geese, out of the throne room, two dragging the semi-conscious priest behind them. Herod's advisers clustered around his throne, trembling and whispering feverishly.

'Stop your infernal mumbling,' Herod snarled. 'What is it that you whisper of now?'

His chief adviser stepped forward. 'We speak of the caravan, Your Majesty, that draws nigh to Jerusalem from the east.'

A second counsellor bowed. 'The caravan is of exceeding wealth and pomp, Your Majesty. It is the talk of all Jerusalem.'

Herod sat back heavily on his throne. 'Yes, yes, my magus informed me. They are Parthians – interferers ... king-makers! They fell kings from thrones at their whim!' He bit his fist, his eyes gleaming with insanity. Sweat poured from his furrowed brow below his crown. 'It is a plot. The Parthians take me for a usurper – they would murder me ... dethrone me. And put this ... this infantile king of the Jews...'

'Nay, Your Majesty. This caravan belongs to a king, Aretas, sovereign ruler of Arabia.'

'Aretas! The king of Petra – why, he is no philosopher, no magus's accomplice.' Herod relaxed visibly. He exhaled deeply and readjusted his wig.

'He is a pragmatic man, one who has seen bloodshed.'

Herod's eyes glittered. 'Does he come in peace or war?'
He bunched his robe in his fist, trembling. 'War!' he
whimpered. 'He seeks revenge. He comes to murder me
and annex Judea to the Nabateans!' A thread of spittle hung
suspended from his chin. He was seized by paroxysm,
coughing up blood into his handkerchief.

His chief attendant held out a sealed missive. Herod
snatched it and tore it open, eyes wild, scanning the
contents.

'He would honour me and solve our border disputes.' He
wiped his brow with a silk handkerchief. 'He seeks peace.'
He exhaled heavily in relief and held out his trembling hand
to his cupbearer, who immediately placed an ornate goblet
of wine in it.

'This upstart king could well threaten Aretas, also.'
He sipped from his cup delicately. 'Get word to his
ambassadors that my palace awaits him. He shall indeed be
my welcome guest.'

Herod caressed the goblet thoughtfully. 'The royal
houses of Petra and Judea would do well to make alliance.
Together we shall destroy this upstart king!'

⌐⌐

Herod turned to a tall, sinister figure to the right of
his throne. 'Mephisto, relay to me the Necromancer's
counsel.'

Mephisto chanted, and slowly the thirteen Warlock
Kings of the West materialized next to him, unseen by
Herod. Dracul, their ruler spoke, echoed by Mephisto,
almost as an alter ego, speaking with him in a strange,
unearthly unison. 'Let them make careful search for the

child and report back, that you may find him and destroy the newborn king.'

⤺

Gabriel thundered bareback on his stallion, through the lush rain forests, across the vast bulrush meadows of the Eastern plains of Eden in the First Heaven, his flaxen hair flying. He came to a halt leagues beneath the holy mountain, near the base of the throne room's rubied entrance, outside the western labyrinths of the seven spires. He dismounted and entered the underground entrance to the sacred caverns. Seven hidden chambers in the mountain each ascended into the inner sanctum of the labyrinths. Gabriel walked, head bowed, his path lit only by the flaming eternal torches high against the cavern walls.

As he ascended higher into the chamber, an unaccountable dread clutched his heart. His ascent continued, deep into the heart of the labyrinths, until he reached the sixth burning lamp. Nine tall, silent warriors stood with flaming broadswords. The Watchers, guardians of the hidden sanctum of Yehovah. They raised their flaming swords to Gabriel, bowing in acknowledgment.

Gabriel continued through the dim passage, ascending until he saw them: Yehovah's dread warriors, the Watchers of the seventh flame.

The Watchers beheld him, and as one they lifted their flaming swords, which had barred his way to the seventh chamber. Ever so slowly, Gabriel walked on through the huge iron grid, magnetised towards a blazing light at his left. The Watchers drew back and disappeared. He moved deeper into the cavern. In front of him blew a stormy wind, and out of the wind burned a great indigo cloud and great lightning and flashings came from out of the inferno. Gabriel stared ahead in wonder. There before him, stood Jether, in the very midst of the burning flames, his arms raised, his staff, the staff of the white winds held high. His hair and beard flew in the tempests that rose from the indigo cloud. Blue lightnings blazed from the staff. His face glowed as burnished bronze, his skin burning translucent. Dimly visible in the midst of the coals of fire, lay seven enormous gold-bound lapis lazuli codices, their pages blazing with a fierce blue fire – the codices of the White Judgement. Gabriel watched as two majestic flaming cherubim became visble through the flames, the first lifted the top codex from the midst of the burning coals. He stretched forth his hand and passed the sacred tome to Jether.

Jether clasped it, holding it high. 'The Codex of the First Judgement!' he cried. 'The secret counsels of Yehovah are unveiled!'

⌒

Herod nodded and slowly opened the voluminous red velvet curtains. Before him stood King Aretas, Balthazar, Caspar, Melchior, and a hundred magi, with coffers of gold and precious stones. Herod bowed deeply to King Aretas, who bowed as well. Herod looked at the overflowing caskets, simpering like a child. He sat down on his throne, motioning to Aretas to sit opposite him on a smaller, ornately gilded throne.

'Your royal name has travelled often across the desert plains to me, great Sheikh Aretas of Petra and Arabia, Aretas the noble, the warrior, protector of his people.'

'Your royal name is one of fame and renown throughout the eastern plains, O Herod of Idumea, Herod the Great, feared by all.' Aretas bowed again.

A smile of pleasure spread across Herod's slack-jowled face. 'You come to Jerusalem not only to seek peace, Aretas. You seek a king other than myself. Of this I am convinced.'

Aretas stared deeply into the old king's eyes. He was debauched and evil, but he was no fool – even near death, a formidable enemy. This Aretas knew. 'I seek to pay my respects to Herod the Great, but yes, you are correct in your assumptions. There is another that I seek, O Herod.'

Balthazar stepped forward and bowed deeply. 'Your Majesty, we seek the one who has been born king of the Jews. We saw his star in the East and have come to worship him.'

Herod's eyes narrowed. He clutched Aretas' arm and drew him away from the magi. 'You are a brilliant man, Aretas . . . ' Herod lowered his voice ' . . . to have realized the threat of a new king who would ravage our kingdoms, and to have allied yourself with the very magi who can locate his presence.'

Herod turned back to the magi and smiled agreeably. 'My chief priests tell me that the newborn king is to be found in Bethlehem. Go, make careful search for the child. And when you find him, report to me, that I, too, may go and pay my homage to him. My armies are at your disposal, as is my hospitality.' He clapped his hands.

'Our minor disputes – the Dead Sea Valley, Syllaeus – are all behind us. Melech, show my royal guests to their quarters.

CHAPTER SIX

CHRISTOS

THE PRINCELING DARSOC stood at the head of the Grey Magus, his cultured, sinister demon sorcerers. Ruthless and cunning beyond compare, the Grey Magus were Lucifer's finest informants, serving as his senior intelligence corp. Archivists, Philosophers, Intellectuals. They stood, a hundred strong, their white hoods pulled down over their faces, shadowed in the darkness.

'Shepherds! Pah!' Alastor, Grand Wizard of the Black Courts snarled to Darsoc. 'This is no king's dwelling!' He turned his black charger around impatiently. 'You and your magus waste my time!'

Darsoc stood, not a muscle moving, every sense alert. Alastor threw back his silver turbaned head, his squat blood red cat eyes gleaming with disdain.

'A fool's errand!' he spat. '*We* intend to return to the Black Courts in possession of the facts!'

'Then ride, Alastor,' Darsoc's words were spun like silk laced with venom. 'You would not want to disappoint your unforgiving Master ... Grand Magus Charsoc. And forfeit your jewels ... and advancement.' A small evil smile played on Darsoc's lips. 'Or your head.'

Alastor turned his black charger to face his company of Black Court Wizards. 'Turn back, there is nothing here – we ride to Persia!' he cried, thundering away on his monstrous fire breathing stallion, his blazing staff held high.

Darsoc threw back his hood. His pale, fine features exuded a strange luminosity. It was only on closer scrutiny that it was noticeable how his once perfect skin was now marred and his beautiful grey eyes glinted a dark evil. The gusts blew his long strands of hair across his white cloak.

'I smell the scent of the revelators on the winds,' he hissed. He held up a grey gloved finger to his pale lips.

A tremendous wind blew overhead, accompanied by the sound of a monstrous beating of wings. Instantly the sky was filled with thousands upon thousands of giant white eagles, their wingspans a hundred feet, their collars and talons of molten gold.

'The scouts of the White Knighthood.' A malicious smile spread across Darsoc's face as he watched Alastor and his company of Charsoc's Black Court Wizards ascending into the black skies in the direction of the East. 'Michael is here ... ' he murmured, a gleam in his cruel eyes. 'We wait.'

King Aretas, Balthazar, Caspar and Melchior led the great caravan, seated on white Arabian steeds. Balista and Ayshe, Aretas' manservant, followed close behind. Balthazar gazed up at the star, now stationary, fixed directly above a summit that lay in the distance, then pulled on the reins of his horse, gesturing to the party to do likewise. He dismounted, his heart pounding, swiftly leading the way up the terraced hills of Bethlehem guided only by the solitary lamp that swung from the centre of a rope hung across the entrance of a lone inn ahead of them. He stopped outside the low structure, built of rough stones. It consisted of an enclosure where a small herd of cattle were huddled together, tied up for the night. Above the enclosure were six small stone rooms. Balthazar walked slowly past each low chamber, studying the inhabitants closely, then turned to Aretas and Melchior and shook his head. Frowning, he walked further out to a crude stone grotto attached to the inn as a stable. Four small dogs, their ribs sticking through their mangy coats yapped at him relentlessly, nipping at his feet. He covered his face with his robe as the pungent stench of waste from cows, mules and camels hit his nostrils, stopping outside the filthy area where the mules and horses were tethered. Hesitantly, he peered inside, then turned, gesturing to the party to follow him. Aretas frowned. Balthazar nodded. Aretas shrugged in assent as Gaspar and Melchior followed Balthazar further inside the stable. There among the hay and straw spread for the food and rest of the cattle, sitting cross legged on a mat in the far corner of the threadbare room sat a young girl, scarcely more than a child. Her thick waist-length tawny locks framed her fine olive features with its high cheekbones, aquiline nose and soft rosebud mouth. She stared at the guests, exhausted, but her brown eyes were exultant. Her gaze turned to the babe in her arms. As one, the magi fell prostrate. She placed the infant gently back down in the manger, then walked across the straw floor towards Balthazar.

Aretas watched silently from the doorway, staring at the empty stable, the wooden manger, the only furniture in the room. Balthazar fell to his knees, tears falling down his wizened ebony cheeks. 'All these years ... these aeons, we have faithfully guarded these,' he whispered. Kept them safe for the Jewish Messiah prophesied by the great Hebrew Daniel.' He bowed his head, trembling.

A pale Gaspar gently laid the gifts at Mary's feet. 'The cup of frankincense; the box of myrrh...'

Melchior stepped forward. 'The gold rod of Aaron. With these we pay homage to the Messiah.' He knelt, his head bowed.

Mary lifted her head, brushing the long dark tresses of hair away from her enchanting face. 'We humbly receive your gifts,' she replied.

'We thank you.' Joseph quietly watched from behind the manger.

Balthazar raised his hands. 'That I would live to see this day.' He lifted his head and turned to Aretas, who still stood pale, and silent by the door. 'Aretas, come.' Balthazar's eyes shone. 'It is He whom our forbear Daniel longed for.'

Joseph held out his hand to Aretas, who shook his head. 'I am not a religious man...' he stated firmly.

Balthazar grasped his arm firmly and guided him over to the sleeping babe, no longer wrapped in the snug swaddling bands of his earlier months. Aretas stood back, his hands held before him. Mary smiled tenderly and held out her hand to Aretas.

Again he shook his head impatiently. 'Forgive me . . . I do not believe as these . . . '

Mary continued to smile at him, her gaze locked to his. She took his brown, hardened hand gently in her small olive one.

'Tell them I do not believe . . . ' Aretas looked pleadingly to Balthazar. Mary looked compassionately at him with her liquid brown eyes as if he were dull of understanding, and placed his hand over the babe's.

Aretas fell backward as if jolted by a violent, shocking force. Balthazar, Mary and Joseph stared, astounded, while Aretas' entire body shuddered as in the throes of a violent fit. His breathing became short and shallow, and he flung his head from side to side, raising his hands to his face before crumpling to the floor.

Balthazar stared down at him in horror. 'Forgive me . . . ' He raised his face to Joseph's. 'We must assist His Majesty at once – we will remove him from your midst.'

Joseph frowned. 'He is in no state to be moved, sire.'

Mary nodded in agreement, her eyes filled with consternation. She placed her hand on Balthazar's.

'There is a space at the back, with the innkeeper. Let us take him there till he is stronger.'

Balthazar nodded and turned to Gaspar, who stood trembling. 'I will stay with King Aretas. Look after our caravan.' Gaspar nodded, dumbstruck, and exchanged a bewildered glance with Melchior.

Balthazar turned to gaze at the newborn infant once more, then grasped the king's hand in his; his fingers were still shaking violently. But it was when Balthazar looked into Aretas' face that his blood ran cold, for the young king was staring straight ahead, his eyes wide open. He had been struck completely blind.

CHAPTER SEVEN

THE REVELATION

LUCIFER SAT BATHING his legs in the balmy amber and gold pools that shimmered under the pale, gloomy moons of the West horizon, sipping pomegranate elixir from his golden goblet. He turned to Marduk on his left. 'These kingmakers, the magi – what did they find?' He plucked a blue fruit from the silvered vines that flourished in his nocturnal orangeries, slicing it deftly with a small sharp blade.

Marduk nodded to the palace sorcerers, who stood petrified behind the ornamental pools. 'The nova was moving, Your Majesty,' the chief magus replied. 'They left Herod's palace at dawn. They were to report back to Herod, sire, as you ordered.'

Lucifer sat silently, waiting. He placed a sliver of the fruit on his tongue and swallowed.

'We received rumours they did not return, Your Majesty,' the chief magus stammered.

Lucifer stared, his mind reeling. Marduk drew his face close to Lucifer's.

'They left by a different route.'

Lucifer handed his cup to his cupbearer, his expression inscrutable, and rose as Balberith dried him with a gold cloth. He strode through the Western terraces, Balberith following, through the orangeries back into the throne room, dressed only in his white silk loincloth, then snatched his satin robe from Balberith's grasp and flung it over his shoulders, enraged. 'Rumours...' he roared, waving the sorcerers away. They scuttled down the marbled chamber, past the Luciferean guard and out through the throne room gates. 'Rumours!' he bellowed.

Alastor moved to the black gates, consulting in deep whisperings with Marduk meanwhile Lucifer paced up and down before his throne, hands behind his back, staring at his reflection in the polished black floors. Marduk hurried back up the nave of the throne room, strangely perturbed.

'Charsoc's Black Court Wizard's are returned, Your Majesty.'

Lucifer did not look up from his pacing. 'Grant them audience,' he commanded.

Immediately the gates opened to reveal Alastor's corpulent black cloaked figure. Behind him hovered his company of silver turbaned wizards, their black staffs issuing orange fire.

Lucifer stood facing his Northern balconies, his back to them. 'Where is the newborn king?'

Alastor walked slowly up the nave of the throne room

towards Lucifer, the only sound in the throne room, his narrow crimson pointed shoes that squeaked with every awkward step. Charsoc materialized at the Black Gates. Silent. Observing.

Alastor stopped halfway up the nave.

'We found no king, Your Majesty.'

Lucifer turned, his face contorted with fury, then flung open the massive golden doors of the north wing. The nova had drawn nearer, far nearer to earth and blazed furiously.

'The nova yet burns.' He clenched his fists in fury. 'WHERE is the infant king that is born in the East?'

Darsoc and his Grey Magus entered the throne room. The Grey Magus stood, a hundred strong. Breathtaking. Their strange beauty, bewitching. Tall and pale, their waist-length platinum hair fell smooth as glass over their billowing white velvet cloaks fastened with delicate silver clasps intertwined with live asps. Darsoc slid silently over the lapiz floors towards Alastor and the throne.

'We found no king of noble birth, sire,' Alastor stopped in front of Lucifer, 'but only a peasant babe wrapped in swaddling clothes, before whom shepherds worshipped.'

Marduk scowled impatiently. 'Shepherds! You waste His Excellency's time.' Lucifer grasped Marduk's arm to still him, his nails digging deep into Marduk's flesh. Marduk frowned, perplexed, but obeyed.

Alastor turned his head back to the approaching Darsoc, then dropped to his knees, 'No – my Lord,' an evil sneer spread across his flabby features. He raised his shadowed eyes to Lucifer's. 'It is *Darsoc* who wastes your time with shepherds,' he rasped. 'We, the Grand Wizards of the Black Courts were prudent. *We* turned back to Persia.'

Charsoc slowly caressed the silver serpent on his staff, observing Alastor intently, deep in contemplation.

Lucifer walked over to the huge open doors, staring out a long while at the nova.

'Darsoc – my wicked prince.'

'My Lord,' Darsoc bowed deeply to Lucifer, then knelt beside Alastor.

'Tell me about these shepherds.' Lucifer's voice was solicitous, soothing, his back to Darsoc.

Darsoc lifted his shadowed eyes. 'Alastor deemed it a distraction, Your Excellency … a mere diversion…' he answered, his voice listless but cultured.

Lucifer turned and stared at him, his face inscrutable. 'But *you*, my loyal and cunning slave…'

'There came a great commotion in the Second Heavens. A vast company of the heavenly knighthood descended.'

'Their purpose?' Charsoc strode up the nave directly towards the throne.

'They were scouts.' Darsoc's voice was measured. 'Of the White Knighthood of the holy mountain, sire.'

Alastor shifted his cumbersome frame, suddenly uneasy, looking from Charsoc to Lucifer.

'Of your brother Chief Prince Michael's Battalion, sire.'

'Michael dispatches his scouts and proclaimers for a peasant babe?' Lucifer frowned and pushed his hair back from his eyes, momentarily confused.

'Pale Fool!' spat Alastor. 'You waste His Excellency's time!'

Darsoc moved his platinum head close to Alastor's silver turbaned one, then pressed his pale grey lips against Alastor's fleshy ear. 'I think not,' he hissed. He removed his silver gauntlets and signed deftly to a tall, pale form, shrouded in a white velvet cloak who instantly materialized next to him.

'I am one of the Grey Magus designated Jequon.' Jequon spoke in a low silken voice. 'Chief archivist of the Grey Magus.'

'And what did your archivists document, Jequon?' Lucifer inquired softly, his back to Alastor.

Jequon stared down at his long, pale trembling hands, then looked back at Lucifer's back. 'My archivists documented the pronouncements of the white knighthood.' Sweat broke out on his temple. 'Relay the declaration, Jequon.' Charsoc commanded. 'It may distress my sovereign Emperor...' Jequon bowed again to Lucifer. Charsoc rested his hand ominously on the hilt of his glinting Necromancer blade. 'Relay it. Word for word.'

Jequon took a deep breath. 'That... that this day a child is born – this day in the town of David...' Jequon looked up at Lucifer, his courage deserting him 'A saviour who is...'. Not a muscle of Lucifer's face moved. 'Who is... Christ...'

Lucifer swung around in astonishment to face Charsoc. The blood drained from Charsoc's face.

'*Chris ... tos,*' Lucifer hissed, appalled. A terrible horror contorted his features.

'...The Lord,' Jequon gasped, his eyes never leaving Lucifer's. A strange smile played on Darsoc's pale lips as he watched Charsoc walk unsteadily towards Alastor, his whole body trembling.

Alastor stared in shock from Lucifer to Charsoc. 'An error, my lord.' He stood to his feet, his chins trembling. 'An error.' Charsoc murmured.

With one savage thrust, Charsoc impaled Alastor on his necromancer blade. Alastor stood choking on his own blue blood, retching.

Then with one sudden, brutal thrust, Charsoc sliced straight through Alastor's neck. Alastor's head landed on the floor with a thud. 'Errors are never tolerable,' Charsoc muttered. His blade slipped out from his hand and clattered onto the empty floor.

'Errors are *never* tolerable!' Like lightning, Lucifer swung around to Charsoc, his own sword raised directly above Charsoc's neck. 'Your magus have failed me, Charsoc!' Charsoc's entire body shook uncontrollably, sweat poured from his temple.

'This Nova ... this King...' Lucifer grasped Charsoc's long hair savagely in his fist and wrenched him so close that Charsoc could feel Lucifer's hot breath burning against his cheeks. 'This King is none other than *Christos*! His blood – is it undefiled?' Lucifer gave another cruel wrench on Charsoc's hair. 'You know as I, the tenets of Eternal Law.' Charsoc stared at Lucifer, horror struck, his mind reeling. 'If his blood is undefiled, he will exchange his soul for the souls of Men and wrest my kingdom from me!' Lucifer roared.

Lucifer stood, silent for a full minute, then flung Charsoc savagely from his grasp. He stumbled to the floor beside the unfortunate Alastor. Alastor's head vanished. Then his body followed, disappearing straight to the Abyss.

Lucifer flung his broadsword down, then strode to the window and threw open the curtains, raging blasphemies at the star still overhead in the Second Heaven. 'Yehovah's genius! He sent Himself! Tricked by my own preconceptions, as He knew I would be!' He pushed past Charsoc to where Darsoc stood, trembling.

'His Messiah will have no palace, no royal robes. His Messiah is born of dust and clay! Tell me, Darsoc, the destination of the infant king,' he hissed, his face only inches away from Darsoc's own.

'I followed . . . I followed your royal orders, sire,' Darsoc uttered in growing dread. 'My Black Murmurers followed the magi back through the desert towards Persia.'

'The infant is with the magi?' Lucifer circled him.

Darsoc held out an unsealed missive, his pale fingers shaking uncontrollably. Lucifer snatched the missive, then crumpled it in his hand, his face contorted with sheer hatred.

'The child has *vanished!*' he snarled.

Lucifer leaned heavily against the pillar, running his fingers through his raven locks, muttering to himself in an evil, peculiar angelic tongue as one demented.

'My brothers deceive me,' he muttered. He turned to Charsoc, still trembling on the floor. 'Investigate the circumstance of the infant's birth. Find out what Jether is up to. Do not dare fail me again, Charsoc!'

He wrapped his robe tightly around himself.d.

Then he turned to Marduk. 'Stir up the demonic hordes that torment that imbecile Herod day and night. Infect his dreams that he may have it in his heart to kill all males under two years old. The swaddling prince shall not escape my wrath. Summon Belzoc!' he cried. 'Great prince of Persia, Prince Michael is his! Prepare our war chariots! Amass all regents to make war against my brothers. Astaroth!' he screamed, 'Alert all powers, principalities, and rulers of the darkness of this world . . . the great satanic princes . . . Nakan and his Necromancer Kings, the Thrones of Folcador, the Warlocks of Ishtar . . . Call them to assemble on the great plains of Perdition. And *find* my brother Michael. Where Michael is, *there* will be the child Christos, also!'

Lucifer hissed. 'Then we strike!'

CHAPTER EIGHT

THE SEVENTH STONE

J ETHER SAT on his jacinth throne in the seventh chamber, deep in the underground crypts of the labyrinths, pouring over the great blue codex. Gabriel stood across from him, studying him intently … waiting.

'The codex unveils Yehovah's plan, his secret counsel prepared aeons before the advent of the Race of Men.' Jether closed his eyes in reverence.

'Yehovah prepares a place for the infant king in Egypt, in Alexandria. There is one king of Arabia; his name is Aretas. He has been chosen to bear his name. He will aid the infant in his flight.'

'Lucifer has not seen the codices?'

'Lucifer was long captivated by the codices of fire. They have lain in the labyrinths for aeons before his origin,' Jether

78

said. 'His soul yearned to gaze upon their pages, but no, he has not looked upon their contents.'

'And what of Charsoc?' Gabriel questioned. 'He was privy to the sacred mysteries. Keeper of the sixth stone.'

'Charsoc…' Jether's expression grew hard. 'He well knows of their existence. The sixth chamber of knowledge was his abode but the chamber of the seventh flame was sealed from him.'

'So the sacred mystery of the Messiah is safe from their polluted sorceries.' Jether closed the book; its golden inclusions of pyrites shimmered like little stars out of the codex's deep blue lapis casing. He looked up at Gabriel.

'I go to retrieve the seventh stone.'

Gabriel stared at Jether, incredulous. 'Six stones resided here within the Labyrinths,' he whispered. 'One went missing … from the sixth Chamber … at Charsoc's defection.' Gabriel stared at Jether intently.

'No angelic being has ever laid eyes on the seventh stone…'

'The seventh stone – the stone of fire, possesses all the combined power of the six. It lies beyond the ordinances of heaven.' Jether's eyes grew dim with wonder. 'It lies beyond the treasuries of winds and hail, beyond the seven seas of wisdom. In the very cradle of the universe.'

Jether carefully picked up the codex and deposited it into a large crevice in the cavern wall into the great silver casket of the sacred writs.

'It will protect the infant while he walks as one of the Race of Men, until its seal is lifted when he will face the ultimate test … against Lucifer himself.'

Jether placed his cloak around his shoulders and clasped it with shaking fingers. 'We have no time to waste. The child *must* be sealed with the seventh stone. At present he is vulnerable. Unprotected. You, Gabriel, make haste to Joseph. Instruct him of Yehovah's plan to take the infant to Egypt. Aretas is Yehovah's instrument to lead them to the monastery at Alexandria.'

'I will leave at once for the land of the Race of Men,' Gabriel said.

Jether nodded. 'I dispatch Vesper, my warrior eagle, with a message for Michael to leave the Eastern horizons. He must journey at once to the caravan. He is the infant's only protection from Lucifer's evil scheming until I seal the child at Alexandria with the seventh stone of fire.' Jether removed a small ampulla filled with myrrh and cassia oils from his robes. Gabriel knelt before him.

'Time is against us.' Jether anointed Gabriel's temple, then laid his hands gently on his head in a blessing of consecration.

'Avoid the eastern corridors,' he whispered. 'The Black Murmurers traverse them incessantly. I prepare for my journey.'

⟿

Balthazar had paced the small square room all night in his supplications, pleading to the God of Daniel to help Aretas, his king and his friend. He bathed Aretas' fevered head with the rags that Mary had given him, soaked in myrrh from the caravan's store, in the hope it would bring him back to his right mind.

He paced the room for hours, praying, pleading. Yet the

ancient Balthazar sensed that Aretas was being weighed in the hands of the omniscient. He would wait.

It had been past midnight before Aretas' hands stopped trembling, and nearing dawn when Balthazar could first make out his first incoherent ramblings and Aretas opened his eyes again. And it was daylight before he rose from the pallet on the floor and took his first unsteady steps.

But when he finally took Balthazar's hand in his, his hand was steady, his eyes were clear, and his face exuded a peace that Balthazar had never before seen in the proud, head-strong young king.

Aretas tried to speak, but no words would come, only tears that flowed. The tears that Aretas could not stop. Tears of a king's past bloodsheds; tears of a king's thousand murders; tears of a king's thousand debaucheries and treasons ... and the tears of a man's thousand regrets. And so it was that he wept in the ancient astronomer's arm, so that Balthazar's robes were soaked from Aretas' weeping.

And then, suddenly, he grew calm.

'The babe is in great danger. We must protect Daniel's Messiah and the holy family.' He looked around him. Ayeshe, his ageing faithful steward, stood outside the door. 'Ayeshe, prepare my royal guard!' He stood up. His voice clear and strong. 'My royal ancestors were bequeathed a monastery in Alexandria by an ancient caste of magi of the Royal House of Egypt. It will be a safehouse for the infant king. We ride to Egypt!'

⁓

High up on the Eastern elevation of the Black Palace, the sharp steel of broadswords glinted as Lucifer and his chief of armies, Lord Astaroth, Grand Duke of hell, thrust and parried as they did each dawn, an integral part of Lucifer's rigorous physical regime about which he was fanatical almost to the point of narcissistic. This dawn, however, he seemed strangely distracted. Astaroth's broadsword hit Lucifer's chest a ferocious blow, and Lucifer doubled over in agony. The strapping Astaroth laughed triumphantly and turned his back. Like lightning, Lucifer brought Astaroth gasping to the ground, his hands twisted beneath his torso in agony.

Lucifer raised his fencing mask, a smile of satisfaction on his face. 'That is why I am king of hell' – he threw his broadsword down on the lava floor and took a cloth from Araquiel to dry his face – 'and you, Astaroth, are but a Duke ... albeit Grand ... '

The scarred but still handsome colossus shook his blond mane, still dazed. Lucifer looked fleetingly down at the fallen warrior. At times, Astaroth's bearing was eerily reminiscent of Michael. From the back, he could be Michael's double. In worlds long departed, Astaroth had been commander of Michael's finest legions, his most trusted general. Michael's closest compatriot. Lucifer's expression darkened at the thought of his brother. And now, Astaroth was Lucifer's champion, commander-in-chief of Perdition's armies. Did Astaroth have regret? Lucifer wiped his face with a silk cloth. He would never be sure.

'Prime your legions,' he growled. 'We ride tomorrow at dawn.' Astaroth bowed in reverence, striding to the far portico, then mounted his black winged stallion and rode the skies in the direction of his vast battalions war chariots gathering on the vast plains of Perdition.

'Your Excellency.'

Lucifer turned. 'I still smart from your folly, Charsoc.' His mouth tightened.

'I redeem myself, Your Majesty. Our demonic scholars and sorcerer sages have examined the circumstances of the infant's birth. My archivists confrm their findings.'

Charsoc moved towards Lucifer.

'The infant was indeed born of a woman of the Race of Men. The birth was witnessed. The Black Murmurers have verified their findings. He was born one of the Race of Men, like any other in a town named Bethlehem. His mother is a Hebrew girl. A youth. The Father – one named Joseph. The possibility, however, exists that a created egg could have been implanted by Yehovah in the host.'

'Christos incarnate . . . ' Lucifer rubbed his chin, deep in thought. 'No possibility is to be excluded . . . What of the egg's conception?'

'As is the way of the Race of Men, the infant's conception is the result of two germ cells: the egg from the mother, the seed from the father. In the Race of Man, these share equally in the inherited mutations of the sin nature – all deriving from the fall. The egg *still* has to be fertilized by seed from the father, Joseph, to enable its conception and replication . . . ' Charsoc smiled triumphantly. 'It is the way of *all* of the Race of Men.'

'I am well versed in the biogenetic engineering of the Race of Men.' Lucifer paced back and forth. 'Every drop of blood the child produces is as a result of the introduction of the male sperm. The fetal and maternal blood do not come into actual contact, separated by the double layer of chrorionic epithelium.'

83

He turned his face to Charsoc's, an unnatural gleam in his eyes. 'What if they have an *alternative* plan – a plan to deliberately by-pass the male seed...?' Lucifer's expression grew dark. 'And *prevent* the inherited mutations.'

'A substitute seed?' Charsoc frowned.

'A seed that is *not* of the Race of Men.'

Lucifer stood staring out beyond Perdition's magenta horzons. 'One that is *incorruptible*...'

Charsoc turned to Lucifer, thunderstruck. Lucifer nodded.

'Yehovah.' Lucifer declared.

'Sire!' Charsoc gasped. 'It is strictly forbidden – prohibited by the tenets of Eternal Law issuing from Yehovah himself. You know firsthand – your generals who left their first estate by having intercourse with the daughters of men. Their punishment for their transgressing of the Eternal Law was to be to be cast in eternal chains into the lowest regions of the netherworld – Tartarus.'

'I am well aware. The pits of gloom until the Day of Judgement,' Lucifer murmured. 'So – if Yehovah fertilizes the created egg, he would be culpable of cohabiting with the Race of Men, just as the fallen host banished to Tartarus.'

Lucifer walked to the far side of the Eastern Wing housing Perdition's royal avaries, pacing restlessly up and down before hundreds of colossal gilded cages that housed his sinister scavenger scouts.

'My brothers will have their schemes, their well formulated conspiracies but when it comes to the issue of Yehovah – He is bound to his own Eternal Law. He cannot transgress it,' he muttered, 'even to save the Race of Men.'

He unclasped an aviary door and gently clasped a hissing

vulture scavanger chick wearing a diamond collar, in his gloved hands. He caressed its black feathers soothingly, his sapphire eyes shadowed in thought.

'Against my deeper instinct, I find myself persuaded,' he spoke softly to himself. 'Yehovah will have no part in the conception of the Christos seed.' He spun around. 'No!' He strode over to a hellcage filled with screeching pale blue-eyed writhing bat-like creatures and grasped one by its long slimy rat tail. 'There will be no incorruptible seed, Charsoc!' he declared. The scavenger chick screeched deafeningly, opening its cruel curved beak, its red fangs visible. Lucifer dangled the shrieking bat creature face down, the chick crushed its head with its ferocious fangs and swallowed it with one bite.

'Good boy, Cagrino.' Lucifer stroked the chick's head. 'The Christos-infant had to have received its genetic inheritance through the father's seed,' Lucifer murmured. 'He partook of the inherent sin damage present in Joseph's seed and blood, therefore the Christos infant's blood is defiled.' Lucifer frowned. 'Only one with undefiled blood, free from inherent sin damage can exchange his soul for the souls of the Race of Men and release them from my rule.'

He placed Cagrino gently on a velvet cushion back into the gilded cage and clasped the door, deep in contemplation.

'Yet He comes to destroy my kingdom. I sense it.'

Lucifer walked over to the Eastern terrace and stood surveying his armies. Hell's immense and terrible militia were assembling on the smouldering volcanic wastelands of hell. 'Why is he here on my planet?' he whispered. 'We must destroy him before he grows in strength.'

'There is a *way*, Excellency.' Charsoc held up a missive with the First Heaven's seal. 'The vulture shamans took a revelator eagle "into custody".' Charsoc waited. 'It was Vespar.'

Lucifer's eyes narrowed. 'Vespar...,' he echoed. He turned, immediately alert.

'He carried this missive from Jether the Just...' Charsoc hesitated, a sinister smile on his face. 'It was addressed to your brother, Prince Michael, sire.' Lucifer strode over to Charsoc and snatched the letter from his grasp, Charsoc watched intently as his liege lord examined the note.

'Jether meets Michael and the infant king near Alexandria, with the great seal – the seventh stone,' Lucifer murmured, a strange exhilaration in his gaze. He stared out towards the horizon, his back to Charsoc. *Remembering.*

'The seventh stone's power is indomitable. It holds in itself the combined powers of all six stones of the labyrinths. Once the infant is sealed with the stone of fire, we, the fallen, are powerless against him. Our only opportunity is...'

Charsoc moved towards Lucifer, clasping his arm with his bony fingers. 'The breach in time, sire, before the infant reaches the monastery and Jether. His greatest vulnerability.'

Lucifer stared at him with an unnatural glint in his eye. 'He comes to destroy my kingdom. Instead I shall destroy him. You have surpassed yourself, Charsoc.' Lucifer held out his hand with the great damson ruby of Satan. Charsoc knelt before him and kissed his ring. 'You are pardoned.'

'Thank you, my lord... my king.' Charsoc bowed deeply.

'The disciples of hell assemble!' Lucifer cried. 'Instruct

Astaroth to marshal them for war without delay to the land the Race of Men call Egypt. We slay the infant king!'

⤳

The fierce, relentless desert winds blasted across the caravan, it was nearing dusk, and the party had been travelling through Egypt for what seemed an eternity. Dozens of camels, laden with frankincense, gold, and treasures of the East, headed the enormous caravan across the vast desert plains, their progress impeded by raging sandstorms. Ten elegantly caparisoned white Arab stallions paced in the caravan's centre. Mary clutched the swaddled baby tightly to her breast, her features almost hidden by her hood, but her eyes resolute. A sudden chill blew over the caravan, and the sky grew dark, as an immense shuddering began. Mary covered the babe and held him tightly to her.

⤳

'Jether! Jether!' The pressing cry filtered from the colossal balconies of the Royal Amber Chamber that hung high above Jether's private monastic cloister quarters in the Tower of Winds, down to where Maheel and Issachar were assisting Jether in his varied preparations for his journey to the cradle of the universe.

Obadiah carried an empty silver amulet over to Jether, who threaded it deftly on a long silver chain.

'Jether! Jether!' Looking up, Jether and Maheel watched Xacheriel making his precarious way down the wide polished amber spiral steps of the Royal Chamber. He clung distractedly to his embroidered purple and golden taffeta toga as he descended, his curled satin slippers sliding dangerously on the steps. Dimnah clung desperately to his arm, hindering rather than aiding his progress.

Xacheriel misstepped, and they both tumbled in a precarious heap of purple and gold into Jether's private libraries, landing in an undignified sprawl on the gleaming amber floor.

'Drat and bumble...' Xacheriel mumbled, scrabbling for his monocle, now buried under mounds of newly bound Annals. He glowered at the trembling Dimnah as though it were all the youngling's fault.

Jether shook his head. He placed the silver amulet around his neck and closed the clasp, then strode over to the languishing pair, followed closely by Maheel. He stared down at Xacheriel's enormous feet, which were crammed into a pair of tight cerulean satin slippers obviously several sizes too small. One of Xacheriel's rare leanings to vanity. 'You didn't, by any sheer chance...' Jether addressed Xacheriel, '...place any of your newly concocted time-travelling lubrication grease under your ceremonial slippers, did you?'

Xacheriel glared indignantly up at him. 'I was conducting a voltage experiment in the hologram chambers.' He scowled sheepishly. 'My – my latest time-travelling experiment – and wandered over into the Red Zone by mistake,' he declared dramatically. 'A temporary *lapse* of my instruments. The grease aided my hasty departure.'

Maheel shook his gentle white head.

'You know we have cautioned you again and again not to travel on those coordinates.' Maheel frowned in concern. 'It is dangerous, my dear Xacheriel. Hazardous at best.

Charsoc's spies frequent that time lock, and they are most ruthless with their methods of torture.'

'Yes, yes . . . ' Xacheriel gave a dismissive wave.

'The demon werewolves frequent the time corridors in the Red Zone,' Jether said darkly and deliberately. Xacheriel paled momentarily much to Jether's relief. Dimnah's mouth dropped open, enthralled. Jether decided to press the point while he had the advantage.

' . . . As do the flesh eating Necromancer Kings . . . ' Jether glowered. Xacheriel's hands trembled visibly. 'One of the myriad advantages of not being constituted of matter.' He consoled himself, then yanked his enormous scarlet spotted handkerchief from his inner pocket and wiped the sweat that suddenly poured from his brow. Dimnah's mouth hung wide open in awe. Issachar strode up behind Jether.

'You needed me?' Jether asked Xacheriel. 'I leave to retrieve the stone of fire.'

Xacheriel frowned, then smacked his temple violently with his large hand. 'Yes . . . Yes . . . of course!' Xacheriel strode round in circles, ordering his thoughts.

'It is a *terrible* tale, revered Jether,' he declared ominously. Issachar yawned loudly and deliberately. Jether glared at him from under his eyebrows.

'A *terrible tale*.' Xacheriel's big hands shook. 'One that affects your journeyings,' he whispered. Jether frowned, placing his hand gently on Xacheriel's shoulder.

'Calm yourself, Xacheriel, old friend. Breathe deeply.'

Xacheriel inhaled, his great chest heaving. 'On my way back past the Red Zone, in the Second Heaven, I encountered the Revelator scouts. Gabriel's firstcore rank of Eagles.'

Jether waited patiently, knowing he would eventually get to the point.

'They had in their custody one nasty-looking-and-smelling-customer. Vulture-like organism – mangy feathers.'

'A vulture shaman – one of Charsoc's scouts.' Jether nodded. Dimnah's mouth gaped so wide that Jether reached over and physically closed it with his hand.

'Dimnah!' Xacheriel barked.

'Anyway, the nasty-looking feathered life form had *this* – he called it his "trophy".' Xacheriel scrabbled in his voluminous pockets, eventually fishing out a great silver and diamond collar bearing the seal of the eagle revelators. He passed it to Jether, dabbing gingerly at his eyes with his handkerchief.

'Vespar...' Jether uttered, stunned. Xacheriel clasped Jether's old fingers awkwardly in his own.

'I am sorry to be the bearer of miserable news, old friend.' Jether extricated his trembling fingers from Xacheriel's iron grasp, then swiftly turned over Vespar's collar. The scarlet insignia that signalled a missive was in flight was still in place. Jether stared past Xacheriel, his features frozen in horror. For he knew with a terrible certainty that if Michael had received the missive, he would promptly have replaced the scarlet insignia with a gold one from the royal house signifying his receipt of the communique. It was the simplest rule of the corridors, adhered to by one and all of the First Heaven's legions.

'The insignia is in place.' Jether's voice was barely audible. 'Vespar did not reach Michael with my missive. Consequently, Michael did not receive my instruction to leave the East and escort the child to Alexandria.' Jether held on to the balustrade for support, his hands trembling.

'The infant travels as we speak. Unprotected.' He turned to the elders, his face white as a sheet. They stared at him, appalled.

'Far worse. If Lucifer discover the missive, he knows I meet the infant king near Alexandria, with the seventh stone. He will be mobilising hell's armies even as we speak.'

Jether hurried up the amber stairs, the elders following close behind.

'Send Sachiel to Michael. He must leave for Egypt without delay.' He turned to the elders on the stairway.

'We no longer have the element of surprise. Prime Raphael and our armies for assault. We leave at dusk.'

CHAPTER NINE

THE HORDES OF HELL

HELL'S IMMENSE and terrible armies mobilised on the smouldering volcanic wastelands of hell. Folcador, hell's fearsome archduke and Lucifer's finest general, a ferocious demon with the face of an angel and the wings of a griffin, rode fierce and proud in his black war chariot, leading a hundred legions of the fallen. Astaroth, grand duke of hell, rode the skies, his war chariot pulled by the fierce white ice dragons of Siberia. His barbaric generals – Pruslas, Barbatos, and Rashaverak – marched below, the menacing Black Horde marching behind.

Forneus, the great and scheming marquis of hell, rode the skies on monstrous, coiled Leviathan, followed by twenty-nine legions of silver-tongued winged serpent demons.

The vast companies of Dark Grey Magus on their

headless three-humped camels, rode alongside the dread warlocks of Ishtar on the backs of werewolves and dragons. Overhead in hell's crimson, murky skies flew the demon Witches of Babylon on Leviathan, and Hera and the Banshees of Valkyrie on their flying giant serpents. Marching to the rear was the great, macabre company of Necromancer Kings, leading their armies of living skeletons.

Belzoc, barbaric prince of Persia and Lucifer's commander-in-chief, led twenty thousand of hell's legions, riding their black war chariots pulled by hell's formidable dark-winged stallions.

Lucifer stood, menacing and proud, in his monstrous black war chariot, its silver wheels sprung with jagged war blades. The crimson flame on hell's infernal flag flew proudly.

The sinister Shaman Kings stepped forward; behind them marched the vast company of hooded shaman drummers.

'Armies of hell, I salute you!' Lucifer cried. The slow, menacing throb of war drums pulsed beneath his voice. 'Slaughter the usurper king before he is sealed!'

A terrible, blood-curdling roar went up from the armies of hell as the rulers of the dark world thundered towards Egypt's skies.

$$\backsim$$

One by one, fine hairline cracks started to appear on the great idols of Egypt in the great temple. The shuddering built to a crescendo with an overpowering roar as, one by one, the imposing golden images crashed to the ground. Temple priests ran for their lives, the idols continued to fall until not one remained standing.

Mary bowed her head and stared down at the sleeping babe. She shivered. Thousands of silent sinister looking vultures had descended towards them this past hour, circling the caravan, casting strange dark shadows across the desert.

Aretas frowned. 'We must make haste,' he said. 'There is danger in the wind.' He flicked the reins and galloped to the head of the caravan, strangely troubled.

⤙⤚

Raphael, resplendent in his full ceremonial battle armour, rode past the front line of the armies of the First Heaven in his platinum war chariot, pulled by twenty winged stallions. He stood tall, imperial, the valiant general of Yehovah's armies on the mount of the North in the First Heaven.

To the left marched Gabriel, attired in his ceremonial war regalia, followed by his vast company of the revelators, his swift and agile archers, in their suits of gleaming silver armour. Their great bronze crossbows reached from the ground past their heads. At the ready.

Overhead flew a million of the Revelator 'scouts', occupying the length and breadth of the skies – the First Heaven's huge white-feathered warrior Eagles, with their beaks and talons of gold, their wingspans over one hundred feet. The archangel princes led Michael's battalions. Juhdiel the Daring led a thousand legions. Uriel the Fearless rode ahead in his enormous silver chariot, leading four hundred legions of the First Heaven's finest swordsmen, followed by his multitude of warrior princes. Jether and his twenty-three royal compatriots, the angelic monarchs, were mounted on their royal white chargers, standing in a semicircle, their lances raised.

Gabriel drew the Sword of State from its jewelled sheath and raised it high above his head. 'We fight for Yehovah, that truth and justice may prevail!' he cried.

'We protect the infant king!'

The deafening roar from the First Heaven's armies resounded through the First Heaven. Jether rode over to where Raphael and Gabriel stood surveying heaven's armies, he clasped Raphael's arm.

'My spies inform me that Lucifer sends Belzoc, prince of Persia, ahead to slaughter Michael before he reaches the infant.' Jether lowered his eyes. 'Hell's depraved champion would settle an old score.'

'He defeated Belzoc once over the Hebrew Daniel,' Raphael declared.

'With Yehovah's strength, he shall defeat him again.'

Jether frowned. 'One clean thrust of the sword of justice, and Belzoc is banished to the Abyss to await the Judgement. Your aeons as Lucifer's commander-in-chief will serve you well against their malevolent strategies.'

Raphael spoke with a hard fierceness. 'Once Belzoc is slain, speed is Michael's advantage ... Lucifer will be close behind. They are evenly matched.'

'You have your fastest warriors?'

Raphael nodded. 'My swiftest legions are my escort.' Raphael pulled down his golden visor. 'The Messiah's kingdom come!' His twenty winged stallions and war chariot thundered into the lilac skies, followed by a hundred thousand of his legions war chariots. Jether stared after them, strangely troubled. He turned to Gabriel and placed his hand upon his shoulder.

'You are prepared for Nakan and his necromancer sorceries?'

Gabriel gestured to the amulet around his neck. 'Well prepared, revered Jether. Our arrows dipped in the sacred ointment from the labyrinth's sixth spire.'

'The entire destiny of the Race of Men rests on the outcome...' Jether looked silently into Gabriel's eyes. They clasped hands, and Jether embraced him.

'Yehovah be with you, noble Gabriel. Press any advantage against Lucifer. Tell Michael to bring the child safely to me. I shall be waiting.'

Jether placed his hand on Gabriel's shoulder. 'I go beyond the treasuries of the hail, Gabriel,' he whispered, 'to the wake of the universes – to retrieve the seventh stone. I await you at Alexandria.'

⁓

'Your Majesty, Your Majesty!' Ayeshe galloped up alongside Aretas at the front of the caravan, his stallion whinnying in terror. Ayeshe tugged at his arm with his scrawny brown fingers. 'The noise, sire – it frightens the camels!'

Aretas nodded; the royal servants exchanged looks of trepidation. 'Stay in my place, Ayeshe.'

Aretas pulled on his stallion's reins and galloped to the back of the caravan. He turned his Arab steed around and scanned the vast expanse of desert. He could hear the great thundering of horses' hooves far behind him, but the desert was empty. Flat. A vast plateau stretching to infinity. And then the hair on the back of his neck crawled as watched the desert sand a full league behind being kicked up, as if by the hooves and shadows of a great army on horseback, drawing down on the caravan.

The string of horses and camels started to move faster, and the Arab steeds whinnied with fear.

A second great thundering was now coming towards them from the opposite side of the desert. The white steeds of the caravan now panicked visibly as the camel riders struggled to keep their beasts under control. Joseph and Ayeshe, chilled with fear, watched the desert plains, as the two waves of invisible moving sand converged towards the caravan. Aretas galloped over to where Joseph rode with Mary and the babe.

'Some strange magic is afoot,' he cried. 'Surround the infant king!'

Immediately Aretas' royal guard surrounded Mary and the sleeping infant. 'Full speed – make haste!'

Aretas rode next to Mary, keeping a grim eye on the infant. Jesus slept peacefully.

⌒

Belzoc and his ferocious hordes closed fast, riding from the West, gaining ground on the now galloping caravan. But suddenly a small white throng appeared ahead of them on the eastern horizon. Michael and his lone company of warriors advancing towards the caravan from the East.

Michael stood tall in his flaming chariot pulled by twenty winged seraph stallions, racing along a full league above the stark desert plains, leading a hundred angelic warriors astride their white steeds.

Belzoc pulled the reins brutally, bringing his vicious black steeds up short on the desert plain, and turned hell's monstrous black chariot to meet the oncoming Michael head-on. They faced each other on the sweltering sand, less than a length apart.

'Belzoc, prince of Persia,' Michael cried, 'prepare to war!'

Belzoc stared in relish at the empty sands yawning leagues behind Michael, then turned to the hundreds of thousands of his black-armoured Persian angelic legions behind him.

'Michael, chief prince of Israel ... Your armies are late!' Belzoc spat, giving Michael a menacing grin, then swung his six-foot black blade savagely in the air, 'Prepare to die!' Immediately his savage hordes let out a bloodthirsty roaring, stampeding towards Michael's angelic warriors. Thousands of the savage hordes of darkness raining blows on the ferociously fighting warriors of the First Heaven, broadsword against broadsword.

Michael's and Belzoc's chariots thundered across the sand towards the caravan, their flaming wheels grinding against each other as they raced neck and neck.

'Your swordsmanship has grown soft, Michael, since our last skirmish over the Hebrew Daniel!' Belzoc shouted derisively. He pushed his filthy braided hair away from his face. Caked with dirt, it hung down past his brawny thighs.

'You have never forgiven me for defeating you in front of your armies, Belzoc!' Michael cried. Sparks and rivets flew from the princes' chariot wheels, the stallions straining to breaking point as, all around them, the violent battle played out.

'This time you shall pay with your life, chief prince of

the royal house of Yehovah. I shall exhibit your head on the gates of Hades.' Belzoc spat on the ground, wiping his mouth with a grimy arm.

'By the setting of eleven moons, you shall be banished to the penitentiary in Tartarus!' Michael yelled, never taking his eyes off his enemy. He followed Belzoc's gaze far in the distance, to Mary and the sleeping infant.

Michael stood still, all senses alert, his gaze fixed on Belzoc. Belzoc moved suddenly and, with his immense strength, jumped across from his chariot onto Michael's, ploughing his sword through the air at Michael's neck. Michael neatly evaded the stroke and slammed his sword down across Belzoc's chest, catching him off guard and knocking him, winded, to the floor of Michael's chariot. Enraged, the demon prince thrust savagely at Michael. Belzoc thrust. Michael thrust back. Belzoc rose leering to his feet. The ring of steel on steel resounded across the desert, as the chariot veered furiously ahead.

'I shall feed Christos' tender flesh to the wild dogs that roam these mountains...' Belzoc smirked. He thrust his sword through Michael's thigh, then drew it out savagely, and hundreds of small curved barbs tore Michael's flesh to shreds. Michael fell to the chariot floor, collapsing to his knees in pain.

'My latest addition – rips to the very bone,' Belzoc leered lecherously. I shall tear Christos limb from limb.' Sweat poured from Michael. Incensed, he attempted to stand but collapsed, overwhelmed by the excruciating pain. Belzoc shoved him to the floor, towering over him triumphantly.

'This day – you go to the Abyss, Michael!'

He raised his broadsword over Michael's neck, then turned his head to follow Michael's gaze over to Raphael's war chariots thundering towards them, now visible on the horizon. In that instant, Michael grasped Belzoc's tangled black mane hanging at his thighs and wound it in his fist in an iron grasp, savagely wrenching Belzoc's head down onto the chariot floor with his great strength, then swung his sword across and through Belzoc's neck one clean thrust, severing his head from his body. Thick black blood spurted up in twin fountains.

'Till the great judgement!' Michael kicked the body off his chariot onto the sand. Belzoc's head vanished. Then his body followed, disappearing straight to the Abyss.

'The Messiah's kingdom come,' Michael cried, saluting grimly at Raphael overhead.

∽

Jether hovered at the cusp of the ordinances of the heavens and the treasuries of the hail, the scorching luminous white waves of the seventh sea of wisdom churning beneath him, at the very edge of the wake of the Universes, his silver robes billowing in the tempests, his long white hair and beard flying in the rushing hail blizzards. His face was burning in ecstasy. His veined hand clasped a burning azure sapphire the size of a duck's egg. In its epicentre burned a fierce crimson flame – the seventh stone of fire.

Jether reached into the folds of his robes and produced a silver amulet. He opened the case, placed the stone of fire within, and closed the clasp, then placed it around his neck on a silver chain. And mounting his white-winged charger, he rode the colossal flashing thunderbolts of hail towards Alexandria.

⁓

Michael turned his monstrous chariot around to follow the disappearing caravan that held the infant king, then looked back to the West. Stampeding straight towards Michael on their headless winged chargers rode the legions of the sinister Necromancer Warlock Kings of the East, followed by their vast armies of living skeletons. These were the foulest, most depraved and feared of all Lucifer's armies, their sorceries vile and potent. This he well knew. And he was trapped in their pathway.

He glimpsed Gabriel out of the corner of his eye, racing towards him from the left through the skies, with a hundred legions of archers. The only way to destroy a Necromancer King's power was with a silvered arrow drenched in sacred ointment from the censer on the white altar of the labyrinth's sixth spire, sent straight through the heart. This Michael also knew.

'We shall eat you alive, Prince Michael!' cried Nakan, iniquitous Warlock King of the East, as his headless charger raced alongside Michael's thundering chariot. Michael felt a sharp pain and clutched his wrist. A tiny silver barb had penetrated the skin. He stared at it in dread. Necromancer poison. 'First I shall peel the skin from your torso,' Nakan hissed, his foul oiled tones reverberating strangely in Michael's head as his demon magic began to take effect. Michael grasped for the poisoned barb, flailing at it clumsily. 'Then I shall sip your thick, glutinous blue blood from my goblet.'

Nakan held a golden goblet high in his left hand. Sweat poured from Michael's temple down his cheeks, his eyelids grew heavy . . . far too heavy. Nakan smiled a slow evil smile. 'Once your eyelids close, Michael my pretty,' he hissed, 'you have only five seconds before the Abyss.'

There was a sudden dull thud. Nakan stared down at his chest in disbelief; a second later, his head turned to green vapour before Michael's eyes. A thousand more arrows found their marks among the horrified Necromancer company.

Gabriel thundered through the skies towards the chariot, his gaze locked on the fast weakening Michael, now collapsed, his head flung down on the chariot floor. Gabriel's huge seraph wings billowed behind him as he rose through the skies and landed directly in Michael's chariot. He wrenched Michael's head from the chariot floor, just as Michael's eyelids closed heavily.

Gabriel grasped for the tiny steel barb in Michael's wrist and pulled it from his flesh, deliberately forcing Michael's eyelids open with his free hand. Instantly, the effects of Nakan's demon magic started to drain from Michael's limbs. Gabriel exhaled in relief, gently pushing the thick blond hair matted with sweat away from Michael's temple. The recovering Michael grinned sheepishly and saluted feebly from the chariot floor. 'Close shave!' he mouthed, then he stared frowning beyond Gabriel.

Gabriel turned to follow Michael's gaze. Rakkon, Jatir and Obadiah led by an exhilarated Xacheriel on his flying white charger, were launching hundreds of flying iron cannonballs towards Hera and the flying demon witches. Directly behind the younglings a pack of drooling demon werewolves headed straight for the dramatically gesticulating Xacheriel. Xacheriel, blissfully unaware of the impending danger, was lambasting Jatir on his erroneous co-ordinate calculations. Gabriel saluted to Michael, then thundered back into the skies towards the ancient elder. Michael staggered to his feet, clasping the stallion's reins. He glanced back to see the vast company of the Black Horde led by Dagon thundering on the horizon towards Raphael and Uriel's battalions. He swiftly loosed his lead charger from the chariot and jumped astride its back, then thundered across the desert after the disappearing caravan.

Then Michael's blood ran cold, for he sensed a terrible evil, a malevolent presence. He turned.

There, only three lengths behind, stampeding towards him astride his monstrous winged stallion, his broadsword lifted high, his six black seraph wings extended, raced the king of hell himself. Lucifer … escorted by the thirteen Warlock Kings of the West.

CHAPTER TEN

ALEXANDRIA

THE CARAVAN TRAVELLED across the sweltering desert plains, the ancient granite walls of the monastery of Archangels becoming visible far in the distance on the horizon. The walls were thirty-five metres tall and three metres thick, carved from the huge mountain behind the monastery fortress.

Mary gazed up towards the formidable stone monastery, then looked questioningly across at Aretas, who smiled gently. 'The Monastery of Archangels,' he said.

'He will be safe there.'

⤶

Michael and Lucifer raced bareback on their stallions, thundering neck and neck across the desert. Overhead flew the thirteen Warlock Kings of the West, astride their monstrous dark winged Leviathan racing towards the Monastery of Archangels.

'I shall yet see you to the Abyss Michael, my brother.' Lucifer drove his rapier savagely into Michael's wounded thigh tearing the wound freshly open. Michael clasped at his leg in agony, incensed, the blood spurting over his palm gushing down his thigh.

'But I have come for a greater prize than Michael. I come for the supreme trophy…' Lucifer spat. Michael grasped for his bayonet with his free hand.

'Your supreme trophy awaits you, brother…' Michael thrust the bayonet brutally straight towards Lucifer's right shoulder. 'In the Lake of Fire!' Michael cried. The bayonet found its mark, ripping Lucifer's flesh savagely. Lucifer erupted with an agonized roar. He glared at Michael venomously, then raised his javelin with his left hand. With one last desperate thrust, he savagely ripped Michael's leg from thigh to knee, sending him hurtling violently onto the desert sands.

A sadistic smile of triumph spread across Lucifer's face as he thundered past his maimed brother, catching up to the Warlock Kings. Michael pulled himself to his knees, blood pouring onto the sand, then staggered in agony to his feet and remounted his stallion. In the distance, he could see the caravan already drawing outside the monastery gates.

⤳

The caravan drew up outside the formidable black iron gates of the Monastery of Archangels. At the crest of the gateway, a sign was engraved in gold Arabic script. The towering gates slowly swung open revealing ten priests of the ancient caste of the Archangels, dressed in simple cassocks who stood at the entrance. The great caravan began its entry through the towering iron gates.

Jether turned to face the desert.

Lucifer and his stallion was thundering towards Jether over the desert sands. Above him, the thirteen dread Warlock Kings of the West raced through the skies, their long black capes billowing, their pale green parchment like skin and hooked noses visible underneath their crimson hoods, riding their monstrous scaled dark-winged Leviathan. Searing crimson flames erupted from the monsters enormous jaws as their powerful black webbed seraphim wings beat the air frenziedly.

Jether strode over to Mary, her attention riveted on the babe nestled in her arms. He lifted the infant from Mary, never taking his eyes off Lucifer and the approaching Warlock Kings. Removing the silver amulet from under his robe, he unclasped it, revealing the seventh stone. Deliberately, he raised it high in the direction of the oncoming Leviathan.

Fierce crimson lightnings forked from the stone towards the mammoth winged monsters, striking their flaming yellow eyes. The pack of Leviathan screamed in unison. A blood chilling eerie high-pitched screaming. Seething black smoke spewed from their nostrils, then one by one, the creatures plummeted like lead to the ground, hurling the Warlock Kings violently onto the desert sands.

'No-o-o-o!' Lucifer roared, lashing his stallion savagely with his razored cat-o'-nine-tails, drawing blood. The stallion extended its black wings, soaring into the skies over the great palms on the road to the monastery, directly towards Jether.

Jether removed the stone of fire from the amulet, his eyes, hard as iron, never leaving Lucifer. The blue stone glistened, the crimson flickering fire at its centre blazing fiercely through the sapphire.

'The seal!' Lucifer screamed, thrusting his barbed spurs deep into his stallion's flanks.

Jether made a strange mark of a cross on the baby's forehead with the blue stone of fire and instantly, a blazing incandescent lightning radiated from the sapphire onto the infant's forehead. The fire of Yehovah's presence. Aretas and the monks fell prostate.

Then monstrous, iridescent flames a league high leapt up, encircling the monastery walls, erupting in a ferocious firestorm that exploded through the desert skies engulfing the armies of hell and flinging Lucifer from his airborne steed down onto the desert floor. Michael flew through the skies, watching in wonder from his stallion, his savage wounds healing swiftly in the consuming fire.

Lucifer lay, gasping and winded, trembling in terror, shielding his eyes from the torrid conflagration of light, his skin blistering in the unrelenting, scorching inferno. The Warlock Kings' frenzied screaming mingled with the demented cries of Lucifer's ravaged fallen armies, echoing through the Egyptian skies.

With a mighty shudder, the gates closed.

Michael wrote at an old wooden desk in the monastery chamber. He was clothed in a simple white robe; his golden armour hung next to the cloister window. To his right lay an open missive bearing the black seal of Perdition. 'Yes, He is safe,' Michael wrote. 'Fled to Egypt, hidden safely in her bosom. Growing in stature and favour, both with Yehovah and with man.'

He stared out through the window onto the roof of the monastery, where the boy played under Mary's watchful eye. Michael dipped the pen in the inkwell.

'He wears the seal. You cannot touch Him, Lucifer – not until Christos places Himself into your hands...'

⚭

Lucifer gazed out from the portico of the Black Palace, at the Earth far in the distance. He crumpled Michael's missive in his fist.

'No matter, Michael,' he breathed, his eyes gleaming with venom. 'I will wait.'

And so Christos became one of the Race of Men.

Sealed by the seventh stone, protected from Lucifer's unbridled wrath and Herod's murderous schemings, he spent his days and nights sheltered under Egyptian skies in the Monastery of Archangels in Alexandria. And Michael and I and Jether, chief of the twenty-four heavenly elders, ministered to Him.

The great king of heaven.

CHAPTER ELEVEN

MONASTERY OF ARCHANGELS

LATER – 1 AD

THE YOUNG BOY sat in the moonlit cupola on the monastery roof, intently carving a piece of wood. His fingers still bore the soft chubbiness of babyhood, but His strokes were deft and sure. His long, dark hair curled in tendrils around His gentle face. His eyes danced, mercurial as the changing hues of the Mediterranean. Michael and Gabriel stood on the far side of the roof, watching as He sang softly to himself.

'It is almost time,' said Michael.

Gabriel nodded gravely. 'Joseph senses it. I meet with him at dawn.'

'Aretas will be here by morning.' Michael watched as Jesus walked from the cupola to the far edge of the monastery roof, His beautiful features bathed in the moonlight. He closed His eyes and threw His arms up to the night sky. An unearthly light encompassed Him and His face shone like burnished copper.

Gabriel looked on, mesmerized. 'He talks with Yehovah.'

Looking down at his feet, Michael stared at the plane, mallet, measuring line, chalk, and several wooden carvings that lay on the flat roof. He knelt and picked up the beautifully carved objects one by one: a fish, a cup ... he stopped at a strange, crafted shape of a cross and stared up at Gabriel, unusually overcome with emotion.

'I have seen it in my dreamings in aeons past,' Gabriel bowed his head, 'and now again for many nights.'

'I have seen it also,' Michael whispered. 'After Lucifer's banishment, I ventured to the Holy Mountain, to the seventh chamber. It was there I saw it.' He clasped the cross fiercely.

'They will do terrible things to Him. I cannot let Him be harmed!'

Ever so gently, Gabriel pried the cross from his grasp; he would not let Michael look away. 'The penalty MUST be paid,' he said.

Michael turned angrily to see Jesus looking at him with a terrible sorrow. The boy closed His eyes as though greatly pained.

'*Nay, My fierce and noble Michael – stay your sword.*' The words of Christos from the seventh chamber from aeons past echoed strangely in his ears.

'*There is much I must suffer still at the hands of the Race of Men. Let this one thing be your comfort in the moons ahead: that these are the wounds of love.*'

Michael stood staring at the child, then, trembling, held out the wooden cross. Jesus reached His small hand out and took it from the strong, sinewed hand of the archangel. Michael wept.

～

King Aretas strode across the courtyard of the Monastery of Archangels. Followed closely by his royal stewards, Jotapa, and her keepers. Aretas clasped Joseph's shoulder.

'You have food and water to last the journey. I have pressing matters to attend.' He nodded in the direction of the monastery. 'I will catch up with you this dusk and escort you myself with my royal guard to the borders of Judea. Herod is dead, but his son Archelaus is still to be reckoned with. A safe house in Nazareth is prepared for you. The child will be safe there for a season.'

Joseph gripped Aretas' hand.

'We are deeply indebted you, Your Majesty. To the royal house of Aretas...' Joseph broke off in mid sentence, and Aretas followed his gaze to Jotapa and Jesus, who stood staring at each other with extreme curiosity. Mary observed the children tenderly from the centre of the small caravan. Jotapa curtsied, her unruly black curls falling across her face. The younger Jesus grinned and, with the awkward fingers of a toddler, gently moved her hair away from her eyes. Aretas watched in amusement as Jotapa giggled bashfully, then ran towards her father.

She turned to stare back impishly in Jesus' direction, then tripped over her robe, her hand landing heavily on a sharp rock that pierced straight through her palm. Jotapa stared at the blood running from the deep wound, then started to scream hysterically. Aretas ran and instantly hoisted her to his chest, the blood from her palm flowing down his robes.

Jesus walked towards them, grave, then reached out His hand and gently placed it over Jotapa's palm. Instantly the blood dried up. Aretas frowned. Jotapa instantly quieted, staring at her palm transfixed, watching the skin growing over the wound until only the tiniest of scars remained.

Aretas turned her palm around, examining it in wonder. Jotapa buried her head in his chest. Aretas shook his head, rechecked her hand, then tenderly mussed Jotapa's hair, kissed her fiercely on both cheeks, and handed her to her keeper. Immediately the young princess started to scream, this time in a fit of temper, flailing with her fists against the maidservant's chest. Jesus watched her, amused at her display.

Aretas stared at her sternly as her keeper took her, still screaming, through the monastery doors; then he walked over to Jesus and knelt down on one knee, clasping the boy's hand. 'Thank You,' he murmured.

Jesus stood silent. Earnest.

'You will be safe now.' Aretas looked tenderly into Jesus' eyes.

Jesus nodded, His gaze intent on Aretas. He felt in the folds of His tunic and brought out the perfectly carved wooden cross. He pushed it with His chubby fingers into Aretas' strong brown ones, then pointed to Aretas.

'King Aretas...'

Then He pointed to Himself. 'Jesus' friend.'

Aretas clasped the three-year-old tightly to his chest, his eyes closed for a brief moment, unusually overcome by emotion. Then he swooped Jesus up into the air and sat Him directly in front of Mary on the white royal stallion. He signalled to Ayeshe.

'Move!' commanded Ayeshe, and the caravan instantly moved as one set out from the monastery gates.

Slowly Jether walked over to Aretas. He placed his hand gently on Aretas' shoulder.

'May the gods protect Him,' murmured Aretas. He clasped the small wooden cross tightly in his hand. They stood in silence watching the caravan travel across the vast Egyptian desert. Jether turned to the priests in the courtyard.

'Seal the Monastery gates!' Jether cried. 'Until the time of His great return.

And so the infant king returned to Nazareth, where his boyhood was spent in one of hundreds of white stone flat-roofed houses that lay glittering in the sunlight, nestled in the dusty, narrow streets of the little Eastern town.

His mornings were spent at his father, Joseph's right hand, growing skilled in his vocation as a craftsmen in his carpenters trade, learning diligently as they reconstructed houses and carved ploughs and yokes, working with stone and wood. On occasion, beside himself with excitement, he would accompany Joseph and his older cousins walking the dusty roads back and forth to join the labour pools in the bustling urban metropolis of Sepphoris, Herod Antipas's ambitious new rebuilding project.

But much of his boyhood was filled with the simple dazzling sunlit Galilean afternoons that overflowed with the bright boyish, ringing laughter with his little band of friends as they ran scurrying through the emerald fields rich with oceans of wildflowers and orange and pomegranate blossoms.

And his nights were spent on the roof of the small stone house or wandering the silvery Galilean hillsides under the light of the eastern stars, communing with his Father, Yehovah.

And so the holy child grew, waxing strong in spirit, increasing in wisdom and stature and in favour with God and with man,

Preparing his heart . . .
Preparing his mind . . .
Preparing his soul . . .
     . . . Preparing for his confrontation in the wilderness with
his adversary, the prince of the damned.

Chapter Twelve

MEGGIDO

4 AD

I T WAS NEARING dusk. The eight-year-old Jesus
stopped to catch His breath, surveying the hills of
Galilee, to the north, and the majestic snow-crowned
Mount Hermon. Then He turned His gaze to the west,
where the the magnificent purple Mount Carmel rose,
beyond which lay the fringe of silvery sand of the Great Sea.

To the east lay Tabor and the unending string of exotic
caravans from Arabia, Africa, and India, wending their way
along the bustling eastern spice trade routes that linked
Egypt with Syria.

But it was the great plain to the south that commanded
the young boy's full attention.

He clambered over the stones, up the rocky slopes of the
Nazareth Ridge, His eyes filled with an ardent fervour,
oblivious of the carpet of richly coloured flowers and sharp

MESSIAH – THE FIRST JUDGEMENT

stones under His feet, His attention riveted on the monstrous magnificent valley that sprawled before Him.

Finally He stopped, gasping for breath, having reached the summit of the eastern slope, the soft breezes ruffling His long, dark curls, His bare feet sinking into the thyme and mountain flowers beneath Him. Staring.

Staring at the Great Battlefield of Israel ... Esdraelon, the Valley of Jezreel. Armageddon.

Far away in the distance, across the fertile valley, stood two imperial figures: Michael and Gabriel.

'He sees the future,' Gabriel whispered. 'The final war ... '

'Armageddon.'

Jesus stared at the great plains before Him, now filled with a vast multitude, every nation represented in the violent, bloody panaroma before them: Chinese, Arab, European, American, African, Australian soldiers, their bloodthirsty cries of battle mingling with agonized screams of the dying. The Prince of Peace watched, pale and silent, as the Son of Perdition and the great kings of the earth gathered with their armies, a great and terrible multitude two hundred million strong ... waiting ...

Huge hailstones fell from the skies onto the terrorized militia. The colossal teutonic plates of the earth shifted and the mountains shuddered as their foundations collapsed, levelling them – the Alps, Himalayas, Andes, all melting like wax. A thousand great and terrible whirlwinds rose from the south, merging with the colossal frenzied eyes of force five hurricanes, raging from the East and West Coasts of North America. Monsoons seethed from the Far East. Tsunamis erupted from ferocious seas, and now the moon turned to blood in the sky.

And then, as He viewed the 200 million man army before him, He saw men's flesh literally rotting away as they stood, soldiers' eyes disintegrating in their sockets, their tongues melting in their mouths as the valley of Jezreel became like a winepress, blood rising up to the horses' bridles.

Jesus bowed His head.

Instantly the horrific scene before them vanished, and Michael and Gabriel were gone.

Jesus held His head in His hands, breathing rapidly in shallow gasps, then lifted His face and gazed once more at the now tranquil, fertile emerald plains of the valley.

'In the latter time He has made it glorious, by the way of the sea, beyond the Jordan, Galilee of the nations,' He whispered. 'The people who walked in darkness have seen a great light...'

He stared up at the cloudless blue skies, at the lines of pink-backed pelicans and yellow-billed storks as they fluttered overhead, winging their way to the Lake of Galilee.

A strange aroma of frankincense filled the air. Jesus turned.

There, just paces away fom Him on the eastern summit, stood Lucifer, studying the eight-year-old boy ... his adversary.

'Why are you on my planet, Nazarene?' His voice was soft but his blazing blue eyes were filled with loathing. He moved closer to Jesus. 'What is it You want?' His voice was low, mesmerizing. He circled the boy.

'When the seal of the seventh stone is lifted, You shall know my vengeance.' A slight smile played on Lucifer's lips.

'You shall indeed suffer, Nazarene – away from Him.' Then he was gone.

Nothing stirred, just the soft gusts of mountain air that blew Jesus' locks, and the faint aroma of frankincense that still lingered on the breeze.

CHAPTER THIRTEEN

THE GATHERING

TWENTY-TWO YEARS LATER

J ETHER STOOD ON the high place of the Tower of Winds, the retreat of the ancient ones and Yehovah's trusted elders, who formed the high council of heaven. His fuchsia ceremonial robes blew in the blue angelic tempests. His crowned head was bowed, and his lips moved fervently in supplication.

Michael and Gabriel strode through the lush gardens towards him, followed just paces behind by Obadiah, Tirzah, and seven other younglings, who carried piles of tomes and piled them on the large, circular golden table surrounded by twelve jacinth thrones.

'His request for access has been granted?' Gabriel laid his sword down against the battlements.

Jether nodded. 'The codices of the White Judgement require the presence of Lucifer to witness the reading of the tenets pertaining to Jesus of Nazareth. Yehovah has granted

Lucifer entrance to the First Heaven for this gathering. Eternal Law cannot be revoked.'

Jether moved to the golden table, where the angelic zephyrs of wisdom and revelation raged in eternal cyclones, then sat down heavily on one of the jacinth thrones. The zephyrs immediately subsided to a gentle breeze. 'The conditions set by the codices of the White Judgement affect Christos' time span on earth. They must be witnessed by all angelic parties, ourselves and our fallen compatriots alike...'

Jether broke off in mid sentence, his gaze suddenly locked on to a silver speck flying over the rainbows that arched majestically over the Seas of Zamar.

Gabriel moved to the battlements and stared out over the pearl sands. 'It is his chariot.'

Jether nodded somberly, his eyes never once straying from the silver speck.

Michael frowned. 'Surely he has not been granted access to the entire planet of the First Heaven?'

Jether shook his head. 'No. He is confined to the Tower of Winds during his stay, but nonetheless we must prepare our minds...' He turned to fix his gaze on Michael and Gabriel. '...and our souls. He is on holy ground here. He will appear in his former state. Remember, he suffers no ill effects from Yehovah's presence here when he has been summoned by Yehovah Himself to fulfil Eternal Law.'

Jether stared at the brothers grimly. 'This day, he will be as breathtaking as when he was prince regent, his throne second only to Yehovah's. His soul, too, will seem to take on his previous beauty. Never forget, my princes, it is merely a mask, no more than a shortlived façade. His sorceries are deep-rooted.'

Far in the distance, the thundering grew louder as Lucifer's magnificent chariot became visible through the rainbow's aurora, riding on the shafts of lightning, pulled by eight of his finest winged stallions, their glistening white manes interwoven with platinum.

The chariot landed on the grand lawns of the high place of the Tower of Winds, its huge platinum wheels ploughing through the manicured lawns, churning up deep, unsightly furrows in the turf. Instantly the grass grew back, covering the enormous chariot tracks.

Lucifer alighted from the chariot. He knelt next to one of the enormous wheels, his eyes ablaze with wonder as he caressed the lush new blades of grass with his long fingers. He shook his head in fascination, seemingly mesmerized by the swelling, budding blades.

Michael stood, his arms folded, watching Lucifer intently.

'Heaven!' Lucifer declared. 'No decomposition ... no decay ...' He rose to his full nine feet. 'No death!' He swung around giving Michael the full intensity of his gaze. 'Why, Michael what wonders I have missed in my own atrophied planet!' He smiled his old magnificent smile.

Michael studied him, against his own better judgement. At their last meeting Lucifer's features had been gnarled and scarred, but today, as in times of old, he was perfect in his beauty: the wide forehead and straight patrician nose, the wide-set, haunting azure eyes and passionate, full mouth. He was as splendid as before his banishment. Imperial. His presence compelling. Michael lowered his eyes from his brother's gaze. For he well knew that Lucifer read his soul.

'Why, Michael, it is all as it used to be!' Lucifer smiled. A soft, indulgent smile. 'Nothing has changed.'

'*Everything* has changed, Lucifer,' Michael retorted.

Lucifer threw back his head and laughed loudly. His laughter rang through the gardens as he walked towards Michael.

'No, Michael, *nothing* has changed, for you are still solemn.' He clasped Michael in a warm embrace, kissing him on both cheeks. Michael stood coldly, then stepped back.

'And Gabriel...' Lucifer studied his youngest brother, then walked over to the sapphire fountains, the water cascading down as glistening blue mercury. He held out a goblet to catch the elixir. 'Ah,' he sipped delicately. 'Frankincense and whitecurrant!' He turned to Gabriel and smiled his old magnificent smile.

'You are still vexed with me?' Gabriel lowered his eyes from Lucifer's magnetic gaze. 'You know my thoughts, Lucifer. They do not change, no matter what guise you choose to take today. Your outward beauty does not reach to your soul.'

Lucifer winced mockingly. 'Ah, too much time with Michael has made *you* solemn, too.' He plucked a silvered sweetmeat from the great, spreading tree hung with thousands of white blossoms and delicacies, and popped it in his mouth, savouring it. 'Strawberry and persimmon.' He closed his eyes in rapture. 'With a hint of curds!'

Lucifer breathed in the invigorating aromas of the myrrh and frangipani that swirled in the gusts over his head. 'Jether the Just...' he murmured. For a split second, his eyes hardened. 'My old mentor, who taught me all I know of Yehovah and His mysteries...' Jether glimpsed the fleeting venom behind his dazzling smile, but then the venom was gone.

'I brought an old friend, so you could reflect together on aeons past.'

Lucifer gestured in the direction of a white albatross who perched on Lucifer's chariot. 'Your bosom companion, one who used to occupy these very thrones.'

The albatross transformed into a tall, thin figure with white hair who walked towards them. Jether stepped back. Appalled. Charsoc stood, tall and regal, in the splendour he once possessed in his former state as ancient imperial monarch. His hair was now as white as Jether's own; his white beard swept the floor, and his once blind eyes were now the same pale grey-blue as Jether's – and seeing.

Michael grasped Jether's arm to strengthen him.

'You have no place with us here.' Jether stood between Charsoc and the golden table. 'You forfeited your place at this table in worlds long departed.' His eyes blazed with indignation.

Lucifer grasped Jether's shoulder; Jether flinched.

'Oh, but you see, venerated Jether, He *shall* be at this table.' Lucifer's fingers dug into Jether's shoulder. 'He is to be my witness. It is the prerequisite of Eternal Law. Today I discover why Christos trespasses on my planet!'

Jether, his face turned to stone, took his throne; Michael took the right-hand throne, Gabriel the left. Lucifer sat on the throne opposite Jether, with Charsoc at his right.

Lamaliel entered the garden, followed by Methuselah and Zebulon, Issachar, Maheel and Jehosaphat.

All took their places at the table, as a panting Xacheriel, still with his violet laboratory galoshes followed at the rear. He sat down heavily on the only remaining throne next to Charsoc. In front of him lay a lone crown. Jether nodded and gestured to Xacheriel's head. Xacheriel scowled, then grudgingly removing his orange sou'wester and replaced it with the jacinth crown. He folded the sou'wester carefully in half, then placed it in front of him.

Charsoc scrutinized the sou' wester distastefully, then carefully opened an enormous crimson carpet bag with its mother-of-pearl handles.

'You brought your knitting?' Xacheriel gave Charsoc the full force of his darkest glare from under his knitted eyebrows. 'Or do you return the sixth stone which you *stole* from us?' he snapped. Jether shook his head darkly in Xacheriel's direction.

Charsoc smiled languidly, then removed a small gold container which he placed on the table. He opened the lid, dipping his long fingers in the clear liquid, then ran them deftly through his hair and beard, inhaling deeply in ecstacy.

Xacheriel sniffed loudly in Charsoc's direction. 'Mandrágora...,' he muttered testily, glaring at Charsoc, wiping his suddenly streaming red eyes. He sneezed deafeningly into his handkerchief, then leaned over and snapped Charsoc's container shut heavily.

'We address pressing matters.' Jether's tone was brisk. 'Time is misspent on coiffures, Charsoc.'

Charsoc turned his gaze to Xacheriel, slowly and deliberately scrutinizing the High elder. His gaze moved from Xacheriel's curd-stained apron, past his blueberry splattered beard to his uncombed, knotted, wiry silver hair visible under his crown.

'I think not.' He gave Xacheriel a purposeful, slow, patronising smile, then pulled on a pair of soft white goatskin gloves and sat his hands entwined.

Xacheriel spluttered, infuriated.

'Compatriots ... compatriots.' Jether raised his hands. 'Restraint, *please*.' He rose, clearing his throat.

'I bid you welcome, Chief Prince Michael, commander-in-chief of the armies of the First Heaven, Chief Prince Gabriel, Lord chief justice of the angelic revelators. Lucifer, ruler of the Race of Men, Earth, and the nether regions, king of Perdition. Charsoc, chief magus and apostle of the fallen. My esteemed Elders of Yehovah's High Council.'

Lucifer stood. 'First, I must be assured....' He walked slowly around the table, stopping directly behind Gabriel. 'My claim stands in the Courts of Eternal Law, does it not, Gabriel?' He laid his hand heavily on Gabriel's shoulder.

Gabriel sighed. 'Your claim against the Race of Men was received and recorded in the courts of heaven. Judgement was duly passed against the Race of Men.'

Michael stared at Lucifer sceptically. 'This you well know, Lucifer.'

Jether opened a tome. 'I paraphrase from one of our earlier recorded gatherings.' He picked up one of the tomes of Eternal Law, his nimble fingers rifled through the pages.

'A claim was lodged against mankind in the courts of heaven by Lucifer, sovereign ruler of the Race of Men. The aforesaid Lucifer placed the Race of Men on trial. Records from the archives of Perdition were as a result meticulously scrutinized and cross referenced with the Records of the Race of Men registered in the codices of the First Heaven. Every generation of Homo sapiens from the time of Eden was investigated. It has been proven beyond reasonable doubt that the Race of Men has persistently and without penitence committed desertion and has transgressed Eternal Law. Yehovah cannot judge Lucifer and his fallen angelic host and not mete out the same judgement to the Race of Men. Their transgressions are identical. Both Lucifer and the Race of Men were granted free will. Both Lucifer and the Race of Men have transgressed against Yehovah and Eternal Law as an act of their own volition. Judgement was duly passed.'

Lucifer nodded. 'Excellent, Jether. Your records are meticulous.'

He raised his hands in exhiliration. 'Every man's soul is mine – to be with me in hell and the grave and in Tartarus. And when my judgement comes, they will burn with me in the Lake of Fire!'

'Yes.' Michael glared at Lucifer fiercely. 'The Race of Men will share your fate.'

'There is no remittance,' Charsoc said emphatically.

Jether pursed his lips. 'We have been through this, time and time again.'

Lucifer held up his hand. 'We must be assured.'

'There is no remittance,' Gabriel said softly. 'Only one with undefiled blood can pay the penalty.' Gabriel opened a second tome.

'Conditions of the Race of Men to pay the penalty of judgement according to the tenets of Eternal Law: the life of the soul of the Race of Men is in the blood, as pertaining to the constituents of matter. Therefore without the shedding of undefiled blood, no remission of judgement exists for the Race of Men.'

'Undefiled blood . . . ' Lucifer murmured.

'Tenet 7728891977 of the Code of Eternal Law.' Jether passed his palm over a second tome, and bluish lightning arced from his palm through the pages of the codex. The modulated voice narrated:

'If one undefiled from the Race of Men is willing to shed his lifeblood on behalf of the Race of Men and become a substitute for judgement, the said Race of Men, its past, present, and future generations, will be released from eternal judgement by the death of that one. One undefiled soul can be exchanged for the souls of the Race of Men. This is binding Eternal Law.'

'Humour me. Read the definition of "undefiled", brother.' Lucifer studied Gabriel's face intently as he read.

'Definition of "undefiled" as pertaining to the Race of Men, as laid down by Eternal Law,' Gabriel declared. 'The substitute's blood must be pure and untainted from the mutation of the fall of man.'

'Ah – the Nazarene's blood.' Lucifer's eyes moved from Michael to Gabriel, stopping finally on Jether, where they lingered.

'. . . Yehovah would not think to use the Nazarene as a substitute, Jether?'

The whole table fell silent.

Lucifer moved from Gabriel to Jether. 'I have studied the Nazarene's conception intimately. Yehovah cannot banish my angelic generals to Tartarus for leaving their first estate and cohabiting with the Race of Men and then seek to

breach his own Eternal Law by fertilizing the Christos egg.'
Lucifer looked down at Jether. 'Is this not so, Jether?'

Jether stared ahead, silent for a long moment. Finally he
spoke softly. 'You speak truly. Yehovah cannot breach His
own Eternal Law.' Charsoc smiled triumphantly at the still
sneezing Xacheriel, who glared at him darkly.

Lucifer smiled a slow evil smile. 'Therefore the egg *had* to
be fertilized by seed from the Race of Men ... from the
father, Joseph, to enable its conception and replication. The
Nazarene's blood is defiled by inherent sin damage; He does
not qualify.' His gaze locked greedily on the great lapis
lazuli codex, bound in gold, its pages blazing with a fierce
blue fire. 'Forget the bloodlines!'

Lucifer raised his arms to the heavens.

'Long and impatiently have I waited to discover the
reason for his *intrusion* on my planet!'

'And now your wait comes to an end.' Jether stood. 'His
objective on the planet earth reads simply thus: To proclaim
the kingdom of the First Heaven to the Race of Men.'

Lucifer stared at Jether in bewilderment, taken aback.
'That is it?'

Jether stared at Lucifer grim. Lucifer ran his fingers
through his long unbraided locks, mystified.

'That is it.' Jether repeated, his voice hard.

Lucifer surveyed the table, examining his brothers' faces.
Uneasy.

'He exchanges deity, immortality, divine Kingship ... for
wooden tables and saws in a dusty hovel?'

Jether continued his staring.

'We have much sway in the Race of Men, sire,' Charsoc
said, slowly removing his soft white goatskin gloves,

methodically finger by finger. 'They will give no heed to a carpenter from Nazareth . . . '

He threw his gloves down on the table in disdain.

Lucifer's eyes narrowed. 'You were shortsighted before, Charsoc, to our ruin.' He rose. 'I am not so easily persuaded.' He circled the table. 'They will take no heed of a carpenter . . . *unless*' he swung around to Jether, 'unless the carpenter is not a carpenter – but a sorcerer – *a miracle maker!*'

He leant over Jether until his face was only inches from Jether's own.

'He has no right to use His supernatural powers on my planet?' he whispered. 'He is a *trespasser.*'

'His status changes if He passes the test.'

'Test! *What* test?' snarled Lucifer. 'Ah! – *Now* we unveil Yehovah's scheming strategy.'

'The test of obedience to Yehovah. The test you put before the first stewards of the Race of Man, namely one Adam and Eve. Eternal Law cannot be broken.' Jether sat, leaning back in his throne.

'The Nazarene turns thirty not many moons from now. The day the seal is lifted, He will face you as Eve did in earth's Eden, in worlds long departed. That is why we are here.'

'A second Eden,' Charsoc murmured in wonder. 'It is expedient for us, master.'

Lucifer walked over to the battlements. His long raven hair blew violently across his face, his ermine cloak flew in the raging tempests at the edge of the Tower.

'A second Eden.' He stared far into the distance, over the Eastern plains of Eden to the Hanging Gardens where the two massive trees of Life stood, their fruit glistening gold in the lightning, almost wholly enveloped by swirling white mists. 'How fortuitous.' His gaze moved to the north of the two trees where the colossal golden, ruby-encrusted door was embedded into the jacinth walls of the Tower.

' – but fortuitous for who?' He stared at the Rubied Door, his expression dark.

'What does the carpenter gain if he passes my test?' he whispered, his back to Jether.

'He secures the right to proclaim the Kingdom of the First Heaven on your planet – no longer a trespasser.'

'And what of His powers?'

'If He passes the test, His access to the supernatural powers of the First Heaven is secured. But He will make use of them as one of the Race of Men.'

'Aha! It is as I presumed – He would entice them with His sorceries.' He turned from the battlements.

'And if He fails?'

'He suffers the same fate as Adam. He becomes your subject. One of the Race of Men under your control.' Jether gestured to Lucifer's sceptre lain on the table. *'You will be His King.'*

Lucifer stared at Michael, a wicked fire in his eyes.

'I am gratified I attended our little tête-à-tête, Michael. I am surely not disappointed. And *when* is our contest to be?'

'When the Nazarene reaches the age of thirty years, as counted in the Race of Men. In but a few moons, the seal of the seventh stone will be lifted. He will face you as one of the Race of Men.'

Lucifer nodded, a peculiar smile flickering on his lips.

'And the terms of the Nazarene's residency rights,' Lucifer's eyes narrowed, 'on *my* territory, Earth?'

He walked over to the table and sat back down in his throne.

'They are laid out in the White Judgements.' Jether opened the codex.

'Christos will be known in the following residency document as Jesus of Nazareth – the Nazarene, one of the Race of Men. At the age of thirty, as predetermined by the Race of Men, Yehovah's protection – the seal of the seventh stone will be lifted. Jesus of Nazareth is bound by Eternal Law to confront the ultimate challenge of obedience as did the first steward of the planet earth, Adam – as one of the Race of Men. The testing must be conducted in exact like manner to that previously encountered by the aforesaid Adam and Eve. A test of obedience. To Yehovah or to yourself as Sovereign of the Race of Men.'

Jether nodded to Gabriel.

'As ruler of the Race of Men, you may lay before Him three separate temptations of your creation,' said Gabriel. 'If He overcomes these temptations, He secures the right to proclaim the kingdom of the First Heaven among the Race of Men.'

Lucifer leaned back, studying Gabriel in enjoyment.

'If He fails even one of your tests, according to Eternal Law,' Gabriel continued, 'He becomes your subject and forfeits His right to proclaim the kingdom of heaven among the Race of Men. If He fails . . .'

'If the Nazarene fails . . .' Lucifer echoed Gabriel's words, toying idly with his sceptre. 'If He fails . . . He will spend the

rest of His life in obscurity in Nazareth, making tables for old, fat women in dusty marketplaces.'

Michael glared at the smirking Lucifer.

'The contest will be between the two contenders,' continued Gabriel quietly, deliberately ignoring Lucifer's comment. 'According to Eternal Law, the tempter must be the self-same one who caused man's demise in the first place.' Gabriel closed the tome. 'Lucifer contended with Adam and Eve; Lucifer will contend with the man Jesus. The contest shall take place in the land of Jesus of Nazareth's origin. The only ones present shall be the two contenders. Christos in His present form as one of the Race of Men – Jesus of Nazareth, and Lucifer, present ruler of the aforesaid Race of Men.'

'So – if the Nazarene obeys even just *one* of my commands, He is mine!' Lucifer snarled. He stood, suddenly bored with the proceedings. 'I have demands! He is to fast all sustenance. For forty days. Before the contest.'

Jether nodded. 'Your demands will be duly noted by Eternal Law.'

Lucifer strode towards his chariot, his beautiful features starting to mar. 'I await the contest eagerly.' He lashed his stallions. 'The Nazarene shall rue the day He was born on my planet!' he cried, then rode high into the shimmering skies of the First Heaven towards Perdition.

Jether stood and smoothed his robes. Grim.

'The gathering is closed. Let us prepare. I will stay and close the tomes.'

CHAPTER FOURTEEN

AD 26

ARETAS, STILL NOBLE and regal, his once jet black hair now greying, was in his sixty-eighth year. 'Aretas, Lover of his People' was the name affectionately given him by his subjects. He gazed out upon the vast expanse of Arabian desert, far beyond his formal pavilions and ornamental palace gardens. Then he flung open the portico windows, inhaling the heady perfumes of Nabatean spices. The Nabateans were exceptionally skilled traders, conducting a flourishing commerce between.

China, India, the Far East, Egypt, Syria, Greece and Rome. Petra now had a profitable trade with the seaports in frankincense, myrrh, and spices, as well as trade with Egypt in bitumen from the Dead Sea, and the silk trade with China. From its origins as a fortress city, Petra had become a wealthy commercial crossroads between the Arabian,

Assyrian, Egyptian, Greek, and Roman cultures, controlling the routes not only eastward from Petra across the Negev to Gaza, but also northward up the King's Highway to the outskirts of Damascus.

Over the past thirty years, Aretas had poured his life out as supreme monarch of Arabia, and his people had reached the height of their economic and cultural development. He had built new towns and improved old ones, constructed irrigation systems, and expanded the agricultural base. And the status accorded Nabatean women had been the fodder of Arabian marketplace gossip these past ten years, much to Aretas' amusement. Their women not only now inherited property but could buy and sell it in their own right. Jotapa would be proud, as would her gracious, long-departed mother, his beloved queen, who had died in childbirth. He smiled, well satisfied. He had ruled his noble people with devotion. With might and with justice.

He smoothed his robes. But this dusk, his attire was simple. A tunic of a pale lilac silk covered his loins, rather than the rich deep-purple silks of his formal royal garments. He was determined. Tonight he would lay aside his station as Aretas the king, and for one fleeting evening he would be simply Aretas the man.

His entire royal household was already en route with the festival tents to his summer encampment at the Gulf of Aqaba, and at this very moment his manservant was saddling his favoured stallion, Aswad. He would ride as he had when he was very young – so young that his face had been hairless and smooth. He would ride the desert paths that he had ridden with his father decades before, across the white sands to the Gulf of Aqaba, with its crystal clear waters fringed by the lapping white palm sands.

He would relish the sensation of the warm water lapping against his skin as the steady northerly breezes from the Negev Desert fanned him.

There was a soft knock at his chamber door, and Malichus, his cupbearer, entered. He held out a scroll.

Aretas smiled. A missive from Jotapa!

'Thank you, Malichus. Inform Yohanna that I am ready.'

Malichus bowed in reverence, backed away, and closed the chamber door.

Aretas tore open the missive and studied the contents, imagining Jotapa's spontaneous, abandoned laughter and her soft voice.

. . . My husband, though a hard man – like all kings, surely! – treats me with grace. Yes, all is well here in Judaea – except, of course, for your absence, dearest Papa . . . But when I am lonely my soul is comforted by the gardens of the princes; they bring me close to you, and to Arabia . . .

Like yourself, I hear many stories of the Hebrew here in Tiberias, Papa. There are inside the palace walls that His feet tread these shores. I shall make discreet inquiries of the Hebrew's whereabouts.

Aretas folded the letter carefully. He looked down at the beautifully carved wooden cross on his desk. How long had it been since he last saw the infant king? He cast his mind back to the gruelling journey from the monastery in Alexandria back to Judaea. He had ridden for days across the desert, escorting the child and his parents to the borders of Judaea. He vividly remembered how the three-year-old had insisted that he keep the cross – had thrust it with His small, chubby fingers into his palm and closed Aretas' strong, brown fingers over it. And indeed it had comforted Aretas. There were times when he felt that it had a strange power. He shook his head.

Over twenty-seven full years had passed, and he had never seen the infant king again. But his spies came on occasion, filled with wild, unsubstantiated tales of the Hebrew's eloquent, earnest soliloquies and fierce, courageous confrontations with those Jews the Hebrews called Pharisees. Aretas laughed at the thought of those pampered religious exploiters of the commoners, with their soft, lily-white hands. Aretas was comforted. The Hebrew was discerning. Aretas would ask Jotapa in his next missive to keep an eye on his compatriot king – his friend.

Aretas laughed out loud. An Arabian king and *the Hebrew*. He caressed the cross and laid it gently back down on his desk.

He raised his hands to his head and unbraided his long, curly hair from its ribbons, picked up a spear from his collection, placed it over one shoulder, and strode through the portico doors. Aswad stood patiently tethered in the Garden of Kings. The stallion's chest was broad, his back was short but strong and his shoulders sloped, the source of his immense power. His noble head was held high. Aretas lovingly stroked the silky black mane.

'Aswad,' he murmured. The stallion nuzzled him affectionately, his clear black eyes gentle, as Yohanna, the royal saddler, released the tether.

Aretas hesitated, then took a step back, his gaze moving

far upward towards the eastern chambers of the golden-roofed royal palace. A solitary lantern was burning, and a form stood at the window. Aretas nodded in acknowledgment. For a fleeting moment his shoulders slumped, and a terrible weariness clouded his countenance.

'Malichus,' he said, seeming suddenly older than his seventy-four years, 'tell Zahi, he is in my prayers and in my heart while I am gone.'

Then he mounted Aswad, leaned over, and whispered in his ear. At once the magnificent black stallion sprinted forward, its black high and hollow hooves kicking up the sand as they raced like the wind past the grand pools, past the royal hunting parks, across the white desert sands, out towards the Red Sea.

～

Jether closed the last tome, placed the quill pen beside it, and rubbed his eyes wearily. He rose from the table and walked towards the cascading fountain.

'So the contest hastens.'

Jether froze at the sound of the distinctive elegant tones.

Charsoc smoothed his voluminous mulberry taffeta sorcerer's vestments and adjusted his lilac silk neckerchief with pale jewelled fingers. He stared at the cascading fountains around the lush gardens.

'You are too self-assured, Jether, my compatriot.' He held out a goblet to catch the elixir, then sipped delicately. 'Tayberry, my favourite extract – one of the wonders of the First Heaven!'

'You outstay your welcome.'

'And *you* underestimate the fog that this Race of Men

contends with on that muddy little orb – Earth. It dulls their senses, Jether; it veils their souls.' He drank the elixir down with one elegant swig.

'It veils His soul . . . the Nazarene . . . thirty years, Jether,' he whispered, circling Jether. 'Thirty-one years encased in matter, born of a woman.' His voice was very soft. Compelling. 'Birthed of the mud and dust that clouds their sense – it clouds His, also. Each and every dusk, Jether, the memory of Yehovah fades from the Nazarene's mind, until it becomes just a distant imprint.'

'He will pass the test,' Jether said quietly. He walked alongside Charsoc as he had done each dusk thousands of aeons past when they used to walk – two bosom friends engaged in intimate conversation across the same manicured lawns.

'The Nazarene has forgotten Yehovah. Now His soul will play to fame and recognition . . . to all that dwells in the fallow breeding ground of men's souls.' Charsoc's eyes glittered. 'Do not be deceived, Jether. This is no walkover. Lucifer is well prepared. If He obey's even one of Lucifer's commands – His soul is ours.'

Jether gazed out over the battlements to the Sea of Zamar. 'We do not underestimate,' he said softly, his back to Charsoc. 'We well know the fight for His soul.'

Charsoc reached inside his robes and removed a missive embossed with the seal of Perdition. 'My master's demands. An extra proviso that he would incorporate in the tenets.' Jether stared at him. Sober. Waiting. 'He would choose the location of his contest with the Nazarene.' Charsoc held out the missive to Jether. Jether took it and placed it in his robe.

'I will deliver it to Yehovah.'

Charsoc's face was raised to the skies, and a strange ecstasy played on his features. His eyes were wide open, drinking in the vast panorama of lilacs and vermilions that he had once loved so well. His long white hair blew loose in the tempests. For a fleeting moment, Jether studied him. It was almost as it had been.

Slowly Charsoc turned. 'You pity me, Jether.'

'I know you miss our world,' Jether said softly.

'Do not grieve for me.' Charsoc looked long and hard into Jether's weary pale blue eyes. 'I sold my soul aeons past.'

A long serpent writhed across Charsoc's legs. He reached down and grasped the snake, which became a silvered cane with the head of a serpent. He lifted his face to Jether's, his pale eyes expressionless – sightless once more. 'Even I do not know what I am capable of.'

And then, just as in days of old, he vanished into the white, rushing mists.

⤴

2021
AQABA, JORDAN
— JASON —

The event was going brilliantly, better than even Julia St Cartier could have imagined. The contemporary open-air set designed by her London events company, 'Lola', had been phenomenal. The caterers had outdone themselves, the live satellite connection to VOX Communications had gone without a hitch, and any international journalist worth his or her salt had been waiting next door in the crowded pressroom since dusk. She decided to give herself a short but desperately needed luxury of a powder room break and walked through the marquee, checking as she walked how many new bottles of champagne would be needed. She glanced over to the enormous helipad where the Princess of Jordan had landed earlier, other VIPs were now arriving in quick succession. Suddenly her heart turned to ice. There he was – striding down the helicopter steps. She couldn't mistake *that* stride and the severe set of his face – it was Jason De Vere.

Her heart raced. Why, he never came to these functions! He *hated* them – would complain for days after being dragged to one. There must be a new merger or some spectacular opportunity for him to appear, even though it was his brother's big moment. She watched as he embraced Adrian and they launched instantly into deep conversation.

She continued walking to the powder room, her mind all at once a fog. This was the first time she had seen Jason up close and personal since their divorce thirteen months earlier. Maybe the leopard had changed his spots; maybe their split had given him a new lease on life.

She pushed open the powder room door, staring blankly at her reflection in the huge, gilt-framed mirror. She felt tired tonight – old – as old as she was – forty. 'Get a grip on yourself, girl,' she murmured. Why should she care? She and Jason were over. He had his new life; she had hers. Trembling, she unclasped the travel compact and touched up her eyeliner and brows, then dabbed on a hint of clear gloss and touched up her foundation. All age defying. She smiled. She idly wondered if her expensive cosmetic creams actually worked. She closed the compact and shook her highlighted blonde mane. *Okay, into the lions' den.*

She walked out back into the marquee, fighting her way past the dance floor and through the growing crowd, her eyes intent on the floor. Suddenly, a pair of large, black-shoed feet barred her way.

Heart sinking, she slowly raised her head. Jason De Vere stood in her path, his whisky glass already half empty, his face flushed. He'd most likely had two since he arrived, she thought cynically. He was staring at her.

'Jason ... what a surprise.' She stared back at him, blankly.

'Julia.' He continued to stare at her. Silent.

Julia rubbed her neck. 'I have to go. I'm running...'

Jason looked around them. 'You're running the event. Congratulations. Pity the lawyers didn't know that before you took half my assets.' he drawled sarcastically.

Julia glared at him. Fuming. Her deep-brown eyes flashed. Only Jason could make her *that* infuriated. *Instantly.* She walked away.

Jason grasped her arm. Hard. His fingers dug into her flesh.

'Sorry ... sorry, okay? It's been a tough day.'

Julia unclasped his hand. Incensed.

'And mine's been tougher!' she spat.

'Of *course*,' Jason retorted mockingly. 'Your needs always *were* the overriding factor.'

'Don't you dare.' Julia's voice trembled with rage. '...*Dare* ... *dare*. Jason Ambrose De Vere...' Her eyes flashed dangerously.

'*Eighteen years*..., I spent eighteen years of my life subordinating my entire life to your needs.'

'*My* needs!' Jason slugged down the remains of his

whisky. 'You spent more time at your goddamn New York designer hairdresser than you did at home . . . ' He glowered at her. 'Or in the bedr – '

He caught himself. Not the time to risk being slaughtered in cold blood, in full view of a thousand of Adrian's guests. She dragged him by the arm out into the kitchen galley.

'Do you *have* to make a scene?' Julia hissed.

Jason placed his whisky glass on a passing wine steward's tray and raised both hands in submission. 'Okay, okay. Fine – I was a selfish, boorish husband. It's *all* my fault. Let's try again. I'm sorry. Apology accepted?'

Julia glared darkly at him.

'I mean it, Jules, I was a terrible husband . . . I took your advice, went to therapy – they told me I had intense deeply buried anger and resentment. Okay?' He raised both his hands.

'You . . . you actually went to therapy?' Julia stared up at him in amazement. Stunned.

He nodded.

'That's remarkable.' Her eyes narrowed. 'How many times did you go?'

Jason tugged at the knot in his tie. 'Once,' he said sheepishly. Julia rolled her eyes in frustration.

Jason looked around at the festivities. 'Seriously, I'm really impressed with Lulu.'

Julia glared. 'It's Lola,' she snapped.

'Lola . . . deeply impressed. This is great – really great, Jules.'

He reddened. He rubbed his collar, looking like an embarrassed schoolboy.

'Lola...' he murmured. 'After your mother? I'm really glad for you.'

Julia's eyes softened. He was sincere; she knew him that well. He was truly glad for her.

'What brings you here?' Her expression softened slightly. 'You hate these things.'

'Adrian. It's his big night. He took a real beating over Melissa's death.'

Julia's eyes moistened. 'It was tragic ... *and* the baby.'

'I felt his big brother should be here and support him. I can't stay long.'

Julia nodded.

'Humanitarian of you,' she muttered sarcastically. He followed her out of the kitchen back into the marquee. Jason gently took her by the arm, guiding her through the crowds.

'Julia, I miss Lily. I want to see more of her.'

Her jaw clenched. 'Jason, this is not the time – or the place.'

'Well, you always said my timing was atrocious. At least some things never change.'

She sighed and turned to him. 'Jason, our daughter is crippled ... in a wheelchair. It's not as though she can spend weeks at your New York penthouse while you're at work. Face it, you were never home when you *had* a family – what's changed?'

'Then let her come when Mother's in New York. Let her stay with Mother more often, and at least I can see her.'

Julia nodded. It was reasonable. She loved Lilian De Vere deeply. *And* trusted her.

'I'll think about it.'

He nodded.

'I have to go.' She walked away, back towards the podium.

'Julia...,' he called.

She turned. He stood staring at her, unable to bring himself to say what was in his heart. She stood waiting, then turned and walked away.

'Damn!' Jason made his way to the bar. 'Whisky – make it a double.'

Julia watched him, unobserved, from the far side of the marquee as his expensive minders instantaneously circled him, guiding Jason deftly past the crowded dancefloor towards a group of VOX's wealthy billionaire investors. She watched as he stopped to shake hands with a second group – Chinese ministers from Beijing. She could read him at a glance – he was already bored with the proceedings – making smalltalk.

He had aged. At forty-four, his thick jet black hair was almost silver. He was well worn although still ruggedly handsome, his tanned face already creased with numerous lines. And he'd lost weight. It suited him to be so lean, she thought. He was unhappy. Restless. She could sense it. She sighed. There were times when it was hard to live without him, but it was far harder to live *with* the driving, unrelenting force that was Jason De Vere.

She caught sight of Adrian, heading towards the pressroom.

Tonight his face was drawn. The recent deaths of Melissa and the baby had hit him like a bodyblow. He looked gaunt, not his usual charming self. He was five years younger than Jason. Tall and slim. Cultured. Educated. His sense of humour was fabulous. He was genuinely funny. And likeable.

Unlike his brother Jason, who had few friends, thousands of enemies and was as blunt as a proverbial sledgehammer.

A tanned, manicured hand rested softly on hers. She turned. 'Adrian!'

He gave her his endearing, lopsided half smile. 'Hiya, sis. You've done us proud tonight.' He kissed her affectionately on both cheeks. 'The predators await.' He nodded in the direction of the pressroom.

Julia smiled. 'You okay?' She straightened his tie, as she had done so many times before when he was home from boarding school at Gordonstoun when he was just fifteen.

He nodded. 'I'm coping.' He said softly. Julia studied the man in front of her. Just two years younger than she, he had matured from an awkward though brilliant teenager into a most attractive man. He had married young, straight after university – and well – into a top British political family. Melissa Vane-Templar was beautiful, elegant and brilliant, newly-qualified as a barrister. Her father, Viscount Miles Vane-Templar, Leader of the House of Lords, had been like a father to Adrian. Melissa had died four months ago giving birth to their first son, Gabriel Lance who was stillborn. Straight after the funeral, he had furiously thrown himself back into his work and been almost single-handedly responsible for creating the most impressive and ambitious peace process in the history of the Western world. The final accord was to be signed next month in Damascus. And 'Lola' was sole events co-ordinator.

Adrian kissed Julia tenderly on both cheeks. 'Thanks, sis. I could do with an escort.'

She turned to catch Jason glaring at them from the bar, across the room. *Why*, she thought, *he's jealous.*

She laughed softly, enjoying his discomfort and placed her arm deliberately through Adrian's.

Jason slammed his glass onto the bar top and strode back towards the helipad.

Julia stopped by the pressroom door, watching the big black helicopter with the De Vere monogram on its side, taking off into the Aqaba skies, carrying Jason De Vere to Amman, no doubt to board his Gulfstream.

She sighed.

CHAPTER FIFTEEN

BETRAYAL – AD 27

J OTAPA SANG SOFTLY to herself the ancient Arabian lullabies she had loved so well when Aretas had sung to her as a child. She walked with a light step in her flowing white silk garments, along the imposing marbled corridors, past the Judaean king's magnificent works of art, and out into the colourful rose arbors on the sumptuous palace grounds that led up onto the Royal pavilions. She continued through gardens of exotic palms until finally she came to a secluded ornamental garden with a gurgling fountain. Jotapa placed a silver goblet under the fresh, clear running water and drank long and deeply. She turned to stare at the breathtaking views of the lake, drinking in the exotic beauty of the surrounding territory of Galilee. Today the lake was as a deep blue pool and, its surface smooth as glass.

Her gleaming ebony hair, intricately braided with hundreds of small, fine freshwater pearls, fell past her narrow waist. Her large eyes, blue as the Mediterranean, danced in the exquisitely featured face. Her slim olive-skinned fingers were covered in diamonds and pearls – gifts from her husband of seventeen years, Herod Antipas, tetrarch of Galilee and Perea. She was breathtaking – the Arabian princess.

Jotapa hesitated beside a stately palm tree. Hearing soft voices, she caught sight of her handsome, well-manicured husband, standing below her by the palace portico, with his chief adviser, Caspius. Jotapa beamed, about to make her presence known.

'A missive arrived at dawn from Rome, Your Excellency ... from Herodias.'

Jotapa stopped in her tracks. She could hear Herod's crisp, cultured tones effortlessly.

'Herodias has sworn she will not marry me until Jotapa is repudiated. She demands it. Our affair is no longer secret – Jerusalem's scandalmongers create mischief.'

'Herodias has accepted your proposal of marriage, sire, and has drawn up a contract to move into your household on your next return from Rome. It is, however, in both your and the princess Herodias's contracts that the daughter of Aretas is to be renounced ...'

There was a long silence.

'... thrown out.'

Jotapa's blood ran cold. She stayed, hardly daring to breathe, hidden behind the palm's foliage.

Herod Antipas paced up and down the path, his face drawn.

'I would have got rid of her years ago if not for her father, that confounded warmonger Aretas!'

'Then repudiate her *immediately*, master.'

'If I divorce her, her devoted father will wage war on me with his horde of bloodthirsty Arabs!'

Caspius's evil eyes narrowed as he placed his hand heavily on his master's bangled arm. 'But, master...'

Jotapa leaned forward, straining to hear him, hardly believing her ears.

'There are other means...'

There was a long silence.

'It must have no repercussions, Caspius. If there is any hint of villainy, the Arabians will slaughter us without mercy.'

Great, noiseless sobs racked Jotapa's petite frame. She held her head in her hands, distraught, her gleaming raven locks falling with the tears down over her slim, jewelled fingers.

'My Egyptian physicians are most skilled in the arts of poison... There will be no evidence.'

'And I could finally marry Herodias.' Jotapa watched as Herod smiled calculatingly. 'Make haste, Caspius. There is no time to lose. I leave for Rome at dusk and return twenty days hence. On my return, I shall invite the princess to my chambers, and we shall dine.'

'It will be done, Your Excellency. On your return.'

⟅⟆

Jotapa ran, stumbling, falling, back up the lower path towards her golden-roofed palace chambers. Tears mixed with ochre coursed down her high, elegant cheekbones as she wrote in Syriac with a shaking hand. Ayeshe, her father's faithful old Arab manservant, bequeathed to her on her marriage, watched her with tears in his own eyes as well. Jotapa folded the letter hastily with trembling fingers.

'Ayeshe, go to my father.' She took a deep breath in between sobs. 'Tell him that Herod seeks my life. He must save me. I will tell the king I am ill, and ask permission to convalesce at Macherus while he is Rome.'

She pushed the letter into the old man's hands.

'Saleem will organize all necessary preparations for the journey. My father's generals must meet me there and escort me straight to Petra.'

Jotapa pushed Ayeshe out the back way and watched, trembling, as he mounted the white Arabian stallion.

'Ride like the wind, Ayeshe,' she whispered as the stallion tore out of the palace gates. 'Oh, Papa!' she sobbed.

⟿

A tall, haggard-looking young man with long, unkempt hair stood on the edge of the river. He wore a rough garment of camel's hair tied with a leather girdle; his limbs were burned nut brown by the relentless Judaean sun. The crowds thronging the river Jordan stood riveted to his every impassioned word. His voice carried deep conviction, and his emerald eyes burned with fervour in the handsome, angular face.

'I am the voice of one crying in the wilderness. Make straight the way of the Lord.'

He returned to his task of baptizing the unending procession of men, women, and children, when an enormous chariot, pulled by six white steeds decorated in golden ornaments, turned and stopped at a vantage point above the river. It was Herod Antipas's royal chariot. The baptist looked up from his baptizing and fell silent. He bowed his head, praying. Then grasped the shoulder of one of his disciples.

'Ari, take care of the people. I have a message to deliver.'

His jaw set, he pushed swiftly past the eager, clamouring throng until he stood in the crowd just an arm's length from the royal carriage, which had started to move slowly back on its way.

'Stop! Stop, I command you!'

Herod's soldiers grabbed the baptist and shoved him roughly to the ground as the carriage came to an abrupt halt.

Slowly, the curtain parted, and a veiled face stared out directly at the man lying on the ground. A finger with a long painted fingernail pointed directly at him. A loud whispering rose up from the throng. The baptist lifted his bloodied mouth from the dust.

'Bring the creature here,' Herodias commanded.

The soldiers manhandled him towards her. He struggled violently, his eyes flashing with anger.

'Mmmm ... very handsome.'

John stared at her boldly, and Herodias removed her veil, revealing her ageing but still sensuous features. Her crimsoned lips pouted provocatively.

'And not afraid.' She stared at him, fascinated.

'You are a man of God, the rabble say – so much wasted passion.'

A guard bowed deeply before the chariot.

'He says he has a message for you, Your Highness.'

'You have a message?' She ran her finger over her lips.

'For me? Bring the baptist nearer, that he may tell me his message.'

The guards dragged John forward. Herodias reached out her soft, white ringed hand and caressed John's face slowly and sensuously. He lifted his eyes to hers.

'I have a message from the most high God. You are an adulteress, and incestuous. You sin against the most high God. You are under judgement.'

Herodias turned pale and began to tremble uncontrollably; her limbs became like water. Then her eyes blazed with fury. 'You are a fool!' she cried. 'You insult a queen-to-be! Herod Antipas shall hear of this.'

John looked at her in the eyes, bold and at peace.

'You shall pay for it with your life!' she hissed. '*When I* am queen I shall seize you and throw you in the dungeons in Macherus!' She seized the whip from the driver, and brought it violently down on the nearest horse. 'I shall silence you, baptist!' she yelled as the carriage pulled away.

~

The seven pale lilac moons of dawn glimmered on the First Heaven's horizons as Michael and Gabriel raced, bareback on their stallions through the foaming silver waves towards the Palace of Archangels. They raced neck and neck, slowing as they caught sight of Jether in the distance. Michael slowed his stallion to an even canter. Gabriel followed until they reached the shore where Jether stood, grave. They dismounted.

'The hour has come, my princes.' Jether said softly. He held out a parchment embossed with the seal of Perdition in his hand to Michael who took it, scanning its contents.

'The High Council received an extra proviso from Lucifer forty moons ago.' Jether's voice was soft. 'Yehovah sets the time but Lucifer, in his capacity as sovereign ruler of the Race of Men demanded the right to choose the location of his contest with the Nazarene. His proviso was accepted by Yehovah. He has stipulated through the royal courts that the location of the contest will be divulged only to his blood brothers. And to only one of you. That one must set foot on his domain before the fading of the twelve moons of Perdition.'

Michael's eyes flashed with a dark fury. 'What new foolishness is this?'

He passed the missive to Gabriel.

'You must deliberate between yourselves. As of course, is his intention.' Jether lowered his tone. 'We are well aware.'

'I will go,' said Gabriel softly. 'He will only seek to incense you, Michael. And do it with deliberate intent.' Michael's chin set. 'Yes – he may incense *me*,' he stared angrily back at Gabriel, his emotions strangely charged, 'but his seductions could still hold sway over *you* . . .'

Jether placed his hand gently on Michael's arm. Michael bowed his head, immediately penitent.

'Forgive me, Gabriel,' he said softly, 'his sorceries reach us even here.' Jether sighed.

'He has no power here. Your souls have long been freed from his hold. Have faith in each other.' Jether studied the two brothers intently. 'Have faith in Yehovah.' Jether took the missive from Gabriel and placed it in the pouch at his waist.

'Your escort stands ready at the Western Gate. Lucifer awaits his brother at his summer palace above the

Babylonian plains of the Race of Men. Choose wisely. Choose swiftly. The moons of Perdition fade even as we speak.'

⤚

Aretas paced the four corners of his ornate festival tent, Jotapa's missive crumpled in his fist. He stopped, smoothed the page, and reread the letter for the third time. His black eyes glittered hard with wrath.

Ayeshe knelt before him, trembling. Aretas turned to his chief general. 'Saleem, wake your generals from their beds. Prepare the royal guard. Ride through the night. Our enemy is time. Do not dare return without my daughter.'

He lifted his hand to Saleem, then strode through the tent's entrance and gazed out across the white sands to the full moon illuminating the lapping azure waters of the Gulf of Aqaba. He turned to his chief of staff, standing silently in the shadows.

'Break off all amicable relations with my son-in-law.' His voice was quiet. Dangerously soft. 'We will make a pretext for conflict, concerning the boundaries in the land of Gabala, as soon as Jotapa is safe and it suits our purposes – and inflict a severe and ruinous defeat on Antipas. Jotapa's honour must be avenged at all costs.' His eyes glittered black with revulsion. 'As weak and wretched a prince that ever disgraced the throne of an afflicted country ... Mahmoud, pack the tents immediately. Wake the royal servants. We depart at dawn back to Petra.'

He put his hand gently on Ayeshe's white head.

'You have done well, my devoted servant.'

Aretas turned and strode back out across the tent court to

the large carved stone a 'Beytel', that rose behind the tent. On the top of the altar lay the small carved wooden cross from Alexandria. He picked it up and held it tightly to his chest, raising his eyes to the heavens.

'Help me, Hebrew.'

CHAPTER SIXTEEN

TERMS OF ENGAGEMENT

LUCIFER FLUNG OPEN the colossal doors of his newly constructed summer palace and walked out onto the eastern terraces. He watched in gratification at the lone chariot that flew through the clouds, its escort long turned back to the mid heavens, thundering towards his recently constructed monstrous alabaster edifice.

Lucifer himself had been the grand architect of the palace and its exotic hanging gardens suspended leagues above about the sweltering Babylonian plains in the Second Heavens. Branches of myrtle, willow, and juniper trees hung low over the upper terrace walls, while thousands of almond, date palm, ebony, and terebinth trees flourished along the lower terraces. Nightshade, pomegranate, plum, pear, quince, fig, and grapevines were entwined over a hundred terraces and arches supported by hundreds of colossal alabaster columns. Brilliantly coloured flowers of every hue dangled from the ramparts. Below, in the inner sanctum of the palace, were over a thousand golden-vaulted chambers and underground crypts that housed his vast libraries of iniquities – the records of every genealogical line of the Race of Men.

He raised his face to the skies and moved his palm across the heavens. Instantly, the plains of Perdition appeared. Lucifer stared at the twelve pale magenta moons of Perdition rapidly fading from the desolate smouldering horizons of hell.

'The moons fade – you are just in time, brother,' he murmured. 'Marduk, unbolt the palace doors – I would bid my brother welcome.'

⌒⁀

The platinum wheels of the royal chariot sank down into the green lawns of the hanging gardens. Instantly six of Lucifer's attendants stepped up and bowed deeply as the carriage door opened.

Lucifer stood in the enormous arched entrance of the palace. He surveyed the tall, muscular figure who stepped out of the carriage and onto the palace lawns with satisfaction. Michael's loose golden mane fell well below his broad shoulders onto his emerald velvet cloak. He wore the white ceremonial robes of his battalion trimmed with gold. His strong, chiselled face was set, his green eyes inscrutable. Lucifer smiled in pleasure.

'Ah, Michael . . . ' He strode towards Michael and kissed him warmly on both cheeks. 'I knew you would come, brother.'

Michael stared at him coldly. 'Your mind games are wasted on me, Lucifer.'

'Of course, my brother, you were never cerebral like Gabriel,' Lucifer smiled again, indulgently.

'No matter.' He grasped Michael firmly by the shoulder and led him through the winding corridors. 'I have something I wish you to see...'

Together they strode through the winding palace corridors under Lucifer's magnificent frescoed ceilings, descending downwards into the thousand golden vaulted chambers beneath the palace. Finally they stopped at heavily guarded enormous gilded doors. Twelve Luciferean Guards bowed deeply in reverence, then unchained the doors. Lucifer walked into the chamber, followed closely by Michael. There, ahead of them, manacled to a colossal alabaster altar was a carved golden casket with golden cherubim – the Ark of the Race of Men.

'The Ark...' Michael murmured in awe.

'Ah...' Lucifer's eyes gleamed with exhilaration. 'How well I know my brother. Long has Michael wished to gaze on that which is no longer his.'

'Stolen ... I believe would be a more appropriate word.'

Lucifer winced.

'Michael, *Michael* – How undeserved. Not stolen – *appropriated*. I did not take it, it was placed into my hands by its stewards themselves.'

'Your methods hold no interest for me. You stole it. By manipulation, by your evil scheming you reign king over the Race of Men.'

Lucifer picked up the golden key and slowly opened the casket. Twelve golden codices occupied the ark, the covers of the large books embedded with jacinth, diamonds, sapphires, chrysolite, and multitudes of other precious stones.

'The title deeds to the earth and its solar system, the Second Heaven above the earth,' Lucifer said, 'bequeathed by Yehovah to the Race of Men.' He swung around. 'Bequeathed by the Race of Men to *me*. I reign Prince of their world. This is Yehovah's covenant, bound by Eternal Law ... Adam's defection – my greatest triumph...' He spun around. 'So far.'

He strode from the chamber through the lower corridors out onto the sapphire pathway of the lower terraces. Michael followed him down the majestic pavilions of cedars and great oaks to a portico surrounded by magnificent gushing waterfalls. The scent of frankincense permeated the pavilions.

Underneath the portico stood a sumptuously decorated table lavishly set for three. Balberith took Lucifer's cloak, then Michael's, placing them on a podium behind them. Lucifer reclined back in an ornately carved ivory chair, then motioned to Michael to do likewise in a second.

'So...' Lucifer smiled languidly. 'The Nazarene has reached the age of thirty years, as counted in the Race of Men. Yehovah's protection is lifted.' He held out his cup to his cupbearer who filled it at once with a thick gold and strawberried elixir. 'Drink, brother...' Lucifer addressed Michael. 'You have a long journey,' he paused, '...home.' Michael held out his goblet to the cupbearer who filled it.

'You are well?' Lucifer enquired. Michael nodded. 'Gabriel is well?' Michael's eyes narrowed. Slowly he nodded.

'You are concerned about our health?' Michael asked, a rare mischief flickering in his eyes.

Lucifer studied him lazily. 'I have missed your dry humour.' Lucifer picked up a soft sugared rose-coloured delicacy, and placed it into his mouth. 'I have missed much of Michael.' He turned his full sapphire blaze to Michael.

Michael lowered his eyes, he had been away from Lucifer's presence for aeons yet could suddenly feel the familiar seduction drawing him close. Lucifer's danger, Michael considered, lay in his very intensity. His reverie was broken as a tall muscular figure sat in the chair to his right, his hair as blond as Michael's, his stature as imperial.

'Your Majesty. I present Astaroth ... Grand Duke of Perdition,' Balberith announced. Michael stared at Astaroth, his soul suddenly strangely filled with a thousand unheralded emotions from worlds long past. Astaroth laid his helmet down on the table. He bowed his head in deference.

'Chief prince Michael of the Royal House ... welcome to Perdition.'

Lucifer watched intently, 'How touching.' A small smile flickered at his lips. 'Two old comrades in arms.' He studied Michael's face. 'How long is it since you fellowshipped, brother?'

'The fellowship is broken.' Michael said coldly. 'Astaroth chose his bed.'

Astaroth stared at Michael a long while. Enigmatic. 'And I lie in it.'

Balberith and his courtiers placed huge silver dishes of steaming boar and venison down before them. Michael brought his head close to Astaroth's. Lucifer watched him out of the corner of his eye.

'Do you have no regret, Astaroth?' He spoke in an undertone. 'You were one with Gabriel and I, a prince of the Royal house. When you lie awake at night, do you not feel shame for your treachery – for all that was and could have been?'

A fleeting vulnerability crossed Astaroth's features, he looked deeply into Michael's gaze, then back to Lucifer, then stared out at the waterfalls. Michael stared over to Lucifer in exasperation.

'It seems you have Astaroth's tongue.'

'Under iron control. I rule by force. Coercion. I take no prisoners.'

'Yet each and every one is a captive.' Michael's voice was very soft but fierce.

Lucifer spun around. 'I tire of my brother's conversation.' His voice held a soft venom.

'And I tire of my brother's diversions.' Michael replied heatedly. 'Where is the contest to be held, Lucifer?'

'My dull and dogged Michael ... you become uninteresting.'

Lucifer reclined back in his chair and sipped from his goblet.

'O – Where *is* the second Eden to be? Which ancient wonder of my planet earth – which magnificent edifice is to be our backdrop?' Lucifer tore off a boar's leg with his hand and sank his teeth into it voraciously. 'Shall I meet the Nazarene at the Mausoleum of Maussollos; or the Pharos at Alexandria ... Michael?'

Lucifer threw up his arms dramatically. 'Is it to be the Sphinx at Gaza ... the Statue of Zeus at Olympia made of marble and beaten gold,' he continued. 'Many moons I have spent to find a location fit for the Nazarene.'

'I have no time for your indulgences.' Michael glared at Lucifer impatiently.

'Marduk!' Lucifer idly picked up a silver casket, toying with it with his ringed fingers. 'My younger brother's temper turns ill.'

He passed the casket to Marduk. 'Read the contents aloud to my fractious brother. The location that I, Lucifer have selected for our contest.'

Marduk unclasped the casket and removed a scroll. He opened it.

'The contest will be fought, mi'lord at the location named Mount Quarnel.'

'Mount Quarnel?' Michael exclaimed, snatching the missive out of Marduk's grasp. 'Mount Quarnel is a *wilderness*, Lucifer!'

Lucifer studied Michael, his expression inscrutable.

'A wilderness...' Lucifer smiled at him tantalizingly. 'How *careless* of me ... Two Kingdoms contesting for the Race of Men on a desert tract – one that obsesses him so.' He took another huge bite of the boar's leg and chewed for a long moment.

'It is fortuitous, Michael.' Lucifer moved his head to Michael's, his voice an undertone. 'The Nazarene will be scorched in the desert – without food forty days – fainting from hunger ... it will be greatly to my advantage.'

Michael bowed his head to Astaroth. 'I have what I came for. I take my leave.' He rose, then snatched his cloak, incensed, his hand on his sword. 'I shall be there to witness your defeat, Lucifer.'

Lucifer stood, his arms outstretched. 'You miscalculate, brother!' Balberith draped his cloak over his shoulders.

'Don't you see?' he hissed. 'If the Nazarene obeys even one of my commands ... just *one*, Michael ... He will be my craven subject. Just like Adam before Him. To do my will. Yehovah's pathetic little rescue mission is thwarted.'

Lucifer bowed to Michael. 'The seal is lifted.' Michael watched him striding down the corridors, his indigo cloak billowing after him. 'The Nazarene is mine!' he cried. The faint aroma of frankincense lingered in his wake.

⌒

Michael flung the doors of Gabriel's southern chambers wide. Gabriel slowly turned from the balcony. 'You are back safe, brother. I am comforted.'

His gentle features were haggard.

'I have been tormented by dreamings, Michael – I have seen his very intention.' Gabriel walked towards Michael. 'He will lay his kingdom at his feet – the Ark, the title deeds, the books of judgements, the book of iniquities. It is in his hands to give to whom he would choose.'

Michael nodded, he unclasped his sword belt and placed it wearily onto a jacinth throne. 'He chooses the Nazarene.'

'Let us walk.' Gabriel and Michael walked together across the vast diamond floors of Gabriel's chambers, beneath the soaring vaulted ceilings until they reached the arched door of his private retreat that led to his glass house palace that hung over the very edge of the Crystal Sea. The soaring glass house's floors were of lush lawn and covered in foxgloves and lupins of every colour of the rainbow, grand pools flowed into waterfalls that fell leagues down into the Sea. Gabriel strode over the flowers that sprang up under his feet and dived into the deep silver pools. He surfaced.

'Christos is birthed of mud and dust.' He pushed his hair back from his eyes. 'Encased in a body of matter. He confronts Lucifer and his evil scheming as one of the Race of Men. If He falters even once . . . '

Michael stared eastwards out towards the shimmering Rubied Door far in the distance. 'Yehovah's plan to liberate the Race of Men from Lucifer's tyranny is lost.'

Gabriel nodded, his gaze dropping to the silver casket still clasped in Michael's left hand.

'Where is the contest to be, Michael?' Gabriel whispered. 'A second Eden?'

Michael followed his gaze past the Rubied Door to the vast golden bulrush meadows of the Eastern plains of Eden. The brothers watched the sheer majesty of the undulating rainbow horizons in silence.

'No, it is far from any Eden, Gabriel.'

Michael bowed his head, a terrible suffering on his strong features.

'The contest will be fought at Mount Quarnel, north of Jericho. He will face Lucifer in a wilderness, surrounded by wild beasts.'

CHAPTER SEVENTEEN

THE VALE OF TEMPTATION – 27 AD

J ESUS SURVEYED THE vast expanse of barren, stony wilderness, His strong, imperial features set as stone. His long dark hair, lashed by the fierce desert sandstorm, thrashed against his bare, sun-scorched shoulders in the wind. He stumbled across the harsh, rocky terrain, faint from hunger and exhaustion. In the distance, a second figure walked towards Him. Lucifer stopped ten yards away, dark hair flying, majestic, noble. They could almost have been brothers, although Lucifer stood a clear three feet taller, his six wings spread behind him, his scarlet cloak blowing behind him. The dark seraph.

In the distance, Astaroth, Dagon and Moloch stood silent, high on the mountains, behind them thousands of the fallen host waited, menacing, covered in shadow, in their monstrous black War Chariots.

Jesus looked resolutely at Lucifer. He studied the Nazarene's crystal clear gaze.

'So this is what it's come down to...' He laughed manically. 'The great Yehovah ... Christos, sovereign ruler of the universe, ensnared in matter. Jesus of *Nazareth*...'

Jesus was silent.

'The seal of the seventh stone has been lifted. You are unprotected, Christos.' Lucifer walked towards him menacingly. 'You have none of your former powers now – you must pass the tests as one of *them*. It is the condition of the Codices.'

Jesus continued to gaze at him. In silence.

Lucifer spat. 'That I would ever see such a day – Yehovah, Almighty Creator, denying Your deity and taking on their inferior form. Lower than the angels. It *insults* me,' he spat.

Lucifer's eyes narrowed. 'But maybe You are not *He*. I require proof...' He swung around. 'If You are the son of God, then prove it. You fast and are faint from hunger – turn these stones into bread.'

Jesus stood completely still as Lucifer moved closer. He leaned down and picked up a stone; it turned to bread, freshly baked ... still steaming.

Jesus bowed His head. He had been without food for nearly forty days, and His famished body was starting to rebel violently.

Lucifer took and ate. Revelling in Jesus' torment. 'Satiate Your hunger.' He held out the fresh bread.

'Matter requires sustenance to exist,' He smiled, 'unlike the angelic.'

He studied Jesus with narrowed eyes, then tore more of the bread and bit into it deeply. With great relish.

Jesus bowed His head. His voice was faint. 'It is written by My Father: man shall not live by bread alone but by every word of God.'

Lucifer studied Him for a long moment, then moved his hand across the skyline. Immediately he and Jesus stood on the lofty pinnacle spire of the temple of Jerusalem. Lucifer watched Jesus intently, drawing nearer to Him.

'Thirty years away from His presence, away from the very elixir of life – You suffer, Christos; I sense it,' he whispered.

A terrible grief crossed Jesus' face. 'Hearken back to your days of glory!'

Lucifer knelt on one knee and bowed his head. 'Behold, O God our defender, and look upon the face of Thy chief princes, for one day in Thy courts . . .' A slow cruel smile spread across his face as he raised his arms raised to the heavens. ' . . . is better than a thousand elsewhere.'

Jesus said nothing as He watched image after image of Lucifer and the archangels bowing before His throne. An agonized sob rose in Jesus' throat, and He turned to Lucifer, suddenly vulnerable.

Lucifer was ready. 'I suffer as You do, Christos, each and every dawn.' He reached out his hand, still wearing his ring with the royal crest of the House of Yehovah. Jesus stared in recognition at the royal seal, and an intense, searing yearning coursed through Him.

Lucifer smiled. 'I *know* what it is to be desolate, Christos – away from Him.'

Jether walked slowly out of the entrance to the Holy of Holies, his white head bowed in silent supplication.

'Lucifer revisits Eden as the tempter.' Gabriel turned his face away.

'This is no Eden,' murmured Jether, his face ashen. 'He is now to be tempted under all the pressing conditions of the fall.' He walked towards the edge of the hanging gardens, looking out towards earth, and raised his hand. Instantly Mount Quarnel came into view.

Michael watched Lucifer and Jesus of Nazareth in horror. 'He launches the whole fiendish arsenal of hell against Him. He has meticulously planned it.'

'We wait, Michael.' Jether placed a firm hand on his arm and bowed his head.

'Have faith.'

~

The tempter continued, 'A carpenter's son from Nazareth cannot herald in a kingdom *unless* they proclaim You their king ... They do not understand Your deity, Christos,' he whispered, 'even in Nazareth, the carpenter is a prophet without honour...'

Christos bowed His head.

'You – the Great King of the First Heaven have made Yourself lower than the angels, Christos – for the sake of what? The Race of Men? You have granted them free will, and yet they embrace *me!* They do not *care* that You were born one of them. The sacrifice of the great Christos is passed over, completely disregarded in the Race of Men.

An evil smile played across Lucifer's mouth as he caressed

the ring. 'What visions of despair, what desolations have filled Your soul these forty days and nights, Christos – visions of a mission aborted ... a mission failed?'

'The Race of Men seek signs, Christos. They seek wonders. Descend, heaven-borne, into the midst of the priests, Christos ... prove to them Your deity ... Jump,' he hissed.

Lucifer moved his arm across the skyline, and instantly a panorama unfolded before them. Jesus watched, transfixed, as images played of Himself jumping off the spire to shouts of acclaimation. He watched as the Pharisees and Sadducees hailed Him as King. He stared, almost mesmerized, at the chief priests and priests falling in homage before Him as he walked through the temple courtyard.

Lucifer's wheedling tones broke through His reverie.

'Yehovah will give His angels charge over You to keep You,' he whispered. 'Michael will save You ... then they will all hail You as their true Messiah. ... Take the short cut, Nazarene ... Show them Your power ... Jump...'

Lucifer drew close to Jesus. They watched in silence together as the massive temple gates opened and the priests' trumpets blasted through the pale dawn silence.

Jesus looked up, pale and trembling. 'Thou shalt not tempt the Lord thy God.'

Lucifer paled. He pulled his heavy velvet cloak tightly around him in fury, then moved his hand across the heavens. Immediately he and Jesus stood on the summit of a vast mountain, in the full blaze of sunlight, where they shared a bird's-eye view of the entire earth.

Instantly the horizon changed, and the sounds of millions

of voices from heavenly choirs; of tabrets; pipes, violins – wondrous sounds beyond human or angelic comprehension – titillated His senses.

'The splendour of Eden ... the breathtaking elements of earth in all its glory...,' Lucifer murmured seductively. 'Observe the beauty, the majesty...'

Lucifer circled Jesus.

Jesus stared, strangely captivated, as a thousand images played out in vivid technicolour. 'Nations rising and falling, kings and kingdoms...,' Lucifer whispered.

Jesus watched hundreds of millions of soldiers – Chinese, American, British, Japanese, Arab, and Russian, their flags all emblazoned with Yehovah's royal seal – marching.

'This is why You are here, Christos.'

'To proclaim Yehovah's kingdom. You need not pass any test for indeed I will bequeath all the nations of this planet to You now. *All* that was delivered to me in the title deeds of the Ark of the Covenant of the Race of Men.' A slow strange smile spread across his features. He bowed down before Jesus.

'I *give You* my kingdom.'

He waved his hand. Asmodeus and six fallen angels walked towards them carrying the Ark of the Covenant of the Race of Men upon their shoulders. They placed the great golden ark before Jesus' feet. Slowly Lucifer opened the lid. Inside were the twelve glowing golden codices, the title deeds to earth and the solar systems. 'I grant You the rulership of the Race of Men.'

'And...,' Lucifer gestured to the millions of the shadowed fallen host in their war chariots waiting on

174

the horizon, 'I give You – the armies of the fallen ... once Yours – to be at Your command.'

⤸

Jether shook his head grimly. 'How far has the lightbearer fallen – he offers his damned host that once served Christos back to be His vassals.'

Michael frowned. 'The title deeds – What scheming strategy is this now?'

'He offers the kingdom of the Race of Men in exchange for His very soul.' Gabriel said softly. 'We knew it would be so,' Jether said.

'The very same same strategy that he used to tempt Eve, and Adam after her.' Jether continued. 'If Jesus, weary of the contest, succumbs to his seductions, He has bowed His knee to Lucifer, just as Adam did so easily in the first Eden. He then becomes his subject and forfeits the right to proclaim the kingdom of the First Heaven.'

'It is the rule of Eternal Law,' Gabriel echoed. 'This Lucifer well knows.'

They watched as Jesus closed His eyes.

'He faints from hunger,' Michael murmured.

'He is weary of the contest,' Jether whispered. He covered his head with his hood with trembling hands and bowed his head. In supplication for Jesus of Nazareth's soul.

⤸

'Forfeit the contest, Christos.' Lucifer moved closer; his voice was soft, seductive ... compelling. 'They do not

deserve Yehovah's love. They are renegades . . . treacherous
. . . lovers only of themselves.'

His eyes blazed with fury. 'Men serve me willingly; they
enjoy my rewards. They are reprobates; their transgression
against our Father is unpardonable. Why should You
proclaim Your kingdom when their ears are stopped and
their eyes are dim with their own lusts and self-will? All this
authority over the Race of Men, I will give to You because it
is mine, for it has been delivered to me and mine, to give to
whomever I wish.'

Lucifer's eyes gleamed in exhilaration.

'I *wish* to give it to You, Christos . . .' He moved his face
closer, so close that his cheek brushed Jesus' own. '. . . *if*
You worship me.'

Jesus' head remained bowed; Lucifer's face contorted
into a vicious mask of loathing.

'Now bow, Nazarene,' he snarled, 'As *You* made me bow
in the penitentiary, when You humiliated me before my
kingdom . . . *Worship* me . . .'

Very slowly Jesus raised His head. 'It is written that you
shall worship the Lord your God, and Him only you shall
serve.' His voice was as soft as the breeze but sharp as a
blade.

'Before your rebellion – you worshipped Me as seraph.'
His fierce clear eyes stared directly into Lucifer's shadowed
sapphire gaze.

Jesus' words rang clear and unmistakably through the
skies of Mount Quarnel, echoing in the First Heaven.

'Get . . . behind . . . Me . . . Satan.'

Lucifer shielded his eyes from the blinding light emanating from Jesus' form. Jesus raised His arm. Instantly,

Lucifer was thrust violently to the desert floor, his body shaking uncontrollably in loathing and terror.

⤳

'Yehovah!' Jether cried out in exhilaration. A tear ran unheeded down his weathered cheek.

Gabriel closed his eyes in reverence.

'The kingdom of the First Heaven descends on the Race of Men!'

A great rushing of wind filled the eastern horizon as Yehovah's huge white eagles flew over the steep onyx foundations, under the heights of the clouds towards Mount Quarnel.

Michael stood.

'We make haste to our king!' he cried.

⤳

Moloch stared, paralysed at the searing light erupting from the wilderness heights towards the fallen host, Dagon fell like lead to his knees on the desert floor, gasping for breath.

'Retreat!' he gasped, clutching his throat as hundreds of Lucifer's black stallions bolted, overturning war chariots and stampeding across the wilderness.

'Draw back!' Moloch screamed. 'The Nazarene wreaks havoc against us!'

Uproar broke out among the confused fallen horde as thousands of monstrous war chariots took off into the blazing dawn skies above Mount Quarnel.

Only Astaroth stood silent, his great fists grasping the reins of Lucifer's monstrous war stallions that pulled his chariot.

The stallions remained calm, but Astaroth's entire body shook as he watched from the shelter of the chariot, his gaze riveted on the imperial figure in white far in the distance. He stared transfixed as Christos raised His hands to the skies in rapture.

Slowly, the ferocious light softened and Astaroth moved from the shelter of Lucifer's war chariot to the open plains watching the skies. Michael's company of ten thousand times ten thousand heaven's great angelic company descended on the vast desert terrain of Mount Quarnel, their angelic shofars blowing from the north, south, east, and west of the horizon, led by Michael's golden chariot. Astaroth watched as Michael alighted, tall and imperial in his silver armour. He removed his helmet, shaking his long blonde hair loose from its braids, then strode straight towards the blazing white form, where he knelt before him.

Astaroth turned away, a thousand unsolicited emotions invading his soul.

Then he raised his gaze upwards to a monstrous form that flew straight towards him across the desert, his six dark seraph wings outstretched, his raven hair flailing across his scarlet cloak that blew wildly in the desert winds. His eyes burning with an evil crimson fire. His master – Lucifer.

I lowered my eyes from the malevolent hatred of his gaze that day – the day of his grievous defeat at the hands of the Nazarene.

'I shall wreak my vengeance, Gabriel!' he spat as he pulled his scarlet cloak around his imperial form.

Then disappeared with Astaroth in his war chariot on the flashing thunderbolts.

Following his menacing, iniquitous horde of the fallen.

Returning to his summer palace on the Babylonian plains of the Race of Men ... to conspire against the Nazarene.

2021
PETRA

Nick drew up outside the Movenpick Nabatean Castle Hotel, ten minutes from the entrance to Petra. He handed the keys for his rented convertible to the concierge, then turned towards the mountains, drinking in the spectacular views over the Great Rift Valley. He ran his frail fingers through his long, tousled hair with its fashionable dirty blond lowlights.

'Match me such a marvel save in Eastern clime,' he murmured in his distinct London accent. 'A rose red city . . . '

' . . . half as old as time,' the familiar melodious Arabic clipped English-accented voice softly finished his sentence. Nick turned, an unusual softness on his features.

'The Victorian traveller and poet, Dean Burgon – his contribution to the magnificence that is Petra,' the princess continued. She studied Nick intently. He was frailer than the last time she had seen him, a month ago. Still attractive . . . far too attractive.

Four years ago, at twenty-four, Nick De Vere had been the toast of Western society, sex symbol of the year in all the hottest Western gossip magazines – the rich, pretty young playboy whose prime occupation had been to dissipate the first tranche of his inordinate trustfund in a bevy of exclusive private clubs strung from London to Monte Carlo to Rome, seven nights a week. His antics had been splashed across the front pages of the *News of the World* and *The Sun*, much to his father's chagrin and his mother's despair – and his elder brother's outright horror. Finally his father, James De Vere, had frozen Nick's trust fund the night before collapsing with a fatal heart attack. And now Nick had AIDS. One evening too many – the sex, the heroin, the adrenaline of the chase. Nick De Vere was dying.

'You came?' Nick seemed surprised.

He strode after her and her entourage of clean-shaven bodyguards into the hotel lobby, where she was greeted by the management. Jordanian secret service agents were already stationed at intervals throughout the hotel.

Princess Jotapa stepped onto the lift with the manager. She looked at Nick intently. 'We share a similar passion for ancient artefacts. You said you had discovered an antiquity … something I would find of immense interest.'

Nick nodded.

Your Majesty…,' the manager interrupted, bowing.

Nick glared, furious, as the lift doors closed on him. 'Damn.'

He legged it up the stairs, arriving out of breath just as the princess stepped out and walked through to the terrace. They had seen each other on only one other occasion since the meeting in Alexandria: across a room at an after party in Amman, during Adrian's fleeting Middle East tour.

'You have good architectural taste, Nicholas.' The princess raised her eyebrows. Impressed. 'This hotel was designed by the renowned Jordanian architect Rasem Badran, winner of the Agha Khan Award for Islamic Architecture.'

The manager led Jotapa to a private table at the very end of the terrace and held out the chair for her. Nick followed, scowling at the two secret service bodyguards who stood, earpieces in their ears, next to the princess. He pulled out his own chair and sat heavily, beckoning the waiter over as Jotapa studied the menu.

'Movenpick's pistachio ice cream . . .' Jotapa smiled up at the waiter.

'Mint tea,' Nick said.

The waiter hurried away as Jotapa turned her clear gaze to Nick. 'I would have thought we would meet at the resort hotel.'

'The Al Nadeem Bar has the most spectacular sunset in Jordan.' Nick gazed back at Jotapa intently. A soft, pinkish flush crept from her neck until it reached her ears. She lowered her eyes.

'Saiid, Mahmoud . . .' She waved them back. They both bowed their heads in respect and moved to the far end of the terrace.

Nick nodded in the direction of the minders. 'How do you live in this fishbowl?'

Jotapa sighed. 'I grew up surrounded by bodyguards – it's part of my life.' She smiled gently at Nick. 'I don't resent it, Nick,' she said matter-of-factly. 'I have been entrusted with many, many privileges as a princess of Jordan, and as a princess I embrace the burdens that are also thrust on me. It is my duty to serve my people.'

'But don't you wish that just once you could throw it all to the wind? Be free?' He stared at her amazed.

'No, Nick De Vere, not even once do I consider it. That is the difference between us. You threw everything – fortune, privilege – to the wind to be free . . . ' She hesitated. 'You see, I am free, Nick.' She lay back in her chair, studying him. Amused.

He took out an object wrapped in a beige coloured cloth. 'For you,' he said unceremoniously, laying it on the table. 'Without you, I would have no access to the Jordanian dig.'

'You realize, of course, that your unprecedented access was not just royal favour, but your reward for sacrificing the world stage.' Jotapa smiled, her eyes never once leaving the cloth. 'And for keeping your mouth sealed.'

Nick was silent for a moment, remembering the white mist fading as two huge golden-bound codices became visible in the upper compartment of the casket. He recalled his wonder at the first sight of the pulsing angelic script – he could almost taste the moment when he first traced his finger along the title, the glowing Arabic lettering instantly transforming to English. He pushed the bag across the table to Jotapa. 'Here's to extended royal favour. There.' She looked at him. 'Open it.'

Carefully she unwrapped the cloth, her eyes glittered with curiousity. Lying on the table before her was a bundle of papyrus scrolls.

'Your namesake,' Nick said quietly, 'King Aretas the Fourth of Petra – his daughter Jotapa's private royal journals, unearthed from our dig at Petra.'

She looked up at him. Dumbstruck.

'Where did you . . . '

'In our excavations of the Temple of the Winged Lion.'

Nick pushed back his chair and stood, his tea untouched.

Jotapa reached for his hand. Suddenly vulnerable.

'Did you . . . ' She hesitated. 'The cross,' she murmured. 'The legend . . . '

Nick pushed his fringe from his eyes.

'It didn't . . . ' She faltered.

'It didn't heal me, Jotapa,' he said softly, walking towards the door.

Her face fell, and she nodded in acceptance. He walked through the entrance, then doubled back.

'I didn't touch the cross, Jotapa – I couldn't bring myself to. Your legend still stands.'

And without another word, Nick De Vere was gone.

CHAPTER EIGHTEEN

FLIGHT – 27 AD

ARETAS' GENERALS RACED at breakneck speed on their royal Arabian stallions, flanked by the king's ferocious royal guard. Just lengths behind them the royal guard of Herod Antipas rode in hot pursuit, masked from their view by the fierce Arabian sand blizzards that raged across the desert plains as the party of Arabians fled from Macherus across the vast, barren desert plains towards Petra.

Jotapa sat clinging to the waist of Aretas' most trusted general, the fierce and noble Saleem, her waist-length, gleaming black hair flying wildly behind her as they rode. Her eyes were wide with fear.

Ahead in the distance, barely visible through the seething sand storms, a tall lone figure walked across the sands, His white linen robe blowing furiously in the desert gales. He stood directly in the Arabians' path. Unmoving. He raised His hand. One by one, the Arabian stallions came to a grinding halt in the middle of the barren wasteland, refusing to shift, rearing and snorting in terror.

The stranger moved nearer the horses. Jotapa watched in astonishment as He lifted His hands, deftly making the secret calls and signals that she was certain only her father's royal trainers had access to. Instantly the stallions calmed, nuzzling the stranger's hands.

Saleem kicked his steed, but it refused to move any farther. Jotapa turned her head to the stranger, apprehension mixed with her anger.

'A fool and his sorceries!' shouted Saleem. 'Get him out of our path. Use the whips!' Jesus calmly stood His ground.

Jotapa's eyes met His. Incensed, she glared at Him. He smiled.

Impatiently she dismounted. Saleem immediately took out his whip and moved angrily over to where Jesus stood.

Jotapa, suddenly fierce, grasped Saleem's arm. She shook her head haughtily, giving Jesus an imperious glance. 'No, Saleem, I will deal with this, this *impertinent* stranger.'

Saleem fell to one knee. 'Yes, princess.'

Jotapa stretched to her full imperial height, pulled the black hood of her robe over her head and thrusting her body against the raging sandstorm, marched with immense difficulty directly up to where Jesus stood. He watched her intently, restraining His amusement at her peevishness.

'How *dare* you?' She stood in front of Him, her eyes flashing with arrogance from under her hood. 'Have You any idea precisely whose path You block?'

Jesus bowed His head.

'Look at me, stranger!' Jotapa placed the whip directly under Jesus' chin.

'You address the princess of Arabia!'

With great effort, she pushed His face up to meet her eyeline.

Jesus raised His head, His dark mane lashing against His high cheekbones. His face radiated with such a brilliance that Saleem and his generals held their arms in front of their eyes.

Jotapa stared at Him apprehensively. He was about her age.

Her unruly black locks blew over her face under her hood. Jesus reached out His hand, gently moving her hair from her eyes. She stared at Him, thunderstruck, her mind racing back to a distant far flung memory – a moment in time more than thirty years earlier when the young King and princess first met. He turned her left palm around; she gazed at a small scar hardly visible on her palm.

The whip slid from her hand onto the desert floor. She stared at Him in stunned silence. 'Your father, Aretas, protected My house once,' He said softly. He took her slim painted hand in His. 'Tell him from Me, Jotapa, that his Hebrew friend has not forgotten. My Father shall not fail to protect his house. That My kingdom is come.'

Jotapa stared at Jesus, strangely mesmerized.

Saleem, now recovered, strode towards Jotapa, his sword raised. 'Princess!' he cried, gesturing behind them at Antipas' royal guard, now fully visible, thundering towards them on the horizon. They will slaughter us.' He glared at Jesus darkly. 'With no mercy!'

Jesus smiled. 'There is no need to press the stallions,

faithful servant of Arabia.' His voice was calm. 'Antipas' men have turned back. Ride in peace.'

The hardened Saleem looked over his shoulder, then stared, dumbstruck. The desert sands were empty, silent. The furious gales had abruptly reduced to a gentle breeze.

Saleem frowned, bewildered. Strange tears pricked his eyes. He bowed his head to Jesus and saluted, then turned back to his generals, brandishing his sword high. 'The gods have protected the king's daughter. Let us ride to Arabia!' he cried.

When he turned back, Jotapa stood staring, transfixed, at the vast expanse of desert. The imperial white figure had vanished.

⟿

Charsoc paced up and down the portico of the exotic hanging gardens in Lucifer's newly created summer palace listening to the faint thundering that echoed through the crimson dusk. The sound of the fallen in their monstrous war chariots, returning from Mount Quarnel in Palestine. The thundering grew to a crescendo as the legions of war chariots set down on the rolling lush lawns of the palace.

Lucifer's elite black guard stood at attention, petrified as Lucifer stormed down from the chariot, his cloak wrapped tightly around him, whip in hand, his countenance like thunder. His steel boots pounded ferociously on the sapphire pathway as he strode beneath the canopies of the willow and juniper, down the majestic pavilions of cedars and great oaks, trampling down the beds of lilies fiercely in his path. Close behind followed Asteroth and his elite guard. Storming through the golden vaulted rooms and out onto the great eastern terraces, he threw his scarlet cloak onto the marbled floors. He flung himself down on the silver throne at the head of the immense table, draped in white satin and elaborately set for a huge banquet to celebrate his certain victory over the Nazarene. Six immense golden candelabras, each holding a hundred black tapers, illuminated the terrace. The frankincense burned and sputtered fiercely.

Lucifer sat in silence, and then held out his hand. Nothing stirred. Balberith lifted a silver flagon filled with exotic berry elixirs and, with trembling hand, poured the liqueur into Lucifer's jewelled goblet. Eighty courtiers stood around the terrace, waiting in trepidation. Lucifer sat like stone. Moments passed. Then slowly, deliberately, Lucifer turned the goblet upside down. He watched the crimson elixir pouring out, staining the satin cloth, his expression inscrutable. Then with one wrench, he heaved the cloth from the table, the fine crystal goblets and silvered dishes smashing into smithereens onto the lapis lazuli floor.

Flinging off his outer robes, he dived into the deep indigo waters of the immense pools that flowed outside the terrace's magnificent sapphire balconies.

Lucifer's powerful limbs sliced through the water with a savagery that set the colossus Asteroth trembling uncontrollably. Charsoc walked up through the gardens, to the pool's edge.

'The Nazarene?' Charsoc raised his eyebrows to Asteroth.

'He did not succumb. The Nazarene won the contest.' Asteroth stared at Charsoc, ashen.

'We failed,' Charsoc whispered in dread.

Lucifer heaved himself out of the pool, and Balberith ran to his side with a white satin robe. Lucifer snatched it from

Balberith's grasp and flung it over his shoulders, then slowly placed his feet in the silver slippers laid out for him. He walked over to the very edge of his hanging gardens. Silent. Not a muscle of his face moving. Restraining his rage with iron discipline.

'We leave for Perdition at dawn with the Ark of the Race of Men,' he muttered. Lucifer turned to Charsoc.

'Let us be prudent.' He plucked a golden pomegranate from a tall tree hung with thousands of white blossoms and took a large bite. 'Summon the Darkened Councils of hell to the Black Palace. Summon them from the Second Heavens and from under the earth.' Lucifer's voice was very soft. Dangerously soft. A smile flickered on his lips.

'How much damage can a carpenter from Nazareth *do*?' he shrugged. He held the pomegranate to his lips, then turned back to his staring out across the vast Babylonian plain, his expression sphinx like. The pomegranate fell from his hand onto the grass.

'How much … indeed?' And he ferociously crushed the half-eaten fruit under his slippered feet.

CHAPTER NINETEEN

ZAHI

JOTAPA RODE LIKE the wind on her grey mare, exhilarated, feeling the rush of adrenalin as she raced past the palace pavilions and the amphitheatre, leaving the magnificent Arabian ornamental gardens and the royal hunting parks far behind her. She was back in her beloved Arabia.

She raced across the vast palace grasslands, under the stately rows of ancient palms, past the royal pistachio, cashew, and wild olive groves onto the burning white sands. She slowed the horse's pace down as she arrived at the royal black tents where Aretas' royal relatives dwelled. Six young Nabataea princes, intent on training the royal horses, waved furiously as her mare sped by eagerly, shouting to her, their voices rising in excited gabbled Aramaic salutations as she galloped past.

Finally Jotapa arrived at the entrance to the sumptuous Royal Stables, with its ornate gold fretwork. She dismounted. Aretas was unaware of her arrival, absorbed in fellowship with his favourite Arabian stallion. He whispered endearments and fed him from his hand.

'Papa!' She ran to him, flinging herself into Aretas' arms. Aretas kissed her on both cheeks, and then held her fiercely to his breast. He looked down at her, his eyes moist. Deeply moved.

'I am so thankful you are safe, my child,' he whispered, wiping an errant tear from his cheek with the back of his hand. 'I climbed at dusk to the high place and sacrificed in appreciation to the gods...' He hesitated, 'And to the Hebrew.'

Jotapa nodded. Gently she unclasped herself from Aretas' arms and stepped back and studied the Nabaetan king.

He looked older, much older than when she had left Petra to become a young bride. His hair was greying, and the handsome face was lined, but she loved it. He looked like the wise and mighty sovereign he had become, devoting his life to the welfare of his people. They walked arm in arm out of the stables, their hands clasped together in great affection into the area of the great tents, Aretas leading the great Arabian steed by its halter.

'You remember the legend I taught you when you first learned to ride?'

'I was but four; I rode with Mother.'

Aretas nodded, his eyes suddenly moist.

'And the angel Gabriel took a handful of south wind and from it formed a horse, saying, "I create thee, O Arabian." He

whispered, *"To thy forelock, I bind victory in battle. On thy back, I set a rich spoil, and a treasure in thy loins. I establish thee as one of the glories of the earth . . . "'*

Jotapa continued softly, '*"I give thee flight without wings . . . "'*

'Look at his form,' Aretas murmured. 'Have you ever seen such symmetry, Jotapa? Such beauty? Our horses are the finest in the world – bred for endurance,' Aretas' eyes gleamed. 'agility . . . and speed!'

Aretas stopped in mid stride as they passed one of the black tents. One of the young princes, a small brown-skinned boy of twelve, was whipping a young mare, which was snorting and whinnying. Aretas frowned fiercely, grasping the boy's arm in a vice-like grip.

'You blunt her senses by the overuse of the whip.' He threw the whip down onto the sand, then looked up, noticing spurs on the horse. His expression grew black as a thunder.

'Spurs! You abuse the royal horses!'

'She was rearing, Your Majesty.' The child lay on the ground trembling, his face in the dust. 'She kicked Mahmoud.' He pointed to a four-year-old lying trembling on the sand. Then hastily reburied his face in the sand.

'Your voice trains the horse to habits of gentleness and attachment, so its senses are not blunted by abuse. As it feels the touch of your hand, the coaxing of your legs, it darts away like the wind. If the rider is dismounted in the chase, the horse instantly stops till he has recovered his seat. These are the royal Arabian horses of Aretas, King of Arabia.'

He walked over to the sobbing little boy lying in the dust. 'Hush, Mahmoud,' he whispered, examining the bruised leg. Then, scooping the child up in his arms, he cradled him to his chest, moved over to the mare, and placed him on her back. The mare looked into his eyes with her own clear trusting ones.

'You recognize her, Mahmoud; it is Felah – she used to share your tent – you used her neck as a pillow when you were an infant. Now, speak to her, Mahmoud – as I taught you.'

The boy whispered in the mare's ear. Instantly she calmed down and started a slow even canter around the tents. Gentle. Perfectly calm. Jotapa watched intently as Aretas signed the horse deftly.

'Papa...' she hesitated, 'the Hebrew used your secret signals on our horses.'

'Impossible!' Aretas turned. 'Our horses are trained to respond only to the sign of the king and the royal guard – these signs are an ancient Nabaetan kings' signs. Known only by myself... and my generals.'

I saw him with my own eyes father. I know these signs also from when I was taught as a child. He conversed with our horses just as you do. With the secret signs of a Nabaetan king.'

Satisfied Mahmoud – and the mare – were safe, Aretas led the way through the pistachio and wild olive groves to a private arbor. He clapped his hand, and four servants appeared. One placed goblets of gold and silver on the table.

'Tell me, Jotapa, what kind of man is the Hebrew?'

'There are all manner of stories circulating around Tiberias, Papa. I have heard that He tells His followers that love is mightier than the sword.'

Aretas frowned. 'He is not a warrior I fear.'

Jotapa looked at him mischievously. 'Oh, and, Father, He single-handedly stopped Herod Antipas' forces.'

Aretas smiled. Relieved.

'He had a message for you, Papa. He said that you had once protected His royal house, and that the house of Aretas shall never fail to be protected by Him.' She looked up at him enquiringly. Aretas nodded, strangely moved.

'But did he speak of Rome, Jotapa? When does he plan to overthrow the Roman occupation?'

'He said to tell you that His kingdom is come.'

Aretas frowned. 'The Hebrew's riddles – but He is talking of Rome – I am *sure* of it!' He held out his hand to his cupbearer, who refilled his goblet with wine. 'So He will overthrow the tyrant Antipas and set Himself up as King of the Jews. I shall await His war and then join the armies of Arabia with His armies – the King of the Jews and the king of Arabia shall be a force to contend with – together we shall overthrow the Romans!' Aretas stood.

'Papa . . .' Jotapa looked out towards the veiled windows of the palace's eastern wing. Aretas followed her gaze, his countenance growing clouded.

'What ails Zahi, my beloved brother, your treasured son, the crown prince? His chambers are barred, and the windows are veiled. I sought for his company, but Duza says he is resting.'

Aretas sighed. 'You must be strong, Jotapa.' He paced the grove steadily. 'Jotapa . . . I would have saved you from this anguish. I could not bring myself to write you about what has befallen him.'

Jotapa paled, intuitively. She stared into her father's eyes, trembling, awaiting the words.

'Your younger brother is sick unto death, my child. He has leprosy.'

~

2021

LONDON

— JULIA —

Nick De Vere slammed the black taxicab's door and strode towards the Harrods entrance. He passed four London policemen in body armour holding machine guns. Five police vans were stationed at the top of New Oxford Street. It was a common enough sight in London now. The past five years had seen a new acceleration in terrorist attacks all across the British Isles and Europe. After the dirty bomb detonated in Trafalgar Square, the ancient centre of London had been demolished and abandoned. Security procedures had been revolutionized all over the UK. But last month four huge bombs had been detonated in New Oxford Street, in stores during prime time shopping hours. Two thousand people killed. It had been a massacre. The New London police were taking no chances, and the normally resilient British public was growing increasingly weary.

Nick looked down at his watch – he was late. Two security guards inside the Harrods entrance threw his bag on the conveyor belt of a sophisticated screening centre, then ushered him through the iris recognition system that Adrian during his term as British Prime Minister, had fought fervently to install in every public place in the British

Isles. Today, it was commonplace. Nick couldn't even shop at his local Sainsbury's grocery store without 'IRIS', as she was affectionately called.

He took the elevator up to the third floor.

Julia was waiting for him in the Punch Café, as he knew she would be. It was an exact replica of the original café from the early 2000s. Nick remembered it well. She and Jason used to bring him here for lunch on their frequent business trips from the States when he was young.

There she was, seated at the far end table, near the paintings. Nick smiled. She was talking on her phone. As usual.

Age had been good to Julia. She had always been pretty, but now she was stunning. Quite stunning, Nick thought. Jason had been a fool to let her go.

He leaned over and kissed her freshly made-up cheek. She smelled of Chanel – not the No. 5, he thought. Of jasmine . . . He placed his sunglasses in the pocket of his faded leather jacket, then sat back in his chair and studied her.

She had aged well. Gracefully. She would be forty-one in November, but she could pass for thirty. Her platinum blonde shoulder-length hair was painstakingly highlighted. Her pretty face was perfectly made up. Her big hazel eyes smiled up at him from under her fringe as she continued her phone conversation. She wore faded boot-cut jeans with a simple black and silver belt and a short-sleeved white T-shirt with some designer logo in black. Always a logo with Julia, he thought fondly. Jason was crazy; she was the only thing that had worked in his entire personal life – besides Lily, of course.

Julia placed her fine-boned hand, with its studio tan and polished acrylic nails, on his own affectionately.

Nick smiled. It still amazed him.

Everything – absolutely everything – about Julia St Cartier was processed and contrived. Except Julia herself. From her nails to her hair extensions to her tan, she was thoroughly artificial, yet she was possibly the one solitary human being he knew who had always remained deeply, utterly, madly true to herself. Her complete lack of pretence was disarming.

'Nick...' She smiled broadly. 'It's been too long.'

Nick nodded, taking her hand. 'How's Lily?'

Her eyes reflected his deep concern. 'She's doing well – really well, Nick. She's a survivor, like her father. She uses that wheelchair like it's an extension of her own body... She loves her school. Everything's good.'

Nick thought back on the accident. How long ago had it been? It was one of the big De Vere family parties. Lily, only seven, was exhausted, and Nick had offered to drive her home early. A huge pantechnicon had jack-knifed in front of them from out of nowhere. They hadn't a chance. Nick, though concussed, had only bruises and scratches, but Lily was paralysed from the waist down. Crippled – crippled for life. He had had one beer – well below the legal limit. Julia never needed any convincing that it was all beyond his control. But Jason – well, that was another matter. His brother hadn't talked to him from that day to this.

'Nick... Nick?' Julia said softly. Nick started, suddenly reeled back in from deep in the past. The waitress stood waiting patiently. Julia smiled. 'I'll have the crayfish tails open sandwich on brown bread, and a glass of dry champagne.

Nick shook his head. 'Not hungry – just a pot of Earl Grey.' Julia frowned at him.

'I was with Adrian last week,' she said, as the waitress left.

Nick nodded. 'He told me. You did his big Jordanian gig? He said you were phenomenal.'

Julia nodded. 'It was a nightmare to organize – but it's great publicity for Lola...'

Nick smiled. After the divorce, Julia had decided not to return to her previous role as chief editor of *Cosmopolitan New York*, although they had offered her an exorbitant financial package. Instead she had returned to England and started a small but exclusive PR events firm, running it from her new house in Chelsea. She had named it 'Lola' after her beloved artistic mother, the late Lola St Cartier Deschanel. It had taken off beyond her wildest dreams, with clients such as the England football team, Chanel, and the newly appointed European president, Adrian De Vere.

She hesitated.

'Jason was there,' she said softly. 'I saw him for the first time since the divorce ... in Aqaba.'

'And how *is* my elder brother?' Nick asked, his eyes blank.

Julia grimaced.

'Busy – what else would Jason be? Chasing his latest mergers, cementing deals, drinks with the president...'

'The US President?' Nick raised his eyebrows. Julia nodded. 'He's working with Beijing – some huge merger with VOX Media and the Chinese government. Very complicated ... involves the White House. Uncle Lawrence keeps me up to date; he still sees him occasionally on his trips to New York. And you? Have you heard from him?' The waitress returned with the tea and champagne.

199

Nick shrugged his shoulders.

'Why would I hear, Jules? He cut me off after the accident. No – never a word. Adrian keeps me in the loop, though. Thank God for Adrian.'

Julia studied Nick. 'I know he's been good to you.' She poured Nick's Earl Grey tea into a cup.

'Thanks, sis.' Nick leaned back in his chair. 'More than good, Julia – he sent me to the top clinics, paid all my treatment . . . he kept me alive.'

Julia lowered her voice.

'It's tragic about Melissa – she was so young and beautiful – *and* the baby.'

Nick shook his head. 'Adrian didn't deserve that.' Julia lowered her eyes.

'The medication's working – you look stronger.'

He gave a wry smile. 'You were always a terrible liar, Julia. The treatments stopped working – it's Russian Roulette. 'He shrugged. 'I'm in the hands of the gods.' He took a sip of his tea. 'Not that there *are* any gods.'

Julia bit her lip. 'Uncle Lawrence is so proud of you,' she said softly. 'When Lily and I were with him in Greece, he mentioned you'd made this incredible find in Petra, but it's been kept under wraps for years by the Jordanian government – can't we release it to the press? Get you some serious mileage . . .' She shook her head.

'God knows, Nick, your face has been splashed over the tabloids with all the ghastly inner workings of your personal life . . . the cocaine and the AIDS . . . We could get incredible mileage from this – turn the tables on the London gutter press and paparazzi, kid. Portray you as the serious archaeologist you are.'

Nick gave her a pained look. 'Nah, I can't, Jules – I've given my word.'

She frowned.

'I've taken the money. The price of silence.'

'The Jordanian government?' He nodded.

'It was huge, Jules.' He smiled sheepishly. 'With my trust fund frozen, I had to take it. God – dad hated my relationship with Klaus.'

'And that pretty Jordanian princess ... the archaeologist?' She smiled at him gently.

Nick flushed. 'Yes.' His eyes grew soft. 'She's quite something.' He changed the subject abruptly. 'Dylan Weaver's meeting me at Terminal Four...' Julia frowned.

'The brain...' Nick prompted.

'Your old roommate?' Distant memories flooded back. Of Nick surrounded by tanned, adoring American girls on his summer vacations in Cape Cod and of the pasty, chubby spectacled boy, his best friend from Gordonstoun College in Scotland, who would arrive with Nick, his laptop in tow, and eat them out of house and home. Nick and Dylan had been inseparable.

'He still detests megalomanic Jason,' Nick grinned.

' – but had a crush on you!' Julia laughed. 'That's because I found him the only supplier of British fish and chips and mushy peas on the entire USA East Coast! 'Nick grinned. 'He's chief of IT security for Microsoft Europe...'

Julia raised her eyebrows. 'Impressive!' She took a long sip of champagne.

'You're meeting Uncle Lawrence tomorrow?'

'In Alexandria, at the monastery. How is he?'

'He's good – amazing for nearly eighty-six. He's with

your mother in Bali at the moment, tracking down some ancient monstrosity for the British Museum. He escorts her to New York, then flies straight out to join you in Egypt.' Julia looked at her watch.

'Your plane leaves in four hours. I'll drive you to Heathrow. I've a working dinner appointment at Hampton Court – it's not far out of my way.'

Nick topped up his tea. 'Thanks, sis.'

He was looking forward to seeing that tough old man that was Julia's great uncle – ex-Jesuit priest turned CIA agent, turned antiquities expert – the enigma that was Lawrence St Cartier.

CHAPTER TWENTY

KERF KENNA - 27 AD

I T WAS DUSK, and the flaming torches of the bridal party lit up the main street of Kerf Kenna. Mary, now in her mid-forties, older but still beautiful, stood with the older women in the doorway of the bride's house, her face radiant. She gazed down the road, hoping for a glimpse of Jesus. There He stood, a tall, lean figure in the centre of the crowd, applauding the bridal couple loudly, swept up in the gaiety of the precedings; His face wreathed in laughter.

The handsome young prophet from Nazareth.

Mary passed the garland in her hand to an old woman next to her, then grabbed a jar of oil and a basket of nuts, and ran down the path towards her son. Immediately she was set upon by a horde of excited children, all reaching out their hands. She pushed her hair back from her face, dipping her hand into the basket, she threw the nuts and sweets high in the air. The children shrieked with exhiliration. Then one of them caught sight of Jesus. The five-year-old let out a raucous scream of delight and ran full tilt straight towards Him, with a horde of other children yelling behind him. The children tugged at His robe, their grimy hands feeling inside the folds and bringing out handfuls of sweetmeats. One small boy of two years with unruly black curls, crowded out by the bigger children and unable to reach Jesus, started to cry stridently. Jesus bent down and winked at him, secretly passing him a sticky-looking cake.

The toddler tore the wrapping off eagerly, stuffing the cake into his mouth, his face smeared with the dark sticky substance. Then Jesus hoisted him onto His shoulders, His robe still being plundered by the other unruly youngsters.

Mary studied her son, her mind suddenly racing back to when Jesus Himself had been just such a young boy, running loudly and exuberantly to her, tugging on her garments for sweet cakes just as the children had tonight.

How the years had flown, she pondered.

And the boy had become a man. With maturity his features were now strong and refined. His eyes were still deep mercurial pools, changing hues with His moods as when He was very young. At times, like tonight, she still glimpsed the humour and mischief of His youth. Mary smiled. He had been strong – even when He was small – strong-willed to the point of stubborn when He believed He was right. And courageous. Fiercely protective of those weaker than Himself. Compassionate. How the years had flown. Mary gazed at her son. He had just turned thirty. The thick dark chestnut hair was streaked by the sun and still had a tendency to be unruly, but now it fell down across His broad shoulders like a gleaming mane. He still had His dimples, those had never disappeared ... and *that* smile.

She shook her head. That smile that must have broken a thousand hearts since the age of four. The room became electric whenever Jesus walked in, even as a toddler. The girls had always found Him irresistible. Her old maiden aunts baked Him cakes and had spun childhood robes and sashes for Him. Children adored Him. His boyhood friends were ardently devoted to Him, and His uncle and cousins had always been fiercely protective of the gracious, noble child.

Her expression grew soft, as she remembered how Jesus used to regale all His young friends with His stories of the land of the great Rubied Door. There was one particular dusk that particularly stood out in her memory shortly after Jesus' sixth birthday.

Fourteen of His young friends and neighbours had gathered in the meadow behind the small stone house, clothed in their bright scarlet and blue tunics, sitting cross-legged in a circle. Jesus sat in the centre, on an overturned wooden crate of Joseph's. Jesus' face had shone, almost with an unearthly glow as He told about an enchanted land of crystal palaces and portals that peaked into seven spires. Of labyrinths and hanging gardens, where two silver trees stood and where blue and silver pomegranates grew and flowers sprang back up after being trodden on.

The band of small boys and girls from Nazareth had hung onto every syllable, entranced by the storybook land whose streets were of transluscent gold, where beaches stretched for leagues of pearl sands – and a soaring crystal palace was carved out of one immense diamond – the home of the Great King.

Then Joseph, weary from a day's hard work with his hands, had come quietly and sat, as had the ageing Rabbi and his teenage pupils from the local synagogue. Mary too, had stopped her spinning and sat quietly under the branches of the wide, spreading fig trees to listen. She had watched as the strain and weariness of life seemed to literally ebb away from the men's and women's eyes and faces as Jesus spoke of heavenly councils of ancient angelic monarchs, the governors of heaven, their white hair like cascades of spun silk falling to the floors, and golden crowns upon their heads. And of one called Jether the Just, who reigned over twenty-four. Jesus closed His eyes as He spoke of the chief princes of heaven, the archangels. Of the imperial Michael, commander of heaven's armies, and noble Gabriel, the Revelator.

The breathtaking world that lay beyond the Rubied Door. A world where no tears were shed, no sorrow existed. A world where there was no death, only love and peace and always laughter.

And then Jesus stopped and His eyes misted over. Mary could still hear His awed whisper describing the great golden Rubied Door, ablaze with light, that was embedded into the jacinth walls of the tower – the entrance to the throne room.

And the old Rabbi's eyes lit up with exhilaration as he clutched the boy's hand with his old wrinkled one, drinking in every word. 'Tell us again of the Great King of the Universe.'

And tears would well up in Joseph's eyes, and an awed stillness would fall over the giggling children, so that the only sound was the murmuring of the doves.

'His hair and head . . .' Jesus whispered,

' . . . are white like snow,' the children murmured.

'His eyes flash . . .'

'Like flames of living fire,' the children shouted in awed unison.

' . . . tell us of His great and tender compassions,' the old Rabbi murmured.

And Mary could still picture the exquisite anguish on Jesus' face as He had gazed up to the heavens, His eyes filled with adoration.

'Abba is so beautiful . . . ,' He had whispered in longing, staring out towards the cloudless blue horizon.

Remembering, Mary took in a sharp breath. When He had been but four years old, she had heard Him sobbing in the night and had rushed to Him. He had clung to her, the hot tears coursing down His cheeks. She had raised His heart-shaped face to hers,

'Mama! Mama!' He had cried, hardly able to speak for the intense sobbing. 'I want the Ruby Door . . . I want My Abba! The anguish of an infant separated from His beloved father had imprinted itself on her very soul.

She had never heard Him sob in such a manner again, but on occasion through the years as He grew older, long after midnight, she would find His bed empty, and she knew that He was walking the lush Galilean hillsides under the vast glittering starry skies . . . talking to His beloved 'Abba'.

She held all these things deep in her heart. And pondered them. She started, her reverie broken by the loud uproar that broke out as the young bride neared the bridegroom's house. A nervous-looking young man was pushed forward down the small dusty street by a clamouring crowd of his teenage friends. He walked towards the young bride and took her hand. Jesus and the crowd erupted wildly as the bridegroom conducted her into his house, walking among the excited throng and through the open doorway.

The dining hallroom was brilliantly lit with candelabras and lamps. Massive tables groaned under the weight of the sumptuous provisions for the seven-day feast. Chickens, salads, brightly coloured fruits were crammed together on the tables. A small orchestra played their lyres for the hundreds of guests, standing or seated on couches and cushions. The children and youths whirled and danced with unending energy in the centre of the hall.

Jesus was quickly surrounded by children, clutching at His hands, drawing Him towards the dancing. In no time at all, He and the children were all dancing exuberantly and out of time to the music, singing and chanting loudly and off key. Mary watched from the kitchen, shaking her head in merriment.

The orchestra stopped, and Jesus wiped His brow. He turned to where Peter and John sat reclining on couches. Jesus heaved a sigh of relief and walked over to a couch and sat down, exhausted. Peter passed Him a cup of water, then ripped the leg off a chicken and munched on it, chewing loudly. Jesus looked at him from under His eyebrows. Pained. Peter grinned sheepishly.

'Get some rest, Jesus. First the crowds, now the children … always the children.'

Jesus removed His sandals, closed His eyes in bliss, and leaned His head back.

Mary gently placed her hand on His shoulder. 'They have run out of wine.'

Jesus' eyes remained closed, but He leaned back and clasped His mother's work-worn hand affectionately. He was silent a long while.

'Dear lady, what does this matter have to do with Me?' He smiled.

Mary stood patiently. Waiting. She smiled, looking down at Him.

Finally Jesus opened His eyes and sat up. He looked at her deeply. Tenderly.

'My time is not yet come, Mother.'

She saw that old mischief in His eyes and followed His gaze over to six huge stone jars that lay nearby, customarily used for ceremonial washing, each able to hold up to thirty gallons of water. Suddenly He smiled brilliantly.

Mary grabbed His face in her hands and kissed His forehead. Then she grasped the steward's arm. 'Whatever my son instructs you, do it!'

Huddled in the far corner, his striking features half-shadowed by the flickering lanterns, an educated stranger from the south watched intently as Jesus instructed the servants to fill the jars to the brim.

The man's name was Judas Iscariot.

～

Herodias reclined on her golden throne. Her butler passed her a platter of grapes while four young maidservants rubbed oils into her milk-white skin. She looked languidly up at Herod.

'Oh, let us winter in Macherus, Herod, my dove. I am bored beyond endurance.' She plucked a handful of grapes from the platter. 'And Salome will be there – we would make sport with the baptist.'

Herod sat deep in thought, his mind a thousand miles away. She leaned nearer and grasped his bangled arm.

'Stop thinking about avenging that Arab wench!'

Herod frowned. 'Leave the baptist, my dove. Since he was arrested my sleep has been racked with strange and unsettling dreams. Find another arena of sport . . . I implore you!'

Herodias sat bolt upright. She waved the maidservants away imperiously, then glared furiously at Herod.

'He is vile and insubordinate. He commits treason by his accusations against us. He has cursed us. The rabble of Judaea,' she hissed, 'they all fall under his spell! It bodes ill for us.'

Herod walked over to the palace balcony, staring over the gardens of the princes, towards the lake. Herodias walked over and joined him.

'His oratory is compelling,' he murmured, deep in thought.

'You are *weak*, Antipas.' Herodias pushed him from her roughly. 'You couldn't even dispose of that Arab wench you took as a wife.' She spat. 'She ran back to Papa, and now you have Aretas' bloodthirsty mob screaming for our blood.'

She paced the balcony like a panther. 'Why can't you be like your father – strong, decisive?' He would have had that baptist's head the first day he started uttering his poison!'she declared.

Herod placed his hands over his head, then stood to his feet.

'Prepare the caravan, Caspius! We will winter in Macherus!'

~

Lucifer sat behind his ornate mother-of-pearl desk encircled by his vast private library of angelic antiquities, his expression, one of rare tranquility. He had returned to Perdition only a few moons ago and had been unexpectedly comforted by the familiar surroundings of his Black Palace. The unrelenting pervasive gloom of Perdition agreed with his soul and his mood, after his defeat at the hands of the Nazarene. Here he could forget his humiliation, and bury himself in his antiquities. His music. His myriad intellectual pursuits. Away from the mewling crassness of the Race of Men, he mused.

His raven tresses gleamed and fell unbraided over his favourite cadium orange silk gown, past his shoulders. His long, slim fingers were bare, except for a single golden signet ring embossed with the royal crest of the House of Yehovah. A deliberate token – a reminder of the presence of the 'Nazarene' on *his* planet.

He smiled down at the magnificent young black panther, who lay, purring, its head on Lucifer's jewelled sandals. His latest acquisition to soothe his wounded honour. Another reminder, this time of Ebony, his panther from aeons past in the First Heaven. He picked up a soft jellied saffron sweetmeat and placed it in his mouth, then continued writing in his journal, his beautiful italic lettering filling the linen pages.

Charsoc stood at the arched onyx entrance, a vulture shaman rested on his left shoulder, its eyes glittered red.

Charsoc bowed low. 'There has been an incident, Your Majesty. It concerns the Nazarene.'

Lucifer continued his lettering with his left hand, holding out his right hand to Balberith, who lifted a silver flagon filled with exotic berry elixirs and poured the liqueur filling Lucifer's goblet, Still Lucifer did not look up.

'Of what manner of incident do you speak, Charsoc?' he mumbled.

'It seems . . . Your Majesty, that there has been a matter of transubstantiation.'

'Speak plainly, I command you.' He sipped, darkness clouded his countenance.

'The Nazarene – He is using His powers to change molecular . . . that is, He changes water into wine.'

Lucifer scowled. 'Child's play,' he muttered. He dipped his quill in the purple ink and continued his lettering.

'The terms of His status are altered by His passing the temptations, sire. He passed the test as one of the Race of Men, thereby securing divine right to use His supernatural powers from the First Heaven.' Charsoc said.

'So the carpenter dabbles.' Lucifer shrugged.

'We must be cautious, Your Excellency. He attracts attention. Mostly rabble, it is true, but also those of higher standing – those of influence – our dark slaves of the Race of Men.'

Slowly, Lucifer raised his head.

'You *will* not let it drop, Charsoc, will you.' He sighed and laid down his quill, glaring darkly at Charsoc, who stood quietly by the window, hands behind his back.

'Balberith,' Lucifer closed the soft leather bound book, 'I shall resume my journal at the next moon.'

Balberith bowed and removed the journal from the desk. Lucifer extricated his feet from beneath the panther and rose from his chair. He walked over to the tall loggia doors of the library, deep in contemplation, watching as thousands of cloven-hoofed dauphin scribes rode over the lava plains of Perdition towards the underground crypts of the Black Palace, followed by flying eight-winged demonic scholars with red, fiendish eyes.

'We are prudent. We prepare.' The panther paced beside him, its heavy gold collar studded with rubies. He bent down and stroked its glossy black head

'The gathering assembles. Prepare my ceremonial robes, Balberith. I retire early. We will conspire at dawn.'

Chapter Twenty-one

AD 27

J OTAPA WALKED ACROSS gleaming black marbled floors through the palace corridors, crossing into the eastern wing, to the crown prince's chambers. She pushed open the doors to the huge library. Hundreds of shelves were filled with scrolls from China, India, Persia, and other distant lands.

She continued on towards the immense gilded doors of the crown prince's bedchamber. Two of the royal guard stopped her. The lower half of their faces were covered in thin gauze.

'Duza!' she cried. It was Zahi's boyhood friend and one of her own childhood companions.

He shook his head gently.

Jotapa grasped him by the wrist so tightly that her nails dug into his flesh. He gently but firmly removed her hand. Then gave her a severe look.

'You are *certain* this is your choice.'

'He is my brother – my mother died in childbirth delivering him. He is crown prince of Arabia. He is my childhood friend, my joy, Zahi the tender.' Jotapa's eyes flashed. 'I am certain this is my choice.'

Duza bowed his head. 'He awaits you, princess. He knew you would come.' Duza stepped aside, motioning to the second guard to do the same. They pushed the doors open.

Jotapa walked into the vast chamber, and the great doors swung closed behind her with a thud.

Far across the chamber, by the farthest window, stood a tall, frail figure.

'Jotapa, my princess . . .' He spoke softly. His voice was cultured, refined.

'Beloved older sister, protector, and friend.'

He stood unmoving at the window, his back still towards her.

'Zahi!' Jotapa ran towards him.

Instantly he spun around. 'No! Jotapa!' he cried fiercely. 'You may *not* touch me!'

Halfway across the room Jotapa faltered, staring at him in horror. His face was completely wreathed in a thin, gauze-like muslin material, as were both his hands. Only his eyes were visible, with holes for his nose and mouth. He was frail, his breathing shallow.

Jotapa reached out her hands to him imploringly. Zahi stared fiercely at her, then started to unravel the muslin from one of his hands. Jotapa stared down as the cloth dropped to the floor, then stepped back in distress and sank to her knees, her mind spinning with shock and revulsion.

Zahi's hands were disfigured beyond recognition. The

long, slim fingers that once penned beautiful Syriac and Aramaic letters on his library scrolls were covered with nodules and partially rotted away. Where his thumb had been, only a bloody stump remained.

Tears rolled down Jotapa's cheeks. She stared up at Zahi with passion, watching as the gauze that covered his face grew wet with his hot fierce tears.

They exchanged a long intense glance; then Zahi unfastened the muslin. His lips and ears were distended, swollen three times beyond their natural size, his lashes and eyebrows gone from his staring eyes. She lowered her eyes from his hideous disfigurement.

There was a soft knock, and Duza entered, followed by Aretas' most prominent royal physician, accompanied by a swarthy stranger. Jotapa knew at once, by the immense height of his turban and the length of his sleeves, that he was a Babylonian physician or magician of great importance.

Aretas' physician bowed deeply to her. 'We greet you, princess. Abu Mansur, great priest and choice physician of the caliph of Persia, has traversed the great deserts and the great waters to be our guest. He brings with his ointments the great Indian physician Sushruta's medicines for the treatment of leprosy: chaulmoogra oil.'

Jotapa stood silent, then walked over to Zahi, clasped him to her, and kissed him on the head. She strode out of the room, followed by Duza.

She turned to Duza, her hands planted on her slim waist, her head held high. 'When did my father last visit my brother?' Duza looked at her but did not reply.

'When, Daza? You must tell me.'

Duza lowered his eyes to the floor.

'I command you. Speak, Duza.'

'You command me as a princess or as a friend?'

Jotapa sighed. 'As a friend,' she said softly. ' – a friend of both myself and my brother.'

Duza nodded. There was a long silence.

'He has not entered these chambers for almost five years, Your Majesty.'

Jotapa stepped back in horror. 'Sacrilege!' she cried.

This time Duza grasped her arm so tightly that she winced. He would not let go. 'Do you not comprehend? It is his firstborn son, the precious fruit of his loins. It is his agony that prevents his coming here. He came each dusk and dawn for four years, till it broke his heart and he could no longer bear it.'

'I *cannot* accept it!' Jotapa cried.

'Accept it, Jotapa!' Duza's voice was very stern; he would not let her go. 'Your father spends his royal fortunes scouring the East for the most prominent physicians and magicians. He spends lavish monies and his vast royal treasuries on these priests, physicians, pharmacists, and conjurers – renowned healers such as you saw today. He leaves no stone unturned in the hope . . . '

Duza faltered.

Jotapa glared at him. 'There is no hope, Duza!' she cried.' His doom is sealed. These tricksters, these magicians, these parasites who would bleed my father dry with their potions . . . '

She broke off in mid sentence as Duza paled visibly and dropped to one knee.

Jotapa turned. Zahi stood in the entrance. A terrible sorrow in his eyes.

Duza stared at Jotapa. Incensed.

Zahi looked down at Jotapa with pity.

'Beloved sister,' he whispered, 'while we have breath, there is hope...'

Jotapa knelt, clasping his hand, her tears falling down onto the fresh bandages.

'The Babylonian Rab Mag Daniel's writings speak of the unknown God...' Zahi whispered, staring past her out towards the shimmering dusk skies, a strange ecstacy in his gaze.

'One day He will find me.'

CHAPTER TWENTY-TWO

GERASENE

J ESUS STEPPED OUT of the boat at Gerasene, onto the narrow shore. The horizon was barely visible, obscured from view by the strange haze suddenly descended over Galilee, the residue of far flung sand storms from Arabia. He stared upward at the stark cliffs rising above Him, then bent down and cupped His hands in the lapping lake, drenching His face in the cool, refreshing water. He pushed His long dark hair off His forehead, exhausted, the earlier feverish activity of the day starting to take its toll.

The young stranger from the wedding in Cana walked towards Him across the sand, clutching a large sheaf of papyri.

'Documents, papyri,' Peter grumbled. 'Always something to write or sign . . . You know why he was missing last night,

Master? He was counting money again. Only twenty-three, and he acts like a grandmother.'

Thomas glared at him. 'He is able and prudent, with the gift of administration – something you lack.'

'*Someone* has to count the money, Peter,' Jesus said. 'He has left both his education and his possessions in the south to serve our cause. Let us be generous.'

Judas ignored Peter. 'The agreements, Master. The tax collectors pester me; they eye our purse with relish. The deadlines approach. These must be dealt with.'

Jesus lifted His hand wearily. 'Leave it until the morning, Judas ... The documents can wait.'

Judas uttered an ill-concealed sigh of exasperation.

Jesus placed His hand gently on his arm, and immediately Judas's expression softened. 'Forgive me, Jesus, it is only that...' He looked deeply into Jesus' eyes in respect.

'That we are always so busy.' Jesus finished the sentence softly, looking into the ardent young face.

Judas nodded. 'You are always pressed for time. The crowds demand all Your attention, so I grasp any opportunity that presents itself. It is important that You – that the organization is without reproach in all we do ... that the Pharisees and Sadducees find no deficiencies in our records.'

Jesus nodded. 'We must adhere to the rules.' A faint smile glimmered on His lips. He looked at Judas compassionately, as though at a young child lacking in understanding.

Judas frowned. 'You know that I would give my life for the cause. I am totally committed,' he clasped Jesus' shoulder, '...to You, Master.'

Jesus looked at him for a long moment. 'Yes, Judas, I

know this. I give you My word. Tomorrow morning, before we cross to the far side of Galilee.'

Judas pressed Jesus' hand in gratitude.'Thank You...' Jesus raised His hand to quiet him, as though hearing something. Slowly He turned. Standing by the jagged, rough-hewn tombs at the bottom of the cliffs, completely naked, was a deranged man, staring directly at Jesus. He was filthy and bleeding, puss oozed from hundreds of rough cuts and weals all across his chest and thighs. On one wrist and both feet were broken iron fetters, the chains still dragging behind him on the sand. He stood, foaming at the mouth and snarling.

Jesus slowly raised His head, giving the man the full force of His gaze.

A terrible, unintelligible roaring rose from the naked figure, and he fell down at Jesus' feet in mortal terror.

Jesus moved a step nearer.

'What have You to do with me, Jesus?' he screamed, holding his hands over his head as though in intense pain. 'Son of the most high God!' he shrieked insanely, dragging himself across the jagged rocks to the cliffs, battering his matted head against the hard grey boulders.

Judas watched, ashen. Peter and John looked on in fascination.

'I beg you!' he screamed. 'Do not torment me!'

Jesus held His hand towards the man's head, and Judas watched, mesmerized, as thousands of, looking like fiendish, clawed vapours.

'What is your name?' Jesus commanded.

The wild man opened his lips. 'Legion,' growled a thousand dark decadent depraved voices in unison.

221

Judas nearly fell over Peter and Thomas as they all scrabbled back across the sand, sheltering behind a large rock, staring at Jesus and the demoniac, horror-struck.

'Leave him!'

The screaming changed in tone to high-pitched terror, the wild man clutched his head, screaming as thousands of blackened, dissolute, gnarled figures materialized from the wild man's breath.

'Reveal yourself!' Jesus demanded. The twisted ghoulish figures transformed one by one into fallen angelic beings – a monstrous horde of Lucifer's fallen. Nearly six thousand. Their tangled straw-coloured hair fell over their pock-marked faces, their red eyes glinted in terror. Intent on the Nazarene. The fallen legion waited. Jesus stood, His linen robes billowed in the wind. He raised His arm.

'Not the Abyss ... Christos, we beseech You!' wailed the voices,

The strapping leader of the monstrous horde stepped forward. 'I am Daemuk,' he rasped, 'General of the 102nd legion. My master is Folcador, Grand Duke of hell.' He fell down on one knee before Jesus, his head bowed. 'I beg You, Christos. Do not banish us, the fallen, to the Abyss before the time.'

Jesus moved nearer. Daemuk clasped his head in agony.

'You invade My kingdom. You defile the Race of Men.' Jesus replied, His voice unyielding.

Daemuk gestured to a herd of swine feeding on the mountain.

'Suffer us, the fallen to inhabit the swine, Christos.'

Jesus closed His eyes, then lifted His arm. 'Go!' He commanded, His voice blacker than thunder.

Judas watched from the shelter of the rock in wonder, trembling, as the horde of the fallen vanished and immediately the herd of swine ran violently over the edge of the cliff drowning in the deep waters below.

Jesus pushed His dark locks from His eyes, staring out across the Sea of Galilee. 'The tyranny of satan nears its end. The First Judgement hastens.'

⤴

From above the skies and from under the earth they flew – the menacing powers of evil and terror – to the crypts of the Underlords beneath Lucifer's Black Palace on the desolate smouldering, lava wastes at the edge of hell.

The Darkened Councils of hell were gathered.

Charsoc stood before the great assembly.

'My Master, Lucifer, crowned satan, only true King of the World welcomes your presence.'

Dagon and Lucifer's elite guard drew back a huge magenta curtain, revealing Lucifer, all glorious, seated on the Seat of Satan in the Great Chamber of the Underlords. He was dressed in his white ceremonial robes fringed with ermine. His diamond crown rested on his raven hair. He held his sceptre in his right hand, the great damson ring of satan on his ring finger.

'We are here with only one aim,' he declared, slowly surveying the great assembly of thousands of the dark rulers of the world.

'To cut short the days of the Nazarene.'

A great and terrible roar erupted across the Great

Chamber as the great satanic generals of hell stood to their feet, followed by the thousand stooped hooded Darkened Councils, and the Necromancer Kings.

Lucifer lifted his hand. Instantly silence fell. They bowed as one, and sat.

Marduk walked forward.

'On behalf of our Emperor, Satan, I call upon mighty Philosopher and King of the Western Region of Hell – Chief Elder of the Underlords – Gaap.'

A stooped, hooded figure limped to the front of the assembly. Slowly, he removed the cowled hood from his head. His ravaged face was plastered with large pox-like indentations, his thin scholars hands covered with strawberry birthmarks. He lifted his eyes to Lucifer's revealing colourless iris. His eyebrows and eyelashes were absent.

'I pledge my allegiance, O great Master, Satan,' he crooned, 'My archivists have studied the codices – it is evident – that after passing the contest at Mount Quarnel...'

Gaap brought his head nearer to Lucifer's.

'Each day that he remains on the planet earth – your Excellency – he becomes a greater threat to your role as Emperor ... and *our* reign in the affairs of Men.'

An evil smile played on his thin colourless lips. 'We must cut His time short.'

The Great Doors of the Chamber flung open. Grand Duke Focalar stood in the entrance, hell's fearsome Great Duke and Lucifer's finest general, a ferocious demon with the face of an angel and the wings of a griffin. He strode up the Great Chamber aisle and bowed before Lucifer, stooping to kiss the great damson ring of satan.

'I return from Earth, my Emperor.' Focalar glowered at him from under his huge knitted eyebrows. 'Your kingdom has been pillaged.' Lucifer frowned.

Focalar paced, his hand clasping his sword. 'I was summoned too late. An entire legion banished ... threatened with the Abyss by one of the Race of Men!'

'To the *Abyss?*'Charsoc questioned. 'None of the Race of Men has the power to banish the fallen to the Abyss ...' He stopped short, catching sight of Lucifer's face.

'Except the Nazarene!' Lucifer spat.

'The Nazarene relented, sire,' Focalar growled. 'The disembodied Spirits entered a herd of pigs. They drowned.'

'How many are lost?' Lucifer's voice was barely audible.

Focalar hesitated, then lowered his eyes to the floor.

'An entire legion, Your Worship. One consummate in defiling those of the Race of Men.'

Lucifer stood and walked slowly to the Great Windows, staring out at the Lava plains.

'What next?' he muttered. 'He will mobilize grand armies against me ... plot my annihilation ... He invades my kingdom. Where will this end?'

He turned, surveying the Councils, then gestured to a hooded hunched figure dressed in pale garments who sat on Charsoc's left.

'His Excellency calls Nisroc the ancient. Keeper of hell and death.' Marduk proclaimed.

Nisroc rose from the assembly and bowed deeply in reverence.

'Relay to your Emperor, O Nisroc, the legalities of Eternal Law.'

Nisroc spoke from under his silken hood, his voice spun like silk.

'The legalities that are in enforcement regarding the Race of Men as pertaining to Eternal Law prevent those who are fallen spirits from directly taking the life of one of the Race of Men, your Excellency.'

Lucifer nodded. 'Of this I am aware, O Nisroc the Prudent.'

The ancient Necromancer nodded.

'We, the fallen are bound by Eternal Law. Only one from the Race of Men can extinguish the life of one of the Race of Men.'

Nisroc bowed in reverence and sat.

Charsoc drew his head near to Lucifer's.

'We must find one of the Race of Men who will do our bidding. Who will heed our voice, the voice of the fallen.'

Zilith, governor of the demonic scholars stood.

'Your majesty, in compliance with your instructions, my demonic scholars have been examining the way of the Nazarene and those that surround Him. The religious powers in Jerusalem seek power. He threatens their authority. The masses desert them and instead follow the Nazarene's compelling oratories.'

Zilith stroked his faustian beard. 'He has few friends in high places.'

'And many enemies, your Majesty.' Darsoc of the Grey Magus stood. 'The one who leads they call Caiaphas is weak and ambitious,' he hissed. 'My magus seek him out.'

Lucifer paced up and down. 'We need to strike where he is vulnerable...'

'Your Excellency,' Dracul, ruler of the iniquitous Warlock Kings of the West stood, then bowed, 'we have found a willing and fervent disciple in he whom they call Judas. One of the twelve. He is vain and politically ambitious...' Dracul's cat-like eyes glittered with malice from under his black hood. 'With a weakness for gold...'

'Each day that the Nazarene lives is a threat to my kingdom.' Lucifer raised his sceptre high. 'Release your evil magus. Fill Iscariot's dreams with disturbance. Highlight every weakness. Stir up those around Caiaphas. We cut his time short!'

CHAPTER TWENTY-THREE

SUBTERFUGE

JOTAPA SAT AT her dressing table in her royal quarters. Her maidservant, Ghaliya, braided her long, dark tresses with deft birdlike movements of her fingers.

'Ghaliya...' Jotapa paused, then lowered her voice. 'You have another letter from your cousin?'

Ghaliya nodded, walked towards the door, and closed it quietly, then took out a folded missive from her apron pouch. Jotapa frowned inquiringly. Ghaliya nodded, her eyes aflame.

'It is news of *Him*!' Jotapa grabbed it eagerly. She clutched Ghaliya's hand as she devoured the contents of the missive. 'They say he is a king,' she murmured, '...a king of the Jews. You *must* tell me, Ghaliya. Tell me everything. I must know!'

Ghaliya deftly wove fresh orchids and gardenias through

228

Jotapa's hair as she spoke. 'The stories that circulate – they are...' Ghaliya held her hand to her mouth.

Jotapa nodded impatiently. 'Yes, yes, go on!'

Ghaliya lowered her voice. 'They say that blind eyes see,' she whispered, '...that the lame walk..'

Jotapa covered her mouth in ecstasy.

'That even the dead are raised!'

'He is not of this world – He has a strange powerful magic – I knew it was so!' She hesitated. 'And the bold holy man... he is still admonishing my husband?'

'He condemns your husband's marriage to Herodias as unlawful. A sin against yourself and against God. After the wedding, Herod had him seized. He is imprisoned in Macherus.'

'Imprisoned!' Jotapa's eyes widened in horror. 'This baptist – he is a follower of this Jesus, also?'

Ghaliya nodded. She lowered her voice and put her mouth to Jotapa's ear. 'I heard it said in the palace kitchen that our Jesus of Nazareth called your husband, Herod Antipas...' Ghaliya giggled. Jotapa raised her eyebrows. '...a *fox!*'

'The Hebrew is a man of discernment!' Jotapa laughed out loud. Her expression grew distant. 'I wonder if He realized he is my husband.'

She swung around and placed her head close to Ghaliya's. 'And what of these followers?' She hesitated. 'Those who use the sign?'

'They are *everywhere*, in every station – even Herod Antipas's house steward in the royal palace is a follower.'

'That sombre Chuza?' Jotapa shook her head in disbelief.

Ghaliya nodded vehemently. 'His wife, Joanna ... she

travels everywhere with Jesus and ministers to Him out of her own funds.'

'Chuza holds tightly to his purse – he would never allow it!'

'He is transformed, princess,' answered Ghaliya. 'He is now the most tolerant of husbands . . .' She stopped in mid sentence and bowed her head.

Jotapa looked at her quizzically. 'Go on, Ghaliya.' She clasped her hand. 'It is safe.'

Ghaliya wiped the corners of her eyes with her apron.

' . . . since the Hebrew healed his son,' she whispered.

Jotapa shook her head in wonder. 'He healed his son . . .' she repeated slowly, rising to her feet.

She glided over the marble floors, through the open balcony doors onto the ornate portico, staring out for a long time towards the west wing, deep in contemplation. Slowly, she turned to Ghalilya who was hovering by the doors. 'If the Hebrew can heal Joanna's son . . .' She looked at Ghaliya, an inspired gleam in her eyes, then lowered her voice.

' . . . He can heal Zahi!'

Ghaliya stared at her in shock.

'But . . . your Majesty . . .'

She turned her palm upwards to Ghaliyia, pointing to the tiny scar.

'We have to take him to Him. We will go to Jerusalem!'

Ghaliya started. 'But, Your Majesty, your former husband, Herod Antipas – if he discovers you . . .'

Jotapa swept away her protestations with a wave of her hand. 'Herod stays at Macherus and in Tiberias at Galilee. Jerusalem is far from his thoughts; of this I am assured.' Her face flushed with excitement. She strode back into her chambers, her face lit with exhilaration. 'We will take Zahi to Him, Ghalilya. He will be healed; I know it!'

Ghalilya stared at Jotapa open-mouthed.

'Call Ayeshe, that he may make preparations. Duza will assist us in the subterfuge. My father does not visit Zahi in his chambers – he will not know of his absence. I will tell the king that I go to look after his interests in the incense and spice trade in Jerusalem. I am in charge of much of his household – it is a believable request. Tell your cousin we make haste for Jerusalem. Let her alert Joanna of our coming. It is the Jews' Passover feast – we shall not be recognized in the crowd. We go to Jerusalem – that we may find the Hebrew.'

CHAPTER TWENTY-FOUR

THE VEIL

'THE WORT SEERS of Diabolos have seen a portent.' Marduk said. 'A veil.' He passed the missive to Charsoc who held it gingerly with his gloved hand and carefully opened it. A thin black wisp of hemlock snaked upward. Charsoc scanned the page.

'Tell me about this veil.'

'It is a veil of the Race of Men of the Hebrews,' Marduk replied. 'It hangs in Jerusalem in what is termed the Most Holy Place. In their temple.'

'The veil's purpose?' Charsoc's tone was sharp.

'As is common knowledge to the fallen, since our Emperor's supreme triumph in the East of Eden, the Race of Men have been cut off from direct access to Yehovah's presence.'

Charsoc waved Marduk on impatiently.

'Due to their fallen estate, the slightest direct contact with the power and light emanating from Yehovah will kill those of the Race of Men instantly. The veil that hangs in the Most Holy Place acts as their protection on the rare occasion when Yehovah would choose to visit their High Priest. The veil serves as a reminder that the Race of Men's iniquities render them unfit for the presence of Yehovah.'

'So . . . ' Charsoc fingered the missive, deep in contemplation, 'the veil acts as a divide between the Race of Men and Yehovah's presence. It holds no sorceries of its own.'

'It holds no sorceries.'

Charsoc folded the missive.

'Dispatch our scouts to investigate it. I will inform our Emperor.'

～

Herod Antipas lay back on a soft mountain of vermillion and oyster satin cushions, staring up, half-intoxicated, at the scantily clad young Ethiopian girl who slavishly plucked grapes and placed them on his tongue. A second girl, whose skin was pale as milk, sliced a pomegranate and laid the slices sensuously across his chest. His jewelled crown lay awry on his head, and his hair was dishevelled. The juices from grapes and fruits dripped from his mouth onto the expensive embroidered napkins draped across his chest.

His gaze fell to the hundreds of elegant pot-bellied Roman senators and Galilean nobles sitting at his lavish tables weighted down with the finest meats and fowl and delicacies from all around the Galilean provinces. He watched, satisfied, as his finest generals drank goblets of the finest wines, while a hundred courtiers flanked the great hall, serving the guests' every whim.

A score of voluptuous dancing women, procured from every corner of the Roman Empire, whirled sensuously across the wide marbled floors. Herod lay back, eyeing Herodias, who sat like an Egyptian cat, erect and arrogant.

'Your birthday,' she purred, 'is an occasion to be remembered by all. It should be the spectacle of Galilee, of Palestine ... of Rome ...'

'Administrators, rich landowners, civic leaders, and my army commanders – why, Herodias, you have excelled yourself, my dove.'

Herod brought her small delicate painted fingernails to his rouged lips and kissed them.

'Ah, but, my Antipas, the best is yet to come.'

The entire hall suddenly quieted as the lanterns were dimmed and the music changed from its throbbing, incessant rhythm to one slower and more sensual. Then from a dais, a slim, lithe form, her pale alabaster skin shone through the seven veils of sheer pale rose voile swathed around her sensuous form – so sheer that Herod's eyes stayed riveted to her as she swayed rhythmically in time to the music.

Her waist-length black hair swayed against her bare back to the music as her hands moved across her body, discarding each layer of sheer material until she stood clad only in the seventh sheer veil. She reached down and sensually caressed his swollen pot-bellied abdomen, then raised the last veil from her face, revealing the high cheekbones, the sensual crimson lips.

Herod put his hands over his face.

'Enough! Enough!' he cried, clapping loudly and slowly, until the entire Great Hall was on its feet, applauding.

'More! More!' they cried.

Herod motioned for her to sit next to him.

Herodias watched, alert, and nodded to Salome.

Salome sat down next to her stepfather on the satin pillows, drinking from his goblet and sharing his sweetmeats, whispering diabolical enticements into his ear.

Suddenly Herod rose, swaying in his semi-drunken stupor. He clapped his hands loudly, and instantly the music stopped.

He gestured to Salome to stand on the dais, then walked tipsily up to her.

'Ask of me whatever you will, and I will give it to thee. I swear it this night, by the gods! Whatever you ask of me, stepdaughter, I will give it thee, unto the half of my kingdom.'

A cold smile glimmered on Herodias's face. She and Salome stole from the banqueting hall outside, through the private corridor and into her opulent chambers.

Salome sat on Herodias's luxurious bed, wrapping the purple perfumed silk sheets around her in triumph. Herodias scrutinized her own fading beauty in the hand glass, then turned to examine Salome's fresh, pert features.

'What shall I ask for, Mama?' Salome giggled. 'Up to half the kingdom!'

'The old dithering fool,' Herodias spat. Salome paled. She knew to avoid her mother's violent tantrums at any cost. She sat on the bed, suddenly silent.

Herodias nodded. 'We shall silence him and his vile accusations forever. No longer shall he turn your stepfather and his subjects in Judaea against me, his rightful wife,' she hissed. 'We must preserve our place at the court; we can brook no interference by that viper. He must be silenced. Your very future depends on his being dead. Now, go back to Herod And ask for the head of John the Baptist!'

Salome gasped. Then a small wicked smile played on her lips.

She hurried back through the great hall, then stood before Herod, demure and sweet-faced.

Herod laughed loudly. 'You have chosen – so what is it to be, my sweet? Up to half my kingdom – was there ever such a generous father!'

Salome curtseyed.

'Oh, Herod, great and just – and true to your vow,' her voice was soft but clear, 'I will that thou would give me the head of John the Baptist on a silver platter.'

Herod paled. He shrank in disgust from Salome, appalled. Then he turned to face the great hall, looking first at the senators, then at the merchants, until his gaze stopped at his generals.

'I cannot, Salome. Anything . . . anything but the baptist's head – my treasuries, my jewels, Salome . . . my palaces, even . . . I beseech you . . . '

Salome stared past Herod to the entrance of the great hall, far in the distance, to where Herodias stood, a slim, shadowed figure.

Herod followed her gaze. 'He is a righteous man,' he muttered. 'Not worthy of death.'

Herodias slid over the floors, then sidled up to him, whispering into his ear. 'You made a vow, O great Herod, and a vow must be fulfilled.'

Herod bunched his fists, snapped out of his drunken state, his mind whirling.

'The baptist has done nothing worthy of death. I cannot.' Chuza, his house steward, tried desperately to catch the eye of Joanna, who was praying under her breath.

'You are *weak*, Antipas.' Herodias's imperious whisper seemed to reverberate into every corner of the great hall.

He started. She grasped his bangled arm, her violent, uncontrolled temper rising.

'He turns the rabble against us. They hate us – they loathe me ... They spit at my carriage in the streets when I pass – I, wife of the tetrarch of Judaea! It is his poison; his tongue is as a viper's.'

Herod stood like stone.

'And what of your guests?' she hissed. '*What* will they say when they leave Herod's palace – that he was a man too weak and inadequate to keep his vow?'

Herod's arms dropped like lead weights to his side. He sat down, his hand shaking so violently that he could scarcely hold his wine cup.

'Malchus,' he ordered in a weak, unsteady voice, 'take the guard to the baptist's cell in Macherus and execute him.'

'And bring us his head on a charger!' Herodias screamed.

∽

Lucifer stood on the roof of the Eastern Wing housing Perdition's royal avaries, in front of hundreds of colossal gilded hell cages, feeding his pet carrion scavenger scouts from a large silver urn filled with freshly killed mansouth liver.

Charsoc bowed before him. 'I request audience, mi'Lord.'

Lucifer washed his bloodied hands in a bowl that Balberith held out to him, then dried his hands fastidiously on an embroidered napkin passed to him by a courtier. He flung the napkin onto the floor, then walked towards Charsoc.

'The Wort Seers of Diabolos have seen a portent, your Majesty.' Charsoc bowed again. 'A portent they say is related to the Nazarene. A veil.'

Lucifer stopped in his tracks.

'The veil that hangs in the Hebrews' temple,' Charsoc continued.

'*That* veil...' Lucifer's expression grew dark. 'It hangs in the Holy of Holies.' He tore the missive from Charsoc's grasp. 'The lone place on this planet where Yehovah *trespasses* and visits with the Race of Men.' He scanned the missive. 'The Wort Seers foretell it bodes ill for my kingdom.' Lucifer frowned. 'They saw it torn.'

'It would be a most arduos task to tear mi'Lord.' Charsoc replied. 'My scouts report it is a most unwieldy looking shroud. Forty cubits long, twenty wide, of the thickness of one cubit and wrought in seventy-two squares. It needs at least three hundred priests to manipulate it. It has been said in the Race of Men that bulls tied to each side would not be able to rip the veil apart.'

'Yet my finer instincts tell me the Wort Seers have seen truly – that it holds significance to Yehovah and the High Council in the affairs of the Race of Men. But torn ... why would it be torn?' Lucifer paced up and down the eastern elevation, pensive.

'It *protects* them..' he muttered. 'without it the Race of Men would be struck dead from the radiation of Yehovah's presence.' He turned to Charsoc. 'Instruct the Black Murmurers to watch over this veil. Tell Marduk to report to me immediately of any unusual happenings.' Charsoc bowed.

'You word is my command, Your Excellency. I instruct the Black Murmurers immediately.'

Lucifer walked to the edge of the upper Pavilions, gazing over the desolate smouldering, lava wastes of hell that stretched as far as the eye could see. He looked down at the missive still in his palm, then raised his head to the pale amber horizon. Strangely troubled.

THE HEBREW

THEY STOOD SILENT on the steps of the temple in Jerusalem. Zahi, his face wrapped in cloth, rode in the carriage, veiled from view. Ghaliya sat on the opposite side, playing the rich merchant's wife, with Jotapa, heavily disguised in a maidservant's veils, at her right hand, next to Ayeshe.

'Zerubbabel's temple,' Jotapa whispered. 'Zahi, look – see how Herod has spent vast sums on its beautification.' She stopped in mid sentence as a huge outcry erupted from the outer court of the temple.

There was a sound of loud shouting and the crashing of tables onto the temple floor.

A familiar voice raged like thunder. 'You den of thieves! You *dare* to make My Father's house a house of merchandise

– a bazaar! Your incessant haggling – your profiteering from the poor . . . !'

Dove sellers and moneychangers scattered like geese through the Court of the Gentiles, past the carriage and Jotapa. Sacrificial sheep and oxen milled about and ran through the temple courtyard, to the sound of more crashing . . . then silence.

Hundreds of onlookers gathered outside the entrance to the outer court. Waiting. Jotapa watched, fascinated, from behind her veil as a tall, lean, fierce-looking figure walked wearily out through the temple doors and across the temple courtyard, a makeshift whip of cords clasped tightly in His hands. She drew an involuntary gasp. Yes, it was Him – but – Why – He, somehow looked much younger than her memories of their encounter in the desert. He could barely be thirty.

She studied the man on the temple steps. Then frowned, perplexed. Today there was no trace of the humour or compassion she had seen in the wilderness. His handsome features were grim, the strong chin set. She sighed deeply, lowering her eyes. She had initially found the Hebrew attractive . . . dangerously attractive. But Jotapa was gifted with Aretas' pragmatic shrewdness – she was no fool and she had sensed instantly that He was unavailable. She had known from their encounter in the desert that His only and overriding passion, like the monks of old, was His God. There would be no woman in the Nazarene's life – of this she was somehow certain. She studied Him curiously. His dark eyes flashed like lightning as He wiped the tears from His eyes with the back of His hand – tears of anger, she was sure. She smiled faintly . . . tears of passion.

Why was He so incensed?

She turned to Zahi, bewildered. Zahi gestured towards the temple.

'The temple of the Hebrews has always been a great national treasury,' he said quietly, his voice muffled somewhat by the thin gauze cloth. 'Its vaults contain immense stores of private wealth. The deposits never sit idle, Jotapa, they are loaned at the very highest rates of interest by their moneychangers. I know from our sources that the temple archives in Jerusalem reveal inconceivable debts owed by the poor to the rich. It is not a pretty picture. The Jewish authorities are hated by the commoners. The Hebrew is discerning.' Zahi paused. 'And courageous.'

Jotapa stared, transfixed, as a small boy not more than four years of age, caught sight of Jesus and instantly wrestled himself away from his mother's grasp, tearing across the pavement over to Jesus, nearly knocking Him over in his excitement. The boy latched on to Jesus' legs and buried his head in His robe. Jotapa watched, fascinated, as the terrible fierceness dissolved from Jesus' features. He drew the boy to Him and placed His hand gently on his head, His eyes gazing distantly ahead. The lash slipped from His hand onto the pavement. He tousled the boy's head, then shook his mane of long dark hair out of his eyes and surveyed the courtyard. Still grim. Then drew a deep sigh.

Jotapa watched a dark striking young man who stood just behind Him, trembling with ill-concealed rage.

'Master...' The younger man gripped Jesus' shoulder fiercely. Too fiercely.

Jesus turned to face him, and instantly Judas loosed his grip. Pale.

'Master,' he implored, 'the authorities ... I worked so hard – they were just coming to accept You ... to accept the cause. You withdraw Yourself to Galilee when You could have been crowned king, and they think You're in flight. ... You refuse to show Yourself openly, then publicly challenge the Pharisees – it all bodes ill, Master.'

Judas stepped back, taking in the scene of overturned tables and smashed merchandise. He put his hands to his head.

'We'll never set foot in the temple again ... We're *ruined*. Some are even saying You have a *demon!*' He threw his hands up in sheer frustration. 'I know You are the Messiah, I believe in the cause' – he gestured at Peter and the other disciples – 'more than these men, with their incessant petty bickering. I would die for the cause. I would die for *You*, Jesus. You could put it right. Just take up their challenge and show them one sign from heaven,' he pleaded.

'The fear of man is a snare to our cause.' Jesus turned His face to him. Forbidding.

'And a snare to you, Judas Iscariot,' He stated quietly.

Judas stared at him as though he had been literally lashed across the face. Hot tears rose in his eyes. He stepped back. For a fleeting moment, Jotapa thought she saw a vulnerability in Jesus, but as fast as it appeared, a terrible weariness took its place, as though He bore the weight of the whole world.

Then Jesus gathered the child in His arms, walked straight past Judas and handed the child gently to a large ruddy-faced man. 'We will depart for Capernaum, Peter,' He said quietly; then He walked across the courtyard, towards the street.

'Let us go, princess,' Ghaliya whispered nervously. But Jotapa was rooted to the ground. She shook her head, her gaze fixed on Jesus.

'No, we stay!' she declared. 'We know why we are here.'

All at once as Jesus left the temple steps, throngs of men, women, and children flocked around Him, clutching at His robe, His feet, His hands, until even His disciples could hardly make a path for Him through the crowd.

Jesus studied the faces close to Him, His eyes filled with compassion, then closed. Jotapa watched as an old woman clung desperately to the fringes of His robe, then stumbled in the shoving, pressing crowd. She lay, tears streaming down her face, fallen in the dust of the street. Her tears turned to loud, heaving sobs; then a look of shock came over her countenance and she started to laugh and cry together, as if she had lost her mind.

The crowd continued to push towards Jesus, pressing in on Him from every side, when He held up His hand. 'Who is it – who touched Me?' His eyes scanned the raucous pushing crowd.

Men and women vigorously shook their heads, but Jesus pushed through the clamouring men and women until He stood over the old woman, still lying on the ground. The woman looked up at Him, trembling. 'You touched Me?

She nodded. 'I suffered a flow of blood for twelve years, Master.' She clung to His hands. 'I spent all my money, my life savings, on physicians, and still I grew worse, until – '

'Healing virtue went out of Me.'

'Just now, in the crowd, I tried to touch You, Master, but the crowds . . . I have been so weak, but I clung on to the very fringe of Your robe. Then I was swept away by the crowds.

But … but the bleeding stopped.' She gazed up at Him in adoration. 'I am made whole!'

A brilliant smile spread across Jesus' face. His expression softened and He knelt down until His face was directly in line with the old woman's. Tenderly He took her face in His hands.

Jotapa turned to Zahi. His face was pushed right up against the window, drinking in the entire scene. Jotapa saw a fleeting ray of hope in the eyes that had been without hope for so many years. She left the carriage and ran nearer, much nearer the crowd.

'Old mother, your faith has healed you,' Jesus murmured gently, then drew the old woman to His bosom. Tears ran down the wrinkled face as He tenderly kissed the top of her grey head. 'Go in peace.'

The old woman clung to His hands, covering them with kisses, her face transformed. For a fleeting moment she was beautiful.

That's it, thought Jotapa, observing Him in wonder. *He makes us all beautiful – old and young, man and woman, boy and girl.* It was almost a kind of sorcery – *she considered* – and yet not sorcery at all.

And then Jesus turned. He stared directly at her. She was certain of it.

Jotapa frowned. It could not be – she was too well disguised as a noblewoman's maidservant to be recognized. She turned to look behind her, then turned back.

Jesus was walking towards them. She frowned. She turned to Ghaliya, then back to the tall lean figure drawing rapidly closer. He continued His staring directly at her. There was no doubting it.

'My greetings to the house of Aretas, daughter of the king of Arabia.'

He seemed amused. In fact, Jotapa was sure she caught a trace of mischief in His gaze. Her eyes flashed in annoyance.

'Your temper?' He questioned, the deep dimples showing in His bronzed cheeks. 'It is better kept in check nowadays?'

Immediately Jotapa's eyes narrowed, and she drew herself up to her full imperial height.

'You address the princess of Arabia.' Her nostrils flared in indignation.

Jesus' eyes flickered with mischief. She glared at Him. How He knew her! 'My temper, I can assure you, is in exactly the same state as Yours was today, except that *You* had a whip, and I have none.'

Jesus threw back His head and laughed loudly in delight.

Jotapa frowned, her quicksilver temper starting to rise, but then, as she returned His gaze, somehow she knew with a deep knowing – that it was not her discomfort He enjoyed ... He was enjoying *her*. Despite all her flaws – and there were many – the Hebrew *liked her* – Jotapa – Spirited, strong, haughty princess of Arabia.

And she realized that to each one who clutched at His robe, He was the same. He found the treasure in each soul – searched through the sin and bitterness of each until He found the pearl of great price. With her it was her strength.

And the tears welled up in her eyes, unheeded. Jesus bowed His head slightly, then walked towards her and straight past her, His countenance stern, almost severe. Jotapa turned, her heart pounding, instinctively she knew that He was headed straight for the carriage across the road. The carriage that held Zahi.

She clutched her skirts in her hands, dashing after Jesus, but before she could catch up with Him, He had already opened the carriage door. He put out His hand to Zahi, who immediately grasped it and stepped down onto the dusty road, in full view of all the crowd. A loud gasp went up from the throng surrounding Jesus as they stared at Zahi, his face and hands covered in the thin gauze cloth. A plump red-faced woman clasped her child to her and moved away rapidly, followed in quick succession by dozens of men and women all across the crowd. Jotapa tried to move nearer, but Duza gently held her back.

Jesus looked deeply into Zahi's eyes for a long moment, then whispered something that escaped Jotapa.

Zahi fell at Jesus' feet.

'Who do you say that I am?'

'You are the Unknown God,' Zahi whispered in awe. '... the one whom the Rab Mag Daniel prophesied.'

Jotapa stared in astonishment at Duza.

'He has studied the great Rab Mag's writings these past eight years fervently, day and night, in his library.' Duza said softly. 'There were nights he could not sleep, but still he studied. Searching, searching for the meaning of the great Messiah.'

Jesus smiled gently. An intimate tender smile. Gently, He unwrapped the muslin covering Zahi's face. The crowd, now watching from a safe distance, gasped in horror at the disfigured features. Then Jesus unwrapped the cloth from each hand, revealing the stumps and rotted flesh.

'Go in peace,' He said. 'Your faith has healed you.'

And a gasp went up from the entire crowd, followed by a long, awed silence. In front of their eyes, Zahi's features started to heal. Jotapa watched, incredulous, as the raw distended and rotting skin on Zahi's face began to smooth and heal. She stared down at Zahi's hands. The nodules disappeared; the fingers grew long and straight. She watched as the decaying stump where Zahi's thumb had once been, healed and grew back. She blinked. This could not be! Why, she had believed that Zahi could be healed, but certainly not that his fingers be replaced and as new!

She turned to Duza who was staring in stunned silence, as was the crowd. All were transfixed by the immediate miracle occurring before their eyes. Judas stared, exhilaration on his countenance. This was their *Messiah*.

Jesus clasped Zahi to Him in a long embrace.

Zahi fell to his knees, tears coursing down his cheeks. 'Thank You ... thank You,' he murmured in adoration, staring through tears at the backs of his hands, turning them over in wonder.

And then Jesus placed His hand under Zahi's chin and raised his face to His. He smiled tenderly into Zahi's eyes.

'Zahi, crown prince of Arabia, follow me.'

Zahi rose to his feet, and Jotapa watched as Zahi turned his face to her and Duza. Duza struggled to contain the short, racking sobs that rose from the depths of his soul.

And then Zahi smiled directly at Jotapa. A brilliant, sundrenched smile.

And in an instant, both he and Jesus were gone.

CHAPTER TWENTY-SIX

DARK CHOICES

CHARSOC FLEW THROUGH the forbidding clandestine underground crypts of the damned, his black sorceror's cloak flapping, riding the subterranean zephyrs. The soporific throbbing beat of the shaman drums and the grand haunting arias of the Necromancer choirs filtered upward from the lower crypts growing in intensity as he neared two mammoth black doors adorned with ornately carved golden Seraphim and Gorgons. The entrance to the inner sanctum of the lower crypts of the shadows, the gateway to the Catacombs of Ichabod.

He raised his silvered staff, its head a live serpent. Instantly the massive black doors flung open, revealing the sweltering underground tunnels of the nether regions – the abode of the Dark Younglings.

The air was thick with the eerie hum of demonic incantations, voodoo, hexes, and enchantments as hundreds of Charsoc's dark deformed youngling apprentices industriously poured their gruesome poisons and potions, reciting their black arts and enchantments. Charsoc pulled his black sorcerer's cape tightly around him. He flew through the gloomy tunnels, past the infinite Lower Libraries of Iniquities, their mother-of-pearl shelves crammed with millions of silver tomes and ancient black codices. The menacing rhythm of the shaman drums grew louder as he descended into the crypts of the shadows, the abode of Huldah and his macabre Shaman Kings. The crypt ceilings were festooned with dark menacing troemp l'oeils of damson and deep magentas, barely visible through the shadowed gloom. He flew downward ... forever downward, through the cramped outer shaman warrens that housed the million colossal iron hell cages that incarcerated the sinister shaman vulture scouts who screeched in terror and hissed venomously as he passed by.

Finally he reached a door of beaten gold, its handle one huge uncut ruby. Charsoc placed his ringed fingers on the glittering jewel. Instantly he vanished from the Crypts of the Shadows into the Catacombs of Ichabod.

⟿

Aretas paced the throne room in a dread fury.

Jotapa stood trembling on the far side of the chamber. Duza, Ghaliya, and Ayeshe knelt before the throne, their heads bowed.

'You took Zahi, your dying brother...'

Each syallable strained from his mouth.

'... my firstborn, the crown prince of Arabia, to Jerusalem to see the Hebrew...' He stared, at Jotapa. Incredulous.

'*Without* my permission. And now ... NOW you tell me that he just disappeared ... vapourised into the streets of Jerusalem.' His face was blacker than thunder.

Jotapa swallowed nervously. 'Father ... he was healed – the Hebrew *healed* him.'

Aretas drew himself up to his full imperial stature.

'To add insult to injury...' his dark eyes flashed with fury, 'you have the gall to tell me, your *own* father, that he no longer has leprosy, that ... that the Hebrew just miraculously healed him.' Aretas looked from Jotapa to the clear-eyed Ayeshe, then to the trembling Duza.

'It is true, Your revered Majesty,' muttered Ayeshe from the floor. 'The Hebrew healed Zahi. He is well.'

Aretas strode over to the Beytel and with his sceptre swept the cross to the floor, enraged. 'The Hebrew...'

Ghaliya and Duza flung themselves facedown on the floor.

At last Jotapa spoke. 'Let them go, Father. It is my fault. I commanded them ... I forced them to take us. They had no choice in the matter.'

Aretas' eyes flashed darkly.

'No *choice*? Ayeshe!' He whirled around to his frail aged Nabaetan servant. 'You, who have served me from the cradle – you who are as stubborn as ten thousand unruly mountain she-camels who disobey their masters – did you have a choice?' He motioned for Ayeshe to rise.

The sinewy old Nabatean stood up and looked directly at Aretas, his gaze clear and true. 'I chose this course, my lord. It was indeed old Ayeshe's will to accompany them.'

Aretas threw his hands in the air. 'I am vexed that you do not *fear* me, Ayeshe!' he raged.

'This is a terrible day for a king of Arabia.'

'I do not fear you,' Ayeshe said softly. 'But I love you, my ageing king.' The old man bowed his head.

Aretas groaned in exasperation. 'Never did I think I would live to see the day when it was a greater thing for my servants to love me than to fear me!' He glared at Ayeshe.

'I was there, sire when –'

Aretas waved him silent. His expression softened. 'Yes, yes, my old caretaker, you recount the events of the infant Hebrew too many times – I was blind; then I saw.'

Aretas rolled his eyes in frustration. 'And you Duza, bosom companion of my firstborn son – did my daughter command you, too? Are you succumbed also to the will of a woman?'

Duza lifted his head. 'Your Majesty, the pain that the disease inflicted on the prince was more than could be borne, both for himself and for your soul, sire.'

Duza placed his forehead back down on the marble.

Aretas thrust his arms heavenward in despair.

'So your motive, too, was borne of love.' Aretas set his cup down hard on the table. 'Love, love...,' he mumbled, '...where is the *respect* that should be shown to a king of Arabia.'

He looked at Jotapa, his countenance softer. 'You say the Hebrew touched him and he was made whole. You are *sure* of this, Jotapa. You saw it with your own eyes?'

'And the eyes of all these witnesses before you, Father,' Jotapa whispered.

Tears welled up unheeded in Aretas' eyes. 'You ... you saw it, then...' he stumbled. His eyes pleading with Jotapa.

Tears streamed down Jotapa's cheeks. 'His flesh is healed, Papa, as clear and smooth as a newborn babe's. Your son, beloved of your soul, is whole and free and has peace in his soul.'

Aretas looked, speechless, from Jotapa to Ayeshe and then to Duza. Deeply moved.

'His fingers are grown and strong again, Your Majesty.' Duza's voice was clear. 'Word travels in Jerusalem that he writes ... for the Hebrew, as His scribe.'

Aretas walked to the great window and gazed out towards the Royal Hunting Grounds. He stared for a long while at the lions that prowled across the exotic grasslands.

'He is not safe there. The stories of these followers of the Hebrew circulate even to Arabia. The Hebrew has powerful enemies: the Pharisees, the Sanhedrin ... the Romans. They all fear His sway and authority over the masses, and now Zahi is one of them – a ...' He could not bring himself to say the word.

He turned from the window. 'He is a ... follower of the Hebrew. Is this true?'

'Yes, Father, Zahi is become a follower.'

'It will bode ill for Zahi – my soul feels it.' He sighed deeply, then bent down and picked up the cross from the floor. 'Then so be it. I, Aretas, sovereign ruler of Petra and Arabia, bestow my blessing on Crown Prince Zahi. May his ways prosper and his soul find peace.'

He turned to Duza. 'Duza, your king commands you. Go

to Jerusalem. Seek out my blessed son and bind yourself to him, day and night. Serve Zahi, fruit of my loins, fruit of all Arabia. This is your solemn duty.'

And he replaced the Hebrew's cross upon the altar.

∽

Charsoc sat on a throne of ivory horn in the Catacombs of Ichabod. Green vapours snaked up from the monstrous warlock cauldrons of bubbling hemlock and hellbroth, potions of bladderwrack and deadly nightshade brewing on the towering garnet altar opposite the throne. Numerous cankerworm slithered between the thousand black tapers of belladonna sputtering on the altar, behind which hung the huge magenta veil that led to Perdition's second Unholy of Holies, governed by the dreaded high priests of the fallen – the Warlock Kings of the West.

'Enter, high priests of the fallen,' Charsoc cried.

The magenta veil fluttered, then the thirteen Warlock Kings of the West materialized in front of the altar. They stood, ten feet in height, their pale green parchment like skin glowed with a luminous sheen. Their noses were hooked, their hunched backs covered by long black capes, their jet black hair was poker straight and fell past their waists, their heads were crowned with pointed black hats entwined with living serpents.

'Jether and the elders of Yehovah are gathered?' Charsoc asked.

Dracul, ancient ruler of the Warlock Kings bowed deeply before Charsoc. His beady amber cat-like eyes glittered from his long bony countenance 'The Black Murmurers advise us they assemble as we speak, O master. In the labyrinths of the seventh spire,' he rasped, green sulphur issuing from his pale purple lips.

'This day we uncover their scheming,' Charsoc declared. 'Yehovah's powers are formidable. We need our strongest magic.'

'The seventh chamber is impenetrable,' Ishtar hissed.

Dracul nodded. 'Even our combined sorceries are inadequate to penetrate the seventh spire.'

'But this is!' Charsoc removed a silver amulet from his robes and held it up. The Warlock Kings fell back as one, clutching their temples in agony. Charsoc replaced it swiftly in its amulet. 'The stone of fire from the sixth chamber. My former abode.' He lowered his voice. 'The sixth stone. Its flame is dying. Near extinguished. It cannot exist in our kingdom of the fallen. But its power will strengthen as we draw nearer the labyrinths. We will use it for one final assault upon their assembly.'

And what of Jether?' Dracul leered.

'Jether's powers fade,' Charsoc hissed. 'His magic grows weak.' He rose, holding his staff high above his head. '*I* will deal with Jether.'

CHAPTER TWENTY-SEVEN

GALILEE

J ESUS GAZED ACROSS the Sea of Galilee, its deep
mercurial blue waters glistening in the fading sun. He
glanced down at a tiny girl, no more than three years of
age, who sat on His lap. She clutched Him tightly
around the waist, her head buried in His chest so that only
two long untidy curling, braids were visible, tied with scarlet
ribbons. Surrounding Him in a semicircle on the white sand
were at least nineteen children between the ages of two and
fifteen. Six boys, aged around twelve years of age sat cross-
legged on the rocks opposite Him, greedily devouring
mounds of roasted fish, fresh from the nets and stuffing
great handfuls of dates into their mouths, totally engrossed
in their feast. Jesus watched them in enjoyment. Three older
youths griddled sardines on the open fires.

The small girl with the scarlet ribbons raised her head,

sucking her thumb. She looked up at Jesus lovingly and sighed, then deliberately removed her thumb from her mouth. 'Jesus,' she lisped, 'Rubied Door...' Then she buried her head back deep into Jesus' robes.

An unnatural stillness fell. Even the greedy devourers stopped eating their fish and wiped their oily mouths with their sleeves, waiting for Jesus to speak. His eyes grew distant. Remembering. 'Far away from Galilee, far beyond the moon,' His voice was hushed, 'lies the kingdom of the First Heaven.'

A twelve-year-old boy frowned, 'Why can't we see it, then, Master?' He shook his tight black curls, which fell over his eyes, veiling the mischief hidden there. He was joined in soft laughter by his some of his peers. Jesus sighed long sufferingly.

'Reuben, must I teach you a refresher course on physics?' The boys erupted into raucous laughter, this time at the scowling Reuben's expense. Jesus looked over to a fifteen-year-old youth with even tighter black curls and a straggling black growth of beard, who was busy griddling fish. 'Stephen, teach your brother his lessons.'

Stephen looked over at Reuben through his curls, then spoke. 'The fall of man made fundamental changes in certain laws of physics and biology.' Stephen left his fish and stood proudly on the sand, gesturing with a stick. 'The nature of *subjective* time has changed since creation. The First Heaven is governed by a different set of physical laws. Here in Galilee we are contained or limited to a "one-dimensional" time frame, so we cannot walk through walls or on water.'

Jesus nodded in approval. 'Jesus walks on water,' Rebecca lisped, then ducked her head back into Jesus' robe. Jesus stroked her head tenderly. Stephen continued. 'Jesus, being from the First Heaven, enjoys a multidimensional quality of time. Yehovah is bound by neither time nor space, for He existed *before* the universe was, before the creation of space or matter or time. Just because you cannot see another dimension with your eyes doesn't mean that it isn't there. That is just plain ignorance. And ignorance is *sad*,' Stephen stressed contemptuously, nodding in Reuben's direction. The fiery Reuben scowled, darting towards him like lightning and punched him in the arm.

'Know-all!' he muttered.

'Boys, boys,' said Jesus, shaking His head. 'Have you learned *nothing* of the principles of the First Heaven? Love your neighbour as yourself – *especially* your brother, Reuben.' Jesus frowned at Reuben, but His eyes twinkled. Reuben's face creased into a sheepish grin. 'Well enough, Jesus, I'll learn my lessons.'

'Tell us the tale, Jesus!' a lively four-year-old exclaimed. 'Of the great war in heaven.'

'Again, Judah?' Jesus sighed. 'Long ago, Judah, before this world as you know it, and billions of years before Galilee was created, a great angel existed, one of three great princes of heaven: the Light-Bearer.'

The younger children clung to Jesus' every word, while the older ones soon grew more interested in their feast of fish and dates. 'He was filled with wisdom, perfect in his beauty. But the great King longed for companionship. So he decided to create a new race, the Race of Men, from his own DNA. But the Light-Bearer, grew jealous of the idea of the Race of Men and launched an insurrection – a war – against the great King.'

'I don't like him,' a small voice shrilled.

'What was his name?' a second shrill voice piped up.

'Sataneal,' Reuben whispered to another in a hushed undertone. 'He was *bad*...'

The twelve-year-olds dropped the remains of their fish on the sand, now captivated.

Jesus looked at them out of the corner of His eye. 'Was there a great battle?'

Jesus nodded. 'I saw Satan fall like lightning,' He spoke softly. The older boys stared at Him in admiration. 'He and his renegade third were banished ... He came immediately to tempt the Race of Men away from God. And in this he met great success. And so the title deeds that the great King had entrusted to the Race of Men now legally belonged to Lucifer, who was made their sovereign king.'

'Oh, no! He is king of the *world!*' shrilled a ruddy-faced five-year-old in horror.

'Is he king of Galilee?' The smaller children huddled together in alarm, their eyes wide. Another child, a little older, frowned at them. 'You're with Jesus, scaredy-cat – He casts the demons out. Lucifer's scared of Him because He's the great King's Son!' Two of the small children stuck their tongue out at the eight-year-old.

Jesus went on. 'The great King loved the Race of Men passionately. He was not prepared to lose them for eternity. So He decided He must leave the First Heaven and be born as one of the Race of Men.'

'And get back the title deeds,' Judah declared.

Jesus raised His eyebrows. '*Excellent*, Judah!'

Judah stood to his full three feet, hands on hips. He

brandished a stick, then shook his unruly red curls. 'Who will fight sataneal?' he cried.

Jesus placed Rebecca gently down on the sands and rose to His feet. He walked over to the edge of the shore of Galilee, His sunstreaked hair blew away from His handsome, noble face. He stared out at the last rays of dusk sun that fell across the lake casting their mysterious shifting shadows on the water.

'I will fight sataneal, Judah.' His voice was very soft. 'At a place called Golgotha. The war between the First Heaven and the kingdom of darkness will be waged.' He turned to the children, who stared up at Him in wonder, then turned back to the horizon, His eyes blazing with fervour. 'The war of the First Judgement.'

CHAPTER TWENTY-EIGHT

MANDRAGORA

THE INCANTATIONS OF the Warlock Kings of the West grew in intensity, their darkening wings suddenly visible. In an instant, Charsoc and the entire Warlock coven vanished, spinning through the catacombs on their broomsticks, accompanied by Dracul's demon harpies to the lower boundaries of the time corridors where a pack of snarling wort devourers waited. Their escort.

Charsoc signalled and he and the Warlock Kings ascended into the time corridors, their black hair and robes flying, veering left, then right, through the winding time passages, beneath oceans, through spiral galaxies and interstellar clouds, diving downwards into super massive black holes, then upwards gyrating at the speed of light through multiple star systems until gradually the first

MESSIAH – THE FIRST JUDGEMENT

glimmering outline of the First Heaven's magnificent horizons materialized.

The coven hovered before the twelve pale blue moons that were now rising from the Eastern horizon, observing the shifting hues of the First Heaven's horizons as the lilacs transformed to amethysts and then to a deep indigo.

Charsoc opened the silver amulet around his neck. The stone of fire was cold and grey, barely flickering. Charsoc waited until finally the stone began to blaze faintly with an orange fire.

He turned to address the Warlock Kings.

'Unprotected, the effects of Yehovah's presence on Warlocks will at best asphyxiate us, at worst destroy us and deliver our souls screaming to the Abyss. The only antidote is thus: each one of you must hold the stone and willingly embrace its power.'

Dracul and the Warlock Kings drew back as one. 'Its power is not yet strong enough to destroy you,' Charsoc removed the stone from the amulet with his gloved hand. 'but it *is* strong enough to immunize us for a brief time against the consuming fire.' He frowned. 'But I warn you, when it wears off, we have no defence.'

He removed his glove and clasped the stone with his bony fingers in triumph. 'It will also render us invisible.' His face contorted in agonized pain, his entire body shook violently as the fierce orange lightnings coursed through his limbs. Then the lightnings stopped. He thrust the stone to Dracul, who grasped it, at once uttering a tortured scream. Dracul's limbs shook uncontrollably. Swiftly the Warlock Kings thrust the stone from one to another, drawing off its power.

'We arrive uninvited.'

Charsoc placed his staff on the stone, a luminous fire blazed from the serpent's mouth, instantly he and the Warlock Kings became invisible.

The fiendish troupe flew past the twelve pale blue moons, upwards through the indigo horizons towards the labyrinths of the Holy Mountain. Gradually, the seven spires of the layrinths became visible through the flashing lightnings. They flew over pearl beaches, past the Palace of Archangels, across the vast onyx expanse of the Mount of the North and over the immense, towering jasper wall. They flew through swirling white mists and thunder and electric-blue lightnings towards the mammoth golden tower of the Crystal Palace that peaked into seven spires, surrounded by its magnificent rolling gardens that seemed to hang from infinity as if held by an invisible force.

Outside the looming golden gothic seventh spire, they came to a standstill. Charsoc disappeared through the walls of the labyrinths followed by the Warlock Kings, their path lit only by the flaming eternal torches high against the walls of the caverns, which were fuelled by the burning coals of the seven spirits of Yehovah. They ascended upwards. Still upwards.

Finally they arrived outside the seventh chamber. Charsoc waited, unobserved by the Watchers of the seventh flame, who stood, barring the entrance. He put his ear to the wall of the cavern, listening intently, then passed straight through the walls of the seventh chamber, followed by the Warlock Kings.

Jether stood in the very centre of the chamber, surrounded by the seven elders of the High Council of the First Heaven who were seated on seven cornelian thrones.

Behind Jether, in the furthest depths of the cavern, a stormy wind raged, and out of the wind burned a great indigo cloud. Charsoc moved nearer. There, dimly visible in the centre of the coals of fire, lay the enormous gold-bound codices – the codices of the White Judgement. He stared at them, as one transfixed, then raised his head studying Jether and the elders. He nodded to Dracul. One by one, the Warlock Kings surrounded the elders who remained oblivious to their presence.

'Revered elders, 'Jether declared. 'The day of the First Judgement hastens. We are here today for the unveiling of...'

Xacheriel sneezed violently. 'Drat and bumble!' He fumbled in his voluminous robes for his handkerchief. 'A thousand pardons, revered Jether!' he spluttered, his eyes streaming. '...Mandragora,' he muttered. Issachar frowned.

'Revered elders,' Jether continued, 'today we unveil the undisclosed tenets of the Codice of...'

Xacheriel let out another earsplitting sneeze. Jether raised his hands in despair.

'Mandragora?' Xacheriel mumbled. 'I'm allergic to it.'

'Mandrake Root – in the *seventh* chamber?' Jether looked at him doubtfully.

Xacheriel nodded vigorously.

'How do you *know* it's Mandrake Root?' Issachar glared dubiously at Xacheriel.

'Mandrake is a plant of the fall. It cannot grow in the First Heaven,' said Maheel in his soft breathy voice.

'My excursions to the red zone,' Xacheriel mumbled. 'The flesh-eating Necromancers use it for their hexes...'

He sat, glowering at Issachar, his arms folded, with his spotted handkerchief now crammed out of both nostrils.

'I tell you...' Xacheriel's eyes and nose streamed, 'it is *Mandragora*!'

'Issachar is right, Xacheriel old friend,' Jether placed his arm gently on Xacheriel's. 'It is impossible to smell mandragora here in the First Heaven.'

Zebulon looked up from his supplications. 'Yet revered Xacheriel, I, too, smell the pungency of nightshade.'

Jether frowned, his eagle eyes alert. He raised his hand then placed his finger to his lips.

'Let us be circumspect. We switch to the ancient language – the speech of antiquities.' He lowered his voice, then continued in a strange unintelligible ancient angelic tongue. Charsoc smiled slowly, for he well understood their dialect.

Jether lowered his head. 'It would seem we may entertain intruders unaware,' he declared gravely.

'Intruders?' Xacheriel spluttered, his eyes streaming.

Jether shook his head, mystified. 'There is not one who exists with the power to invade the seventh spire. Yet, I too, sense a dark intrusive presence.' He rose to his feet and raised his staff.

'Disclose yourself!' The chamber was met by silence.

Xacheriel gave another blustering sneeze. Jether walked towards the great indigo cloud that blazed at the far side of the chamber. He raised a second staff with a golden seraphim carved on the top of its rod, the Staff of the White Winds. Then placed it into the very heart of the flames where the indigo inferno blazed fiercest.

Jether's hair and beard flew wildly in the tempests that

rose from the indigo cloud. He raised the staff, his voice dark with authority. 'I command you in the name of Yehovah – Disclose yourself!' Indigo forks of lightning blazed from the staff's rod towards the left of the chamber.

The High Council watched. All stretched out their staffs.

They stared, transfixed as only a ringed hand materialized, its bony, ringed fingers clasped tightly shut around an object.

Jether moved forward, then swiftly placed the full force of the burning staff on the hand. Instantly the remainder of Charsoc's body materialized in front of them.

'Aha! I told you – *Mandragora!*' Xacheriel spluttered, scowling at Issachar. 'Charsoc *showers* in it!'he exclaimed triumphantly.

'I hold the sixth stone of fire . . . ' Charsoc hissed. A gasp went up from the elders.

'From the sixth chamber.'

'Pickpocket!' muttered Xacheriel under his breath.

'Only the pure can hold the stone,' Lamaliel whispered.

'I *am* the pure,' Charsoc hissed. 'Pure evil . . . pure good – both are the pure.'

'The pure has become corrupted,' Jether walked directly towards him, his face like thunder.

'Then wrest it from me, Jether the Just – as I intend to wrest the codices of fire from you.' Charsoc swiftly lifted his sceptre. Immediately Jether was seized from his feet – hovering eighteen inches off the floor. Charsoc brought the sceptre down. Jether was flung violently across the cavern floor, gasping for breath. Instantly, the thirteen Warlock Kings materialized in front of the elders, their gnarled green features twisted, hair flying. Xacheriel smashed his staff hard against Charsoc's back, while Issachar pushed him against the cavern walls. Dracul's long pale hands swiftly grasped Xacheriel and Issachar's throats, while Ishtar and Loki grabbed the elders' staffs.

Jether staggered to his feet.

'We bid you welcome, Warlock Kings of the West!' he cried, strangely exhilirated. 'Dracul – Long has it been since you crossed my threshold.'

Dracul leered at him. 'It holds a certain . . . *je ne sais quoi?*' He shrugged. 'My old tutor. I am deeply indebted to your instruction. It has served me well in the employ of my master, Satan.'

Jether watched Charsoc out of the corner of his eye moving towards the Codice of Fire lain on the table.

Dracul moved nearer, he raised his broomstick, instantly it became a live hissing serpent.

'It would seem you sink to the lower boundary of harlotries since your defection.' Jether observed. 'I regress momentarily to your kindergarten tactics, Dracul.'

Jether raised his hand imperceptibly. The serpent metamorphosed into a hissing black cat. 'The mislaid part of your costume, I think.'

Dracul's serpent transformed back into his staff.

'Before this day is out, Jether,' he hissed, 'you and your compatriots shall be our captives behind the magenta veil of the Unholy of Holies.'

Jether's expression grew stern. He lifted the Staff of the White Winds. 'I think not, Dracul.'

Dracul was instantly thrust violently against the wall of the cavern, thrown to the ground, gasping for breath. He glared up at Jether with loathing, raising himself up from the ground with his long green hands, his eyes filled with malice.

'Jether the Just – ' Dracul and the fast recovering Warlock Kings moved towards Jether. A ferocious evil pack.

'No, Dracul! 'Charsoc cried. 'We have greater fish to fry than old sorceror's long past their prime. I intend this very day to bring my master, Lucifer, the secrets that the Codice holds.' Charsoc, pushed Maheel aside and strode his way to the head of the table. He stood staring down at the Codice of Fire.

'Secrets of the First Judgement.'

Issachar strode towards Charsoc.

'Leave him, Issachar!' Jether cried, watching from the corner of his eye.

'The codice will discern its reader. Charsoc too easily forgets the sacred mysteries of Holy Lore.'

Charsoc stared down at the Codice hungrily, then opened the cover. Jether watched him intently from the far side of the chamber. He turned the first page. It was blank. Charsoc frowned. He turned a second page, then a third, frantically, he rifled through the Codice. Each page was empty. Blank.

He turned to Jether, vehement hatred in his eyes. Jether held his gaze. 'You have been found wanting.'

Charsoc continued his frantic rifling of the pages, unnerved, each was blank.

'Yehovah knew of your intrusion,' Jether spoke in a low voice, 'the very second the thought was conceived inside your dark and twisted mind.'

Charsoc flung the codice to the floor. His face dark with loathing, he strode over to the flaming indigo cloud,

'Only the uncorrupted can touch the flame!' Jether cried.

Charsoc turned to Jether in triumph.

'You lose power, Jether,' Charsoc spat, 'Your magic grows old and weak. Mine is strong.'

Clutching the sixth stone of fire, high above his head, Charsoc stepped into the very midst of the burning indigo flames.

Jether watched as Charsoc's face began to glow as burnished bronze, his skin burning translucent. In the very midst of the coals of fire, lay the six enormous gold-bound lapis lazuli codices, their pages blazing with a fierce blue fire. Great flashes of lightning came out of the fire as two flaming living creatures, became visible through the indigo flames: the mighty cherubim of Yehovah. Each living creature had four faces, the face of an angel, an ox, a lion, and an eagle. Their enormous eight golden wings were covered with eyes and outstretched. The first Cherub lifted the top codex from the midst of the burning coals, then held out his hand to Charsoc. Charsoc stretched out his right hand, his left still grasping the stone, to the flaming Cherub, then gasped. A moment later, he screamed.

A hair raising, blood-chilling scream. The skin was melting off his hand like wax, his bones visible beneath. Desperately he tried to unclasp his hand from the Cherub's powerful grasp with his left hand.

The stone of fire fell down … down … into the blazing inferno.

And instantaneously Charsoc was gone. Dracul and his Warlock Kings with him. Vanished from the seventh spires.

CHAPTER TWENTY-NINE

LAZARUS

JESUS WIPED THE fresh tears from His cheeks and moved through the garden, past the roses, closer to the rock-hewn vault where Lazarus's body, having been anointed with myrtle, aloes, and spices, now lay. He paced back and forth, deeply disturbed in His spirit, smelling the stench of the prince of demons – of the author of death himself. Oblivious of the mourners' violent wailing, He turned to a bunch of straggling relatives standing some way off, staring pale and afraid.

'Roll away the stone!' He commanded.

Tentatively, the men in the party approached and, under Jesus' direction, removed the great grey stone from the front of the great hewn cave. Then, as one, the men fell back, shrinking in terror.

Jesus' countenance was fierce. He walked undeterred

towards the opening. Then He stopped, sensing the great impenetrable wall of death that rose up around Him as a sombre, cold barricade. His eyes narrowed. Facing Him was Moloch, Lucifer's champion, prince of the slayers, with his rabid depraved battalion.

'What do you want with our prize, Nazarene?' the fallen princes of death hissed in caterwauling unison.

Moloch rose to his full eleven feet of height. A fallen angelic prince of great stature. His tangled black hair fell across his craggy, mangled features. 'My demon slaves summoned me. The smell of strange sorceries linger on one named Lazarus. My master, Satan, king of death and hell, has command of this body,' he growled, his voice a strange mix of dark discord. 'The Light-Bearer now bears darkness. He has greater sway than You on this planet, Nazarene,' he hissed. Jesus moved towards him. 'You are too late. We have already escorted the subject Lazarus to the underworld, to join the sleeping dead,' he laughed maniacally.

He took out a strange-looking, tarnished sceptre – his eyes glinting a demonic red gleam. 'I, *too*, understand Eternal Law, for I was trained by Charsoc the Dark – you trespass, Nazarene!' he snarled. '*We* are the kings of Earth. You have no place with us, Jesus of Nazareth . . . or with our booty!'

Jesus gazed at Moloch, His countenance fierce.

'You have nothing in Me.'

A strange blinding brilliance issued from Jesus' form, taking the form of a hundred blazing lightnings. 'Keeper of hell and of Death,' Jesus cried. 'One who holds power and sway over your kingdom speaks. Yehovah!' He cried.'

The tomb shuddered violently, illuminating the terror-ized princes of darkness. Moloch fell to his knees, his arm shielding his eyes from the scorching flames. 'You torment us before our time, Nazarene!' Moloch shrieked. A horde of hundreds of clawed black bat-like creatures fled from the chamber of hewn rock, while the cave shuddered as if in the throes of an earthquake.

'Lazarus!' Jesus cried. *'Lazarus, Come forth to the land of the Race of Men!'*

⤳

Lucifer stood tall in his flaming golden chariot surveying the massive iron gates of Perdition. Eighteen of his finest fire breathing panthers ran alongside the chariot, their coats glistening black, their golden manes braided and plaited with diamonds, their heavy golden collars studded with emeralds. Marduk rode by Lucifer's side, inspecting the throngs of listless, ashen, grey-mantled lost souls of the dead, which continually poured in unending masses through into hell and the Underworld.

One woman moved out of the rank and file of the lines, she fell to the ground, clawing at the burning dirt beneath her hands. 'They lied!' she stared up at Lucifer, shaking uncontrollably in horror. 'They told me you were a fable, a fairy-tale king of the damned.'

She scrabbled up, desperately clutching at Lucifer's robe. Two of Dagon's fallen horde savagely manhandled her and kicked her to the ground, where she lay sobbing dementedly.

Lucifer wielded his cat-o'-nine panther tails, a slow satisfied smile spread across his face. 'This brings me joy,

Marduk,' he said, holding out his hand to his cupbearer, who passed him a goblet of black elixir that slid like treacle down Lucifer's throat. 'It exceeds my highest expectations. The whole of their lives on earth, they think I am a fable, a figment of their imagination.' He stared down at the demented woman on the ground, tearing at her hair and skin. 'They lose their minds when they arrive here and discover that I am more real than they of flesh and blood. It is great sport.'

He stopped as a horrified wailing sounded from beyond the vast iron gates. A great bellowing and roaring erupted from the demonic princes guarding the entrance, followed by agonized screaming.

Lucifer watched from a distance as a brilliant light blazed across the massive iron gates of Perdition encircling the fettered, grey-robed souls that thronged through the gates; then it engulfed one particular figure. The grey-mantled soul instantly vanished, leaving the grey shroud lying on the burning pitch. Marduk trembled, holding his eyes, which burned strangely with a searing pain.

Lucifer pulled on the reins of his steed and galloped over to where the grey mantle lay on the ground. 'Bring the guards responsible!' he roared.

The great demonic princes slowly rose to their feet, trembling.

'*Where* is my property?'

The sentinel princes bowed their heads as one as Lucifer got off his horse. He knelt down in the pitch next to the grey shroud, caressing it slowly between his fingers. Scorching flames engulfed his hand. He withdrew it, clutching his palm in agony, a terrible hatred twisted his features.

'Where are his bearers?' he spat.

The ground in front of the gates shuddered. Moloch and his battalion of slayers stood trembling at the gates.

Lucifer turned his panthers around to face Moloch. The craggy prince clutched his scorched face; his tongue was seared. 'The Nazarene – He is to be feared...' Moloch whimpered. 'The Nazarene lays siege on my kingdom,' he uttered.

Lucifer watched in disbelief as hell's champion reeled to the ground.

'Marduk! Summon Darsoc and the Grey Magus to the Crypts of the Shadows this dusk. I shall remove every trace of the Nazarene from my planet.' He brought down his cat-o'-nine panther tails savagely on his winged stallions.

'Now we strike!'he cried.

⸻

2018
JFK AIRPORT, NEW YORK CITY
— LILIAN —

Jason De Vere sat in the private executive lounge, scowling at the smiling attentive Vietnamese attendant holding out a plate of prepackaged snacks to him. He hated airport food almost as much as he detested the mass-manufactured in-flight dinners. Thank God for own personal Gulfstream jet.

He rose, glancing impatiently down at his Breitling. Where were his mother and Lawrence St Cartier? He paced impatiently up and down the lounge, a scowl on his face: tall and lean in his crumpled linen suit, his silvering hair severely cropped. He sighed loudly and sat back down in the hard airport lounge chair. Scowling again. No one but his mother could get him to wait two hours in an airport. The fact that he was now majority owner and CEO of the fastest-growing media conglomerate in the world was irrelevant to her. He was her eldest son, and she had been insistent that he meet her personally off today's flight.

His expression softened. His mother. She never failed to amaze him. Since his father's death, she had become chair of the De Vere Foundation, responsible for multi billions of dollars annually, and yet she was, without doubt, the most level-headed, down-to-earth person he had ever known.

Lilian De Vere was an indomitable force – she had to be, to survive the formidable De Vere ancestry. He loved her. Jason reddened at the very thought of it. 'Love' – such a strong word, but when he thought of his mother it was true. She understood him; she always had. From the moment he was born to the time he fought it out with his father about going to New York Film School, she had always understood the untamed spirit that needed to be let loose. And she had fought for him. At every turn. He would never forget it. She was no fool. Could read a person's character at a hundred paces and yet she was genteel. Soft of spirit.

Lilian would stay in New York for the spring, in her penthouse in the Santiago Calatrava Tower in lower Manhattan – the apartment that James De Vere had bought for her in 2017 for $45 million. She would be wined and dined by all her dead husband's friends – ageing executive bachelors and divorcés, multibillionaires every one. She was still beautiful and enjoyed the attention, but never took their bait – there was simply no reason to. She had loved James

De Vere intensely, and she was content with her memories. And she had Lawrence.

She had known Lawrence St Cartier when she was young, so young that her hair was black and her skin was dewey. And loved him. Lilian De Rothschild had met James De Vere at the same time, and he had swept her off her feet and she had chosen the wealthy, educated son of one of America's leading banking dynasties over the brusque, penniless young Scottish priest. Lawrence was not the marrying kind, but they had remained deep friends. Shortly after her marriage, Lawrence had joined the Jesuit order, then in his early thirties left the priesthood and joined the CIA. Lilian trusted him with her life – and her soul. As did her cynical eldest son. Although not related by blood, Lawrence and Jason had a connection that even Jason's nearest and dearest – of which there were few – found perplexing. Only Lilian understood, for she understood them both.

Jason watched as they came through the gates, arm in arm. Lilian, in her late seventies, was slim and elegantly dressed, her silver hair rolled in an elegant chignon, her face barely lined. Accompanying her was the thin, silver-haired Englishman immaculately dressed in a pressed shirt, Saville Row trousers and grey silk cravat. He was in his eighties, with a silver moustache and his ever-present pipe jutting from between his teeth. Trailing them both, obscured from view under Cartiers eclectic assortment of suitcases was his fourteen-year-old Egyptian assistant, Waseem.

'Jason!' Lilian flung her arms around his neck, smothering him. He blushed, awkwardly kissing her in return, then turned to Lawrence, who shook his hand with vigour.

'Jason, my boy!'

Lilian and Lawrence followed Jason and his bodyguards down the private covered walkway, towards the gleaming black Bentley waiting on the tarmac.

'Mother . . .' Jason tapped her arm as one of his four aides opened the Bentley's door for her. Lawrence St Cartier leaned over and kissed Lilian on the cheek. The Bentley purred away.

Lawrence St Cartier disappeared behind the airport escort, back through the doors, followed closely by the heavily-laden Waseem and headed for the Egyptair desk to make the six-thirty flight to Alexandria.

Nick De Vere would be waiting for him at the Monastery of Archangels.

CHAPTER THIRTY

LOWER THAN THE ANGELS

GABRIEL WALKED STEADILY through the narrow pearl arbor covered with pomegranate vines laden with lush silver fruit, shielding his eyes from the intense shafts of crimson light radiating from far beyond. He walked past the heady perfume of the magnificent hanging blossoms of the Gardens of Fragrance, through the vale, until he came to an inconspicuous grotto at the very edge of the Cliffs of Eden surrounded by eight ancient olive trees.

Trembling, he pushed open the familiar wooden gate and walked over to the simple bench in the centre of the grotto, carved of olive wood, staring out towards the the colossal Rubied Door, ablaze with light, embedded into the jacinth walls of the tower. The entrance to Yehovah's throne room.

'You have seen His death.' Gabriel turned. Jether stood to his right.

'I have seen many things these past dusks.' Gabriel shuddered.

'Dreamings too terrible to utter.'

Jether laid his hand gently on his shoulder.

'And yet, He has to take His course. There is no other way for the Race of Men.'

They sat together in silence and gazed a long while at the shimmering rainbow that rose like an immense bow over the First Heaven's horizons.

'But, why –' Gabriel turned to Jether, his expression suddenly fierce.

'The Race of Men do not heed Him.'

'There are some who care, Gabriel,' Jether said softly. 'Those who will not follow Lucifer and his fallen. Their hearts yearn for Him, knowing not that it is He they long for. He knows these ones – past, present and future generations of the Race of Men who will follow Him, fight for His cause. These are his subjects. He will be their King.'

Jether walked to the very edge of the cliffs, gazing down at the sheer drop between the cliff face and the throne room entrance where the fountains of life flowed from Yehovah's throne thousands of leagues downward to the Waters of Eden, then north, south, east, and west to water the First Heaven. There was no bridge across.

'That is why, Christos is, for a brief while lower than the angels.'

Jether turned.

'You come often,' he smiled gently at Gabriel, '... to Christos' garden?'

Gabriel nodded.

'I feel closer to Him here. It brings back memories of

different times,' Gabriel's voice was soft, '...times before the shadows fell.'

Jether sighed.

'We have not been given the capacity to see all things as Yehovah. As Christos, Gabriel. Even as the angelic, even as seers, we see only in part.'

Gabriel closed his eyes, listening to the exquisite birdsong issuing from from the thousands of amethyst linnets perched on the branches of the Great Willows in the Gardens of Fragrance.

'We see through a mirror darkly...' Gabriel murmured, 'even as the Race of Men.'

Jether nodded.

'We the angelic have this in common with the Race of Men, it is true. We walk by faith, Gabriel. Trusting in His Choices. Assured of His decisions. One day, we will see all things – even as they are revealed to Him. Until then, this is our test. To trust. In devotion. In dedication. To execute His commands unequivocally. The very same test that Lucifer failed.'

'Lucifer offers the Race of Men many things.' Gabriel pondered.

'But the greatest yearning of all men's hearts is not his to give.' Jether turned to Gabriel.

'To truly belong. To be counted for. To truly be loved for who each one is and was created to be. Birthed from the very heart of Yehovah. It is only back in the very heart of Yehovah that the Race of Men will find their peace. Their reason for existance. This is what Lucifer knows and fears the most. This is the true knowledge that if the Race of Men discover it, will cause Lucifer's kingdom to crumble.'

Gabriel rose and walked towards Jether, still standing at the edge of the cliffs.

'He will suffer greatly at the hands of the Race of Men.'

Jether stared out again towards the Rubied Door.

'It is a sacred mystery. To marvel at for all eternity. The Councils gather on the Tower of Winds. Come – we must prepare.'

CHAPTER THIRTY-ONE

JUDAS

M ARY, LAZARUS' SISTER, sat at Jesus' feet, her head on His lap, her waist-length copper hair still unplaited, wet and matted from wiping the excess perfume from His feet. Jesus stroked her hair tenderly, deeply affected by her lavish gesture of devotion. She gazed up at Him in adoration, the fresh tears still staining her pale freckled cheeks, her sturdy nail-bitten fingers grasping His tightly. In that moment her plain face seemed almost beautiful.

The strong fragrance of Indian spikenard still pervaded the room. Its alabaster flask lay on the floor, completely drained of its costly ointment, next to a living, breathing Lazarus, who was being pulled and prodded by the constant stream of clamouring friends neighbours and curious strangers who were still lining up outside the house to see for themselves this notorious miracle that had occurred right here in Bethany – and to gaze on the handsome young prophet from Nazareth.

Judas continued in his incessant pacing up and down behind Jesus and Lazarus. Tonight, his rage had reached its threshold. Normally he prided himself on being the epitome of political correctness, but even his carefully controlled temper had its limits.

He clutched the purse tightly in his hands.

Jesus looked up from Mary studying Judas slowly, gazing down for a long while at his hands grasping the purse so tightly until Judas flushed a dull red that spread from his ears down through his neck to his chest. Jesus met his gaze, His expression unusually hard.

'Let her alone, Judas.' His words were slow and measured.

'Why are you bothering her?' He clasped Judas' arm firmly. 'She has done a beautiful thing.' Finally Judas could contain his frustration no longer.

'This oil could have been sold for three hundred denari and given to the destitute!' he exclaimed.

Jesus lowered His gaze to Mary's. 'The poor are always with us, Judas,' He said softly. 'Whenever you wish, you can do good to them; but you will not always have Me.'

He placed His hand over Mary's head protectively. 'Mary has done what she could. She came beforehand to anoint My body for the burial. And wherever the good news of Yehovah's kingdom is preached throughout the world, what she has done tonight will indeed be told in memory of her.'

Judas stared directly into Jesus' stern gaze, his own black

eyes burning with a wild intensity. He stood a full minute in complete silence, then kicked aside the empty flask in rage and strode past Lazarus, slamming the door behind him.

~

Zahi lay on the pallet in the guest quarters of Joanna's house, listening for sounds from the upper chambers. Over two hours ago Judas had stormed into the house, incensed, up the stairs, and slammed his door. Zahi hadn't heard him stir until now. Judas closed his room door and carefully locked it. Zahi could hear his footsteps on the stairs; then the outer door to Joanna's house slammed. Looking out of the window, he glimpsed Judas walking hastily down the narrow street. His hair glistened, freshly washed, and his face was bathed. He clutched the common purse and a larger bag tightly to him. No doubt off on another of his frequent trips to Jerusalem.

Zahi reflected once more on the evening's events. Judas had been indignant, mortally offended. Zahi could still hear his stinging words, 'That was a whole year's salaries!' he had cried, 'It could have been given to the poor!'

Judas' family had scrimped and scraped all their lives just to give him an education.

To him it was an act of unrestrained sacrilege. To Jesus, it was an act of lavish devotion. To Judas it was a year's wages; to Jesus, who regaled them with stories of the First Heaven's gold streets and Rubied Doors, it was a drop in the ocean.

Zahi reflected. To the household of Aretas, it was not even the cost of one ruby from the immense coffers that filled his father's treasuries. The Hebrew thought like a king. How deeply he understood Jesus' discernment on matters of wealth. Money was merely a tool. To be used, not worshipped.

What was it the Hebrew had said? 'Where your treasure is, there will your heart be.' Zahi pondered over many of the Hebrew's sayings which seemed mysterious and indefinable, and yet here he was, totally healed from leprosy. Since walking with the Hebrew, he had seen blind eyes open and the lame walk. Zahi had walked with warriors and with eastern kings since he was an infant, but never – no never had he walked with such a King as this.

He was in a dilemma. For many months now he had felt an uneasiness about Judas's handling of the treasury purse, and had taken it upon himself when Judas was away on one of his increasingly frequent trips to Jerusalem, to conduct his own private audit into Judas's dealings with the common purse. It had taken two whole nights, from dusk till dawn, but his findings had confirmed his deepest apprehensions. Money was missing. Consistently. The amounts were never large enough to attract suspicion; indeed, only someone with mathematical training would notice them at all. But Aretas had been a stickler when it had come to Zahi's education. Both he and Jotapa had been educated in every aspect of the palace's extensive trading rituals since they were old enough to read and write. Zahi's mornings had been filled with endless lettering and ciphering, auditing the royal financial records under Mahmoud's meticulous eye, and there was no room for error. By the time Zahi was twelve, he had progressed from reviewing Aretas' local royal accounts and was now auditing the great stacks of records that arrived each dawn from the Nabatean trading routes. Much to Aretas' elation, Zahi's red lettering grew swiftly to be the scourge of the shrewd Chinese, Persian, and Indian traders who conducted business with the palace. Every inflated sale of spices, incense, or silks the eagle-eyed boy underlined, meticulously recording each missing amount until he had traced the fraud to its author. Aretas had revelled in the knowledge that the young crown prince had single-handedly put a stop to the of some of the wiliest traders in the Eastern Hemisphere.

Zahi tossed and turned restlessly. He had scrupulously checked and rechecked his findings. There was no doubt. Small steady amounts were missing from the purse. And Judas must be growing more confident, for in the past three months several much larger sums had disappeared. Until last week.

Judas must have become suspicious, because his treasury papers were now hidden on his person at all times, and he clutched the common purse to himself even when he retired at night. Zahi wondered if Jesus knew of the petty pilfering that was going on under His nose. Earlier tonight he had watched Jesus observing Judas and the common purse more closely than usual. Perhaps Jesus had done His own investigating. And where was Judas tonight? Zahi would have to tell Jesus of his discovery.

And it was while thinking on all these things, that Zahi fell into a deep and dreamless sleep.

CHAPTER THIRTY-TWO

THE TROPHY

MICHAEL STOOD ON the pearl sands of the First Heaven, gazing out at the pale moons setting behind the copper-hued cliffs of Zamar. A soft warm zephyr blew his flaxen locks; then the scents of frangipani and myrrh from the orangeries filled his nostrils.

He stared up past the looming crystal orangeries of the Palace of Archangels up to the derelict west wing of Lucifer's palace – to the huge carved pearl balcony where his elder brother had so relished watching him and Gabriel thundering through the shallows on their white stallions.

A sudden icy chill blew up. A thousand amethyst linnets suddenly took to the air in a flurry away from the Gardens of Fragrance. Michael frowned. He watched as they flew, their wings fluttering furiously, winging their way over the Crystal Sea. He wrapped his cloak around him, strangely uneasy.

The fragrance of frankincense suddenly permeated the sands.

'Lucifer.' Michael turned. Fierce. No one was there. 'Desist your sorceries...'

A moment passed; then Lucifer appeared in front of him, his head covered by a large grey hood, his ravaged features hidden.

He gazed up past Michael, to the balcony.

'Brothers...,' he whispered, a great pain fleetingly crossed his face, 'for Eternity.' Lucifer murmured. They stood in silence for a few moments.

'Those days are long gone, Lucifer.' Michael turned his blazing gaze onto him. 'By your own hand, you ensured their demise.'

Slowly Lucifer removed his hood, revealing his marred ravaged features.

Michael breathed sharply inward, then lowered his gaze, sickened.

'The ravages of sin,' Lucifer murmured with a wry smile. 'They leave their mark.'

'You appear only in your fallen state when unprotected by Eternal Law. I therefore take it that you come unsolicited,' Michael observed dryly.

'Quite so,' Lucifer murmured. 'I am here uninvited...' He bent down and ran his fingers through the pearl sands, closing his eyes in rapture. 'The sensations of the First Heaven...' He raised his gaze far in the distance, beyond the translucent Crystal Palace to the colossal ruby-encrusted doorway encircled by the shimmering rainbow. He shielded his eyes from the fierce rubied rays.

'Sweet agony,' he whispered.

'You were in Eden, the garden of God; every precious stone adorned you.'

Lucifer turned in the direction of the familiar voice. There, standing beneath the orangeries, his face half hidden behind the fragrant white frangipani, was Jether. Lucifer's expression grew hard.

'You were on the holy mount of God...' Jether walked down the gilded steps towards him. 'You walked among the fiery stones. You were blameless in your ways from the day you were created...' Jether stopped directly in front of Lucifer, 'till iniquity was found in you.'

They stood regarding one another across the pearl sands.

'Jether, my old mentor. My physical demise – a small price to pay for my greatest triumph.' They held each other's gaze in silence.

'So you will kill Him,' Jether said softly.

'You are too much the seer,' Lucifer replied.

Michael and Jether stood facing him. Sombre.

'Yes, His slaughter is imminent in the Race of Men.' A small, evil smile played on Lucifer's mouth. 'As He breathes His last breath, my dark scribes will verify the Nazarene's death in the courts of Perdition.' He walked away from them, down the sands. 'Then we escort Him to hell.'

Lucifer raised his arms to the shifting lilac skies. 'The Nazarene – my prize for eternity.'

Michael and Jether watched him in silence.

'The Pupil supercedes his mentor,' Lucifer spat. He

glared at Jether with unconcealed loathing. 'You have lost, old man.' Then he vanished.

Michael and Jether looked out at the frothing surf on the celestial lilac sea. 'He plays into our hands,' said Michael.

'He is to soon be caught in his own tangled web,' Jether replied, his piercing eyes vigilant. 'The day of the First Judgement hastens. It is now just a matter of time.'

Charged by Darsoc's Grey Magus, Judas Iscariot stood in the council room in the palace of the high priest Caiaphas, before the chief priests of Jerusalem, and sold his soul for thirty pieces of silver.

And from that moment he looked out for a convenient opportunity to betray Jesus of Nazareth.

CHAPTER THIRTY-THREE

GETHSEMANE

T HE FIERCE WINDS of the Kidron Valley blew through the ancient olive groves of Gethsemane. Jesus knelt under one of the spreading gnarled olive trees, His face fallen on His chest. Heavy welts of blood mingled with sweat, dripped from His forehead and down His cheeks, onto the damp grass beneath Him.

Then, inexplicably, an exquisite aroma of spikenard and frangipani permeated the olive grove – the perfumes of the Gardens of Fragrance of the First Heaven. A soft, diffuse light settled, shimmering in front of where Jesus lay unmoving. Gradually His eyelids flickered in vague recognition as the exquisite aromas pervaded His senses. With intense effort, He moved His matted head towards the soft, healing balm of brilliance and opened His bloodshot eyes. A tall, shadowed figure slowly became visible.

There facing Him, looking down on Him with exquisite tenderness, stood an imperial form, its face shrouded by a luminous white cloak. Behind the figure, in a semicircle, stood the entire council of twenty-four heavenly kings, attired in dazzling ceremonial white robes of the First Heaven. A circlet of gold rested on each white head. Jesus recognized Lamaliel, then Methuselah and Xacheriel, His trusted heavenly elders, the stewards of Yehovah's heavenly mysteries.

Slowly, Jether removed his hood, kneeling down next to Jesus on the grass. 'Hark back to the world beyond the Rubied Door,' he whispered, his voice infinitely tender. 'Before You were encased in the dust and clay of the Race of Men, Christos.'

'I am trapped in this mire and clay, Jether,' Jesus uttered, His voice wavering. 'I cannot heed Him...'

Jether looked at him a long moment, his expression filled with tenderness and love. From the folds of his robe he removed a small silver vial, then poured the thick, clear elixir over Jesus' head. It ran down His forehead onto His robes.

Instantly Jesus was transported away from the ancient olive grove in Jerusalem. He flew upward through the heavens and solar systems and still upward, past planets and galaxies, and onward still upward, past golden walls and seven spires, until He caught sight of the twenty-four ancient kings, kneeling in a semicircle beneath the magnificent hanging blossoms of the Gardens of Fragrance, their crowned heads bowed, their mouths moving silently in supplication.

Jesus gasped, looking around at the eight olive trees of

His garden, drinking in the tangible glory of the First Heaven. Ahead of Him, across the vast cavern, shafts of light blazed from the immense golden Rubied Door embedded in the jacinth walls of the tower. He stumbled down onto His knees, His face raised to the blazing crimson light, tears coursing down His face.

'Father . . . ,' He wept.

Slowly the colossal Rubied Door opened. Jesus flung Himself prostrate on the ground as a great thundering erupted and the rainbow around the Holy Mountain ruptured into lilac and intense blue lightnings that appeared to illuminate up every universe in the galaxy. And then, through the thunder and the roaring, through the lightning . . . a voice resonated. A voice that shook the very heavens and the universe in its wake.

Jesus stood, His arms outstretched, His eyes closed in ecstasy, as the voice echoed through the fibres of His being to His very core like a thousand softly flowing waters – a sound infinitely more beautiful than imagination had ever the capacity to conceive: gracious, noble, valiant. The voice of His Father. Intense with yearning, filled with grace and exquisitely tender – Yehovah.

'Beloved Son . . . '

Jesus lifted His face to the gentle, shimmering, all-consuming light, His face enraptured in the presence of His beloved Father.

'I have not forsaken You.'

Jesus sobbed in esctasy as Yehovah's voice saturated the pores of His being.

'Your eternal sacrifice is for the Race of Men.' The crimson shafts grew more intense. Jesus inhaled sharply.

Through the shafts of light, at the entrance of the Rubied Door, on the very edge of the great chasm, stood a form of immense stature, swathed in a blazing wreath of light, His arms outstretched towards Jesus.

'That they, too, may know Me.'

And then, through the light, in the place where the form's countenance would be, what seemed like two immense shining black orbs became visible, gazing out of the brilliance. Gazing ... Gazing ... gazing with intense adoration and yearning upon Jesus. And then a tear fell from Yehovah's eyes, down ... down ... towards Jesus.

Slowly the Rubied Door faded from Jesus' sight, and the lightnings subsided, and the soft, warm breezes of the First Heaven transformed into the chill winds of the Kidron Valley.

'*That they, too, may know Me . . .* ' The words echoed gently in Jesus' soul. Jesus closed His eyes. 'Your will be done,' He uttered.

He raised himself unsteadily from the dirt, then gazed around in the darkness.

Only Peter, James, and John still lay against the gnarled trunks of the olive trees, sleeping, their heads on the damp grass.

The silence was shattered by the sounds of breaking undergrowth, accompanied by hushed voices coming towards them, the darkness broken by the glare of swinging lanterns and torches on poles. Peter shot to his feet, his expression fierce, staring towards the lights. John and James stirred.

Judas strode towards them, holding a lantern at his face,

freshly bathed, his raiment crisp and clean, his companions hanging far back in the semi-darkness.

'Hail, Master!' he called, walking directly up to Jesus.

But Jesus' attention was drawn to the silhouette of a tall, cloaked figure who stood in the shadows, just paces behind Judas's right shoulder.

Lucifer stood haughty, triumphant. He stared at Jesus intently, an iniquitous smile on his face.

Jesus lowered His eyes from Lucifer's gaze as Judas leaned over and kissed Jesus lovingly, first on the right cheek and then on the left.

Jesus stared at Judas. 'Would you betray and deliver up the Son of Man with a kiss?'

Judas lifted his right hand to his own cheek. On Judas's fingers lay a strange crimson liquid. He fell back. Ashen. Trembling.

Jesus raised His eyes to meet Lucifer's.

'Remember, Lucifer.' His voice was soft as a breeze but razor sharp. 'Your kiss on My cheek, many moons past, in the First Heaven, when we walked together in My garden.' Lucifer stared down in dread at the darkening crimson stain on his hand; his features contorted in agony from the sharp burning sensation in his right palm.

'. . . When many worlds have long risen and fallen,' said Jesus, His voice barely audible, 'the Lamb will be slain.'

Lucifer stared steadily at Jesus, his face twisted with trepidation and loathing.

'I shall separate You from Yehovah. You shall share my fate – an eternity away from Him. The vaults of hell await you, Nazarene.' Then he wrapped his cloak tightly around him. And vanished.

A band of Jewish officers and servants from the high priest's palace broke clumsily through the undergrowth. They were followed closely by a Roman detachment, armed with swords and staves. A riotous, disorderly crowd of volunteers and curious strangers followed.

Jesus sighed. 'Whom do you seek?' He called out.

'Jesus the Nazarene!' one called out.

'I am He,' Jesus said softly.

A raucous uproar erupted from the officers and the unruly rabble as a mob of surly-looking men advanced towards Him, their staves upraised. The chief priests followed behind them.

Jesus lifted His hand, and immediately a strange power fell over the advancing throng. They fell back in dread.

'Who are you seeking?' Jesus reiterated patiently, as though addressing slow children. 'I told you, I am Jesus of Nazareth,' He continued. 'If you seek Me, let these go on their way.'

The head of the Roman detachment seized Jesus roughly by the shoulders. Immediately Peter let out a loud roar and recklessly drew his sword, striking Malchus, body servant of the high priest, and slicing off his ear. The whole party erupted and in the ensuing uproar, the Roman captain loosed his hold on Jesus.

'Peter,' Jesus laid His hand on Peter's arm steadily, 'permit them to seize Me,' He said quietly, placing His hand on Malchus's ear. Malchus backed away from Jesus in terror, feeling in astonishment his healed ear.

Peter lowered his sword, stared wildly at Jesus, confused, then tore frantically through the trees. James stood trembling, rooted to the ground, then lifted his robes and fled after Peter, followed immediately by John.

Jesus stood alone. 'And you . . . ' He turned His fierce gaze onto the chief priests, who stood staring at Him, petrified, their eyes filled with hatred.

'Why have you come to arrest Me as some wild, blood-thirsty insurgent, wielding swords and clubs. I taught in your temples and synagogues every day, in full view of you. You could have arrested Me at any – '

A burly Roman soldier savagely threw Jesus to the ground. He nodded, and six of his detachment seized Him brutally.

Zahi stood trembling, hovering on the outskirts of the belligerent mob. His linen garments had been hastily flung around him after Joanna had hastily roused him from his slumber. He stood, trembling behind the tree, watching as the crowds seized Jesus, pushing Him mercilessly down the ravine, west towards Jerusalem. An uncouth youth glared at him and ran towards him.

Zahi fled in terror. The Hebrew was in grave danger; He needed allies. He would send Fariq, royal messenger at once to Aretas' spring encampment; His father had protected the Hebrew once. As an infant.

Zahi would appeal to Aretas.

CHAPTER THIRTY-FOUR

THE WITNESS

KING ARETAS AND his entire royal household were encamped at the Nabaetan city of Mampsis in the central Negev. He and his compatriot kings and caliphs of Persia, Edessa, and Arabia were holding royal summit for the spring, with the blessing of Rome, to Aretas' satisfaction and Herod Antipas' fury.

Jotapa pushed past Ayeshe, into Aretas' festival tent. She was out of breath, dishevelled, and her black hair flew loosely escaping from its braids.

'Papa! Papa!'

Aretas looked up from his ornately carved desk, weary from his royal papers.

'Fariq, your royal rider – he eats with Ghaliya in the kitchen tents, exhausted. There is news from Jerusalem?' Jotapa asked. Aretas nodded. Grave.

'Zahi?' Jotapa trembled.

Aretas shook his head. 'The Hebrew,' he said quietly, laying his quill down. 'The councils meet in Jerusalem.' Jotapa drew up a velvet bolstered chair next to his and earnestly took his old hands in hers. Aretas continued. 'They would condemn the Hebrew to death.'

Jotapa stared at her father. Apalled.

The king took a deep breath and stood. He paced up and down, then stopped next to the tent entrance. 'Fariq rode these past hours with the royal missives. His stallion recovers in the royal stables. They have arrested the Hebrew; it is certain. I was not going to alarm you till it was confirmed.'

Jotapa stared up at him, trembling. 'It is *rumours* – propogated by the enemies of the Hebrew – those fat-jowled Sadducees!' she exclaimed.

Aretas shook his head sadly. 'Alas, it is no rumour, Jotapa,' he said softly. 'Zahi was there. He saw it all first-hand.'

'Zahi...,' she uttered. Ashen. 'He was there ... at the Hebrew's arrest?'

Aretas held out a missive to Jotapa, written in Zahi's meticulous italic script. She tore it open and read the first lines, devouring each word.

Gently Aretas wrested it back from her grasp. 'He says they seized the Hebrew as though He were a wild vagrant...' Jotapa gazed at her father bewildered. 'An insurrectionist...'

Aretas folded the missive and placed it in a leather pouch. 'At the Valley of Kidron. Zahi was a witness. He fled. He asks for my intervention with Rome and the Jewish authority on the Hebrew's behalf.'

'But Zahi is *wrong*, Papa!'

'My mind is set.' Aretas walked down a path lined with rows of date palms. 'The Hebrew was sent bound to the Sadducee Annas after midnight, then to the halls of his son-in-law, Caiaphas. A private interview was conducted. At dawn He was led to that lavish architectural monstrosity the Praetorium ... But Pilate has washed his hands of the matter.'

Jotapa ran to catch up with Aretas. 'The Hebrew does not need your intervention,' she cried, breathlessly.

'Jotapa – do you not grasp the severity of the situation? Your brother and the Hebrew are in grave danger.' Aretas stopped dead in his tracks. 'My daughter, I did not want to tell you this, but you have forced my hand.' He sighed. 'At this very moment, the Hebrew stands before Herod Antipas.' Jotapa started to shake violently from head to foot.

'But Herod loathes the Hebrew,' she whispered. 'It is certain?' Jotapa gasped, hardly able to speak, for the ice-cold vice that gripped her heart. Aretas nodded. 'The wicked prince that once was my husband will slay Him in cold blood, just as he did the baptist.'

'No.' Aretas shook his head firmly. 'The coward Antipas suffered a great political setback from murdering the baptist. He will be more circumspect with the Hebrew. Indeed, he may well revert the whole matter back to Pilate. Zahi is still free, as are the others of those they call His disciples ... But the Hebrew has many powerful enemies, both among the Sanhedrin and in Rome. You must be brave, Jotapa. Yohanna prepares the horses as we speak. I leave for Jerusalem with my royal guard to consult with Pilate immediately.'

'No, Father!' she cried. 'The Hebrew would not want you to use your influence.'

'I swore to protect Him!' Aretas roared. 'And I would protect Zahi!' Aretas' hands trembled violently.

'My son...' Aretas took a deep breath, fighting for control of his emotions. 'My son ... is an academic, a studier of scrolls. He is no warrior. The rabble who follow the Hebrew are no match for the Roman armies. I will send my royal guard.' He turned his back on Jotapa and walked back towards his royal tent. Then stopped in mid stride. Haggard. 'I *must* send my royal guard,' he whispered.

Jotapa looked after Aretas, a terrible sorrow on her face. 'Papa,' she cried, 'do you still not know who He is – the Hebrew, the one you so loved?'

Aretas shook his head wearily and continued walking, he turned at the tent entrance.

'Jotapa, this talk of miracles and wonders and blind eyes that see – my child...'

Aretas looked at her almost pleadingly. Suddenly older, much older than his sixty-seven years.

'I am a pragmatic man, Jotapa. I am confused. Thirty years is a long time not to see and yet still to believe. You tell me that my first-born, the son of my loins, is healed, but I have not seen Zahi. I know not whether it is myth or something more – whether the Hebrew is man or more.'

He sat heavily on a stone chair, ran his fingers through his greying hair. 'At times, Jotapa,' he murmured, 'my imagination runs away with me.'

He turned to her. 'But I am a king. Kings of Arabia dare not trust their imagination...' He stared out to the Negev, past the royal hunting parks, to the horizon. '...I cannot.'

'Father,' Jotapa grasped his arm, 'remember that day, the day you talked of incessantly when I was but a child – the day the Hebrew took your hand as a babe, and you lost your sight?' Aretas growled.

'You used to say, Papa, when you taught me at bedtime when I was a child, that you lost your sight but gained your inner soul.'

Aretas sighed deeply. 'He will be safe,' Jotapa declared. 'It will be a miracle, just like the healing of Zahi and your compatriot, King Abgar of Edessa, and all the other miracles He has wrought. Her eyes glittered with conviction. 'Let this be your sign, Father.' She looked into Aretas' eyes pleadingly.

'You wear me down, Jotapa!' he glowered, though the severity of his features gradually softened.

'Very well.' He rose wearily to his feet. 'Let it be as you declare. Let the Hebrew defeat the Roman Empire with His strange powers,' he proclaimed. 'I shall tell Zahi that I stay in the North. He and Duza must return here at once under my protection.'

Aretas walked over to the carved altar at the back of the tent and picked up the small wooden cross. 'The Hebrew shall prove He is a worthy King. I, Aretas, king of Arabia...' he held the cross high in his right hand, 'put the King of the Hebrews to the test!'

⌒

Jotapa sat fidgeting, mounted on her black Arab stallion. Next to her, on a second stallion, sat Ayeshe. Ghaliya had packed provisions and water into four saddlebags.

'Ayeshe...' Jotapa lowered her voice. 'You should not

ride! My father will have you whipped for accompanying me.'

The old man gave her a broad, toothless smile. "I nursed your father since he was an infant.' His face was stern. 'He will not *dare* have me whipped. I am ninety years old. I was there at his side when the Nazarene healed his soul. He became a great king of Arabia, Aretas the Just, lover of his people, because his soul was clean.' The old man's voice softened. 'Your father is ailing, princess. You go for Zahi and the Hebrew; I go for a king's soul. I will go with you – I have chosen.'

Jotapa nodded. 'You have chosen well, Ayeshe. Zahi waits for us in Jerusalem.'

Ghaliya's hands trembled as she curtsied to Jotapa. Jotapa took her servant's hands in hers; Ghaliya's eyes were wet with tears. 'Go, my princess. Be an eyewitness. Return to your father with the stories of our Lord's victorious armies. He will believe then, and all Arabia will be saved.'

'I go to Zahi and to the Hebrew, Ghaliya. I will bring back such a report, my father will never doubt again!'

The two stallions raced off into the night. Ghaliya wiped her eyes. Then she turned. Far in the distance, in front of the royal festival tent of meeting, a lantern burned, and a figure stood in the darkness, watching as the stallions galloped away. The light from the moon fell across his face.

It was King Aretas.

CHAPTER THIRTY-FIVE

ANTONIA – AD 28

THE DUSTY, OVERCROWDED streets of Jerusalem were heaving with the news of the dynamic young prophet's arrest. Jesus of Nazareth, darling of the masses, was to be crucified. The horrifying whisper had reverberated through the bustling Passover crowd like a blazing wildfire. Women threw their aprons over their heads and wept unashamedly in the streets; crowds of strong men picked up their staves and swords, all making their way through the crammed Passover streets to the Praetorium.

It was barely dawn. The agitated mob of men, women, and children that congregated outside the judgement hall was swelling rapidly. Weeping old women had spun cloth for Jesus; harried young mothers had risen at dawn and baked bread for Him. They held their babes to their breasts, praying fervently for Him. Paunchy middle-aged men who saw their own lost fire of youth in Him clutched swords and clubs, ready to protect Him with their lives.

But the largest of the multitude were the swarming horde of youthful zealots, who, away from the rigid oversight of the Sadducees and Pharisees, all aspired to be like the young prophet from Nazareth. He was their hero. They were determined: today Rome must go. A new and powerful revolution was stirring in the streets of Jerusalem – one that would overthrow Rome. This was their moment; they would fight for Jesus of Nazareth.

Accompanying these youths were thousands from the provinces, who had journeyed to Jerusalem for the Passover, each with a tale of how they had been healed, delivered, touched, transformed, regaling the clamouring crowds with their stories of blind eyes being opened, lame limbs walking, diseased flesh made new.

The youths' incessant roar rose through Jerusalem's reddening dawn skies. 'We want Jesus!' they cried. 'Give us Jesus!'

All at once, the glowing skies grew dark with strange and clouds as a freezing wind sprang up blowing eerily across the mob. Thousands of macabre black chariots surrounded the judgement hall. Invisible to the Race of Men. A hundred of Lucifer's satanic militia stood, towering at each side of the crowd, led by Folcador and his dark legions. Silence fell upon the crowd as the Roman procurator, Pontius Pilate, dressed in his lavish robes strode out and sat down in a carved, cushioned chair. He sighed deeply, then nodded to the soldier at his right.

Zahi watched, hardly daring to breathe as Jesus stumbled out for the third time that dawn, shoved roughly from behind by a Roman soldier. Zahi paled in shock. Stunned beyond belief. The crowd stared transfixed in revulsion and horror.

Jesus of Nazareth stood silent under the Praetorium's colossal wings of white marble. Silent. His chest and limbs an unending mass of bloodied, purple open welts. Blood seeped from His open wounds dripping fresh onto the marble floor next to Pilate's golden-shoed feet. The once dark, handsome features were battered and bruised, marred beyond comprehension, the high cheekbones bloody and grazed, and Jesus' eyes, which once held such beauty, were purpled and swollen to almost twice their size. The vibrant, handsome young prophet from Nazareth was almost unrecognizable.

Pilate beckoned Him forward. 'I find no fault in Him,' he declared. The procurator nodded once more, and this time a scowling insurgent was dragged onto the podium, next to Jesus.

'It is your custom that I release one prisoner for you at the Passover.' He hesitated, surveying the crowd before him. 'So shall I release for you this "king of the Jews" ... or this murderer, Barabbas?'

Huldah, overlord of the Shaman Kings, signalled to the shaman drummers encircling the arena. In compliance, as one the macabre shamans placed black shofars of rams' horns to their lips and blew. A low decadent subliminal aria sounded across the crowd, and immediately a strange web-like substance enveloped the young zealots as thousands of minuscule bat-like demons the size of locusts flurried out from the blaring shofars. Their bloodsucking talons ripped into the youths' scalps, slashing at their ears, noses, eyes.

The youths stood, in a trance, oblivious to the demons' harrassment.

Hundreds of bat-like locusts landed on Zahi's hair, their talons digging into Zahi's scalp. Zahi shook himself as if in a strange fog. His mind suddenly filled with strange and unsolicited thoughts. The Hebrew must have lied. He was just a jumped-up prophet from Nazareth, a failure. Why had Zahi left treasuries, a palace, a kingdom, for this failed prophet from Nazareth?' He clasped his hands over his head. His mind felt numbed, drugged.

Then he stared down at the perfectly formed soft, pink flesh of his hands. This was no figment of his imagination. He shook his head as if to dislodge the errant thoughts. He yearned for the strong, disciplined armies of Arabia to burst through the streets of Jerusalem and carry the Hebrew and His followers away to the sanctuary of Petra. Aretas would not fail him. He would wait. He looked around him, perplexed, at the youths around him who a minute ago had been demonstrating furiously against Caiaphas and the Jewish leaders, screaming for Jesus' release. One by one, the screaming, passionate voices had quieted as though afflicted with a strange stupor.

An ugly roaring grew from another large group of the gathered youths near where the demons had landed. A belligerent raucous chanting.

'Not this man,' they began to hiss in derision. '...Bar-Abbas! Give us Bar-Abbas!' 'Bar-Abbas! Give us Bar-Abbas!'

Bar-Abbas...Bar-Abbas...Bar-Abbas...' the chanting became inflamed by the hundreds of curious onlookers lingering about the Praetorium grounds in hopes of witnessing some gruesome spectacle. A strange unholy smog filled the atmosphere, and as the crowd began to inhale the tepid air surrounding them, their eyes glazed and their faces grew pallid and grey. Then thousands of dark, hunched wort devourers swarmed like a pack of wolves among the crowd and as the clawed demons spewed a sticky tarlike substance from their fangs, whispering satanic enchantments, a horrifying, new chanting began.

'CRUCIFY the Nazarene!' they cried. 'Crucify the Nazarene!' The demonized creatures clawed more deeply into their skulls. 'Crucify Him ... Crucify Him...' the macabre mantra rose through the skies.

Jesus stared, through bloody, glazed eyes, far in the distance towards the monstrous black chariot that was descending swiftly through the darkening clouds over Jerusalem.

Lucifer lifted his visor, his eyes glued to Jesus' blood-spattered face. And smiled in triumph.

CHAPTER THIRTY-SIX

THE PLACE OF THE SKULLS

THE SKIES OF the First Heaven were eerily silent. Deserted. Nothing stirred save for the eastern horizon that was completely filled by Yehovah's white-feathered warrior eagles hovering over the steep onyx foundations, under the heights of the clouds.

In supplication. Silent. Waiting.

The twenty-four ancient Kings of Yehovah lay prostrate, their faces flung to the ground in the Gardens of Fragrance. In supplication. Silent. Waiting.

Jether the Just, knelt at the entrance to the throne room. His head flung on the jacinth floor. In supplication. Silent. Waiting.

A vast, stormy whirlwind blew from the entrance of the great rubied throne room, and out of this whirlwind burned a great, blazing cloud of blue fire, filled with flashes of lightning. Rumblings and thunderings emanating from its centre. The Great White Throne of incandescent light was descended in the Holy of Holies. Seated on the throne was the One whose unspeakable brilliance of His being shone as the blinding radiance of a million, million suns of the brightness of jasper and fiery sardius – the Ancient of Days, Yehovah.

Silent. Waiting. For His only begotten Son. The Prince of Glory. To be crucified at the hands of the prince of the damned.

~

Ten thousand times ten thousand of heaven's great angelic company were gathered in formation on the vast onyx plains of the Mount of the Congregation on the farthest sides of the north of the First Heaven. Their heads raised, right hands on their chests. Kneeling before their commander-in-chief.

'My noble Angelic Warriors.' Michael's tone was fierce but measured. 'This day, we face the most exacting undertaking of our Angelic Chronicles. What you are to witness will test your mettle to its very core. We patrol the Place of the Skulls as observers. Provocation, no matter how brutal or vile serves as no justification for reactionary behaviour.' Michael paused. 'Discipline. Restraint.' He paced back and forth, his fist clenched around his sword. 'Precision. Lucifer and his hordes' provocation this day will without doubt inflame even the toughest of angelic champions. Draw on every ounce of your rigorous training.' Michael dropped to one knee. 'For you will surely need it,' he whispered. He raised his head to Gabriel, who stood far off on the very top of the gleaming onyx mount, the Sword of Justice raised.

'Rise, fearsome dread warriors of Yehovah's armies!' Gabriel declared.

As one, the Hosts of Heaven rose. Silent. Their noble, burnished faces grim.

Michael lifted the Sword of State, leapt into his chariot. Michael saluted, drew his silver helmet down over his face, then rode followed by the First Heaven's fearsome angelic legions in their War Chariots.

To the Place of the Skulls.

Golgotha.

⮐

Michael rode through the strangely deserted skies of the First Heaven, the First Heaven's armies thundering behind. His soul was filled with a terrible foreboding.

Swiftly he left behind the shimmering indigo horizons of the Second and Third Heavens, riding the dark flashing thunderbolts, at last entering the strange swiftly falling dusk that was descending over Golgotha like a thick, shadowy veil, drawing ever closer to the Place of the Skulls. His angelic host hovered well back in the murky skies.

The sweltering Palestine heat hung heavily in the darkening sky. Through the descending gloom, Michael's gaze was drawn to three figures nailed to three wooden crosses on the enormous stark boulder. A lone, frail figure was nailed to the centre cross, His hair matted with congealed sweat and blood. Michael stared, horrified, unable to lower his gaze.

Jesus' head was bowed, His tangled, bloody hair was fallen over His bruised face, His body covered in wounds and putrefying sores, marred beyond recognition, His eyes stared

313

ahead, listless and dull, unseeing, His tendons crushed, His veins lacerated by cruel iron nails. Jesus of Nazareth.

Slowly Jesus lifted His head, and for a moment His eyes became clear. Through the cloud of pain, a fleeting smile of recognition glimmered on His parched lips.

'Michael,' he mouthed, His eyes lingering on the purple flag that flew high and proud from the pure golden cherubim and seraphim statues on Michael's war chariot. The flag of the royal house, emblazoned with Yehovah's golden seal. Then suddenly, Jesus' eyes filled with a deep apprehension.

Michael knew that he smelled devilry on the sultry breeze. He followed Jesus' clouded gaze. There in the distance, beyond Michael's angelic warriors, Satan's champion, Moloch, prince of death, proud and terrible, rode the darkening clouds over Jerusalem. His legions of fallen satanic princes, the butchers of Perdition, held Perdition's banner of death billowing out behind them as they drew closer to the Place of the Skulls. The great satanic princes rode, followed by the fallen Archangels of Ashtoroth, the Thrones of Folcador, and the Shaman Kings, their long, tangled black hair flying, yellow eyes narrowed, green mucus dripping from their thin, purple mouths.

Michael hid his face from Jesus' searching, loving eyes, then rode higher above the descending clouds, the hosts of heaven following close behind as Lucifer's hordes began their descent towards Golgotha. The menacing black clouds descended swiftly, carrying the fallen hosts' gleaming black war chariots nearer to the three wooden crosses. The satanic princes watched with a brooding fascination from their chariots. Silent. Menacing. Millions of hell's rabid demonic battalions lined up behind them across the horizon. A dark depraved host of fallen angels and demons, waiting for the spoils of war finally to fall into their clutches. Today they would reap hell's great trophy: the Nazarene.

Suddenly there was a great stirring in the heavens. The battalions of dark chariots moved aside, creating a pathway in the clouds for the mammoth dark-winged stallions that drew the monstrous black iron war chariot that carried the king of darkness himself. Thirty stallions surged through the skies, their monstrous veined webbed wings beating rhythmically to the dark arias of the Necromancer choirs of the damned. Slowly the war chariot descended on thunderbolts, directly above the Place of the Skulls, opposite the central wooden cross.

Lucifer rose from the chariot and stepped out onto a thunderbolt. He stood, arms folded, tall and imperious, Imperial ruler of hell's infernal army, his inscrutable sapphire gaze riveted on the contorted, blood-spattered face of the Nazarene nailed to the wooden cross below him. Lucifer raised his arms to the heavens.

'Omniscient Father.' A deranged, almost wrenching sob escaped him. 'I would have spared you this . . . ' He surveyed the straggling crowd that surrounded the cross below.

'Look what they have done to You, Nazarene . . . ' his strangled whisper was barely audible. ' . . . this Race of Men – Yehovah's obsession,' he spat.

With enormous effort, Jesus struggled to lift His head from His chest, His gaze became lucid. He held Lucifer's gaze for a long moment. His fierce, noble gaze penetrating to the very core of Lucifer's soul. Then Jesus' head fell back onto His chest.

Lucifer turned his head to see Michael at attention standing in the distance, directly opposite him. 'How the tables are turned now, brother,' he hissed. Jesus struggled again to raise His head. Michael watched helplessly as Jesus' eyes filled with the unfathomable distress of His separation from His Father. Alone. Vulnerable. A slow malicious smile of triumph spread across Lucifer's face.

'Oh how Thou art fallen ... Nazarene ... '

Michael stared ahead, his fingers trembling, grasping the Sword of State.

'I shall kill His only begotten, Michael, that *I* might again be His only begotten,' Lucifer leered.

'*Never* will you be His begotten, Lucifer,' Michael whispered, his voice soft but forbidding. 'You, the unrepentant,' he raised his face to Lucifer's, his green eyes blazing with passion, 'are cut off from Yehovah and his mercies for all time.'

'This very day, Michael,' Lucifer hissed, 'the Nazarene will be incarcerated in the vaults of hell.'

He looked back to the dying figure on the cross, an evil fire flickering in his eyes.

'I return to Perdition!' Lucifer lashed his stallions savagely. 'I unleash the Catacombs of Ichabod!' he cried, then took off and rode the thunderbolts, disappearing into the darkening purple skies.

Chapter Thirty-seven

GOLGOTHA

J OTAPA MOVED SWIFTLY through the thinning crowd that, now tiring of its sport, was turning for home. She was exhausted, worn out, having pushed Ayeshe and the royal Arabian stallions to the limits of their endurance to reach Jerusalem in record time. And even so, she was too late. Tears fell down her cheeks, sobs wracking her body as she pushed her way against the straggling throng. She and Ayeshe had ridden to meet Zahi at Joanna's house, only to discover that the trial had been accelerated. The Hebrew had been crucified.

Joanna's house was deserted. Zahi was missing, perhaps in hiding – she couldn't be sure. It was all such a disaster!

Huge sobs racked her small frame. Her mind was racing. Why had she stopped Aretas from journeying to confer with Pilate? Aretas as king of Arabia wielded influence with the

Hebrew leaders and the Romans. The Hebrew would still be alive. He could have taken refuge in Arabia and preached to the masses, who would have received Him as their own.

Jotapa moved onward. Nearer, much nearer to the three crosses. She lifted her face to the centre cross, then placed her hand over her mouth to still her scream. The Hebrew was unrecognizable, bloodied and unidentifiable save for His eyes – those clear, piercing eyes that were now glazed over with pain.

It was her fault that He was dying ... her far-fetched notions of His kingdom and His Father, the king who would come and overthrow Rome and save Him. She moved closer. His torn flesh was already buzzing with flies. Birds of prey circled low overhead. Jotapa's flesh crawled. Exhausted, grief-stricken, and miserable, she fell on her knees in the mud, pushing her unruly locks off her grimy face with dusty gold-ringed fingers, too weak to lift herself up from the dirt.

Slowly she raised her head. A tall young man wearing a kingfisher blue cowled hood dressed in vestments of the very affluent, stood back from the crowd, his gaze never moving from the figure on the cross. She stared mesmerized, strangely drawn to him.

Slowly he turned his imperial face to hers. His beautiful features were flawless: the perfectly carved cheekbones; the long, fine platinum locks; the regal countenance. His gentle grey eyes were red-rimmed from weeping.

'Do not grieve for Him, daughter,' he murmured. 'You could not have saved Him.' He placed his hand gently on her shoulder. She frowned, bewildered, as a warm, gentle tremor surged through her being, invigorating her entire body. A strange comfort surged through her. She frowned. She had grown up surrounded by monarchs. The Hebrew had influential followers. This man was no commoner, his bearing was that of a prince. He was of royal blood, she was certain of it.

The young man turned his back to her, gazing back up at the cross, his lips moving fervently in supplication.

Jotapa tore her gaze away form him and rose unsteadily to her feet, searching around for Ayeshe, who was lost in the crowd. A short way from Jesus of Nazareth's cross stood Mary, His mother, and three of His disciples. Below Him, five red-faced drunken Roman centurions played dice. A few yards from them, her lithe old Nabatean servant stared up at the cross, transfixed.

Jotapa watched as Jesus' mouth moved, each word sheer agony. She leaned nearer, straining to hear.

'I . . . thirst . . . '

One of the soldiers staggered to his feet as a second threw him a filthy sponge. Drunkenly, the first tried to thrust it in their jug of Posca – that Jotapa knew to be the cheap soured wine of the legionnaires, but the jug fell onto its side. The second snatched the sponge and, with his filthy hand, soaked it in the spilled wine.

Jotapa gasped, her grief swiftly turning to fury. 'Ayeshe!' she commanded. 'Bring me the basket of medicinal herbs – hurry!'

She ran a few paces, grabbing a branch from the hyssop vines nearby, then scrabbled in the basket, bringing out a medicinal sponge. Raising herself to her full imperial height, she pushed through the drunken soldiers, catching the last dregs of wine in the sponge. She turned to the centurion and smiled coquettishly, holding the hyssop stick out to him.

'He thirsts.' She smiled pleadingly. 'Please...' She gestured to Jesus.

The centurion looked at her with half-drunken interest. 'You His sister?' he drawled.

Jotapa nodded vehemently. 'Yes ... yes, I am His sister. Please help Him.'

She held her breath as the Roman soldier staggered to his feet and stumbled over to the centre cross, his companions laughing raucously all the while. He turned back to stare at Jotapa, who nodded eagerly, once again gesturing to Jesus. She held her breath, desperate to soothe His raging, burning thirst.

She held her breath as the centurion thrust the hyssop stick to Jesus' lips. Jesus drank from it. Tears fall down Jotapa's cheeks. 'Thank you! Thank you!' she sobbed, her eyes riveted on Jesus' face.

Thunder clapped, the dark clouds opened in fury, and the rain started lashing down.

Jesus opened His eyes. Looking straight at Jotapa, the faintest smile flickered on His lips. She stared at Him, transfixed. Then His head fell back down onto His chest.

Somehow, although she knew that it could not be so, she sensed that He knew she was there. Knew that she had tried to help Him. That He had been comforted.

'Come, princess,' Ayeshe cried above the storm, wrapping her in her cloak.

'I cannot leave Him,' Jotapa cried, rooted to the ground.

Ayeshe's eyes grew fierce. 'In a moment it will be too dark to see the way back, princess.' He grasped her arm. 'Zahi is ours,' he added. 'The Hebrew is not of our world. His God will take care of Him.'

And Ayeshe drew her after him down the hill, following the drenched and horrified crowd away from the terrible scene. She hesitated as they passed the young man, who stood with his hands raised in jubilation, gazing upward in wonder, oblivious of the rain lashing down on him.

She turned back to the cross, then to Ayeshe. 'We must find Zahi!'

◠

Lucifer vanished from the Crypts of the Shadows into the Catacombs of Ichabod materializing before the towering garnet altar.

He strode swiftly past the monstrous warlock cauldrons of bubbling hellbroths and bladderwrack pushing past the great magenta veil, until he stood in the Unholy of Unholies.

The thirteen Warlock Kings of the West knelt in the Inner Sanctum. They were clothed in the glistening white high priests garments of the Fallen, chanting incantations, their hands raised but Lucifer's attention was fixed solely on the three colossal shadowed Catacombs of Ichabod that lay behind them.

Eighteen misshapen three-headed Shaman-Ogres stood, the height of the gates, a hundred feet high, guarding the Catacombs. Each spiked Catacomb Gate was bound by monstrous iron shackles.

Dracul lifted his bony luminous green face to Lucifer's.

'We are prepared for the unleashing of the Iniquities of

the Race of Men from the Catacombs, Your Excellency.
The Shaman-Ogres await your command.'

Lucifer nodded.

The gargantuan Shamen Ogres let out a deafening roar,
then tore the iron shackles from the iron Catacomb Gates
with their monstrous strength. The thirteen Warlock Kings
of the West raised their hands, their long white capes flying
in the tempests of Ichabod.

'Unleash the Iniquities of the Race of Men!' Lucifer
cried.

As one, the Shaman-Ogres strained their weight against
the first mammoth Gate. Slowly it swung open. Instantly a
million black raging cyclones and clawed grotesque demons
erupted ferociously engulfing the Unholy of Unholies,
knocking the Warlock Kings and Ogres violently to the
ground.

Only Lucifer stood in the midst of the ferocious swirling
black cyclones, drinking in the iniquities in sheer exhiliration. Then the black cyclones erupted violently straight
through the Crypts of the Shadows, through the cupola of
the Black Palace in a savage churning black mass headed
straight for the Place of the Skulls.

⌒

Michael walked up the Nave of the throne room towards
Jether. 'I return from Golgotha. 'He bowed his head.
'Lucifer opens the Catacombs of Ichabod.'

'It has begun. He visits the entire rebellion of the Race of
Men on Christos.' Jether whispered. 'Past, present and
future.' He bowed his head, his hands trembling.

Michael clasped his shoulder.

'Lucifer's triumph will be shortlived. He plays into our hands. It will soon be over.'

'That they too may know Him,' Jether uttered.

⤳

The ferociously seething cyclones swirled above a rapidly growing gulf above Golgotha. Jesus' hair blew violently as every particle of His being was instantly immersed in a violent light storm that coursed like an electric tempest through His being, lifting Him inches from the cross, then thrusting Him violently back against the coarse wood. He raised His face in horror to the black swirling gales that raged overhead, visible only to Gabriel and the legions of the First Heaven and those of the fallen.

The cyclones crashed through the gulf, their ferocious power unleashed on Jesus as generation after generation's evil depraved ravings of the Race of Men and hell's demons descended towards Jesus – a lewd wave of unending filth. A million, million blasphemies, the wicked darkened imaginings of the Race of Men resounded through the Place of the Skulls.

'Eloiiii!' Jesus screamed, his voice drowned out by the discordant, raging profanities, 'Father … Fa … th … er … ', His agonized scream rang out through the darkening skies as His body jerked with violent convulsions.

Moloch and his slayers watched from their chariots in exhilaration.

⤳

The Catacombs of Ichabod fell silent. Nothing stirred. Finally Lucifer lifted his head. Then raised his hand.

'Release the Maladies of Ichabod!' he cried. Instantly the eighteen Shaman-Ogres pulled the second mammoth gate open. A grisly spine-chilling shrieking of a million, million harpies erupted from the Catacombs. There was silence for a full minute, then an infinite horde of purple bloodied harpies spewing hot sputtering aids viruses and living writhing cancers, erupted from the yawning cavern. Millions of leech-vampires of Infirmities, with eeled bodies, scaled wings and bat-like heads writhed in the seething cosmic tempests, disgorging plagues and leprosies from their ulcerated pale grey mouths. An evil smile lingered on Lucifer's lips as they surged up through the cupola of the Black Palace, their translucent wings flapping frenziedly through the Skies of Perdition, headed in straight for the Place of the Skulls.

⬅

The bloodied harpies and leech vampires descended on the centre cross like a violent seething shroud, their pincers and talons ripping into Jesus' limbs, their ulcerated lips leeched onto His chest expelling their infected viruses until His skin became a mass of purpled bloodied welts, a living writhing mass of rotting flesh. Leprous nodules covered His lips and eyes, swollen thrice their size, swelling cancers multiplied and spread across His abdomen and chest, a white film covered His eyes until Jesus stared ahead completely blind. Gabriel lowered his eyes from Jesus' hideous disfigurement.

⬅

From the First Heaven, Xacheriel stared in horror at Jesus. 'Every plague and disease Lucifer has conjured up in his sweltering crypts of Perdition he now visits on Christos...'

'He bears the full brunt of Lucifer's malevolent maladies calculated ahead to destroy the Race of Men.'

⤺

'*Eloi* ... *Eloi*...' ('Father ... Father...')

Jesus' blood-curdling cry reverberated to the revelator eagles gathered on the eastern horizons, to the angelic companies gathered in formation on the vast onyx plains of the mount of the congregation, to the ancient elders of Yehovah lying prostrate in the Gardens of Fragrance. '*Eloi*...' ('Father!')

Jether, knelt inside the rubied entrance, his face raised to the throne. The chilling scream echoed down the deserted corridors of the Tower of Winds, through the seven chambers of the labyrinths of the seven spires, through the vast, stormy whirlwind that blew from the entrance of the great rubied throne room, to the great, blazing cloud of fire and lightning – resounding before the Great White Throne of incandescent light descended in the Holy of Holies, until it reached the One whose unspeakable brilliance of His being shone as the blinding radiance of a million, million suns. The Ancient of Days.

His agonized screams resounded off the throne room walls.

Jether raised his head from the jacinth floor, his eyes red-rimmed from weeping, and stood.

'Jesus of Nazareth comes forth from the land of men bearing the darkness of Perdition, bearing the Iniquities of the Race of Men.

And then the being seated on the white throne spoke. His voice resounded through the incandescent white light, through the labyrinths, and out to the entrance to the Holy of Holies . . . Filled with sorrows. Full of compassions.

'Open the doors.' Yehovah uttered.

Michael turned to his Generals and trembling, raised his sword.

'Yehovah's Judgements commence!' he cried.

⤸

Fifty of Michael's battalion pushed the colossal Rubied Door that soared thousands of feet. A league down the nave of the throne room, in front of the altar blew a fierce stormy indigo whirlwind of thunder and lightning, and out of the whirlwind burned a great blazing cloud.

From its epicentre a great and terrible roaring filled the throne room chamber. Deafening peals of thunder resounded from the walls of the chamber, as though the very atoms themselves were pulsating. Blue lightning bolts, shot through with burning white fires, brilliant as the orbs of a thousand suns, flashed from the magnificent throne that was now faintly visible through the glare, more than a league down the great nave. Seven blazing torches burned in front of the throne as seven flaming columns of white fire, and in the midst of each torch glowed the coals of the spirit of Yehovah.

Jether walked slowly into the blazing cloud of the whirlwind. 'Behold the lamb of God, slain for the iniquities of the Race of Men awaits the Judgements of Yehovah.' He collapsed to his knees.

⤸

Gabriel stared up at the bruised and battered figure on the centre cross from under his blue cowled hood. Jesus' eyes were dull, His hair matted and bloody. A strange darkness was descending down on the city, towards the Place of the Skulls. Gabriel gazed, transfixed as the thunderous churning indigo skies forked open directly above the stark knoll. Ferocious blue bolts of lightning swirled furiously above the yawning gulf.

'The Judgements of Yehovah,' he uttered in horror. Jesus raised His face in dread to the swirling violet whirlwinds of Judgement of the First Heaven that raged overhead.

The whirlwinds crashed through the gulf, their ferocious power throwing Him violently against the splintered wood of the cross as the first blue bolt of lightning struck Jesus' body.

∽

'Christos bears the Judgements of Yehovah for the iniquities of the Race of Men,' Maheel whispered, frozen.

∽

Gabriel watched in horror as a second bolt of light and wind struck Jesus' body, then a third, His back arced back and forth against the jagged wood in agonized pain, sweat pouring from His pores. A terrorizing sound erupted of the torment of a million, million damned souls, souls that rejected Yehovah. The screams from the penetentiaries of hell. Demented, wailing chilling screams resounded from Golgotha's skies. The blood-curdling screaming of a thousand, thousand future generations destined for the Lake of Fire echoed across the Place of the Skulls.

~

'He takes the place of the murderers, paeodophiles, adulterers, all that enact the darkened deeds of the Race of Men...' Jether shook his head in wonder. 'That those of the Race of Men who would accept His sacrifice may go free.'

~

Moloch caressed his cat-o'-nine-tails, his mind racing back to his encounter with the Nazarene over Lazarus, gripped by a strange unease. Then as another cyclone came raging towards the cross from the darkening skies Jesus began to scream. A chilling, tortured, agonized screaming. A slow evil smile of understanding spread across the butcher of Perdition's features.

'He is separated from Yehovah. Butchers of Perdition – prepare the Nazarene's chariot!' he roared. 'He is ours!'

'*Eloi...Eloi!*' ('Father...Father!') Jesus' agonized spine-chilling scream rang out through the Palestine sky. Moloch and his butchers cackled with demonic laughter as a fourth and fifth whirlwind of judgement erupted from the throne. Jesus screamed in agony as the whirlwinds struck His temple with an intense ferocity.

Gabriel pushed his way through the violent winds until he reached the very base of the cross, his face just inches from Jesus' mangled, lacerated feet. '*Eloi...*' ('Father!') Jesus screamed frenziedly in agony. '*Eloi...lama sabachthani?*' ('Why have You forsaken Me?')

'We are here, Christos...' Gabriel whispered, his hand

clutching the wood of the cross. His entire body trembled uncontrollably. 'He has not forsaken you...'

Jesus' eyes flickered open momentarily. A single tear rolled down His cheek.

'That they, too, may know Him...' Then Gabriel laid his head onto Jesus' feet, sobbing wretchedly, his long fair locks mingling with Jesus' blood.

Then as suddenly as the whirlwinds had erupted, the Place of the Skulls fell silent.

꒰

The Rubied Doors closed with a shudder.

꒰

Jether stood to his feet and staggered towards the secret passageway to the Tower of Winds. 'I make haste to Golgotha.'

CHAPTER THIRTY-EIGHT

THE VEIL

JETHER MOVED SWIFTLY through the thinning crowd towards the knoll, staring up at the figure on the centre cross, from under his cloak. His gaze unwavering. The rain lashed down on his cheeks, the furious winds blew his cloak almost from his shoulders. But his attention remained steadfastly on the figure on the cross before him as the strange and terrible darkness descended like a shroud across the city of Jerusalem.

'Have mercy, God!' A petrified woman shrieked behind him as she ran to catch up with the last of the stragglers leaving the hillside, racing vainly against the darkness.

Out of the falling gloom, in front of the cross, Jether could faintly recognize the shadowy forms of the virgin mother and her faithful consolers.

And one other.

The tall figure was peculiarly dressed. Swathed in a great emerald chequered velvet cloak of exceptionally fine cloth, his features hidden under a wide-brimmed, pea-green suede fedora, the hat of a style not seen anywhere in the world of men. There was something about his manner, his bearing, that Jether found disquieting.

Lightning struck again, and this time its bolts reverberated with such intensity on the Place of the Skulls, that Jether thought the entire knoll might collapse in two. A third strike illuminated the sharp, bony features of the cloaked form. Jether recognized him instantly.

It was Charsoc, the grand magus, Lucifer's dark sorcerer, watching with pale, sightless eyes through his evil twisted spirit as only a fallen angelic being could. He tipped his hat to Jether in passing acknowledgment and continued his incessant staring at the Nazarene nailed to the cross.

Jether wrapped his cloak tighter and, mustering all his strength, thrust his body step by step against the ferocious gales until he stood only a pace away from Charsoc.

'Could your carrion's heart not even leave Him alone until His last?'

Charsoc smiled faintly.

'Ah!' he said, his eyes not leaving Jesus for a second.

'Your discernment is accurate, as usual, revered Jether. We await the pickings of the slaughter eagerly. But today I am, you could say, the controller of the proceedings. It is my responsibility to ascertain the second His last breath in our domain is extinguished. I shall immediately verify my findings in the courts of Perdition; then He is legally our

property. Our prince of carnage awaits in his chariot.'
Charsoc motioned to where the sadistic and menacing
Moloch stood, his craggy face raised. Leering from the
thunderbolt.

'The butcher of Perdition – it is a moment I shall greatly
relish.'

He gestured towards his own white gaping eyeballs.

'It may have escaped your memory, but I have the
Nazarene to thank for my eternal sightlessness. And after
our little tête à tête in the seventh chamber, have no naive
expectation that my mercy shall exceed my vengeance,
Jether.' He caressed his scarred bony fingers.

'I am thin-skinned.'

Jether lowered his eyes.

'And what *are* your procedures?' he asked. His voice
dangerously quiet.

'The second the Nazarene breathes His last on this
planet, Moloch and his butchers have orders to seize Him.
He dies on this planet, with defiled blood, as one of the Race
of Men – therefore, we the fallen have jurisdiction over
His body. He is ours. And our emperor, Lucifer, is His
sovereign king. He will make a grand bargaining chip with
Yehovah, I don't doubt. But don't think, Jether, even for a
moment that He will be returned to the First Heaven in the
same pristine condition in which He left ... His torture of
today is but a pale shadow of what awaits Him in the
Penitentiaries of the lower vaults of Perdition...'

Still Charsoc's eyes never left Jesus' form.

'There is already revelry in the vaults of the damned,
awaiting His arrival. He shall be exhibited on the gates, but
first Moloch shall lash Him to the black altar with barbed

332

cords and torture Him with the hellhounds until He revokes Yehovah.'

'Your fall from grace has almost surpassed your master's, it would seem.'

Charsoc smiled slowly. 'The Nazarene fades,' he observed dryly. 'The life forces of the Race of Men ebb from Him swiftly.'

Jether stared at Jesus' lacerated veins, the gaping wounds from the recent scourging which were already turning gangrenous, the bruised and broken body, so bloodied it was marred beyond recognition.

Then, through the raging pain, Jesus lifted His head.

Charsoc followed His gaze, noting that He looked straight and deliberately towards Jether. For a fleeting moment, Charsoc could have sworn that a strange and exhilarated triumph lit the glazed and bloody eyes.

Then the voice that stilled the waters, that calmed the raging storms, that commanded satanic princes to be still, that opened blind eyes, and shattered the bowels of death uttered its last.

'Tetelestai!' ('It is finished!') Jesus screamed in exhilaration.

'Tetelestai! Tetelestai!' he cried.' It ... is ... finished!' He screamed, screamed until His voice was hoarse. Screamed until the last of His life force ebbed from Him in total exhaustion. Screamed until He expelled His final agonized dying breath.

Jether stared, trembling. 'His soul exchanged for the souls of the Race of Men.' Jether whispered, tears mingling with the hot rain on his cheeks, his face raised to the heavens in wonder.

Charsoc watched, a strange uneasiness filling his soul. Mystified. Then Jesus' head dropped onto His chest.

⤿

The heavy, glistening white veil of the First Heaven hung before the incandescent white throne beyond the Rubied Door, in the throne room of the First Heaven. Millions of angels lay prostrate. Unmoving before the throne.

Two resplendent great hands of light grasped the veil. Then with one movement, rent it from top to bottom.

'That they, too, may know Me!' Yehovah cried.

⤿

All at once, a great cacophony of the damned erupted from the bowels of the earth – a hellish din of triumph rising from the nether regions as the satanic shofar sounded.

And then, suddenly, from every quarter almost simultaneously, a strange, inexplicable silence fell. The infernal caterwauling subsided until there was no sound at all in the heavy, sweltering Palestine sky.

A subliminal roaring began that shook the trees and the three crosses above on the hill.

The earth underneath Charsoc shuddered and he was flung to the ground violently, the rocks sliding beneath his feet as he clung to the boulders about him. But even as Charsoc clawed the boulders for safe refuge, they split into smithereens about him. He lay face down in the dirt, the ground shuddering violently beneath him.

Jether watched in trepidation, the ground beneath him firm, seemingly untouched by the raging cataclysm.

'This man was truly the Son of God!' yelled a Roman centurion in terror, diving for safe cover.

Charsoc stumbled to his feet, levitated through the air, his jet black hair and beard blowing violently in the raging winds, until he stood next to Moloch in the chariot. He hung on to his strange broad-brimmed hat.

'Call for the dark scribes!' Charsoc cried, his eyes lit up in fervent exhilaration. 'We verify the Nazarene's death in the courts of Perdition.'

'The Dark Watchers stand ready to deliver the findings to the First Heaven's high council, to be witnessed in Eternal Law,' Moloch growled.

Charsoc clapped his hands in triumph. 'Moloch, my wicked prince!' He gestured to the now limp and lifeless body hanging from the cross.

'Transport our master's booty to your slayers for the triumphal procession.' Charsoc turned deliberately to Jether. 'Our master awaits us.' He smiled a smile of the damned. 'Escort the Nazarene to hell!'

⌒

Moloch's barbarous satanic vandals wrenched Jesus of Nazareth's spirit from the bruised and battered body on the cross. Instantly it took on the same form as the body it had inhabited, though it was of a different, more ethereal substance. Otherwise it was identical.

Moloch's fallen host manacled Jesus' wrists and ankles with heavy iron fetters that ripped cruelly into His tortured flesh. 'Your sorceries are spent, Nazarene!' Moloch leered. 'Bind His mouth!' he commanded. The butchers bound Jesus' mouth with filthy cloth soaked in deadly nightshade,

335

then brutishly hauled Him onto their shoulders, seizing Him in a vice-like grip.

Moloch raised his whip. Instantly, they were sucked violently downward as though by some ferocious centrifugal force. Downwards ... downwards, thousands of miles downward, towards the molten core of the Earth, the party of the damned descended.

Down through the mouths of seething volcanos. Through boiling seas of molten lava, until they emerged into the strange, churning violent world of floating continents and upside-down mountains that raged at 11,000 degrees Fahrenheit. The blast furnace that was the outskirts of hell.

~

Michael turned to the angelic legions. Ashen. 'Gabriel meets us on the plains of Perdition. Christos commandeers the Ark of the Race of Men. We prepare for assault.'

CHAPTER THIRTY-NINE

HELL'S GATES

THE MASSIVE IRON Gates of Hell soared a thousand feet high into the hazy, bleak gloom of hell's smouldering skies.

Six hundred gargantuan, jaundiced-eyed demonic seraphims nested on top of the colossal black iron gateposts of Perdition, their great scaled claws slashing at the posts. Red hot fires flamed from their nostrils and ears. Their black-veined webbed wings flapped like giant bellows as they patrolled hell's skies, fanning the blistering blue flames of hell's 'Ring of Fire'. Hell's sentries.

The great circular chasm of blue flames blazed miles high, stretching from the base of the gates, encircling the savage, scorching black pitch plains of Perdition.

Lucifer, magnificently attired in his ceremonial regalia, reclined on his black diamond throne, which was carried on the shoulders of twelve satanic princes. His gleaming raven hair, intricately plaited with flaming jewels, fell past his shoulders to his glistening satin garments. On his head rested his crown of state of pure gold embedded with chrysolite and black rubies. A glistening white cloak hemmed with ermine was draped across his shoulders, and his sandals were of freshly molten gold. He held hell's sceptre in his left hand.

The king of hell. Followed by thousands of his menacing satanic warrior princes, who in turn were led by the ghoulish company of hooded Shaman Kings's, hell's macabre drummers. The legion of Necromancers, wizards of the dead, marched near the gates, their great armies of skeletons and zombies filling the plains.

Charsoc walked below Lucifer, next to the procession, his hat and cloak now exchanged for his favoured bright vermillion and orange striped flowing robes of Chief Magus. His sorcerer's hat was pointed, its tip and rim of platinum. His scarlet shoes were long and narrow and curved upwards at the toe with diamond buckles that changed colour with each new dark incantation. Charsoc held his crooked magus rod high. Live serpents writhed from under the folds of his robes onto the burning pitch below.

Ahead of both Lucifer and Charsoc, in advance of the fiendish parade, swaggered the leering Moloch and his horde of strapping demonic butchers, to the ominous rhythm of hell's pulsating war drums.

Jesus, manacled and bound, clad only in the bloody loincloth in which He was crucified, was raised high on the massive oiled shoulders of ten of Moloch's most depraved slayers. They marched directly in front of Lucifer.

The Nazarene – hell's trophy.

As the demonic armies approached the gates, the skies grew black with thousands of screeching banshees. They hovered overhead, hissing asps flowing from their bare skulls, their wings beating furiously as the riotous hellish army continued its march to the slow mutinous rhythm of hell's throbbing war drums.

The 'Ring of Fire' flamed ferociously. Hundreds of the seraph monsters left their nests and swooped down across the gates, their nostrils flaming, smelling the intruder. Their jagged claws slashed, hovering menacingly over the manacled Jesus.

A great shuddering drew nearer as a band of Shaman-Ogres lumbered towards the entrance, then peered through the iron bars, their squat yellow eyes glinting in the semi-darkness.

'We are the keepers of the Gates of Hell and the grave,' a voice rumbled.

'We await you and your trophy, O Satan, king of hell,' Ruber, leader of the Shaman-Ogres growled through the iron bars, leering at Jesus. The war drums stopped, and a heavy silence fell, broken only by the vicious snarling of the five-headed sentry hellhounds.

Twenty of the Luciferean Black Horde, led by Dagon, marched forward out of the darkness. Carried high on their shoulders was a huge black casket. 'We present the keys of hell,' Dagon roared.

The Black Guard placed the casket down before the gate and bowed deeply to Lucifer.

Dagon unlocked the casket and opened it.

Lying on a bed of magenta velvet was an enormous

golden key, engraved with angelic lettering, a ruby embedded in its crown.

Dagon nodded to his militia, and six of them hoisted the key up onto their shoulders and marched over to where Ruber stood, waiting in front of the lock.

Ruber held out his huge leathery hand, lifted the master key upward, and placed it in the lock, then turned it. The sound of a hundred monstrous locks of hell unbolting resounded through the lava plains.

'Welcome to your domain, master. Hell and the underworld await you.'

A hundred Shaman Ogres heaved the iron monstrosity back. Slowly the mammoth gateway opened, the entrance into the molten core of the earth. The underworld of departed spirits. Fiery blue tempests howled through the gates while molten lava rain lashed down on the procession as it passed through. Balberith waited next to Lucifer's magnificent dark-winged royal stallion, tethered inside the gates.

Ahead loomed a raised road of crystal ore, with seething pitch glowing red beneath it. The road became a fluid glass passageway that fell away on both sides into a blasting chasm of molten iron ore that stretched thousands of miles below into the very bowels of the earth. This was the Crystal Corridor of the underworld, some three thousand miles below the surface and some fifteen hundred miles across – earth's inner core.

Ahead, glistening through the crystal core, a league in the distance, stood the Black Palace – Lucifer's imposing palace of black crystal. Inside the palace citadel, resting beyond the magenta veil in the black necropolis, lay the 'Ark of the Race of Men'. Guarded by the satanic warriors of Lucifer's Black Horde, his elite militia.

To the left of the corridor, through the transparent liquid crystal walls, loomed hell's monstrous penitentiaries, which incarcerated the wicked dead.

Millions of penitentiaries housing Lucifer's penal colonies were hewn out of the jagged iron cliffs, which stretched steeply upward thousands of feet and plummeted thousands of feet downward – the labour camps of the damned.

A thunderous malicious caterwauling rose from behind the iron bars – the tormented screams of millions of the wicked dead from the Race of Men, mingled with the cackling roar of hell's prison warders, the wort devourers and banshees that lined the corridor to Perdition, shrieking their incantations of the damned. To the right of the corridor, beyond a great gulf, lay the strange, gloomy shadowlands, the abode of the slumbering Righteous dead. The Grave.

It was one monstrous sheer block of translucent crystal that stretched thousands of miles above the corridor and fell thousands of miles beneath.

The twelve satanic princes laid Lucifer and his throne onto the ground. Lucifer rose. He turned, surveying Jesus, lifted high on the arms of Moloch's Philistine horde as they marched through the tempests and molten rain towards him. He raised his arm. 'Deliver the Nazarene to the underworld!' he cried, then pulled his cape tighter around him and mounted his stallion. Its black veined wings extended, and they flew ahead, straight into the raging tempests.

Instantly the party was sucked downward until the grey shadows of hell dimmed to the oppressive pitch blackness of the lower crystal road, lit only by the flickering lanterns of the wort devourers.

⌇

'On the left, Nazarene...' Lucifer smiled viciously as Moloch roughly pushed Jesus' head to the left, '...the rabble of the Race of Men who reject Yehovah – blasphemers, murderers, rebels...'

Screaming men and women, their eyes veiled with grimy opaque film, clawed blindly at the iron penitentiary walls, their lower bodies burning alive in the seething black lava.

'And now the crème de la crème of the Race of Men – the intellectuals...' Lucifer turned disdainfully towards the chain fences where a group of prisoners, screamed in torment, clawing wildly, the fingers of their spirit bodies torn and bleeding, their nails ripped from clawing the jagged barbed barrier.

'Atheists, philosophers, agnostics – all rejecting the existence of a personal creator. Their god was their own minds and opinions. They scream the most volubly when they arrive in my domain and discover that I was real.' Lucifer smiled. 'When they realize that Yehovah exists,' he shrugged, 'they are driven out of their minds and beg for death.' Lucifer raised his hand. 'Release the hell bulls into the penitentiary, Adzeal.'

A hundred raging snarling hell bulls each weighing two thousand pounds, pawed the lava with their horn hooves, then charged the damned prisoners, their curved horns goring their bodies, throwing them onto a pile of writhing screaming prisoners in the corner of the burning black pitch.

'But then, this is hell. There is no death, only torments . . . And now, Nazarene, my prized ones . . . '

Moloch grabbed Jesus by the hair and swung His head violently to the right, beyond the great chasm. There was complete silence in the strange black gloom of the shadow lands. 'My Master's shadowed realm,' Moloch growled.

Gradually, the black faded to a great grey darkness.

Lucifer's voice dropped to a low, intimate tone. 'The grave,' he whispered in awe.

They rode slowly past the brazen gates of the monstrous great crystal barricades of the underworld – the dim outlines of the millions of men and women incarcerated in the murky ice lay as if in some strange slumbering limbo.

'They are all who have fallen asleep since the beginning of the world,' Charsoc whispered to Jesus. 'All who worshipped *Yehovah*, Nazarene.'

'They sleep the slumber of the righteous dead,' Lucifer hissed, '*Never* to awaken in my domain.'

They passed thousands more of the floating slumbering bodies frozen into the sheer block of ice. Almost godlike in stature, even in their slumber it was obvious that they were nearly seven feet tall, with angelic features and an unearthly glowing radiance that still issued from their bodies.

'Souls from the times of Adam,' gloated Charsoc. 'The glory of the Race of Men has diminished through the centuries – a consequence of the fall.'

'The glory of Perdition,' Lucifer crowed. 'His prophets, patriarchs, all who belong to Yehovah ... who belong to *You*, Nazarene – *all* under my jurisdiction. And when my time is up, according to my claim lodged in the councils of the First Heaven, each of them shall join me in the Lake of Fire.'

~~

Over a hundred million of the First Heaven's angelic warriors assembled on the sprawling bleak plains of Perdition, outside the Gates of Hell. Their armies stretched to the horizon in every direction.

Ahead of the vast angelic legions, positioned directly in front of the monstrous iron gates, rode Jether and the twenty-three ancient heavenly kings, mounted in a semi-circle on their winged white chargers. Imperial and forbidding. Their lances flashed with the lightnings of Yehovah and were upraised in their right hands. In their left they held high the blazing crimson standards with the sign of the cross.

On either side of them marched the heralds, the 'Proclaimers', blowing their shofars, with the banners of the First Heaven lifted high. Following them came ten thousand Great White Knights, their battering-rams at the ready.

Directly behind them, led by Gabriel attired in full battle regalia, marched his vast company of swift and agile archers, the Revelators, in suits of gleaming silver armour.

Overhead flew a million of the Revelator scouts, filling the length and breadth of the skies – the First Heaven's huge white-feathered warrior eagles. Around each eagle's neck was a circlet of gold embedded with rubies: the warriors' homing beacons.

Filling the plain to Gabriel's right, thundered Michael's

imperial knights mounted on their gold-caparisoned war stallions. Their gleaming broadswords were raised high, following the mighty commander of heaven's armies.

Michael rode bareback on his enormous black war stallion, covered from head to toe in his ceremonial golden armour, the Sword of State raised high in his right hand.

Escorting him and his armies were the immense company of the White Winged Lions of Yehovah, their white manes glistening, their enormous white wings extended. Their thunderous roaring resounding across the plains and echoing through the penitentiaries of hell.

The Great and terrible Armies of the Lord.

⌒

Dagon galloped his charger towards Lucifer and Charsoc. 'The First Heaven's armies gather on the plains of Perdition, Your Majesty,' he growled. 'Your brothers, the great princes, lead them.'

'Yes, yes...,' Lucifer said dismissively. 'I hear the roarings and commotion. We knew they would assemble.' He smiled triumphantly at Charsoc. 'We hold their *King*.'

'They have no claim,' Charsoc declared.

Lucifer nodded, grinning evilly. 'Michael well knows that if they so much as set foot through my gates, they trespass according to Eternal Law ... And my brothers are *sticklers* for Eternal Law.' He yawned. 'Relay to my royal brother a message. Tell him I have a tomb specially prepared for the Nazarene: the black sepulchre.'

'And *I* have one waiting for Michael!' Moloch roared.

A mighty roar rose up from Moloch's butchers. 'Tear Prince Michael asunder!' they howled.

345

Lucifer smiled. 'Let us forget my brother's torments for the moment. We have our prize – we hold their King.'

'My Lord...,' Moloch bellowed, his voice full of dark intent. 'Permission for some sport, great king of hell.' He bowed deeply, and Lucifer nodded. 'We would bow before the Nazarene,' he said, leering at Jesus. 'We would crown Him King.'

A grotesque smile lit up Lucifer's face. He nodded.

'Let us crown the Nazarene King!' Moloch roared. At this, a strident wail rose from the wort devourers, soon echoed by the depraved multitudes inside the hellish penitentiaries.

The grim procession slowed at the dark laboratories. A party of cackling, orange-haired, deformed dark younglings emerged from the vast, sweltering underground corridors carrying a cruel-looking iron contraption, still glowing-hot from the smelting cauldron, to Moloch. It was a twisted iron crown of thorns moulded in iron.

Lucifer nodded. 'Crown the Nazarene, that He may be King of hell for a moment.'

Jeering laughter broke out anew among Moloch's legions. Hysterical cackles and demented laughter broke out on every side as Moloch lifted the scorching crown in his brawny arms, high above Jesus.

'Unbind His mouth, that we may hear the Nazarene's screams of agony!' Moloch roared. At once the vandals tore away the filthy cloths that gagged Jesus' lips.

Moloch pushed the cruel, jagged hot iron thorns down savagely onto His captive's skull.

An earth-shaking tremor shuddered, and at once the

crystal road collapsed into the burning pitch, like a magnet sucking the armies of hell down into the orange flames. As volcanoes spurted white-hot infernos around them, Moloch hovered above the jagged remains of the crystal path. One by one, his twelve butchers fell, sucked down by the ferocious flames. Charsoc was flung facedown onto the road, his eye sockets burning, his body twisting in agony. 'The Nazarene!' he cried as a blinding flash illuminated the shadowed penitentiary of the grave.

Lucifer watched in horrified disbelief as the brazen gates at the entrance to the shadowed realm shattered, the iron bars of the penetentiaries smashed to smithereens. Jesus of Nazareth had vanished. 'Where is the Nazarene!' Lucifer screamed. 'Mobilize hell's armies. Take every general, each satanic prince, to the Black Palace. Post them at every entrance. Command Dagon ... Darsoc – safeguard the black necropolis. The Nazarene would commandeer the Ark of the Race of Men!'

He stared past Charsoc, in horror as the slumbering inmates of the shadowed realm started to rouse inside their crystal prison. A blinding purple light flashed, illuminated the shadowlands as bright as a thousand thousand suns.

'Do it now!' he screamed, shielding his eyes as the iron penitentiary cliffs crumbled. 'The Nazarene would overturn hell!'

⁓

The vast armies of the First Heaven stood at attention, waiting in silence. Michael rode to Jether and the ancient ones in front of hell's gates. All twenty-four kings raised their white-crowned heads from their supplications.

Jether nodded to Michael.

Michael raised his hand, and a great, thunderous cry arose across the plains. 'Storm the Gates of Hell!' Michael cried. 'Lucifer is *mine!*'

CHAPTER FORTY

WARRIOR KING

JESUS STRODE THROUGH the marble halls of Lucifer's Black Palace, across the gleaming lapis floors, His imperial countenance set. His indigo robe billowed as He walked under the vast ornamental ceilings, past the sinister frescos that adorned the walls of Lucifer's inner sanctum. He raised His silver lash of cords in His fist, instantly the two enormous black gates to Lucifer's throne room flung open before Him.

Facing Him, a league away down the nave, in front of Lucifer's empty glistening diamond throne, stood ninety ferocious warriors – Lucifer's elite militia generals of the Black Horde. Dagon and his generals stared at Jesus in disbelieving dread.

Behind the throne lay a colossal black garnet altar its gleaming surface covered with thousands of sputtering black tapers permeating the chamber with the aroma of pure frankincense. Above loomed an enormous translucent vortex of black crystal. Beyond the altar lay the Golden Gates of the Chamber of the Black Necropolis that housed the Ark of the Race of Men.

'You trespass, Nazarene,' hissed Mulciber. Thick yellow drool fell from his black tongue onto the crystal floor.

The vigilantes stared defiantly at Jesus, their broadswords raised, their pale straw-coloured eyes narrowed, their mangled faces contorted with evil. Snarling black yellow-eyed jaguars paced restlessly, chained to their depraved masters, their black fangs visible.

'What do you want of us, Nazarene?' Ramuel spat, his eyes glinting with iniquity. 'We are the fallen – you have no place with us...'

Darsoc circled Jesus slowly like a wolf gauging its prey, his axe held high. Twenty of his gigantic minions joined him, their maces, cudgels, battle-axes, and cutlasses raised, their filthy braided black hair dangling past their thighs.

Jesus stood unmoving.

Dagon, towering a full head over his minions, shoved Mulciber and Ramuel out of his path. Fresh goat's blood dripped from his mouth and nostrils. Leering at Jesus through his glazed pale eyes, he shoved his iron ball and chain under his enemy's chin. Jesus deliberately unwound the lash. He could see Dagon's reflection in the crystal floor.

'Look at me when I speak, Nazarene!' he bellowed. He screamed instructions in a guttral angelic tongue to his militia, raising his other hand, which held a cat-o'-nine-tails tipped with jagged glass and serrated iron.

He lifted Jesus' head up, in line with his shoulder, but Jesus' eyes remained lowered, intent on Dagon's reflection.

Then Dagon swung his cat-o'-nine-tails, aiming straight for Jesus' neck.

Jesus swung His lash towards Dagon's whip and sent it clattering to the ground. The demonic horde laughed raucously.

'Butcher the Nazarene!' bellowed Dagon, lunging for Jesus with his sword.

Jesus swung His lash a second time. It tightened around Dagon's brawny neck. He pulled it tighter, till Dagon staggered to the floor, retching for breath. Jesus raised His gaze, and Dagon clutched his eyes with his hands, screaming in agony. Then Jesus turned to face the fallen rebels as the packs of snarling black yellow-eyed jaguars leapt ferociously towards Him, their black fangs snarling.

Jesus signed towards them with one deft movement. The jaguars fell backward as one, whimpering, slinking away through the throne room gates.

'The Nazarene's sorceries!' shrieked Mulciber.

Jesus gazed beyond the altar, past the dark sanctum, towards the chamber of the Black Necropolis.

Dagon followed his gaze. 'Loose the hellhounds, Menelik!' he screamed, writhing on the ground. 'He seeks the Ark of the Race of Men!'

A skeletal creature with vampiric fangs released the lock on a huge iron cage, and fifty black hellhounds, each with five heads breathing fire from their nostrils, raced towards Jesus with bared fangs.

Jesus raised His hand. The snarling hellhounds sprang

at Him, thrown back violently by the invisible shield surrounding Jesus. They fell, stunned to the floor, yelping.

Dagon clutched blindly for his sword, one hand still over his eye. 'I shall destroy you, Nazarene,' he snarled.

Jesus bent down and grasped him by the scruff of the neck, holding him off the floor till he screamed for breath. 'You and your master, Satan, have no claim on Me!'

Jesus flung Dagon to the ground as Lucifer's legions burst through the doorway. A thousand of Lucifer's dark minions stormed towards the robed figure, brandishing their blades and snarling obscenities.

Jesus raised His right hand, and a scorching sheet of flame rose from the floor and descended onto the renegade angelic host.

'The consuming fire!' Darsoc screamed, flailing at his blistering hands.

Nerve-jangling screams resounded throughout the chamber as the fallen were caught by the scorching, consuming waves of fire, to fall, burning alive, onto the ground. Their weapons clattered uselessly on the lapis floor.

Finally, the great and terrible Dagon knelt, trembling in dread, before Jesus. He removed his helmet and held it at his chest, his head bowed. 'We the fallen are conquered by You, O Nazarene.' He held out his sword.

'We are conquered by You,' thousands of dark voices echoed.

Dagon raised his head in terror to where Jesus stood fierce and silent, His head bowed. 'Not the Abyss, Nazarene!' Dagon whispered, his hands shaking uncontrollably. 'We beg You, Nazarene, not the Abyss!' Tortured wails resounded from all across the chamber. Jesus raised His head.

A great thundering erupted towards the terrorized fallen horde. A split second later, they shattered like glass, disintegrating into dust. Vanished, transported to the core of molten fire – the Abyss.

Jesus surveyed the empty throne room, then strode past the black altar, through to the portal of the Black Sanctum. His eyes narrowed; it was unguarded.

He pushed open the massive doors.

⤳

Lucifer's monstrous stallion beat the air frenziedly with its colossal black wings as they ascended past the unending penitentiaries, upward past the penal colonies landing just lengths away from the entrance to the massive iron gates of hell, when an earth-shattering shuddering shook the ground beneath them. Lucifer dismounted, trembling, mesmerized by the horrifying sight before him.

One of the immense iron Gates of Hell was collapsing before his eyes, ripped from its monstrous foundations by the giant battering-rams of the Angelic legions of fire and the White Knights. He watched as almost in slow motion, it crashed to the ground, pulverizing a legion of Shaman Ogres and fifty legions of the damned beneath its crushing weight.

Marduk appeared out of the gloom at his side. He bowed deeply, then grasped Lucifer's arm with his long pale fingers. 'My Emperor, I come with tidings from the Black Murmurers of Jerusalem. They report the veil … in the temple is torn,' he trembled, his yellow eyes gleaming evil concern. '... torn in a strange manner,' he added nervously.

'In what manner is the curtain of the Holy of Holies torn?' Lucifer asked, his face ashen.

'The curtain is rent in twain from top to bottom, Your Excellency,' Marduk replied. 'The Black Murmurers report that it was rent in two at precisely the time as the Nazarene exhaled His last breath at the Place of the Skulls.'

Speechless with horror, Lucifer finally drew his gaze away from the collapsing gates to Marduk.

'It is as the Wort Seers foretold.' He pushed his dishevelled hair out of his eyes.

'The veil is a message. *I*, the lightbearer, am banished from His face forever,' he muttered, 'but He would give the Race of Men *direct access* to His Presence.'

He stared, bewildered, as the vast armies of the First Heaven stormed through the entrance, decimating his great mercenaries of hell. To his right and left, thousands of his own savage Black Horde screamed in terror, beaten back by the ferocious company of white winged lions. Fleeing the tearing claws and bared teeth, the hordes of hell fled, flinging their weapons down, to the sanctuary of the lowest crypts of the shadows.

His giant gorgons lay wounded and bleeding, dying on the ground around him. He raised his face to the heavens; the eagle revelators circled overhead – the new owners of hell's skies. He walked unsteadily a few paces forward. 'No longer separated. Direct access ... but *how?*' he murmured.

Michael stood in the midst of the ferocious fighting outside the gates, his gaze fixed on Lucifer, who stood less

than a furlong away from him, well within the gates ...
unaware of Michael's gaze.

Michael slowly removed his gauntlets and threw them to
the ground, never taking his eyes off Lucifer.

He unsheathed the Sword of State, feeling for the
golden dagger in his boot. Then deftly pushed three long
razor-edged stiletto knives into his military sash behind his
back.

He dodged behind the lions and sprinted forward, just
out of Lucifer's view, through the right of the razed gates
until he came up directly behind Lucifer. He grasped
his arms from behind with his great strength, holding his
dagger at Lucifer's throat.

'Prepare to meet your end, Lucifer.'

Lucifer stared ahead. Caught completely off guard. His
mind racing. His face implacable.

'My devoted brother...,' he murmured, not a muscle
moving.

Then kicked his jackboot savagely into the back of
Michael's unprotected calves shin, the razor-sharp jagged
edge of his spur ripping Michael's flesh almost from the
back of his knee to ankle. 'You *would* have your pound of
flesh...' Lucifer hissed. Spinning around.

Michael stood in agony, the blood gushing from his calf.
A terrible blackness clouded his eyes.

'*You* know the angelic law. You are not on holy ground
here, Michael.' Lucifer smiled slowly. Merciless. Michael
swayed, his sword clattering to the ground. Reeling in pain.

'One clean thrust, and your head shears from your
shoulders,' Lucifer unsheathed his monstrous black gleaming sword of hell, '...and you are banished to the Abyss.'

He raised his gleaming broadsword high above Michael's neck. 'Farewell, brother – till the judgement!' he cried.

Marshalling all his iron discipline, Michael reached back into his sash and grasped the three stilettos he had hidden there, and with a last herculean effort, he drove them straight through Lucifer's neck with a single, brutal lunge.

Lucifer's face contorted in agony. He clutched his neck with both hands, ripping the three scimitar-like knives away with one great thrust. The blood spurted from the three great holes, spurting over his hands and flowing down his torso. He sank slowly to his knees, his broadsword fallen to the bloody dirt.

Michael kicked the broadsword away out of his grasp with his good leg.

Lucifer rent his robe, his hands shaking uncontrollably as he wrapped it around his neck to stem the bleeding. His head fell to the ground. With intense effort, he turned his face to Michael.

'The Nazarene is butchered,' he gurgled through the gushing blood. 'He lies bloodied – dismembered in the molten core,' Lucifer stared up at Michael, a strange malicious elation in his glazed eyes, '... burning in hell.'

Incensed, Michael picked up the Sword of State and held it over Lucifer's head.

'And you, brother, go to the Abyss!' he screamed. A slow evil smile flickered on Lucifer's lips.

'No, Michael!' Jether roared. 'It is his fabrication! He would escape the First Judgement!' Mustering every bit of his strength, Lucifer lifted a shaking finger towards hell's gates. His features contorted with a vicious hatred.

Jether and the twenty-three elders of the heavenly council

stood in the crystal corridor, just inside the gates, their white ceremonial robes blazing with light. Jether hurried over towards Michael.

'Leave his head intact,' he instructed quietly. 'He *must* face the First Judgement. Eternal Law *must* be fulfilled.' Xacheriel passed Obadiah a small vial, the youngling raced over to Michael and poured it onto his lower leg which was instantly restored. 'Shackle him!' Jether commanded.

Lucifer rose unsteadily to his knees from the ground, clasping the robe to his neck, struggling towards Jether, then collapsed, only a few paces from him. 'Jether!' he spat through the blood, his eyes glazed as Raphael and Ariel shackled his wrists and ankles, 'Hell is *my* territory!' he struggled for breath, 'You transgress Eternal Law.'

Jether circled Lucifer slowly, then stopped. 'You have not yet guessed?' His voice was dangerously soft. He looked down, staring directly into Lucifer's eyes, silent for a long moment.

'Jesus of Nazareth's father was not Joseph.' Jether's voice was crystal clear.

Lucifer stared up at Jether, momentarily confused.

'His body was created as the first, Adam, not replicated as is the manner of the Race of Men,' Jether said quietly.

'Joseph . . . ,' echoed Lucifer, bewildered.

'There *was* no conception by the Race of Men, Lucifer. Christos' seed was conceived by Yehovah.'

'Yehovah . . .' Lucifer stared blindly around him in horror, then dragged himself desperately through the dirt away from Jether. His robe fell from his neck onto the pitch.' He cannot . . . He breaches His own Eternal Law . . . ', he gasped.

'Two thousand years ago,' said Jether quietly, 'on Mount Moriah, a covenant was sealed between Yehovah and one of the Race of Men – one named Abraham, willing to sacrifice his son. Yehovah, in turn was lawfully released to sacrifice His own son on *your* planet. There *is* no breach of Eternal Law – Yehovah's conception of Christos' egg stands lawfully sealed by the High Courts of the First Heaven. It would have served you well to pay heed to the pathetic Hebrew rituals you so despise. Jesus of Nazareth's blood is undefiled!'

'*Un . . . defiled . . .*' Lucifer echoed, falling facedown into the lava, his blood draining from his body and mixing with the dirt.

'There will be no hellish trophies, no dancing in the streets of the Damned.' cried Jether. 'He has shed undefiled blood on behalf of the Race of Men. He met the claim – fulfilled Eternal Law.'

Michael knelt directly over Lucifer. 'His soul exchanged for the souls of the Race of Men.' He reached down and grasped Lucifer's tangled hair in his fist, twisting his head to his, looking fiercely into his clouding bloody gaze.

'The highest point of Mount Moriah – its summit is called *Golgotha.*' He let go of Lucifer's head, it smashed to the dirt. '. . . brother!'

'. . . Golgotha . . . ,' Lucifer hissed, choking on his blood, his shoulders heaving with fear and rage, the awful dreadfulness of Michael's words slowly sinking in.

Jether rose and turned to Lamaliel.

'Stem his bleeding with medicinal gossamer,' he instructed. 'He will heal slowly – the iniquity he carries impedes the healing process. But heal he will. He *must* face the First Judgement.'

Michael stood, grim but triumphant. 'He is no longer lawful ruler of the Race of Men. We will now commandeer the Ark of the Race of Men and transport it back to the First Heaven. From this moment *Lucifer is their* usurper king. *Our* King awaits us in the Black Necropolis!'

∽

Facing Jesus outside the Golden Gates of the Black Necropolis stood a hooded, hunched figure dressed in pale garments of shantung. Beyond the gates lay the great golden Ark of the Race of Men, chained to the Black Sepulchre with massive iron manacles.

Thousands of flickering black tapers flamed from the Unholy of Unholies, exuding their soporific perfume of black frankincense into the chamber.

The figure spoke from under his hood. 'The veil to the Unholy of Unholies is torn from top to bottom. It signifies a breach in the regions of the damned.'

He stepped back.

'You are not welcome here, Nazarene,' he murmured.

'Nisroc . . . ,' Jesus said.

The hooded figure nodded.

'I have many pseudonyms, Nazarene. "The Pale Horseman," "Death," and "the Reaper" are the ones commonly acknowledged by the Race of Men.'

He raised his pale, hooded eyes to Jesus.

'Your voice is familiar, Nazarene. It has resounded in my selpuchres once before . . . '

'Lazarus . . . ,' Jesus answered softly.

359

The pale horseman nodded.

'I, Death, could not hold him. One who held power and sway over my kingdom had spoken.' He raised his hood. 'One greater than I.'

Jesus looked long into his pale gaze.

I, Death, am subject to the precepts of prevailing Eternal Law and to Yehovah's councils.' Nisroc circled Jesus. Hovering. 'What is Your claim, Nazarene?'

'My claim, Nisroc the Prudent, is for the Keys of Death.' Jesus declared. 'And the Ark of Covenant of the Race of Men.'

The pale horseman nodded. At last he spoke.

'Ah, the title deeds.' He closed his hooded eyes. 'Only the undefiled can claim the Ark. That one does not exist among the Race of Men.'

Jesus stood silent.

'Your hands, Nazarene,' he said gently. Jesus put forth His palms.

The pale horseman stared in horror at the large jagged wounds, then reached out his long, bony finger and thrust it into the bloody wounds in Jesus' side.

'Aah . . . ' He staggered, losing strength.

'Your blood is undefiled . . . ' He stared up at Jesus in dread, his hand burning crimson as if by some peculiar holy fire.' You are *Christos*!' He uttered in recognition, falling, trembling, prostrate before Him.

'If one undefiled from the Race of Men is willing to shed His lifeblood on behalf of the Race of Men . . . ' the pale rider murmured, 'and become a substitute for judgement, the said Race of Men – past, present, and future generations – will be released from eternal judgement by the death of that one. A soul for a soul. This is binding Eternal Law . . . '

He rose.

'For those of the Race of Men . . . *if* they accept the great sacrifice.'

He took a ring of keys from his waist and unlocked the golden gate. 'At Golgotha,' he proclaimed, 'all these You have secured.'

Michael strode into the throne room, his generals close behind, followed by Jether. They bowed low before Jesus.

'Your Majesty . . . ' Michael removed his helmet and knelt before Jesus.

'Lucifer is captured,' he gasped. 'He is in chains; his generals are incarcerated. The keys of hell are in our possession.'

Michael raised his head, catching sight of the pale horseman. He rose to his feet, fierce, and raised his sword. Jether placed his hand gently on Michael's arm.

He shook his head.

'He is subject to Eternal Law, he will face the great judgement,' Jesus stated softly. 'It is not yet time.'

Michael frowned. Jether stared at the old, wizened figure, his mouth open in wonder. 'You have conquered death, Nazarene.'

Nisroc removed the ring of huge glowing golden keys from his waist. It was encrusted with diamonds and engraved with the seal of Pedition – Lucifer's seal.

'The Keys of Death and the Grave.' Nisroc knelt and handed the keys to Jesus. As Jesus took them, the engravings transformed into the royal seal of the House of Yehovah.

The pale rider bowed to Jesus, then lifted his hand in acknowledgment to Jether. Then vanished.

'He was my mentor,' Jether whispered in wonder, almost to himself. 'Nisroc the Righteous. He fell with Lucifer . . .'

Jesus walked through the golden gates of the Black Sepulchre. Facing them, chained to the Black Necropolis was the great golden casket with two carved gold seraphim on either side. The Ark of the Race of Men containing the title deeds to the planet earth and the solar systems.

Michael drew in his breath in awe.

This day justice is served in the courts of heaven,' Jesus said quietly. 'The Race of Men has been freed from the reign of tyranny. Commandeer the Ark, Michael.' He turned to Jether.

'Jether, faithful steward, prepare the chalice.'

Michael drew the sword of justice from its sheath and raised it high. 'We return the Ark of the Race of Men to the First Heaven!' he cried.

At the far door stood Gabriel. He bowed before Jesus.

'Hell's armies have surrendered, Your Excellency.' Gabriel held out a scroll to Jesus. Jesus took it and read, then walked towards Gabriel, His hands outstretched. He clasped Gabriel's hand in His and raised it, His voice echoing throughout hell, shaking the very core of the earth.

'The Keys of Death and the Grave are Yehovah's – Release the righteous dead!'

⟜

Lucifer stared out through the jagged iron bars of his holding cell in the penitentiary, at the unending millions of freed captives that marched past in triumphal procession, led by Gabriel and his conquering armies. The crimson banners of the cross, the new emblem of the First Heaven, flew high, held by the newly released prisoners, the righteous dead.

Lucifer shielded his eyes from the fierce purple light that blazed intensely like the noonday sun, illuminating every shadowy recess of the shadowed regions of the underworld.

He lay sprawled on the floor, still dreadfully weakened from his wounds, his wrists and ankles manacled with the heavy iron fetters that had once chained Jesus. The manacles tore into his bruised flesh.

He was naked, his robes and crown stripped from him, leaving only a narrow loincloth. His neck was bandaged in the silk medicinal cloth of the ancient ones, dipped in myrrh.

Humiliated before his subjects and his armies ... and before his prisoners. His hands shook with rage; his nails bit deeply into the flesh of his palms. A hundred of Michael's elite sentinels patrolled outside, guarding the cell.

A dark, shrunken apprentice youngling, freshly released from the sweltering underground laboratories of Lucifer's crypts, ran past the cell, shrieking dark obscenities, Lucifer's crown balanced awry on his head. A second youngling swaggered up and down outside the cell, enveloped in Lucifer's oversize ceremonial robes, sneering at his shackled master.

Lucifer put his head to the bars. He watched, frozen, as the sons of Noah marched past, then Abraham, the prophet Daniel, and King David. A tall, lean form lingered outside his cell. Looking down on him.

Lucifer's face contorted into an evil snarl. He raised himself on his elbows.

'Be gone, baptist,' he hissed frenziedly. The baptist turned his head to Lucifer, his fierce eyes blazing with righteous judgement. 'The King of Glory has trampled on death and hell. You are *conquered*, Satan.'

From the far side of the penitentiary, through the bars, he could see the leering, mocking faces of hell's inmates. Their voices rose in derision and his cell filled with their strident disparaging shrieks of laughter as they ridiculed their impotent king. Powerless, Lucifer's clasped his hands over his ears to block out the derisive voices. His body trembled violently in rage.

The cell door opened, and Lucifer looked out from under his matted hair to the tall imperial form who strode over to where he lay.

'You trespass, Nazarene!' he seethed, struggling to raise himself to a sitting position.

The Prince of Glory stood over the prince of the damned. Imperial. Majestic.

'Son of Destruction...' Jesus seized Lucifer fiercely by his hair and wrenched his face upward, His own countenance, black as thunder. 'I held out to you in the First Heaven the silver sceptre of My grace, but you would not touch it.' His voice was soft but relentless. 'Now I hold out the iron rod of My wrath.'

Lucifer stared into Jesus' eyes, his own face contorted with fear and loathing. He cursed slowly and deliberately in a dark, guttural evil angelic tongue, then spat in Jesus' face.

Jesus looked at him a long while. Silent. The spittle running down his cheek. Then He flung Lucifer to the floor before bending and writing in the black pitch dust of the cell floor in a strange angelic script, then strode out of the cell.

Lucifer clawed his way towards the writing. Letter by letter, he read, then placed his hands over his ears. Then screamed. A blood-chilling, spine-tingling scream that reverberated through hell's deep dark recesses. 'You will know my vengeance, Nazarene!'

Then he fell to the floor as one dead.

Michael waited outside the cell door.

'You have My instruction.' Jesus' expression was fierce, gradually His eyes softened. 'We have one final task.' Jesus clasped Michael's shoulder.' Meet Me at the Northern Gate of Tartarus.'

Michael looked at Jesus not daring to believe. Jesus held his gaze, then disappeared into the marching crowd.

Michael removed his helmet and entered the cell. Lucifer was huddled in the far corner, banging his head in rage against the bars.

'He has stormed my kingdom,' Lucifer snarled. Michael looked down at him with contempt.

'The Race of Men no longer fear me,' Lucifer wailed, his arms clutching his torso, rocking back and forth like one demented. 'You chose your path, brother. You reap its rewards.'

'My dominion is stormed … my kingdom conquered.' Lucifer whimpered.

Michael turned to Raphael, who stood awaiting his command.

'Deliver him, chained, to Nisroc, the keeper of death,' said Michael. 'He is to be incarcerated in the black sepulchre until he is summoned to the grand councils of

Yehovah in the First Heaven.' Michael turned back to Lucifer. 'To be bound over for the First Judgement.'

⟿

Michael descended down into the lower regions of the underworld, through the nether regions, past the penetentiaries, down deep beyond the very core of hell itself, until he entered the outer boundaries of the bottom-less chasm located in the very deepest parts of hell. Tartarus. Its location adjacent to the Lake of Fire. Unlisted in the tenets of the title deeds. Under Yehovah's jurisdiction.

None of the Race of Men would ever enter these austere and forbidding gates. This was the prison of the damned angelic fallen host who had left their first estate and co-habited with human women aeons past in the days of Noah – and corrupted the Race of Men. Held in chains of darkness in pits of gloom a thousand leagues beneath the Abyss.

Until the judgement.

Ahead, through the terrible unremitting gloom, Michael discerned the hundred noble angelic legions of the First Heaven that guarded Tartarus and the Lake of Fire day and night under Uriel's command. In the distance, stood a tall imperial form, waiting outside the northern-most gate to the bottomless pits of gloom. The entrance to Tartarus – through the lowest shaft of the Abyss.

The black stone was riddled with orange cracks from the blazing furnace that raged a thousand leagues below them. Uriel stood silently at attention, his legion bowed before their King. Jesus nodded and Uriel walked over to the huge circular lock that had been carved out of the colossal granite boulder a mile wide. Reaching down, he placed the enormous key to the shaft of the Abyss into the lock. Ever so slowly, it started to turn. A hundred angelic warriors grabbed the iron rivets of the boulder, pitting their great strength against the cavernous door. Slowly it opened.

Billowing black smoke erupted from the shaft entrance of the blazing furnace. The warriors were momentarily knocked off their feet by the blast of heat from the flowing river of fire and lava – the molten core.

Gradually, the smoke from the twisting shaft thinned out. The walls of the caverns glowed red hot with deadly coals and the air reverberated with the clamouring screams of the incarcerated.

'I curse Yehovah! I curse Christos!' A thousand whispering, vile obscenities grew in intensity. '...curse His holy presence.'

Jesus raised His hand and immediately the blaspheming faded except for the sound of one lone voice from a thousand leagues below, faintly audible above the roar of the blazing furnace.

'Christos!' The tortured scream drew nearer carried towards them on the smoke. '...have mercy on my tormented soul.'

Jesus walked over to the entrance until He stood directly in the path of the twisting blazing furnace. Untouched.

'Christos...!' The chilling scream pierced the air.

He closed His eyes.

'Zadkiel!' He cried, 'The Son of Man commands you – Come forth!'

And so it was that day that I heard Lucifer's agonized scream of defeat. The Son of God, the Son of Man, in all His glorious and terrible majesty – the eternal Christ, the Messiah – had entered his hellish domain and conquered his kingdom. It was a terrible, blood-curdling scream. Lucifer understood his unparalleled folly: that he had been the pawn to crucify the prince of glory. That by the shedding of His undefiled blood, Jesus of Nazareth, the Christ, the Father incarnate made flesh, had opened a doorway to the Race of Men that they could be reconciled to the great creator of their soul, Yehovah. Lucifer's dominion had been stormed; his kingdom had been conquered – forever ... at Golgotha.

And so he screamed.

No one will ever know what was written in the dust that day.

No one will ever know what transpired in that moment between the Prince of Glory and the prince of the damned ... only that after it occurred, Lucifer harboured an insatiable vengeance against the Nazarene and the sons of the Race of Men.

CHAPTER FORTY-ONE

JOTAPA

THE VAST DESERT sky was still strangely crimson. Jotapa sat outside the tent, her face heavily veiled in mourning. Only her eyes, red and swollen from weeping, were visible.

Ayeshe placed a bowl of steaming lamb's meat before her. 'You must eat, princess,' he said quietly.

Jotapa shook her head vehemently. She clutched Ayeshe's hand in hers so tightly that her rings bit into his fingers. Wincing in pain, he very gently removed his hand and covered her tenderly with a soft blanket.

'Please, princess,' he pleaded, 'eat.'

Jotapa waved him away.

'We have no victory to tell my father of – just a brutal tale of the Hebrew's torturous, bloody death. And worse, his tomb desecrated, his body stolen...' She collapsed in desperate sobbing until her head finally dropped onto her chest, her eyes closed in exhaustion.

A strange breeze stirred. A gentle hand rested on her shoulder.

'You must not grieve, princess.'

Jotapa stirred. A weary anger blazed in her bloodshot eyes.

'He is dead. He whom I loved is dead, and you dare tell me not to grieve, Ayeshe.' Her eyes flashed. 'You forget your place,' she muttered. 'My father shall hear of your indiscretion.' And like a petulant child, she pulled the blankets up over her head, bursting again into a loud sobbing.

'Jotapa.' She froze under the blanket, staring curiously out with one eye at the stranger bending over her, His face covered in an Arab head-dress.

'Daughter of Aretas, king of Arabia.'

Jotapa's eyes widened in recognition as Jesus moved directly in front of her, His eyes radiant.

Tenderly, He removed her veil, picked up the bowl of lamb's meat, and held it to her lips. She stared transfixed into His eyes. Her own never moving from His.

'Eat, princess...'

He smiled. Then He removed his head-dress.

She stared at the beautiful countenance before her, spell-bound by His beauty.

He was the same, the very same. She frowned. And yet, not the same at all.

She studied Him: His deep eyes with the long black lashes, the strong, noble features, the thick dark hair that fell in waves down past His strong shoulders. Yet something had changed irreversibly. Then she looked down at His hands, marred by two fresh gaping wounds. Her mind reeling in shock, again she reached for Him.

'No, Jotapa. You cannot touch Me.' He shook His head gently and moved back. 'I must ascend to My Father and My God – to your Father and your God.'

Tears streamed down Jotapa's soft, pale cheeks. 'You go to see Your Father,' she whispered.

Jesus nodded, tears of yearning streaming down His face, in this, His greatest hour after thirty-three years apart. Jotapa watched Him with infinite tenderness as He looked up at the night sky with intense desire. Suddenly, a violent desert storm blew up from nowhere and the stinging desert sands lashed fiercely against Jotapa's cheeks. Clutching her blankets tightly to her, fighting against the violent winds, she struggled towards the entrance to the tent, where she turned.

Jesus stood in the midst of the raging storm, His face and robes lashed by the sand, staring upward at the open heavens, which parted before Him. Radiant with yearning.

Jotapa stared out from the safety of the tent entrance. She could swear that she had seen figures in the sky. She turned inside to call Ayeshe.

'Ayeshe!' she cried, then turned back.

The storm had stopped as suddenly as it began. Jesus had vanished.

'He is gone to His Father, Ayeshe,' she whispered in wonder.

She sighed, new hope illuminating her eyes. 'And I go to mine!'

Chapter Forty-two

THE CARNELIAN CHALICE

J ETHER STOOD BY the fountains in the Tower of Winds. The zephyrs blew his long, silvery hair and beard as he stared out at the vast armies of heaven, returning through the twelve entrances of the great pearl gates from their victory against Lucifer's armies.

Gabriel strode through the gardens towards him, his face radiant.

'Well done, noble Gabriel!' Jether embraced him fiercely.

Gabriel bowed deeply before Jether.

'I have escorted our King back to the First Heaven. He prepares to meet Yehovah. He bids you come to Him with the Carnelian Chalice.' Tears rolled down Gabriel's cheeks; he wiped them away with his hand uncaring.

'He is in His garden.'

372

A cherub took Jether's stallion while another ushered Jether into the thick, swirling white mists of the First Heaven's Eden. Jether carried an enormous Carnelian Chalice in his hands. On its lid was engraved a simple golden cross.

He walked past the golden trees and through the narrow pearl arbour covered with pomegranate vines laden with lush silver fruits, breathing in the heady perfume of the magnificent hanging blossoms in the Gardens of Fragrance that exuded the aromas of frankincense and of spikenard. He trod over beds of gladioli and frangipani trees, across lawns of golden bulrushes and buttercups with fine crystal stamens in their centre towards the intense shafts of blinding crimson light radiating from far beyond. Across the vale, he came to an inconspicuous grotto at the very edge of the cliffs of Eden, surrounded by eight ancient olive trees.

He pushed open the simple wooden gate.

Standing in the centre of His garden, His face only faintly visible through the rising mists, stood Jesus. He was clothed in shining white garments, His gleaming hair fell past His shoulders.

Slowly He turned, and Jether fell to his knees, his arm shielding his face from the glorious white light emanating from the figure's countenance. 'Christos,' Jether uttered in ecstasy.

Gradually, the white mists faded. Jether stared down at Christos' feet, the jagged wounds still fresh. 'Christos...' he whispered.

'Our task is accomplished.' Jesus' voice was soft. 'We have paid the penalty for the Race of Men.'

He looked around at the great olive trees.

'It was here that Lucifer kissed Me so many aeons past . . . before his treason,' He said softly. 'It was fitting for what was to come.'

Jether nodded. 'It was here that it began, when he was told of the advent of the Race of Men.'

Jesus gazed out as the shimmering rays settled to reveal, a hundred feet ahead, across a vast chasm, the magnificent Rubied Door, ablaze with light, embedded into the jacinth walls of the tower – the entrance to Yehovah's throne room. He gazed out at the shimmering rainbow that rose over the crystal palace.

At length, Christos spoke. 'And it is here that it is completed.'

Jether knelt before Christos, the Carnelian Chalice in his outstretched hand. 'Every drop of blood that was spilt at Golgotha,' Jether whispered in reverence. 'The blood sacrifice for the souls of the Race of Men. Undefiled.'

Jesus took the chalice from him. 'Rise, faithful servant of Yehovah.'

Jether rose to his feet, following Christos' gaze out towards the great Rubied Door. Slowly the colossal door opened, and with it the lightning and thunder grew in intensity, and a tempestuous wind blew.

'You will be summoned, to the Great White Throne, in Eden, on the plains of the Great White Poplars.' Christos raised the chalice in ecstasy, His eyes gleaming in adoration.

'My Father awaits Me.' He vanished into the white, rushing mists. Then He reappeared across the chasm and walked inside the Rubied Door.

CHAPTER FORTY-THREE

MOURNING

ARETAS SAT AT his desk, his head in his hands. 'So the reports are true,' he mumbled. 'He is dead.'

Jotapa knelt before him, her face pale. 'Yes, Papa,' she said softly. 'It is true He died, but ... '

Aretas ran his hands through his still thick, silvering hair. Wearily he looked up at Jotapa. Though she was dressed in her black mourning veils, her eyes shone with an ethereal glow.

Aretas' leathery face was haggard, he must have been without sleep for days, Jotapa thought and his eyes were strangely swollen. She wondered if he had been weeping.

'I had ... ' He struggled to speak, then swallowed hard. 'I had hoped ... ' His hand fell heavily on the table before him. 'No matter ... It was a fool's dream.' Aretas raised his head.

Suddenly, he seemed old ... much older than his sixty-seven years. Jotapa stared at him. Silent, her eyes wide with grief.

'You *did* believe...,' she murmured. She looked at her father in wonder.

'I see now that I was foolish,' Aretas murmured. 'It was emotional ... an illusion.' He looked in her eyes, grasping for hope. 'You saw Him ... die.'

Jotapa nodded. 'Yes, Papa, He died.'

'But He lives.'

She reached out to Aretas, but he shook her off him, a terrible fury clouding his features.

'*Desperate* tales!'

Jotapa drew her face close to his.

'I saw Him, Father.'

Aretas' countenance grew dark like thunder. Jotapa persisted.

'Your friend Abgar, prince of Armenia, has written to Lord Tiberius saying that the Hebrew is risen, that He has appeared to many,' she said, her face flushed with excitement.

'Many graves and tombs were opened, Papa – over twelve thousand it is the talk of all Jerusalem. Simeon, the high priest ... his sons, blood brothers Karinus and Leucius ... their graves were opened. Annas and Caiaphas joined with Gamaliel and Nicodemus and found them in the city of Arimathea – alive! Alive, Papa! Resurrected. They swore by the God of Israel that they had arisen from the dead. They wrote of what they had seen – that they were in deep, shadowy darkness and suddenly Hades was alight with royal purple light shining on them. John the Baptist was there, and the prophet Isaiah! The Hebrew resurrected them, Papa!'

Aretas stood to his feet, hunched and in that moment very, very old.

'I cannot take it.' He stared at her in fury. 'These lies sicken me. Leave me alone!'

Jotapa ran, clutching his robes, but he pulled himself away from her.

'Leave me, Jotapa!' he cried. '*Get out!*' He pushed her away from him. She tripped over the hem of her garments and fell to the floor. Aretas stormed into his bedchamber, leaving his daughter sobbing on the marble floor.

The doors ricocheted shut behind him.

CHAPTER FORTY-FOUR

ECHOES OF ETERNITY

T HE SEVEN PALE lilac western moons glimmered softly on the horizon of the First Heaven. Indigo lightnings struck the seventh spire, far above the rock face of the Holy Mountain. Seven hidden chambers in the mountain ascended into the inner sanctum of the labyrinths.

The secret entrance to the throne room, accessible only by the ancient ones from from the seventh spire, was barely visible, wreathed in the glistening mists that rose and fell in the dawn zephyrs.

Michael stood a thousand feet below, in the gardens that lay behind the rubied entrance to the throne room, outside the western labyrinths of the seven spires. Seven scorching columns of eternal white fire blazed fiercely and unrelentingly at the seventh entrance to Yehovah's palace, underneath the immense flaming rainbow.

'Jether was summoned to the seventh chamber before the western moons arced in the heavens,' Michael said.

Gabriel tethered his white steed to one of the great gnarled willows that flourished on the lawns of the western labyrinths. 'Yehovah delivers His pronouncement concerning the fate of Lucifer,' he said.

Michael clutched his gauntlets in his hand. 'His Judgement hastens.'

'The First Judgement,' replied Gabriel. 'The judgements of the damned . . .'

'And the one who instigated their damnation at the start,' Jether said softly.

The princes turned.

Jether stood at the base of the labyrinths, holding a flaming eternal torch, his head and crown covered by his white mantle.

'It is time, Michael, chief prince of the royal house of Yehovah – He commissions you to leave for Perdition immediately. You will return with Lucifer before the grand councils of Yehovah, for the First Judgement. At the Great White Throne, in Eden, on the plains of the Great White Poplars.' He placed his hand on Michael's shoulder.

'Bring Lucifer to his old chambers in the West Wing. Ephaniah will be waiting with his ceremonial regalia.'

Jether pushed the mantle back from his head wearily.

'He damned the Race of Men in earth's Eden. Heaven's Eden will be where he is judged.'

⌐

Lucifer stood, his hands and feet shackled, outside the huge golden doors of the Western Wing of the Palace of

379

Archangels. Michael pushed open the doors, then pushed Lucifer through into the centre of the enormous chambers. Michael nodded to Sandaldor, one of his High Command, who immediately unshackled Lucifer's hands and ankles, then bowed and took his place with twelve of Michael's command outside the doors. Lucifer stood in the centre of the enormous chamber, dressed only in a stark grey tunic, studying his old chambers. Everything was untouched, exactly as it had been the night before he was banished. The magnificent frescoes, his collection of pipes and tabrets – his viol and bow still lay on his writing table. His Sword of State was placed back in its magnificent jewelled sheath. The enormous rubied palace windows were flung open, and the sounds of the angelic orations from the Mount of Assembly echoed throughout the chamber.

He stared up at the soaring vaulted ceilings with their spectacular panoramas that covered the ornate carved ceilings of the chambers, then walked to the tall casement doors that led onto the shimmering white beaches in front of the Palace of Archangels. A company of white-winged stallions thundered past across the beach and soared into the firmament past the twelve pale blue moons that were now rising from the Eastern horizon. Michael watched, silent as Lucifer stared after them in exhilaration. Lucifer turned, catching Michael's gaze. He walked over to the writing table, then stood beneath the hundred blazing frankincense tapers and inhaled deeply.

He stared at his ceremonial regalia laid out before him. The ceremonial silver half greaves, intricately carved with the emblems of Perdition. His ceremonial jacket of embroidered white silks, his gauntlets of soft white leather. The silver and gold medals. The great diamond crown.

'It is all as it was...' Lucifer murmured, a strange smile flickering on his lips.

He picked up his viol, thrumming the viol's strings as he walked back out onto the balcony. He drew the bow across the viol's bridge with nimble fingers, his eyes closed in rapture.

A dazzling, pulsating light fell across Lucifer, blinding him and completely covering the pearl balcony. He let out an agonized scream, the viol smashing to the marble floor. He stumbled into the chamber, then fell to his knees, desperately making futile attempts to shield his eyes from the blazing light.

Michael slammed the casement doors closed and drew the immense velvet drapes over the latticed windows until the chambers were engulfed in semi-darkness. He stared down at Lucifer, who lay trembling in horror on the floor.

'*Nothing* is as it was, Lucifer.'

Michael rang a golden bell that hung from the velvet curtains.

An old, wizened angelic courtier entered through the door and bowed. 'Ephaniah,' Michael said. 'Dress my brother as you used to in aeons past in his ceremonial regalia of the House of Yehovah. Then deliver him to Sandaldor. He is to be judged. To stand before our King.'

Michael strode through the huge golden doors which slammed behind him.

CHAPTER FORTY-FIVE

THE FIRST JUDGEMENT

THE MAGNIFICENT TRANSLUCENT Pearl Gates of Eden in the First Heaven slowly opened, revealing the vast, lush white plains that were filled with thousands upon thousands of great white poplars. Each exuded a soft, milky radiance. Their trunks and branches were a transparent white, the diamond markings on the trunks spawned real diamonds. Their healing leaves were a pale green, white on the underside, and their branches hung heavy with glistening white blossoms with diamond stamens that were filled with spikenard. The exquisite fragrance filled the plains. A fitting memorial to the One who had been anointed in lavish devotion by one of the Race of Men.

The Great White Plains radiated with the soft white light that hung in the blazing white mists rising from the immense lush lawns of white lilies and foxgloves that grew below the poplars.

In the very centre of the plains stood a thousand colossal ivory columns, holding up a great canopy of the finest spun gossamer. Beneath this diaphanous roof, millions of the angelic host were seated on carved silver thrones divided by a great nave of glistening sapphire panes, leading to the great White Sacrosanct altar. On the altar stood the Carnelian Chalice.

In the centre of the nave the waters of life, bright as crystal, cascaded from the throne room, watering Eden and the Great White Plains. Hundreds of stately white swans drifted down the flowing stream towards the Crystal Sea.

A hundred angelic heralds blew their shofars.

'We herald the holy council of the ancient ones, stewards of Yehovah's sacred mysteries,' they proclaimed.

The blinding white mists cleared, revealing Jether and the twenty-three ancient kings of heaven. They walked solemnly, majestically, through the soaring Pearl Gates towards the twenty-four golden thrones that stood behind the great carved white altar. Jether seated himself on the centre throne, the twenty-three remaining ancient kings following his lead.

Again the herald blew the shofar.

'Gabriel the Revelator, prince of archangels,' he proclaimed, 'long may you reign with wisdom and justice.'

The angelic host's refrain reverberated through the chamber as Gabriel followed the kings through the gates, carrying the sword of justice

'Michael the Valiant, chief prince of archangels, long

may you reign with justice and valour,' the angelic host proclaimed.

'Lucifer the Light-Bearer, fallen prince of archangels, son of destruction.'

The entire assembly fell silent. As one they turned towards the pearl gates.

Lucifer stood next to Michael in his full white ceremonial dress of the First Heaven. His long raven hair was plaited with white pearls and diamonds. His ceremonial jacket glistened with embroidered white silks, and his gauntlets were of soft white leather. He wore his silver and gold medals on his chest. He held the royal golden sceptre of Perdition. On his head rested a great diamond crown. His wrists were manacled with heavy silver shackles, as were his ankles. Michael held his arm in a vice-like grip.

Lucifer turned his head to him.

'This is scandalous, brother.' He looked at Michael with thinly veiled loathing. 'You treat me as an insurgent.'

'The insurgent we know you to be.' Michael pushed Lucifer forward roughly. Lucifer turned his head mockingly to the angelic host. Every head stayed bowed; every mouth kept silent. There was no sound on the vast plain. Doggedly, step by step, Lucifer walked up the great nave of gleaming sapphire panes that led to the Great White Throne. Michael's knights in arms fell into step behind them, solemnly bearing the banners of the royal house of Yehovah. Michael and Lucifer stopped next to Gabriel, a distance away from the ancient elders and the place of the throne. Michael and Gabriel bowed low and knelt in the burning mist that poured over the white plains. Lucifer's attention was strangely drawn to a tall noble figure exuding a glorious light, standing to his right. Slowly the figure turned his head to Lucifer, holding his gaze fiercely for a long moment. 'Zadkiel...' Lucifer gasped. He turned to Michael, bewildered, then bowed his head, his hands trembling with fear and rage.

'Behold, O God our defender, and look upon the face of thy chief princes, for one day in thy courts is better than a thousand elsewhere.'

Jether watched Lucifer intently. Lucifer stood imperious, refusing to kneel. He stayed silent for a long moment, his face down, then closed his eyes. Ashen.

'His memories return to the days before he fell, to his days of glory,' Jether murmured to Lamaliel in wonder.

'When he was Light-Bearer – all-glorious,' Maheel murmured.

A great thundering and lightning sounded, and the blazing white light of the plains transformed to dazzling sapphire, then to amethyst. 'Yehovah descends,' the herald announced.

Lucifer stared ahead, expressionless, though Jether noted that his hands trembled visibly, uncontrollably as the Great White Throne descended.

Before Yehovah's feet, the seven blazing torches burned as seven flaming columns of white fire, and in the midst of each torch were the flaming coals of the Spirit of Yehovah. A rainbow descended also, which stretched across the white plains, surrounding Yehovah's presence.

Ear-splitting peals of thunder shook the plains of Eden. Then all was still.

Lucifer stared ahead to the Great White Throne, pale. He bowed his head from the radiance.

There, seated on the Great White Throne of incandescent light, was the One from whose presence, and from the sight of whose face, earth and sky fled away – the great King of the universe, Yehovah.

But now, a second throne, to Yehovah's right, became faintly distinguishable through the glowing mists. Then, through the Pearl Gates, twelve holy Watchers in ceremonial dress walked in procession up the nave, holding the golden casket carved with golden cherubim on their shoulders. The Ark of the Race of Men. They placed it down directly on the altar before the throne.

Gabriel nodded. Raphael walked forward with a large golden key resting on a velvet cushion. Gabriel picked it up and reverently opened the casket. The twelve golden codices filled the ark, their covers embedded with jacinth, diamonds, sapphires, chrysolite, and multitudes of other precious stones. 'The earth and its solar system, the Second Heaven above the earth, is this day returned to Yehovah, throughout eternity of eternities,' he declared.

Jether stood. 'According to Eternal Law, the Ark of the Race of Men is no longer property of Lucifer, Son of the Morning. It is once again restored to Yehovah's keeping. The great and terrible sacrifice at Golgotha has delivered the Race of Men from the rule of the son of destruction . . . ' He paused. ' . . . *if* they accept the great sacrifice.'

He bowed his head in supplication, then turned to a man, great of stature, his body glowing with a radiance unnatural to the Race of Men.

'Yehovah calls Adam, the firstborn creation of Yehovah.' The tall man, perfect in his symmetry, walked out from the angelic host and flung himself prostrate before the thrones.

Then a glorious imperial figure walked majestically through the white fires, from the throne at Yehovah's right hand. The mists started to fade as the breathtaking form became visible. It was Jesus.

'I accept the great sacrifice of Golgotha,' Adam uttered in awe.

'Rise, Adam, first-created son of man,' Jesus declared.

Adam rose from the floor. Gabriel removed the lid from the Carnelian Chalice, and Jesus dipped His forefinger in the sacred blood.

'The Race of Men, lost by the tree of transgression,' Jesus said softly, anointing Adam with the sign of the cross in blood, 'is regained through the tree of the cross of sacrifice.'

Jesus smiled, clasping Adam tenderly to His breast. Tears flowed down Adam's cheeks.

'He is reinstated,' murmured Xacheriel, 'through the blood.'

Jesus raised His hands to Yehovah. 'The First Judgement commences,' He proclaimed.

Zadkiel rose, followed by twenty-four White Holy Watchers, who carried six monstrous silver and garnet caskets engraved with the seal of Perdition. They placed them before the altar, then raised the lids, revealing six hundred and sixty-six enormous codices sealed with the seal of the House of Perdition.

Lucifer's expression darkened.

'The Books of Iniquities of the Race of Men seized from the archives of Perdition,' Zadkiel declared. Jesus nodded and immediately a hundred youngling scribes swiftly lifted the codices from the caskets until all six hundred and sixty-six codices lay upon the mammoth white altar.

Jether walked over to Jesus.

'Every generation of the Race of Man is registered, Your Majesty. Lucifer and his archivists have meticulously recorded every darkened act; every act of iniquity of the Race of Men against Yehovah.

'Open the Books of Iniquities,' Jesus commanded. The youngling scribes swiftly opened the books.

'I, the slain lamb execute the First Judgement.'

Lucifer stood silent as Jesus picked up the Carnelian Chalice and held it over the open books, watching him.

'Former prince of the world of men, you are already condemned, and sentence is already passed upon you.'

Lucifer's hands shook visibly, the appalling comprehension of Jesus' actions dawning.

'Every drop of blood shed at Golgotha – I shed for the Race of Men – for their reconciliation with Yehovah – for their deliverance from hell and the Lake of Fire.'

Jesus held the chalice high –

'Noooooo!' Lucifer screamed, his eyes wild with horror. 'Every man's soul is *mine* – to burn with me in the Lake of Fire!' Michael grasped his arms in an iron grip, his fingers digging fiercely into his flesh. Lucifer stared, riveted at the Carnelian Chalice, droplets of sweat ran from his temple onto his cheeks.

Jesus poured the blood from the Chalice over the Books of Iniquities. As each drop of blood fell down, the pages blazed ferociously with intense black flames that contorted to a blazing white inferno.

Jether dropped to his knees. 'The First Judgement.'

'The Lamb that was slain.' Gabriel mouthed in wonder.

Michael grasped Lucifer's hair, then brought his mouth up to Lucifer's ear.

'Slain by your own hand.' His whisper reverberated in Lucifer's head. Lucifer stared down in dread at the darkening crimson stain on his right palm. He clutched his hand in agony from the searing pain.

The angelic host all across the plains fell prostrate.

Gabriel fell to his knees. 'Jesus of Nazareth has died as the Lamb – He arises the great conqueror!'

'All power, honour, dominion above the earth, under the earth is Yours,'

'All hail – King of kings – Lord of lords – Your reign is forever!' the multitude of angelic hosts thundered.

'Yehovah would issue His decree.'

A great thundering issued from the throne, through the mist – the roar of a thousand waters. Then the mists rose and the gracious, noble voice resounded through the plains.

'We receive the blood sacrifice of Golgotha for the Race of Men. All who reject My Son remain under the kingship of Satan and his damned – never to enter these gates. All those of the Race of Men who receive the great and terrible blood sacrifice of My Son shed at Golgotha, I now set free from the tyranny of Satan. I declare Myself their Father and their God. I shall set My royal seal upon their heads.'

The mists rose and through the golden hues, the dim outline of a form of immense stature could be seen through the golden undulating mists. Torrential waves of compassions and unending mercies flowed from His being like a vigorous living deluge over the plains. And then, for a moment, a moment so fleeting Yehovah's face became visible. The whole of heaven fell prostrate, as though dead, in the very majesty and awe of Him. Lucifer stayed standing for a moment, then collapsed like stone onto the sapphire floor.

Only Jesus stood. Tears falling down His cheeks, staring ... staring into the beautiful noble face. For His beauty was indescribable, and to those few who had ever looked upon His face – they could not but hear His name and weep. His hair and head were white like snow from the very radiance of His glory, Yehovah's eyes were burning luminous black orbs that reflected His infinite tender compassions, His unending mercies, the gentleness and the beauty of truth. Of justice. Of holiness. Of indissoluble love.

'This is My vow.' Yehovah's words issued from His being like ripples of golden radiance. 'My solemn promise from age to age – from the eternity of eternities.'

And then He smiled. A brilliant tender smile. The understanding of the ages in His smile.

'For the Race of Men is exceedingly beloved by Me.'

Yehovah disappeared back into the mists.

Heaven was silent.

Finally, Jether stepped forward and motioned the angelic host to rise.

'Let it be recorded by the scribes of the First Heaven: the decrees of Yehovah as Eternal Law. The First Judgement reads thus: All members of the Race of Men, past, present, and future generations, who receive the seal of the blood sacrifice of Golgotha, are released from the rule of Satan, son of destruction. All are released from the defilement of the fall of man. All who are sealed have access to Yehovah's courts beyond the Rubied Door and are saved from the flames of the Lake of Fire.'

The angelic host erupted in a jubilant roar.

Jether looked to where Lucifer stood, his head cast down, shielding his eyes from the brilliance of Yehovah.

'Yehovah calls to account Lucifer, son of destruction – Satan, tempter, Adversary of the Race of Men.'

Lucifer lifted his hate-filled eyes towards Jether. Michael clasped his shoulders with both arms. Lucifer shrugged him aside.

'I can walk,' he spat.

Slowly, determinedly, he walked. His eyes were downcast as he placed one foot before the other on the polished sapphire path. Michael walked behind him. Lucifer walked, trembling in terror and rage until he stood directly before the throne. Raphael unshackled his hands.

'Christos . . . ,' Lucifer whispered in dread.

The King spoke in a voice at once soft and filled with the authority of the universe. 'Son of destruction.' Lucifer's head was bowed, his arm shielding his face from the light that blazed from Jesus, Great King of Heaven.

Lucifer lifted his head, inch by inch until he was staring directly at Jesus.

'Ceased is Lucifer, the golden one. Yehovah has broken the staff of the wicked, the sceptre of rulers.' Jesus reached out His hands and removed Lucifer's sceptre. 'Thy pomp is brought down to Sheol.' He looked straight into Lucifer's eyes. Severe. Forbidding He nodded to Gabriel. 'Complete the Judgement, then deliver him back to the fallen. He walked back to His throne and disappeared into the thick swirling mists with Yehovah.

Raphael and Ariel stripped Lucifer of his white ceremonial garments until he stood before the altar clothed in only a white loincloth.

'You have lost, brother,' Gabriel said. 'You no longer have authority over the Race of Men.'

Lucifer grasped Gabriel's tunic and pulled him towards him. 'Unless men *give* it to me . . .' Lucifer hissed. He drew Gabriel closer until their faces touched.

'My brother Gabriel,' he whispered, 'your fallen brother, Lucifer, is yet also a prophet.' Lucifer raised one hand to where the righteous dead sat. The entire assembly fell silent. Michael turned from his position at the Gate exchanging a glance with Jether. Jether nodded.

'I foretold you, compatriots, before my unmerited banishment, that we would see our angelic sanctuary *desecrated* by these replicated mewling, inferior beasts.' Gabriel felt Lucifer's hot putrid breath on his cheeks. 'Here they are in your midst! It is a travesty!' Lucifer flung Gabriel away, then raised his arms to the angelic host. 'Mark me well, my revered angelic compatriots . . .' His eyes flamed with an unholy fire as his voice rose in decibels.

'If *truly* we serve Yehovah, we will protect Him against His splendid and overwhelming love for them.'

'Bind his mouth!' commanded Michael striding towards Lucifer, 'that his odious words fall to the ground, not on our ears.' Michael seized him by the neck and bound his mouth. Uriel marched towards him, his dagger sharpened and ready. Lucifer struggled violently. Michael seized his head in a vicelock. With six deft swipes of Uriel's blade, Lucifer's long raven locks fell to the floor. He was shorn. 'How art thou cut down to the ground . . . ,' whispered Jether.

Lucifer stared into Michael's eyes with a shocking violent hatred.

' . . . and the noise of thy viols; the maggot is spread under thee,' Michael said through gritted teeth. '*And worms cover thee*. Deliver him back to the kingdom of the fallen!'

Raphael and his generals dragged Lucifer up the nave towards the gates, struggling violently. With his one freed hand, he ripped the binding from across his mouth.

'You shall pay for this, Michael!' he cried. 'Nazarene!' he screamed, 'You shall pay for this for eternity-y-y-y-y . . . '

The great pearl gates of the white plains closed behind Lucifer forever.

'It is over,' murmured Michael wearily. Shaken. Suddenly emotional. Lucifer's cry ringing in his ears.

'It is over,' Gabriel echoed in relief.

'He is the master of resurrections.' Jether turned from the gate to the brothers, his expression guarded. 'Only when Lucifer lies burning in the Lake of Fire on the eastern shore, *then and only then* shall it be truly *over*.'

⌒

2021
MANHATTAN, NEW YORK

Lilian surveyed the vast open-plan living room of Jason's Manhattan penthouse. It was stark, almost utilitarian – its one redeeming feature, the plush white 'Nina Campbell' sofa that Julia had fallen in love with when they had first moved to New York City. Strange, Lilian reflected, Jason had rigorously erased every memory of Julia . . . except this one glaring omission.

Lilian smiled. It had been she who coerced Lawrence into introducing his young niece, pretty fledgling London journalist Julia Cartier, to her stubborn young son freshly out of Harvard and attending film school in New York. And how she had loved Julia instantly, the fiery, talented young writer. Julia was so good for Jason – that she was sure of.

They had married young. On Julia's nineteenth birthday. Jason was just twenty-two. And on his twenty-third birthday, his portion of the De Vere trust fund became his to do with as he wished – 200 million pounds at his disposal. To be released in tranches of ten million by the De Vere Foundation board of trustees every five years until he turned forty, when the remainder would be his.

And the world had become Jason and Julia's proverbial oyster.

Jason and Julia's divorce had shaken Lilian badly. Jason had never fully recovered from Lily's accident. Lilian knew that he drank too much. Never – never enough to jeopardize his work, but quite enough to affect his marriage.

He had used his vast personal fortune to leverage the New York merchant banks in his quest for new media companies. His personal media empire, Vox Media was funded by one of the more than nine thousand active hedge funds of the trillion dollar (and growing) industry. Most of the funds were based in New York, and the hedge fund board was made up almost entirely of his father, James De Vere's closest friends. Charles Cussler, Jason's godfather had been an invaluable ally.

Media Acquisition had become Jason's sole obsession. Jason was stubborn … as stubborn as his father James De Vere had ever been. Oh, yes – how alike they were. Both prickly, selfish, driven, irascible, and, most of all, stubborn, but both Jason and James were true, Lilian had concluded. There was no guile in Jason.

Lilian walked over to the drinks cabinet, and picked up the one of the two solitary photographs in the apartment. Jason and Adrian at Adrian's recent presidential inauguration.

She smiled. Jason was starting to look like that actor from the previous decade – what was his name...? Harrison Ford. Jason would loathe that comparison.

And Adrian. Handsome, gifted, generous Adrian. Lilian replaced the photograph.

He had been such a sunny toddler. Always smiling. A people magnet since the age of two. He never sulked. Never pushed for his own, never pouted or fought to get his way. What an easy child he had been! And he was funny. Lilian smiled to herself. Side-wrenchingly funny. A joy.

Adrian had entered his teens and suffered through some of its the awkward phases, but otherwise he had sailed through school at Gordonstoun, achieving first class grades at Oxford University, completing a faculty exchange year at Georgetown University in D.C. specializing in Arab studies, before entering the world of British politics. At twenty-nine, Adrian De Vere had become the youngest British Prime Minister in the history of the British Isles. He had served two full terms and resigned last spring to concentrate on his bid for the European presidency. James would have been so proud. Lilian sighed.

But James De Vere never lived to see Adrian invested. He had collapsed from a fatal heart attack in his study at their home in the Oxfordshire countryside. He was dead even before the ambulance arrived. And then less than eighteen months later, Melissa ... and the baby. Lilian shivered.

Adrian and Jason had always been close. Very close and

since James De Vere's death, they had grown even closer. But even Adrian couldn't persuade Jason to forgive Nick.

Nick. Lilian's expression softened. Her beloved youngest son. Her baby. She believed in her heart that he was the greatest victim of the accident. He had never recovered from the crippling guilt and Jason was determined that he never would if he had anything to do with it.

Nick had been a glorious child. A quiet, handsome boy with a gentle spirit, an honours student, a first-rate archaeology student at Cambridge – but then came the accident. She had watched as her blue-eyed boy had drunk the nights away to forget, dissipating his substantial trust fund on cocaine, heroin and God knows what else. He was beautiful enough to become prime celebrity fodder for the ruthless British paparazzi, and he gave them plenty of material. Then he got AIDS.

Lilian moved to the penthouse balcony and stared out at the view across the Atlantic, deep in thought.

Eighteen months before James De Vere died, he had frozen Nick's trust fund in horror at discovering Nick had broken his engagement to his glamourous British model fiancée – Jordan – for a fling with a German archeologist – Klaus von Hausen. James was old school. And frozen it would remain, for when James died, Jason, as eldest son joined the foundation's board of directors. And he refused to sign.

'Mother,' Lilian turned. Jason stood at the drinks cabinet, freshly showered. He poured her the tomato juice she loved, then himself a whisky. He came up beside her and passed her the glass. They stood in silence for several minutes. At ease. Finally Jason spoke.

'I saw Julia.'

Lilian nodded. She waited.

'At Adrian's event in Aqaba.' Jason slugged down the whisky.

Lilian gently removed the whisky glass from her eldest son's grasp and took his hand. 'I miss Lily.' He shrugged.

She looked deeply into his eyes, then over to the only other photograph in the apartment. A holiday photo. Jason, Julia and Lily on the beach together in France – laughing, relaxed – a family. Jason followed her gaze.

No words passed between them, but Lilian read her son completely.

CHAPTER FORTY-SIX

THE DREAD
COUNCILS OF HELL

LUCIFER LIMPED THROUGH the great bronze portico of the eastern wing of his chambers, out into his ornamental tropical gardens. His hair had grown back in dark stubble on his scalp. His sapphire eyes were clouded with a thin, opaque film. His wrists and ankles were still bruised and scabbed from the shackles of past events.

'Cerberus,' he crooned, feeding his pet hellhound a sweetmeat from his palm.

He moved his palm across the horizon, resting his weight on his silver cane, then leisurely massaged his bruised wrists, surveying his newly erected fortress, which lay light years beyond hell and the shadowed regions, beyond the southern polar caps of Mars, in the Second Heaven under the escarpment of the brooding ice-capped crags of Vesper.

It was a monstrous structure, constructed entirely of molten silver and alabaster. He stared out at the great portcullis and battlements, then smiled. The ice citadel of Gehenna was almost complete – his winter palace. Not a trace of hell's fires would ever cross his threshold again to humiliate him. He must embrace eternal winter until his allotted time was up according to Eternal Law, until the final judgement. *The Lake of Fire*. He shuddered.

Marduk stepped over the threshold, bowing low before him.

'Sandor ... Diablon,' Lucifer spoke without turning. 'All of my warriors who surrendered to the Nazarene and Michael's armies – they are delivered to the Abyss?'

Marduk smirked.

'All the fallen that were conquered are delivered to the Abyss, sire. To the molten core. As are the insurgents among the ranks of the wicked dead.'

'My edict has gone out?' He turned.

'Your edict has gone throughout the penitentiaries of hell, great Majesty. There will be no whisper of the Nazarene's visit to the courts of the damned. It is punishable by the Abyss.'

'Well and good, Marduk. The missives are sent?'

'The stygian missives are circulated to all the dread fallen, sire. The satanic princes of Babylon and Grecia – the principalities of Belphegor. To the fallen archangels of Astaroth ... The Thrones of Folcador, the Warlocks of Ishtar.

All the great principalities of evil and terror above the earth and under the earth gather for the dread assembly of vengeance, my lord.'

'Tell Charsoc my winter palace must be prepared for their coming.' Lucifer looked down at the lapis floors beneath his feet.

'As soon as it is prepared, demolish this palace, that there be not one stone left standing – that there be no trace of the Nazarene's presence remaining in my kingdom.

'It shall be done, my lord.'

Lucifer put his hand to his head, running his fingers over the new growth of hair. They gleamed black with a malevelant evil. Vengeance.

'Every trace, Marduk. When the council is over, the Nazarene will have ceased to exist!'

⤳

Jether and Michael looked up from the waterfalls of nectar, far beyond the horizon, to a lone figure who stood in the gardens of the labyrinths outside the seventh spire, gazing out towards Earth. 'He is returned again from Earth,' said Michael.

Jether nodded.

'It draws Him continually.'

Jesus stood silent, watching the earth as it spun slowly on its axis. The lightnings and thunderings from the spires at the top of the mountain struck continually all around Him. His face betrayed a deep yearning.

'He is torn,' Jether murmured. 'By two worlds – ours in the First Heaven, and the world of the Race of Men.'

'We cannot feel what He feels,' Michael whispered. 'We have not been one of them.'

Gabriel knelt in supplication under the great willows. He raised his head.

'I have watched each dusk as He leaves,' he murmured. 'He returns each dawn.'

'He visits those who accept His sacrifice, who long for His appearing. He yearns for His subjects; He is their King.' Jether's voice was soft.

They watched in silence as Jesus walked towards the rubied lightning bolts that flashed from the secret Portal that led from the seventh spire directly before the Great White Throne.

'He goes to requisition Yehovah. He is touched by their infirmities.'

Jesus walked into the glorious source of the thunder and lightnings, His head raised, surrounded by an unearthly radiance. His face exultant with the rapture. Then vanished.

⤳

The Great Silver Battlements of the citadel of Gehenna glistened in the nine magenta ice suns that rose from the murky, cold skies above the ice-capped crags of Vesper in the Second Heaven.

The wild, barren ice wastelands stretched for miles, surrounding the great forbidding fortress. Freezing arctic blizzards and tempests from Mars circled the citadel continually, venting their fury on the alabaster battlements of Lucifer's winter palace.

Gargantuan white vultures circled the bleak plains, their wingspans reached a hundred feet, their mangy feathers grimy with dried blood.

The menacing satanic princes arrived one by one in their chariots of the damned, each pulled by twenty dark-winged Griffons. From Babylon and Ethiopia, Grecia, and China they came. From Siberia and from Persia. From Gog and Magog. Their great and terrible armies assembled on the ice plains of Gehenna to execute their bidding.

Thousands of the sinister Black Magus rode across the plains on their headless three-humped camels. Close behind flew the Witches of Babylon and the dread Warlocks of Ishtar on the backs of werewolves and dragons, their faces raised in ecstasy to the ice blizzards.

From above the skies they came – thousands of dauphin scribes with cloven hoofs, flying towards Gehenna, and from under the earth they came, Hera and the Banshees of Valkyrie, riding on Leviathan and giant serpents. The Wort Seers of Diablos and the Necromancer Kings. All across the plains, as far as the eye could see, the fallen were gathering.

Answering the call. To hold high court in the Dread Councils of Hell.

Lucifer turned from the window facing the great hall and smiled.

'The disciples of hell are assembled,' he said. 'Let the gathering commence.'

⌒

Lucifer stood under the vast open dome in the centre of the Great War Chamber of Gehenna, his eyes closed, his robe blowing violently in the dark blizzards that blew in from the White Dwarf Pinnacles. The nine magenta ice suns were setting, and in their place rose the seven comets of Thuban, their flaming hoarfrost tails blazing above the bleak ice plains of Gehenna. Hundreds of ferocious snow hellhounds, each with six heads and glowing red eyes, patrolled the plains in packs.

He bowed his head, his arms outstretched, as six enormous black seraph wings extended from his spine. A second later, he was in the ornately carved high place of the war chamber, a thousand feet up. He stood, resplendent in his ceremonial robes, crowned with translucent rays of light in the carved horn pulpit that hung from the high place in the centre of the dome. His back was turned to the hundreds of thousands of fallen gathered in the war chamber. A great oration came forth from his lips. The sound was as the sound of celestial pipes and of flutes and clarinets and of every pipe ever heard in the universe. A discordant song of the damned burst forth from the host of the fallen in response.

The monstrous bells of limbo pealed, rung by the Banshees of Valkyrie from their perches in the basilica belfry.

Lucifer lifted his sceptre, his magenta velvet robes billowing in the violent ice tempests.

He turned to face the damned gathered in the great war chamber – the great assembly of powers of evil and terror – the rulers of the dark world. His intense sapphire eyes blazed fiercely.

The great prince of Babylonia stood. 'We have heard, O great Satan, that your kingdom is plundered,' his voice was spun like silk. 'The Gates of Hell spoiled, the keys to hell and death purloined.'

He sat caressing the razored edge of his jewelled scimitar, an inscrutable smile on his face

The menacing Dragon Warlord of China stood in his robes of crimson dragon robe silks. 'Word has reached us, the fallen, that your empire has been pillaged.' His beady yellow slit eyes glinted with mutiny. 'The crypts of hell are ransacked.' He sat, folding his broad hands across his chest, fingering his great iron mace.

'Word has reached us under the earth...' The ancient leader of the Harpies flew before the throne, her body of a winged monster, her head of an ugly old crone. '...that your power is dissipated,' she warbled, her wings flapping.

The Dread Warlocks of Ishtar stood as one body. 'Persuade us, iniquitous Light-Bearer, dark seraph, that thy kingdom still stands,' they hissed in their dark treacled, seditious voices. 'Or should we choose another to rule over us...? ...should we choose another...?'

The dark, subversive whispers raged through the assembly of the damned. The stooped Darkened Councils and magi sat under the high place, their cowled hoods concealing their faces. Marduk arose from the bench of the Darkened Councils and bowed his head in reverence.

'You have been summoned to the Dread Councils of Hell, princes of darkness and great powers of the damned, by the one and only true king of this world, Lucifer, crowned Satan.'

Lucifer surveyed the assembly. The room fell silent.

'A dreadful day has dawned in the regions of the damned.' His voice shook with rage.

'A day so dire, that none could conceive it.'

'The Day of the Nazarene.' No one stirred.

'Golgotha,' a voice whispered.

A great shudder of terror ran through the entire assembly.

'Golgotha!' the banshees shrieked, clasping their ears.

'We lose our strength!' the Witches of Endor cried.

'Golgotha,' The warlocks of Ishtar clutched their throats. Retching.

'Golgotha!' the Wort Seers of Diablos rasped.

Lucifer stood, his sceptre raised.

'We would settle the score – we seek revenge!' he cried.

The entire assembly stood to their feet as one.

'We seek revenge, O Satan!' they cried as one voice.

'Draw and quarter the Nazarene,' Hecate, the ancient crone, shrieked, her twisted green fingers clasping her throat. 'Steep Him in wolfsbane.'

'Boil Him in burning pitch!' shrieked another.

'Cut off His hands and feet and feed Him to Leviathan,' hissed the Lord of the Warlocks.

Lucifer raised his hands to quiet the assembly.

'No!' he cried. 'You will have your bloodshed later – I vow it. There is a more expedient way, but first . . . '

He cast his eye across the chamber.

Twenty-four fallen satanic princes, his generals, wearing black armour and golden crowns, walked before him, bowing deeply.

'I seek for *loyal* followers . . . '

A thousand of Lucifer's Black Horde stepped forward and sealed the great gates.

'*Devoted* disciples.'

He nodded to Balam. Instantly fifty of his menacing Black Guard surrounded the great prince of Babylonia. The Shaman Kings took savage hold of the dragon warlord.

'Throw the craven traitors into the Abyss!' Lucifer cried.

Huldah and his Shaman Kings dragged the prince and the warlord through the rear hall, out to the ice wastes.

'Wait ... I shall gift you with five hundred crimson-bellied dragons!' screamed the warlord.

Lucifer looked straight ahead in contempt.

Their blood-curdling screams of terror echoed through the bleak ice wastelands, filling the chamber. Then a sombre silence fell.

Lucifer surveyed the assembly in triumph.

'Should you choose another to rule over you?' he whispered.

He strode down the hall, studying the faces before him intently, and stopped in front of the old harpy crone. Again he nodded to Balam.

'No-o-o-o-o-o!' she screeched as two of the Black Horde grasped her wings and carried her off. Her demented screaming filled the Chamber, then died away.

'Who else casts doubt on me?'

One by one the damned stood to their feet all across the Chamber.

'O fallen one, Satan, tempter, nemesis to the Race of Men,' they chanted in unison, 'we declare our allegiance. There is none so great as you.'

'We declare our allegiance. We worship you,' echoed the damned.'

Lucifer smiled.

'I call upon Charsoc, dark apostle, sorcerer.'

Charsoc rose from his throne at the head of the Dark Grey Magi and bowed.

'Mighty Emperor,' he said, bowing again to Lucifer. He turned to address the gathering. 'My revered compatriots of the damned, I recite the articles of Eternal Law: "If one undefiled from the Race of Men is willing to shed His lifeblood on behalf of the Race of Men, and become a substitute for judgement, the said Race of Men, past, present, and future generations, will be released from eternal judgement by the death of that one." This is binding Eternal Law.'

Lucifer raised his head. A sinister smile on his face.

'For those of the Race of Men ... only if they *receive* the great sacrifice.'

Charsoc nodded, his face ripe with evil. 'Each time one of the Race of Men accepts the Nazarene's sacrifice, he is branded with the seal of Yehovah – the seal of the First Heaven on his forehead – the seal of the Nazarene. It is a seal that denotes his transferral from the kingship of Satan to the kingship of Yehovah.'

Charsoc nodded to his liege Lord. 'The seal is not visible to those of the Race of Men,' he hissed. 'It is visible *only* to those of the First Heaven and to the realms of the damned. It represents the shed blood of Golgotha.' Charsoc surveyed the fallen. 'It bestows on its wearer the same powers as the Nazarene.' A ripple of horror spread like wildfire through the chamber.

Dagda, brother of Nakan, now grisly king of the Necromancers, stood up and lumbered to the front of the hall. 'I have seen the seal only once,' he croaked. His voice was thick with iniquity. He shuddered, clutching his black cloak to his cumbersome frame with his fleshy pigmented hands. 'It smoulders on their foreheads like a hideous luminous furnace in our spirit realm and renders us, the damned, powerless against such a one.'

Lucifer paced up and down, his hands behind his back. 'It greatly compromises our power in the realms of men. If a thousand, a hundred thousand, a million of the Race of Men were to wear the seal, it could decimate the realms of the damned.'

Sethunelah, the ancient leader of the macabre Black Magus stood. 'The Spirit is not strong with the Race of Men.' His voice was a soft nightmarish slither. 'They are formed of the mud, and the dust of earth clings to them. They live by their minds, their souls consumed with the affairs of men. They do not comprehend affairs of the Spirit.' He smoothed his black robes with pale bony fingers. 'We the fallen must feed on their weakness.'

Failenn, queen of the demon witches, rose from the back of the assembly.

All eyes were riveted on her. She wore a long, flowing diaphanous dress of white gossamer, her porcelain skin visible beneath it. Her floor-length auburn hair, woven with lilies, fell thick and gleaming down her back. She walked towards Lucifer, her voice beguiling, honey-tongued yet poisonous as hemlock. 'Lure them with our enticements, my lord. Persuade them with our intellects.' She flung around, transformed in an instant into a hideous, hunched crone with wrinkled green skin like a toad's, a long, twisted chin, gnarled and clawed hands. 'Deceive them with our enchantments!' her chilling scream rang out. Lucifer rubbed his fingers together in pleasure.

The Dread Warlocks of Ishtar stood, all ten thousand speaking as one voice.

'Venerated Excellency.' Their dark depraved tones echoed through the Chamber. 'We must dethrone the Nazarene in the minds and souls of the Race of Men until they consider Him as just one of themselves – no greater, no lesser. We will humanize them. Secularize them. They will call Him virtuous. They will call Him good … but they will not call Him *God*.'

'They shall call Him noble,' the Banshees screeched.

'They shall call Him good,' cackled the Witches of Babylon.

They shall not call Him *God!*' the Necromancer Kings cried.

'They shall call Him noble,' the Demon Witches wailed.

'They shall call Him good,' the Warlocks of Ishtar rasped.

The entire assembly stood.

'THEY SHALL NOT CALL HIM GOD!' they roared.

Lucifer and Charsoc exchanged glances.

'And if he is *not* God,' Lucifer murmured, 'he is dethroned … in the hearts and souls of the Race of Men.'

A great cry broke out across the War Chamber. 'Dethrone the Nazarene!'

'Dethrone the Nazarene!'

Lucifer stood, an evil smile on his lips.

'We shall erase His name and face forever from the records of the Race of Men. The terrible sacrifice shall be a mere myth for the weak and stumbling and the babes in arms. The sacrifice on Golgotha shall be in vain, for they shall not heed it.'

Lucifer raised his voice to the heavens.

'Mobilize all armies of the damned to deceive the Race of Men. Above the earth and under the earth, rulers of the dark places. Powers. Principalities. Thrones. Satanic Princes, Shaman Kings, Warlocks, Witches, Magus, Harpies – all who are subject to you – are my loyal subjects. We shall next convene at the turn of the second decade of the second millennium of the Race of Men.'

He ran his pale fingers slowly through the dark stubble on his head.

'The Nazarene shall wish He had never stirred the wrath of the son of destruction.'

⤸

AD 33
FIVE YEARS LATER

Jotapa stood outside Aretas' chambers, folding and refolding the now crumpled, tear-stained missive that had arrived from Jerusalem only an hour before. Five years had passed since the Nazarene's death on the cross on Golgotha.

Ghaliya was now with other believers in Jerusalem and communicated with Jotapa faithfully. The Hebrew's death had not been in vain. Zahi and hundreds like him had insisted on staying with the disciples in Jerusalem. The Hebrew's followers had multiplied in number all over Palestine and Asia Minor.

Two years ago, Zahi and Duza had left Jerusalem, travelling to Phoenicia and the isle of Cyprus, journeying through Thessalonica and finally arriving in Antioch, in Syria. Jotapa smiled through her tears. Zahi knew her exotic tastes and would send her colourful and outlandish trinkets from the marketplaces of the cities where they toiled, preaching of the Hebrew's Father and of the First Heaven. But four months ago, the trinkets and missives had stopped.

And today she had received the awful confirmation from Ghaliya.

First, the brilliant and gifted youth Stephen with the tight black curls, whom Zahi had loved and tutored at nights in all the great languagues of Arabia, had been stoned to death outside the city of Jerusalem. But worse news was to follow. Written in the swarthy fisherman Peter's hand, the missive was only barely legible – but legible enough to send her running from the room, screaming.

The faithful Ayeshe had soothed her with the ancient Arabic lullabies, but neither of them knew how to break the appalling news to the king, Aretas.

'I have to do it, Ayeshe,' she had whispered. 'It is a daughter's task.' And at last Ayeshe had agreed.

Since the night of the conversation of the Hebrew's resurrection, Aretas had withdrawn from Jotapa, from Arabia, and from his God. His body had weakened alarmingly, and though physicians had come from all over Arabia, Persia, and India with their potions, still Aretas grew frailer. Jotapa knew that both Zahi and Duza prayed for his soul faithfully, that he would remain steadfast in his faith in the Hebrew. And now this last hideous blow.

She paced up and down outside his chambers incessantly, then finally nodded to Aretas' royal guard, who at once opened the huge golden doors.

Aretas stood, aged and frail, leaning on a cane, his hands behind his back, staring out at the fountains in the Royal Pavilions.

He turned.

'Jotapa.' His expression was soft.

'I have missed your fellowship, daughter.'

'As I yours, father,' Jotapa replied softly.

He looked down and saw the tear-stained missive

411

clutched in her hand. His face turned to stone. Without a word, he limped across the marbled floor and snatched it out of her grasp.

Unfolding it, he quickly scanned the contents. He uttered a terrible, almost noiseless scream, the papyrus fluttering from his hands to the floor, he stumbled to the window in a daze.

'My beloved tender Zahi . . .' He stared out of the windows, tears streaming down his face, unheeded.

'Crucifed *upside down!*' He turned to Jotapa, his face ablaze with a terrible fury.

'Tell me, Jotapa, WHERE is the love and mercy of the God of the Hebrew? It is a farce!' he raged, slamming his fist on the table. 'A desperate myth for gullible children as they build their dirt castles on the desert floor . . . My son, dead,' he whimpered.

'Never – Jotapa!' He snatched up the cross from the altar and smashed it down on the table. It shattered into three pieces on the marble floor.

'*Never* will His name be spoken again in the house of Arabia. *Never* will the Hebrew's name be heard.' He turned, his eyes flashing dangerously with rage.

'Never again will a Hebrew be our friend.'

Jotapa watched helplessly as Aretas beat his feeble fists against the wall, his arms flailing.

'My son is dead,' he lamented, his eyes glazed and unseeing. His frail body collapsed under him, and he slid down the wall to the floor. 'Zahi . . . ,' he moaned.

CHAPTER FORTY-SEVEN

THE RUBIED DOOR

ARETAS LAY SLEEPING, propped up by seven fringed vermillion satin pillows. Jotapa sat next to him, his frail veined hand clasped in hers. He was restless, thrashing from side to side, his silk bedclothes soaked with his perspiration for the fourth time that day. He drew deep, rasping breaths.

Ayeshe smoothed his brow with old, veined fingers. Too often before, he had heard the death rattle as life ebbed out. Simple as the old Bedouin was, he knew that King Aretas was dying. It was all connected with the Hebrew. Of that, Ayeshe was certain.

Jotapa rose from his bedside, re-lit the sputtering lanterns, then poured out another draught of medicinal potion into the king's goblet. The potion, the latest of a dozen this month alone, had arrived by camel that dawn from the caliph of Persia in the east.

413

Aretas' old compatriot, Abgar Of Edessa had journeyed across desert and plains to visit him, but Aretas would tolerate none of the Armenian king's stories of how the Hebrew had healed him when he lay dying; indeed, Aretas had sent the great and generous king away, grieving for the loss of their old friendship.

Ayeshe shook his head.

'His malady is a sickness of his soul. The potion will do nothing!' Ayeshe threw his hands up in the air, muttering darkly in Syriac under his breath. 'It is *all* to do with the Hebrew.'

Jotapa sighed. 'He is slipping away from us, Ayeshe. He is become a shadow of the great king of Arabia he once was.'

'He has not forgiven the Hebrew for dying on the cross or for taking his firstborn son from him.'

There was a soft knock at the door. Jotapa frowned. It was late, only a few hours before dawn. She reached for one of the lanterns and walked across to the bedchamber door, softly opening it, gasping as a brilliant light radiated through the entrance.

In the centre of the brilliance, facing Jotapa, stood Jesus.

She dropped to her knees.

Her gaze moved upward, from the hem of His indigo silk robe to the platinum sash around His waist.

His face radiated a light so brilliant that His head and hair seemed white as snow, but as the shimmering waves of light settled, she could make out the deep, flaming dark mane. Resting on His head was a golden crown, set with three great rubies.

She stared mesmerized at the high, bronzed cheekbones, the blazing clear eyes that flashed from hues of blue to emerald to brown like flames of living fire. The great King of Heaven. *Her* King. Beautiful beyond imagining.

Jesus walked slowly over towards Aretas. He stopped beside the bed, Jotapa watching from the door. He gazed down at the sleeping king with a look of infinite tenderness and compassion.

'My friend, Aretas,' he murmured, bending over him, gently stroking the thinning silver hair on the dying king's head.

'Blessed are all those who have not seen Me and yet still believe,' he murmured in wonder. 'He looked down at Aretas with a deep compassion in His eyes – a compassion that understood a king's confusion, that forgave a king's scepticism, that washed away a king's bitterness, that embraced Aretas the man. Aretas, the friend who had protected Him as a babe in arms.

Jotapa gasped as her father's eyelids fluttered. Slowly his eyes focused. He frowned, and gazed long and hard into Jesus' face. A fleeting recognition lit his features.

He shook his head in disbelief, and a smile of incredible joy broke over his face. He stared, enraptured, his eyes never once wavering from Jesus' face.

'It is You,' he gasped, attempting to prop himself up with feeble arms. Clumsily he clasped Jesus' strong hands in his two frail ones. Then he frowned. He turned Jesus' hands around until the palms were facing him.

He stared at the harsh, jagged wounds, then cupped his mouth with both hands, horror-struck, the tears coursing down his face.

Jesus smiled and nodded. Aretas buried his face in Jesus' hands, his tears falling on the gaping wounds. Jesus clasped

415

the frail old man to His breast, deeply touched. Jotapa looked up through her tears, laughing exultantly in sheer, abandoned joy.

'My Hebrew friend,' Aretas murmured though his wracking sobs. And Jesus wept. Jotapa stared, transfixed as a shining white seal slowly materialized on Aretas' forehead in the sign of a cross.

'Come, My friend,' Jesus said. 'There is something I must show you.'

With infinite gentleness Jesus eased Aretas out of the bed and, clasping him tightly around his waist, led him over to the huge palace doors that opened onto the exotic oriental gardens. He pulled back the heavy pale rose silk curtains.

There, at the base of the marble steps, stood Zahi, radiant, his arms outstretched to his father.

Aretas looked back to Jesus, his eyes wide and questioning. Jesus nodded.

Jotapa moved towards him, tears streaming down her face.

'You are taking him?'

'If it is his wish,' Jesus said quietly.

Aretas looked at Zahi, then at Jesus, then back to Jotapa. 'It is my wish.' He turned to Jotapa, torn.

'I would go with them, Jotapa,' he whispered. 'I would visit the land of the Rubied Door.'

Jotapa flew into Aretas' arms. He clasped her tightly to him. She held him as though she would never let him go, her tears staining his night-robe. Finally, she looked up at him, her words hardly distinguishable through her sobs.

'I will miss you, dearest Papa . . . Go,' she sobbed. 'Go and be with those you love.'

Aretas kissed her fiercely on the head, as he had done when she was a child.

'You will make a great queen of Arabia!' he declared, then turned to Jesus, who nodded.

And unaided, he strode through the grand doors, down the marble stairs towards his firstborn son, whose arms stretched wide to greet him. He turned once more to look back at Jotapa, and then he was gone.

Jotapa turned from the doors to find Ayeshe, his face awash with tears.

They were alone in the room.

Then Jotapa looked towards the king's bedstead.

Aretas lay dead, the most incredible smile on his countenance. And the three pieces of the Hebrew's cross were clutched in his right hand.

⤳

2021

LONDON

Jotapa, princess of Jordan, slowly folded her namesake's final missive and replaced it back in the bundle of ancient papers. She wiped the tears from her cheeks with the palm of her hand and rose, fingering the small silver cross at her neck.

Her dark hair fell loose past her shoulders, onto the long silk negligee. She walked over to the large double windows and flung open the curtains, her bare feet sinking into the penthouse suite's plush carpet. The black London taxis were still travelling over Westminster Bridge. She stared out past the Millennium Wheel, over the Thames River towards Big Ben and the Houses of Parliament, gazing up at the strange white apparition above the London skyline.

⤳

2021
ALEXANDRIA, EGYPT

Nick stood bare-chested in his jeans on the balcony of the grand old Cecil Hotel, on Saad Zaghlou Square, gazing out at the uninterrupted view of the eastern bay and the yacht harbour. He inhaled deeply, smelling the salty sea air from the Mediterranean.

Tonight he indulged in the rare sentimentality that as an Englishman in Egypt, he relished the fact that both Somerset Maugham and Noel Coward had lingered there on a balcony before him and that even the British Secret Service had once maintained a suite in the old Cecil Hotel for its operations. As good a reason as any to stay there. Plus the added interest of the hotel's Moorish architecture; a constant memorial to the former seat of Alexandria's lavish extravagance.

Nick smiled idly at the incessant hooting and vociferous haggling that drifted up from Alexandria's legendary cafés and patisseries, even though it was nearly one in the morning. He had flown in from Rome to Cairo on the late flight, then driven straight down the major highway that linked Cairo and Alexandria, arriving in the old city just an hour earlier. Tomorrow at dawn he would visit what he considered the only real antiquities site in the area tomorrow – Kom el-Dikka, where a small Roman theatre had been excavated – before driving out to the desert monastery, where Professor Lawrence St Cartier would be waiting for him.

Nick raised his eyes for what must have been the sixth time that evening towards the full moon that glowed high in the Egyptian night sky, at the strange white apparition – then turned and walked inside to the disappointingly nondescript hotel room. He glaringly sighed, studying the predictable wallpaper and the mass produced coverlet on the bed. Then lay back heavily on the hard mattress, closing his eyes. His body was failing rapidly now; he could feel it. He stared down at the ribs now partially visible through his chest. He had lost another eight pounds this past fortnight. His faded jeans hung loose on his hips, held up only by an expensive soft leather belt buckled at its tightest notch.

He knew the exact day and hour when it had happened. It was a Sunday night in Amsterdam. They were rich, young, and bored. Celebrity fodder. Seven of them had used the same needle that night – four guys, three girls – their whole lives in front of them. The heroin had been a kick – the virus lived on long after the adrenalin faded. It was the deadliest strain of AIDS yet – pernicious, invasive.

The sixth had died last Monday. It was all over the British papers. She had been a model. From Manchester. The world at her feet. Her parents were devastated.

Nick felt for the remote, switching it on with his free hand. He changed the channel on Nilesat from some obscure homegrown Egyptian drama, punching the remote until he found Al Jazeera.

There on a replay, beaming from Damascus, was his brother Adrian De Vere. Thank God for Adrian. Nick knew he could never have made it this far without him. He studied his elder brother. Adrian must have taken Julia's advice and hired a top stylist. He was tanned, lean, his dark hair gleaming, looking every bit the sophisticated Hollywood star – except that he was newly appointed president of the European Union and the youngest initiator of a Middle East peace accord in history.

Nick yawned, exhausted, then fell into restless dreams of monks and antiquities, of his brothers, Jason and Adrian De Vere, the remote still clutched in his hand ... And of the Jordanian princess.

~

WASHINGTON DC

Jason De Vere watched from the roof of the chamber of commerce building as Marine One took off from the Whitehouse lawn for Camp David. The president and the Chinese foreign minister had left the gala party half an hour ago, followed by the last of the Capitol Hill senators and the group from the Chinese embassy. Only the usual Washington stragglers and media wannabes still hung around, warded away from Jason by his well-paid, extremely efficient minders.

He put his whisky glass down heavily on the makeshift banquet table and walked across the roof, past the media tents belonging to VOX Communications, his personal media empire. The Chinese and foreign film crews had all derigged, only the BBC and SKY were still rolling up their cables.

Jason smiled. A rare act. Elated. Two years ago, VOX had been ready. Already owning majority shares in broadcast platforms throughout Europe and the Middle East, he had bought out Direct TV, followed three months later by FOX News and its British equivalent, SKY, finally clinching the acquisition of 21st Century Fox. And yesterday VOX had signed one of the biggest global broadcast buyouts of all time, with Beijing – the greatest risk Jason De Vere had ever taken. All things considered. He now appeared to be unstoppable. Not bad for the ripe old age of forty-four.

He looked out at the White House, where he could see the familiar outline of snipers on the roof. His mobile rang.

'Yes,' he answered tersely. 'No, we won't budge. It's as high as we go. My position is unchanged.'

He ran down his messages. No personal calls. In fact, he hadn't received a single personal call since his divorce from Julia had been finalised thirteen months ago . . . except from his mother . . . and Adrian.

Julia. Jason froze.

He had been shocked. More than shocked. Stunned at the intense rush of emotions on seeing Julia last week in Damascus. Their meeting had deeply unnerved him. Bewildered him. He still loved her; that much he now knew. But he didn't dare run the risk of having to deal again with such highly charged emotions. He would never see Julia in person again – never, he vowed inwardly, unless it was a matter of life and death.

He replaced the phone in the case at his hip and stared out one last time at the view of the White House, which was feeding live to M Street uplinking to VOX satellites worldwide. Then once again at the strange white image still hung high above the Washington skyline. He ran his fingers through his close-cropped greying hair. Julia would hate it. That thought gave him a childish rush of pleasure.

He glanced at his watch and frowned. It was Adrian's birthday tomorow. His fortieth.

He made a note to phone France in the morning.

⌇

2021
LE MONT-ST-MICHEL
NORMANDY, FRANCE

A tall man, impeccably dressed in a Saville Row suit, stood staring out of the enormous cherrywood balcony doors of the European summer palace library. In his hands he held a parchment with strange Aramaic letterings. He stared past the hundreds of military police patrolling the perimeters of the double chain-link fence, past the circling gunships overhead, his gaze transfixed on the waxen apparition, visible against the full moon, in the darkening skies above the Atlantic.

A Jesuit priest, dressed in the flowing garb of his order of the 'Black Robes', walked towards him, his antique silver-knobbed cane tapping evenly on the polished mahogany floors. He stopped a few paces behind the man.

'The White Rider.'

The man nodded. His raven hair was fashionably long, falling just below his collar, gleaming blue-black in the moonlight.

'Our sign is in the heavens.'

He turned slightly, the outline of his chiselled features

suddenly visible in the moonlight. His profile was arresting
... strangely beautiful.

'We have waited over two thousand years for our
revenge.'

The man stared out at the monumental view across the
bay. Moving into the stream of moonlight, the Black Pope
gazed in the general direction of the apparition. His hands
trembled with contained rage as he lit a black taper, held it
to the parchment, and watched it burn.

'And now we avenge our dishonour,' Lucifer murmured.
'Our humiliation at the hands of the Nazarene.'

Lucifer smoothed his Jesuit robes, caressed the carved
silver serpent on the top of his cane and gave a slow,
malicious smile. ' ... We avenge Golgotha.'

THE CHARACTERS

THE FALLEN

Lucifer – *Satan*, King of Perdition. Tempter; Adversary; Sovereign Ruler of the Race of Men, earth, and the nether regions.

Charsoc – Dark Apostle – Chief High Priest of the Fallen. Governor of the Grand Wizards of the Black Court and the dreaded Warlock Kings of the West.

Marduk – Head of the Darkened Councils and Lucifer's chief-of-staff.

Darsoc – Princeling of legion of Grey Magus.

Alastor – Grand Wizard of the Black Courts.

Lord Astaroth – Michael's ex general – Lucifer's Commander-in-Chief.

Moloch – Satanic prince – 'Butcher' of Perdition.

Dagon – Commander of the Black Horde.

Belzoc – Champion of Perdition and satanic regent of the dark world of the kingdom of Persia. Ruler of twenty-four satanic Princes of Perdition.

Merodach – Satanic regent of the kingdom of Babylonia.

Gaap – King of the Western region of hell: Chief elder of the underlords.

Nisroc the Necromancer – Keeper of Death and the Grave.

Nakan – Warlock King of the Necromancers of the East.
Dracul – Ruler of Warlock Kings of the West.
Araklba – Newly crowned Princeling of the Dark Watchers.
Sethunelah – Ancient leader of the dark grey magus.
Huldah – Dark Overlord of the Shaman Kings.
Dagda – Newly crowned Ruler of the Necromancer Kings.
Faileen – Queen of the demon witches.
Forneus – Marquis of hell.
Balberith – Lucifer's chief attendant.
Zadkiel – Lucifer's aide. Banished to Tartarus – Abyss.
Ramuel, Mulciber, Vidar, Belial and Ruber – Generals of the Black Horde.
Pruslas, Barbatos and Rashaverak – Lucifer's Generals.

DREAD COUNCILS OF HELL

The Dread Warlocks of Ishtar.
Archangels of Ashtoroth.
Thrones of Folcador.
Black Magus.
The Necromancer Kings.
Demon Witches of Babylon.
Hera and the Banshees of Valkyrie.
Shaman Kings.
The Wort Seers of Diabolos.

FIRST HEAVEN

Michael – Chief Prince of the Royal House of Yehovah – Commander-in-Chief First Heaven's armies – President warring councils.

Gabriel – Chief Prince of the Royal House of Yehovah – Lord Chief Justice of angelic revelators.

Yehovah – Ancient of Days.

Christos – Jesus.

Jether – Imperial warrior and Ruler of the twenty-four ancient monarchs of the First Heaven and High Council Chief Steward of Yehovah's sacred mysteries.

Xacheriel – Ancient of Days Curator of the sciences and universes, one of the twenty-four ancient kings under Jether's governance.

HIGH RULING COUNCIL OF ANGELIC ELDERS

Jether, Xacheriel.

Maheel, Lamaliel.

Issachar, Zebulon.

Jehosaphat, Methusalah.

Raphael – Lucifer's ex Commander-in-chief. Michael's leading General.

Ephaniah – Lucifer's ex manservant.

Uriel, Ariel

Adam – Firstborn of the Race of Men.

Younglings – An ancient Angelic race with the characteristics of eternal youth and a remarkable inquisitiveness, expressly designed as apprentices to assist the Ancient Ones in their custodianship of Yehovah's countless new galaxies.

Obadiah, Dimnah.

Tirzah, Rakkon.

Otniel, Jatir.

Lamech, Kalleel.

EARTH: 2021

Jotapa – (22), Princess of Jordan – 2021.

Nick De Vere – (29), youngest brother – De Vere dynasty – Archeologist. Dying of AIDS.

Adrian De Vere – (39), middle brother – De Vere Dynasty. Ex-prime minister of the United Kingdom, newly appointed President of the United States of Europe, Nobel Peace Prize nominee.

Jason De Vere – (44), eldest brother – De Vere Dynasty. US Media Tycoon. Owns a third of the Western world's Television and Newspaper empires.

Julia St Cartier – (42), Jason De Vere's ex-wife.

Lily De Vere – (15), Julia and Jason's daughter. Crippled.

Lilian De Vere – (76), Nick, Adrian and Jason De Vere's mother.

Lawrence St Cartier – (82), ex Jesuit Priest; retired CIA; Antiquities Dealer – Julia St Cartier's Uncle.

EARTH: AD 28

The Nazarene – Jesus.

Aretas – King of Arabia/Petra.

Jotapa – Princess of Arabia.

Zahi – Crown prince of Arabia.

Ayeshe – Aretas' manservant.

Duza – Zahi's bearer

For more information on the Chronicles of Brothers
including other books in the series,
the characters, live chat with the author
and lots more go to
www.chroniclesofbrothers.net